Alfred M. Lorrain

The Helm, the Sword and the Cross

A Life Narrative

Alfred M. Lorrain

The Helm, the Sword and the Cross
A Life Narrative

ISBN/EAN: 9783337250959

Printed in Europe, USA, Canada, Australia, Japan

Cover: Foto ©Raphael Reischuk / pixelio.de

More available books at **www.hansebooks.com**

THE HELM,

THE SWORD, AND THE CROSS:

A LIFE NARRATIVE.

BY ALFRED M. LORRAIN,

OF THE CINCINNATI CONFERENCE.

—◦—

CINCINNATI:

PUBLISHED BY POE & HITCHCOCK;

CORNER OF MAIN AND EIGHTH STREETS.

R. P. THOMPSON, PRINTER.

1862.

CONTENTS.

———o———

CONTENTS.

6　CONTENTS.

INTRODUCTION.

I HAVE frequently been requested by ministerial brethren to write my life; but I felt so unworthy, in the midst of so many pious and useful men around me, that I was contented with my name to be left written on the sandy shore of time, where a few succeeding waves might soon wash it away from the view of mortals. It is comparatively easy to write the life of another. And some authors will, unconscious of wrong, clothe their subjects in almost angelic vestments, so that the youthful reader almost despairs of a faint imitation of the character. Perhaps there are few of the illustrious dead who would be willing to indorse their biographies. But for one to write his own life—is the tug. Several times, even to the close of my manuscript, I have been tempted to throw the whole batch into the fire. Certain it is, that nothing less than the request of my Conference could have induced me to undertake it.

There is another matter of which we would advise our readers; and that is, our labors were not laid in the pioneer strata—amid Indian onslaughts and huntsmen's adventures. Some of our oldest preachers, who have written their autobiographies, have been able to mingle very exciting matters— "part of which they saw, and part of which they were." We belong to a class a little subsequent. True, we have labored where thrilling traditions are cherished and recited. But they are *traditions;* and if they are not infected with accumulation, in descending to the third generation, they have been remarkably preserved from a great family disease. We do not wish to propagate any thing but what we know to be truth.

We have looked, at the beginning, at the many circuits and stations we have occupied, and we saw that we could not do any thing like justice in giving the Church history of each, with all the thrilling incidents, and private, extraordinary conversions; so we were led to take only a general view of each—and soon found we had to be more and more sparing in our remarks. And this abiding fear of swelling our work beyond all reasonable bounds has restrained our pen throughout. A close-written history of our fields of labor would form of itself a very large volume.

We have also excluded chapters, with all unnecessary head-dressing, which can answer, as far as we can see, no end but to make a large volume out of a little matter. Our difficulty is too much matter; and we have, perhaps, lessened the interest of the work by withdrawing much of the original matter from the manuscript. The time has come for our people to distinguish the comparative value of a large book with much waste paper, and a smaller book with one-third more matter. For the same reason we have avoided giving a list of all the appointments on a circuit—appointments which have long since been altered or deranged, so that the mere record of their names will leave but little satisfaction to any one. And, although we recollect with lively gratitude many noble men and women—who have laid us under lasting obligations, which we will remember, world without end—yet in a Christian Church, where we have met with so many of this stamp, it would swell our book beyond measure only to pay them a passing compliment. It is also true that, among *so many*—and how can it be otherwise?—we have met with some of the meanest of the mean.

We heard brother Finley advise the rowdies at a camp meeting not to meddle with the Methodists, on the score of their being non-resistant. "Because," said he, "they have been converted from all classes; and, if the devil should happen to get out of you into them, they will backslide, and half kill you. There is no greater visible devil on earth than a backslidden Methodist." But we have left all these to their own master— sincerely praying, the Lord have mercy upon them! Some of these, like pet bears, may be recovered out of the snare of the devil, and stand among God's elect. And the Lord forbid that we should be found reviling them, as we also are but flesh and blood, and need greatly the mercy of the Lord.

THE HELM, THE SWORD, AND THE CROSS.

PARENTAGE.

BIOGRAPHIES generally—and we think properly—begin with the homestead. My honored father was a descendant of a pious family of the Huguenots, who were so fortunate as to escape from their father-land to England at the revocation of the edict of Nantes. Family tradition runs the genealogy to an honorable length beyond; but we are satisfied in stopping in an atmosphere decidedly pure. Like God's people of old, "they chose rather to suffer affliction with the children of the Lord, than to enjoy the pleasures of sin for a season." In my very childhood I was awed by the solemn and earnest manner in which my father conducted family worship. Readers will, no doubt, smile at his son saying he was a man of singular morality, chastity, and integrity. Many years after his death, and when we had removed to Ohio, a Quaker, in passing the home of my mother, caught a sight of my father's portrait, and, stopping, he placed his hands on both sides of the door, gazed a few moments on the picture, and exclaimed: "Surely, it is my old friend, Thomas Lorrain! Is thee his widow?" "I am." "Well, I did all my trading at his store for years; and if there ever was a man of pure uprightness and honesty, thy husband was the man."

My mother, on the maternal side, was of a Roman Catholic family. Her father adhered to the Church of England. When a child she sometimes attended church with her father, and sometimes with her mother. So she had the benefit of two ecclesiastical teats; but, according to her own account, found dry nursing at both. She was, however, baptized in the Roman Church. Its splendid ornaments, romantic tales of saints and miracles, and the apparent austerity of its priests, gave her the impression that it was the better Church of the two. Indeed, such was the religious condition of Maryland in that day, it was hard to tell where the ark of God rested. When she was about seven years old, her faith in Roman legends and relics was shaken to its foundation by the following circumstance: She had two maiden aunts who were extremely devout, in their way. They wore, suspended from their necks, amulets, which, they told her, contained pieces of the coat which the Savior had worn previous to his crucifixion. She felt a dread veneration for those precious relics, and

he ran down all *innocent amusements* — such as
dancing, card-playing, etc." My mother could hold
in no longer. "The very people of whom the Savior
said, 'They should speak all manner of evil —
falsely!'" My mother was permitted to attend the
next appointment. A plain and solemn man stood
up, and took for his text—"The day of the Lord is
near, it is near, and hasteth greatly, even the
voice of the day of the Lord; the mighty man shall
cry there bitterly," etc. Every word, look, and motion of the minister deeply impressed her. She said
within herself, "This talk is more like the language
of the New Testament than any I have ever heard."
She was deeply convicted.

As she returned home, across the field, she heard
a voice behind her—"Miss Betsey!" It was the
voice of a colored man, who lived in the town.
"Miss Betsey, did you ever hear a man talk like
that man? He used some high words, and I may
not have understood him, and I thought you might
explain his discourse. I understood him that we
must be born over, get new hearts, and that we
might know our sins to be forgiven." Here my
mother took up the text, and recapitulated the whole
sermon, while big tears rolled down the negro's face.
Another arrow was driven home—the exhortation
of our Savior fulfilled—"Let him that heareth say
come." The carrying out this was a great auxiliary
to the ministry in that day. Preachers were few,
and could not half supply the country. People

would come to town or market, hear a Methodist preach, get under great concern, and when they returned home, as soon as it was known that they had heard a real Methodist, many would come and say, "Do tell us about their doctrine." "Their doctrine is the doctrine of the Bible. The man said we were all sinners; that we might often promise to do better in our own strength; but all our promises and solemn vows were like ropes of sand — no sooner made than broken." "That is certainly true. No man of common-sense will say that he is not a sinner. Well, what then?"

"He said that 'the soul that sinneth, it shall die. If we die in our sins, hell will be our portion forever and ever.' He was no ways mealy-mouthed."

"That seems reasonable; but how can we help it?"

"He added—God had compassion on us, and gave up his Son to die for us, and to lay a broad platform of mercy on which he may be just, honor his law, and pardon penitent sinners, who believe. If we believe heartily and sincerely God will forgive us our sins, and give us an evidence of our acceptance. And this, by the grace of God, is what I am seeking for."

"But how do you intend to seek for this faith?"

"The preacher said, in the use of the means of grace—reading the Word of God, occasional fasting, watching over our hearts, and against our spiritual enemies, earnest prayer; then as God gives us grace, ceasing to do evil, and learning to do well."

"The Lord knows it is high time for us all to be

doing better. Will you not hold prayer meetings in your house, and take some lead in this matter?"

"Yes, if there are any among you who fear God, and are determined to flee the wrath to come, and will join me in prayer, we will have meetings, and if the Lord bless us, we will try to get a preacher to help us." This was the way that the work enlarged. Those who heard said, "Come." And great was the number of believers that was raised up in Maryland. My mother did not join the Church at that time, but she had gained much. The Roman errors which had been so deeply impressed on her tender childhood were obliterated. She learned that the kingdom of God was not meat or drink, but righteousness, peace, and joy in the Holy Ghost; and that God had still a people on earth. She studied the Word of God, attended the means of grace, and prayed much; and for two or three years endured almost continuous conviction.

Before she had passed her teens she yielded, and joined the Church, with a fixed purpose to use all her ordained and prudential means of grace in seeking full salvation. She retired to an upper room, and spent nearly two days in transforming her fashionable wardrobe, and in prayer. In this she was opposed by those whom she loved most tenderly. But her heart was fixed. We have often heard her say since, that without calling into question the religion of others, this with her was a necessity. The Spirit of God so clearly wrote this duty on her truly-

awakened heart that non-compliance would have
been nothing else but obstinate rebellion. The
magnitude of the cross which she lifted can scarcely
be conceived of by the young members of the
Church in this day. It was an irreligious day.
Her relatives and associates moved in the highest
circle of Annapolis. Dancing, card-playing, and
fashionable parties were all considered very innocent
amusements. Extravagance of dress had no moral
boundaries. On the other hand, the Methodist
usages, in regard to external bearing, might have
been like the negro's tree—so perpendicular that it
leaned a "leetle the other way"—with this advantage, it was on virtue's side. Behold her, then, passing through their shining ranks arrayed in what
we now call Quaker plainness, and instead of a high
head-dress, and powdered hair, over an enormous
cushion, a simple cap, unruffled and unadorned.
Jewelry was out of the question. While playing
the last game at cards which she ever played, a
splendid finger-ring, without any known natural
cause, snapped and flew on the table. Yet old men
have told us that this novel plainness had peculiar
attractions; and that a great trouble with the
Church was to prevent irreligious young men running off their girls into unequal matrimony. It is
an underground sentiment in the bosom of every
sensible man, that

" Loveliness
Needs not the foreign aid of ornament,
But is when unadorned adorned the most."

Otherwise I could not have claimed a father of unusual intelligence and classical polish.

My mother was particularly opposed by her stepfather. More than once he threatened to close his door upon her if she attended the Methodist meetings. But undismayed she attended to every duty. After her marriage, when lying upon his death-bed full of penitence and contrition, he desired prayer. When asked who should be sent for, he answered, "Send for Betsey and her husband. If God has any true children on earth, they are. They are tried, faithful, and chosen." And she had the holy triumph of seeing her greatest opposer buried in hope of eternal life. All her oppositions would have been lighter if she had only enjoyed an evidence of her acceptance. This she earnestly sought; and one day, while much engaged in her retirement, she received an overwhelming manifestation of the power of God, and entered into the enjoyment of a spiritual life. We have been thus particular in merely extracting from her written experience, because her case was similar to hundreds of the children of the ancient Catholic families of Maryland, who found a rest in the Methodist Church—that blessed asylum for all who are oppressed of the devil. My converted mother was the little leaven that leavened nearly the whole family.

This pious young lady was subsequently my mother. She raised four enterprising sons, and four lovely daughters. In the last years of her widowhood she was with me in my itinerant movements, and counseled me, and prayed for me. She died in great peace in the parsonage on Madisonville circuit. When near her end I endeavored to console her with the idea of her speedy reunion with her mother, whom she had loved with deathless affection. She looked up with great astonishment, and said, "Why, my son, what straitened views you have of the coming glory! True, I shall see my mother and all my pious friends deceased; but O, I shall see much more than this—I shall see my beloved Savior, who died upon the cross for me. O Alfred, my son, Alfred,

> 'Preach HIM to all, and cry in death,
> Behold, behold the Lamb!'"

I have never heard that line read or sung since without a peculiar touch. And the idea of Jesus being the all-absorbing view of the dying saint has ever since been deeply sunken in my theology. Brother Barrett, of precious memory, once gave me a beautiful illustration of this doctrine in the relation of a dream which he once had.

"Brother," said he, "if you can have patience to hear the recital, I will relate a dream which I had many years since. Indeed, I have always been at a loss what to call it—whether a dream, vision, or trance—for it was certainly distinct from all my mental exercises, before or since, sleeping or awake. In the morning of my ministry, my mind was

greatly harassed in regard to the *Divine call*, as
is quite common, you know, with preachers. Having gone through with a string of discouraging appointments, without perceiving any immediate fruit,
and being greatly depressed with the most hum-
bling views of my own inefficiency, I concluded to
wind up my *traveling* career, at least, and retire.
I had, however, an evening appointment at a private house, where I had not yet been, and concluded
it should be my last. I was late in reaching the
place, and commenced the services immediately.
When the congregation had retired, I felt so exhausted in body and afflicted in mind, that I wished
to sleep. The brother pointed me to the room which
was prepared for me, and I retired without a candle.
As soon as my tired head was laid upon the pillow,
it seemed as if the heavy hand of Death was suddenly laid upon me. I never expect in the final separation of my soul and body—by whatever means—
to experience more physical anguish than was endured on that occasion. The whole body of vitality
and consciousness appeared to be rapidly withdrawing from all my extremities and members, and con-
centrating their forces in my breast. Thence they
ascended into my throat. One more agonizing
spasm and gasp, and my unharnessed spirit was
calmly gazing on the pale body which it had left.
There seemed to be nothing peculiar in the light
that was about me, but matter and things were
as clear and indisputable in my perception as or-

dinary noonday scenery. The next thing that arrested my attention for a moment were certain oddities which were peculiar to the room in which I had lodged, and which I had not seen in the evening because of the darkness. Particularly did I notice some grotesque figures which had been drawn on the wall by children, or those who were as inexperienced in the fine arts as they. In the next moment the room with all its furniture was no more, and my whole mind was riveted on a person who held a milk-white horse, and who commanded me to mount and follow. As we started, I looked back, and saw the farm-house with all its appurtenances, nothing altered in any respect, but every thing wore the appearance and impress of reality. For several miles we passed through a country of commonplace scenery—such as I had been familiar with for several days.

"The roads were sometimes good, sometimes middling, sometimes very bad; but in their general aspect they got better and better as we advanced. By and by the air became more balmy—the landscape more serenely sweet. Extraordinary prospects were scattered here and there; groves and shrubbery of unearthly beauty and texture would occasionally appear, till at last we seemed to be ranging a very paradise on earth. As we ascended a gentle rise, my guide bade me turn to the right. I turned, and beheld a stupendous wall of rich, transparent, and precious stones, indescribably va-

riegated by colors, lights, and shades. And while
I gazed, its wide and pearly portals slowly swung
with a noiseless welcome, and we entered in. Now
the consciousness overwhelmed me that this was not
an earthly but a heavenly paradise. I can no more
describe the celestial scenery than I can the unut-
terable ecstasy that at once possessed my soul. I
must give you, brother, the naked narrative. The
embellishments lie on the other side of the river.
We traveled on a celestial highway, walled with
vines, flowers, and deathless verdure, such as I
thought Eden never knew, till we came to the
head of a spacious, and apparently endless avenue.
Far in the distance stood the dazzling throne.
Well might a prophetic sojourner on earth say,
'*high and lifted up.*' And then the *train*—the
millions of holy, happy ones, who flowered all the
plain! The aromatic air, the sweet and mellow
music and alleluiahs wafted through all the bright
regions on high, I may only mention; conceive you
the glory if you can. My soul for once drank it
in, in rich and generous draughts. In all this blaze
of light my mind particularized some things. The
throne seemed to be sustained by seven pedestals
of transcendent beauty, receding as they rose one
above another, so as to present spacious platforms.
These, with the exception of a space in the center,
were filled with happy spirits. When nearing this
glory, my guide commanded me to dismount and
walk. As I put my foot on the first step looking

to the right, I saw a younger brother who had lately died in the hope of eternal life. As soon as our eyes met, we were locked in each other's arms; and he exclaimed, 'My brother, O, my brother! and so soon!' Relations and Christian brethren crowded around, and I thought I had scaled the summit-level of all glory, and was ready to ask, 'Can heaven give me more?' but just then I glanced my eyes upward, and saw JESUS! Brother, relations, all heaven were dropped like so many playthings, and on the upper platform I was prostrated before my Savior, and Christ was all, and in all." We pursue not the dream beyond its illustration, although it gave to the ministry of our brother a new tone. "I believe," said he, "the highest joy of heaven is Jesus Christ." We indorse this, especially as it was the doctrine of the inspired apostles. St. Paul says, "To be dissolved and to be with Christ is *far better*"—better than all on earth, all in heaven. When St. Stephen was yielding up, he called not father or mother, brother or sister, but "*Lord Jesus*, receive my spirit!" And I enjoy the continuous hope that my mother is with Christ in paradise. If Christ is the brightest bliss of heaven, how necessary it is that we should be conformed to his likeness here, that we may see him as he is, and love the appearing of the Lord. May the Lord conform me—the sinner me—to his likeness, that I may enjoy the highest bliss of heaven!

II.

CHILDHOOD.

ONE can not lightly pass over the period of childhood in reviewing his life. An inconsiderable impediment near the fountain may give direction to the sweeping river. Early childhood! Some say this is the happiest part of human life. This, we think, is questionable. There are some things vastly pleasant to our memory in overhauling the events and circumstances of childhood—the tender care of our parents, the social circle of the family, the absence of anxious care in regard to our provision and defense, and a thousand nameless comforts with that state inseparable—that will be sacredly imbedded in our memory forever. But we easily dismiss from our minds the trials and afflictions, mental, spiritual, and physical, that followed us almost from the cradle; the disappointed hopes, and rudely-crushed toys, which gave us keener anguish at the time than the loss of a ship would give a merchant. We have forgotten the impatience of wholesome restraint, the incessant longing for manhood and liberty, which appeared to be ages distant—and, not the least, the drudgery of the schools, and study, of which we could not

comprehend the end—"creeping like snails unwill-
ingly to school." Still the state of childhood is
interesting. The Lord has made it so. It is a
doctrine full of grace and comfort to Christian
parents, that infancy is a state of justification; and,
if death interposes, the child is assuredly taken
from the evil to come; for no one can arrive at
maturity without being constrained to exclaim,

> "Crosses, in number, measure, weight,
> Were written, Lord, for me."

But such is the amazing love with which parental
affection twines around the stricken one, that the
first outgushings of sorrow overtop all these divine
cordials which God administers to us. Indeed, we
dare not say that they were intended for application till the first showers of parental sorrow have
sanctified the graves of the little ones. Our Lord
is a sympathizing power; and the Gospel does not
harden, but abundantly refines, the higher instincts
of our nature. It seems to us like a mighty frigate
standing down the stream of time, with a weeping
world in convoy. When the tide has slackened, and
the proper eddy is gained, she throws out her signal to tack, and stem the stream, and through the
silver trumpet is heard, "Weep not for your dead
as those who have no hope; for if we believe that
Jesus died and rose again, even so them also which
sleep in Jesus will God bring with him."

A lady, an intimate acquaintance of my mother,
had a little daughter that she almost idolized. She

was suddenly taken away, and the mother became inconsolable. She refused all nourishment, and comfort, and her friends feared she would be destroyed with overmuch sorrow. One night she fell asleep, and thought an angelic messenger came to her, and, with a benign smile, said, "Would you see your Martha?" The mother quickly replied, "O, above all things!" He said, "Then follow me." She followed him through a long passage, till he stopped and touched a spring: a large door flew open—the voice of merriment, revelry, and dancing broke upon her ear—the room was studded with lamps, chandeliers, and reflectors. The conductor pointing to a tall, fashionable young lady, with a face flushed with dissipation, and who seemed to be the idol and leader of the giddy throng, he said, "Behold thy Martha!" "O, no!" cried out the impassioned mother, "she never could have been that tawdry, sporting thing. I was bringing her up in the fear of the Lord, and training her up for heaven." "So you thought," said the mysterious stranger; "but every day she was gaining on your fondness, and you would have got blinder and blinder to her true interests, and you would have denied her nothing; and that would have been the result. But follow me." Presently he touched another spring, and wide and massive doors flew open, and all heaven was exposed to the enraptured mother. She heard the voice of harpers harping with their harps; she saw the white-vested elders around the throne; and

far within the interior glory stood a blithe and
agile form, crowned with glory, and with a harp in
hand, joining in the new song. The conductor said,
"Behold thy Martha as she is!" The mother
echoed back the celestial shout—the joy was more
than earth could bear—the bed shook, the curtains
trembled—the saint awoke in midnight darkness,
exclaiming, "Thy will be done, O God, on earth as
in heaven! Yes," said she, "'taken from the evil
to come.'" This she had often read. This had
lately been breathed into her ears by sympathizing
friends. But now she realized God's truth, and the
truth set her free. When faith lays hold on the
Lord's promise, it is a tower of strength. She
arose next morning, washed her face, combed her
hair, and went forth, with a smiling countenance,
to help to fill up the measure of Christ's sufferings
left behind.

One of the heaviest blows my mother received
was the death of her little daughter, Caroline.
Indeed, the whole family staggered under the
shock. She was a lovely child. The neighbors
around held her to be a perfect sample of human
beauty. She was very young, and I can not believe
she had passed the line of infant justification—yet
her end seemed to be a triumph. The disease was
too rapid to reduce her; her eyes assumed an unusual luster, the fever tinged her cheek with a higher
flush—and a little before her death she awoke out
of a sleep, and said to her mother with a happy

smile, and her peculiar dimples fluttering as she spoke, "O, ma! I have seen such pretty things— prettier than I have ever seen! O, how fine! It made me feel so good!" "Well, my daughter, tell your mother about those pretty things." "No, no, ma, you must not know them; they would make you so sorry." "Why, child, how can any thing that is so pretty, and makes you so happy, make your mother sorry?" "Yes, you would cry—you would cry yourself almost to death." All the eloquence of my mother—and that was not small— could not draw the secret from her; and she would still advert to it, with smiles, till her happy spirit passed away. All were under the impression that the things which made her so happy were closely connected with her death, and she knew that would almost break her mother's heart.

Perhaps one may say, "What childish things to go into an autobiography!" True, they are childish; but remember, reader, that one-tenth of a man's life *is childhood*. And then remember that they can not find a place in a mere biography, because the author knows them not. And then only have patience, and we will begin to grow some. We were writing of infant justification. But those who live have to doff those bandages of Divine mercy, and enter into the world.

We have thought that personal sin, or consciousness of guilt, arises out of a collision of Divine light and human depravity. The child is a sinner by nature, indulges in passions and tempers that arc sinful, but he is unconscious of the wrong. When light shines into the soul, so as to distinguish good from evil, the individual detects himself in evil practices flowing from his depraved nature; his heart condemns him, and God, who is greater than his heart, also condemns him. He is a sinner in an incipient degree at least.

At what period this change of relation takes place, who can tell? Sooner in some, perhaps, than in others; and sooner in all than men are willing, in general, to admit. We so judge, governed by our own experience. As far as *my* memory extends back, I recognized myself as a sinner. I can just remember that, when a disease was raging through the country, sweeping off scores of children, it struck me with great violence. Great were my convictions. My mother had carried me much to meetings. The ministers in that day were very plain in describing the morning of the resurrection, and the judgment-day; and I was conscious of my sins. I feared God, feared the grave, feared what would follow. Ardent desires rose from my heart—call them prayers. All at once a sacred calm, a sweet tranquillity pervaded my mind. The fears of death, hell, and the grave vanished. I could think with calmness on the closing scene. I believe, if I had died then, I should have gone to heaven—not in virtue of infant justification, but as a sinner saved by grace. While I was lying in this condition, my parents were preparing to move to a residence in the suburbs. That day they had taken a hasty dinner in the room where I lay. Having been forbidden strong food for some time, the flavor of fried ham came flowing delightfully on my sense, and when they withdrew from the room I cautiously tottered to the table, and, seizing the largest slice in the dish, retreated to my bed, pulled the cover over my head, and feasted at my leisure. While eating, I felt the glow of returning health shooting to the very ends of my toes and fingers. Then I thought I would live, and not die. That evening I was carried to our new home. When I awoke in the morning the bright sun was shining, a multitude of birds singing in the trees around, and the brightness of my own mind was in unison with the loveliness of the scenery without. This happy frame I did not long retain.

Although ever wandering, yet there was a large development of veneration within me. The elder children—brother and sister—seemed to recognize this, and were willing to clothe me with ministerial honor. They would sometimes put to me very knotty questions in theology. At one time they said, "We have been talking religion, and we have been in a puzzle. You know God made man out of the dust of the earth; but we want to find out who made the Lord. What do you think, Alfred?" Drawing myself up to my utmost dignity: "Yes, God made man out of the dust; and you may easily see that, before he did that, he lay down, and rolled in the same dust, and made hisself." This brought out a screaming laugh, which offended me, for I could see no point to their merriment. This theory was as clear to my mind as my own creation. At another time they got into the habit of holding meetings. And, as the congregation was small, they determined to take a pet cat into the society; but, in order to do this, they must needs have her baptized. Again I was invested with power. We marched down to the branch, they teaching me a short formula. With all solemnity I took puss by the neck, and held her over the water, and said, "I baptize thee—" But the cat had other views; a dangerous scuffle ensued, and it is hardly necessary to say she gained the victory, threw up her bristles, straightened her tail, and rushed away as if horrified at our profane proceedings. This might have been locked up in the cabinet of childhood-secrecy, but a young man who attended in the store, unseen by us, had witnessed the whole ceremony; and we had to bear the expense for years following.

On one occasion I thought I would take a step or two beyond the narrow line which had been prescribed. There was living in our town a young lawyer, who, notwithstanding he was so crippled that he had to walk with crutches, was a great reprobate—most profane and vulgar. His wickedness was spoken of in all companies, and therefore I hated him. One day I was standing in our back porch and saw him hobbling up the steps of the adjoining tenement. I looked down upon him and cursed him as a wicked cripple. In the same moment I felt myself clasped as in a vise. It was my father, who, unknown to me, was standing behind. He took me into the counting-room, and drawing out a fresh cowhide, it seemed to me that he would not stop till he had cut my legs off. It might seem incredible to some, while I add, that although a wicked sailor for several years, and afterward a wild soldier for twelve months, I have never cursed or swore, except lawfully, since that eventful day. I thought what an awful sin it must be to compel my father to punish me so. I never knew him to strike a servant with a cowhide; but he loved his son better than his servants. If my father had smiled at my smartness, and told it to every visitor, I would have, doubtless, gone on for quantity. He was as serious as the grave. I would not put him past smiling, when he made the report to my mother, if it was only at the crankness of my anathema. I believe in Solomon's blisters for children, in cases of necessity. On every Sabbath my mother gathered all the young ones together—white, yellow, and black—and catechised them thoroughly. We did not enjoy the advantages of the Sabbath school in that day. In the course of my ministry I have cherished that institution with peculiar care. But here let me say, if our Sunday school is to cost the abandonment of parental instruction, our loss will be incalculable. The sweet seasons of maternal ministration have followed me through every turn of life.

It must not be supposed we were destitute of daily schools. We attended one of the best grammar schools, as they were called, where we gradually were led up through the rudiments of the Latin language. The doctrine was, we might be prepared for college, or if not, it would give us a better understanding of the English. The idea in that day and section was, that there was no arranged system of English grammar above the outlines that were given in some of our spelling-books, and that in letters almost microscopic. In process of time there came a Yankee, who published that he would teach the English in all its branches, and the English grammar thoroughly. This attracted many to his school. Our schoolmaster was a Scotch minister, and he taught school, and administered to the Episcopal Church for many years in that place. My boyish view of him was, that he was the most dignified and awful personage in the world. He was strict in morality; but it was not considered inconsistent by the majority of the people for him to attend the balls, and occasionally the theaters. He had a black man named Moses, whose highest ambition was to be a fac-simile of his master. As he had all his cast-off suits, it was not very difficult to toe the line. The parson was a bachelor, and as he did not wish to get up in the morning before the fire was made, he let Moses lock him up every night, and take the key to the kitchen, which was in range of the front of the house, and about a hundred yards off. Sometimes Moses indulged in a morning nap. The parson would hoist his window, and put his head out and cry, "Marses! O Marses! The devil's in him. God forgive me!" Whenever he got out of temper, or spoke as he thought unadvisedly, he would wind up with the amend, "*God forgive me!*" He used to keep his head pomatumed and powdered, and the locks on his forehead and temples rolled up in yellow paper all the week. He removed the paper on the Sabbath, and a handsome roll of hair half surrounded his face. Although he had considerable Scotch brogue, he was the best reader I ever heard. In after years he married. Once when very ill he sent a written request for the Methodist Church to pray for him, when some leading members of the Presbyterian Church wondered why he had not sent a similar request to them; he said he did not intend to hurt their feelings, but the Methodists were nearer of kin, and he had great confidence in their prayers. Under the superintendence of the pious Bishop Moore he became more and more pious; lived till he was over ninety years of age; and we trust he is now in heaven. My father, being a classical man himself, intended to give a polished education to his children. My oldest brother was transferred from this school to Washington College, where, in due time, he honorably graduated. We were following suit, when, as we will presently show, the sun of our family prosperity went down.

My father moved his family from Maryland while I was an infant, and settled in Petersburg, in Virginia. I loved Petersburg in childhood—I love it still. Sweet in my memory are my morning walks on the banks of the meandering Appomattox. I loved to sit on the rocky cliffs, where honeysuckles creep and woodbines flaunt, listening to the murmurings of the falls—music that might lull to sleep, even the head that wears a crown. I have traveled far and near, on field and flood, but never saw any population so beautiful—male and female—as the natives of that town, as then impressed on my heart. About the breaking out of the Southern rebellion I read in a paper, that a professed minister of God undertook to rail against the Union in a congregation in that town, when some of the elders retired; this made him more furious, when the congregation began to move, and as some passed out, they paused on the threshold, and looking indignantly back, said, "Treason! treason!" I laid the paper down and wept, and thought, "O, Petersburg! patriotic Petersburg, surely it will take an iron cable to drag thee from the Union!" My father was among the first merchants who opened stores—wholesale and retail—in that town, and many of the country merchants of North Carolina were his customers; his business was fair and flourishing, and we were a happy family. We learned by tradition that Petersburg had been a wicked place, but was getting better.

In my remembrance it had several special attractions. 1. The Spring and Fall races. All respectable ladies, who were not religious, attended in their chariots, often making a procession about a mile in length; and they engaged in all the jockey-talk and excitement of the turf—betting on the black gelding or Wilkin's gray. 2. Periodical balls through the Winter were occasions of great social glee, and considered indispensable to health, although some of the old doctors occasionally whispered that they cost annually two or three human sacrifices. 3. Gander-pulling and cock-fighting were precious amusements of the gentlemen — between meals. 4. Feasting on maple biscuit and wine at funerals. This was a custom that could not be dispensed with without drawing down heavy reflections on the mourners.

The Methodist preacher came along, and he doubtless felt as Paul did when he first came to Athens. He began with the funerals. After winding up their feelings to extreme tension, he would turn his eyes to the sideboard, and begin to descant on the decanter and cake, showing how inappropriate they were to the house of mourning, and he would beg them, if they saw fit to honor him with the solemn duty of preaching over their friends, that they would abandon the revolting practice.

This sore was soon healed. He was a doctor of the healing, and not of the dissecting practice.

As for the ball, the race, and other iniquitous frolics, the Methodist preacher, in succession, considered them as anvils on which the drumsticks ecclesiastical might play perpetually. The attendance on the races declined annually, till a decent woman could not be found on the ground. The ladies anchored their attractions at home, and their lords were kept to their moorings, and they found it profitable for this life at least. The balls became few and far between, and the gander-pulling sunk into oblivion with a hiss; as for the cock-fighting, it fell into the hands of the negroes. It was not unusual to see a darkey, on Sabbath morn, passing with hasty strides through the streets, with something wrapped up in a striped cotton handkerchief, under his arm. On drawing nigh might be seen two little bright eyes, under a splendid comb, sticking out at one end, and shining spurs at the other; and Sambo's face would be illuminated with an arch smile, as much as to say, "You all know it is a rooster, and white folks may come if they will behave." This reformation was accorded to evangelical preaching in the pulpit, and right-living in the Church, imperceptibly and gradually affecting public opinion.

We can hardly hope that that community, during the last forty years, have gone on to perfection. Though our ministers preach the system of salvation in this day as clear as it was dispensed in the apostolic age, as we suppose, yet they do not keep up an unremitting fire on the devil and all his works, as they once did; nor is the discipline administered as scrupulously. We are not croaking. We know that circumstances have materially changed. The enemy's batteries are closer masked, and his bullets are sugar-coated. In the progress of things fairs have been gotten up with the professed, and may be sincere, purpose of improving agriculture, etc. Many good men have attended them for laudable purposes. Before they get back they see what they did not go to see—races as genuine as those which once cost professors their membership. They hear African ditties and conjumingoes sung by feigned — and not very much feigned—negroes; and sometimes they witness a stag-dance, and make their bow to the big woman of Ohio. But many are falling off by the force of common-sense. They find, as it regards the inventions and machinery exhibited at the fair, their intrinsic merit is their highest premium, because it will introduce them to the factory or farm, where we may see their applications in all their practical excellency. As for the trained horses and fat cattle, it has been well discovered that the farms—if they have any—of those who have carried the prizes, present a dreary prospect at home — as dreary as the vision of Pharaoh, only reversed. In his dream the seven lean kine devoured the seven fat ones; in

the last case one fat calf eats up the whole plantation, and the owner is something leaner, notwithstanding the premium. The forced vegetables are
almost poisonous, and a horse, who possesses more
sense than we do—the discernment of invisibilities—would snort over them. So the inhabitants
of a great city drank delicious draughts at their
hydrants, and smacked their lips, for years; but
when they overhauled their reservoir, they found it
full of corruption and dead men's bones.

It is necessary to this work that its readers
should see my early surroundings. My home was
in the heart of slavery; and this, I suppose, has
given me a tender feeling for the African race;
and this feeling abides with those in the free States
who have been raised in the South. The African
knows this, and when he comes among us to raise
money to buy a wife or child, he knows where to
go. This can not be otherwise. Parents in the
South can not lay their fences so high as to separate entirely the children of the two classes. We
went chincapin hunting together, fishing together,
in some branch which was dry for one-half of the
year, and if we got three or four nibbles, we would
fish till sundown. When we got tired at noon, we
would lie down on the bank, packed away like a
layer of herrings. It is no wonder we caught their
brogue. In after years, while I was preaching a
funeral discourse, a strange minister who had been
raised in Kentucky, came to the door, and on ac-

count of the press, stood without where he could not see me. He told me afterward that he had heard only a few sentences, when he said in himself, "That fellow has cracked many a corn-dodger." But now let me say, that there was very little said about the institution, especially before children; yet, whether it was by intuition, or inspiration, or what not, I was, while a white-haired boy, bitterly opposed to slavery. In the large towns, their condition is—comparatively—comfortable. The slaves wear, in their turn, the clothes of their owners, and sometimes scarcely soiled. This is often economical, and the masters escape the charge of their garments being motheaten. In a common family, there could be little saved by putting servants under a different regimen; so they eat the same food, tastefully culled, of course, but with this advantage—"The nearer the bone, the sweeter the meat." Dainties are excepted. In some kitchens they occasionally live better than they do in the great house, because they sometimes add a 'possum, or fresh fish, or other rarities, that are overlooked by white folks. We used sometimes to have high life below stairs. It was there that I first realized how a drunkard felt, by getting quite boosy on eggnog, scalding hot. Still, as Sterne says, "Disguise thyself as thou wilt, O slavery, still thou art a bitter draught!" Even in our town, we had occasional exhibitions of its ugliness. While a little boy, in passing by a lot that was highly fenced

4

with boards, I heard an unusual groaning within.
My curiosity led me to hunt a hole, that I might
see what was going on within. I saw a negro
hoisted up, so that his feet swung clear of the
ground, by a rope fastened to his wrists, and passing over a kind of gallows. This was held by a
fellow-servant, while a white man was peeling his
back with a cowhide. The skin would sometimes
be stripped off like ribbons. The tyrant would
threaten to lay on in proportion to the noise he
made, and continued the cruel chastisement till entirely exhausted. He then took down his victim,
and by the forced assistance of the other slave,
stretched him on the tail of a dray, with his face
down, and brought from the kitchen a tin-cup of
melted tallow and poured it on his wounds. This
seemed to be the most excruciating part of the
whole process. My young bosom was filled with
indignation and wrath, supreme. In after years,
while reading about Moses, when he saw an Egyptian smiting an Israelite, and where it is said, "And
he looked this way and that way, and when he saw
that there was no man, he slew the Egyptian, and
hid him in the sand," I thought I understood how
Moses felt. When I saw this act of cruelty, I felt
if I could secretly dispose of that scoundrel without
exposing myself to the law, I would be doing God
an acceptable service.

But I might mention a case that came much
nearer home than this. My father, for about fif-

teen or twenty years, hired almost a whole family of slaves. They were of sterling integrity, and some of them religious. Aunt Milly, the matron of this colored family, was a dark mulatto, and a very pious Baptist. She had two sons besides her children in our family, who were blacksmiths. One of them came in one day apparently in great anguish, and told his mother that his wife's master had sold her and the children to a Georgia negro-buyer, and that they would pass in the afternoon by our big gate, which was on the Carolina road. When I heard this I became deeply moved, and resolved in my mind to be there. When I arrived, I found Aunt Milly and her son already there. They looked with painful suspense for some time down the road. Presently the sorrowful band was seen advancing with unwilling tread. Several men were handcuffed—two and two. The women and children were not bound. As they came up, Will and his wife rushed into the last sad embrace. The little children grasped his pantaloons. The grandmother's eyes flashed like diamonds, from earth to heaven, from heaven to earth. Only two or three ox drops ran down her cheeks—it was agony beyond tears. I alone was allowed this luxury, and I almost doubled myself down to the earth, and wept as if my little heart would burst. Many of our white acquaintances who knew the worth and sensibility of that colored family, sympathized with them. The negro-trader checked his horse awhile, and seemed to respect this scene of hopeless sorrow, but after a while drove them on. The wife and children cast many a longing look behind. The husband stood like a marble monument of woe, till a turn in the road separated husband and wife, parent and children forever. Many of our citizens used to feel deeply on such occasions, but they seemed to consider them as necessary outrages connected with an institution that appeared to be as firmly settled as the pillars of heaven.

. We never felt a sense of comfortable security while living in that beautiful town. Sometimes reports of intended insurrections would send a thrill of fear through every family. One time a boy came up where we were playing near the school, with dismayed visage, and said, "Boys, as I was coming to school, a negro looked at me and said, 'Ah, my lad, you look white and rosy now, but in a few days your face will be as black as my hand.'" Then we gathered up our playthings, and entering into serious squads, began to rehearse all the latest symptoms of an outbreak that we could drum up in our memory. When the school broke the intelligence was carried to every home.

Sometimes reports would be spread which would be found utterly false. Still they would create uneasiness for the time being. The most formidable disturbance which we ever had was the meditated insurrection of Gabriel—General Gabriel, as some called him by way of derision. The plan was to commence at Richmond, in the most sleepy watch of the night; but there was to be a general uprising through the country. They were to station two men at the door of every house, fire the city in two places, and then raise the all-exciting cry—"*fire! fire!*" As the citizens would rush out with their fire-buckets, as they usually did in such alarms, they were to cut them down. Richmond taken, and being supplied with more effective arms, they were to spread their devastations throughout the State. It was said that they intended to destroy also the colored women, and to supply their place with white ladies. The leaders, in order to forestall any subsequent misunderstanding, had agreed on their future partners, chosen from among the most celebrated beauties of the land. Scythe-blades and reap-hooks were secretly converted into war instruments, and the blacksmiths in the country, who generally worked late in the night, had made a considerable number of pikes, which could in a few moments be attached to staffs.

The secret was faithfully kept till the very eve of its intended accomplishment. There was a gentleman in the country, residing alone on his plantation. He had a boy who had been raised as a pet negro. This boy came into his chamber, and roused him up from his sleep. "Master! master!" said he, "I have brought your horse out, and fastened him to the gate. Arise and fly for your life!"

"Why? what's the matter?"

"The negroes have been meeting several nights at their quarters. I have hung around, listening till I have found out that they intend this night to march to Richmond, and kill all the white people. Fly for your life, master!"

He soon sprang on his horse, and fled. About this time a dismal cloud covered the heavens, sending forth almost incessant lightning. As he rode down the lane, by the bright flashes above he could see the negroes, in almost every field, converging toward the quarters. He arrived at the city, aroused up the authorities, and immediately the military were turned out, and the city under arms. The insurgents had not yet congregated, for they were waiting forces from the country; but squads of insurrectionists were arrested, and the programme fully exposed. In the mean time, the storm that had been threatening so long fell with awful devastation on the earth. Instead of raining it poured in mighty floods. In Petersburg, twenty-five miles off, the storm leveled or broke off nearly all the shade-trees; an arch which ran under Bolingbrooke-street, which was high enough for a man to stand under, was insufficient to carry off the flood, and it burst across the street. We supposed every family was up, for every house was lighted. I remember my father said, "Betsey, God is in this storm, as horrible as it is—it is supernatural. Mark me! this storm is salvation." So it was, and so I have ever believed. God had mercy on white and black. If the insurrection had commenced there might have been a great slaughter of the whites, but it would have resulted in an awful destruction of the blacks; for the other States would have sent their desolating forces upon them. The country negroes were bending their way to the city when the storm broke loose, but they found every branch with their bottoms overflowed. Here some said, "You can see plainly the hand of God is against us." Others charged them with cowardice, and after having a general "knock down and drag out," it was—every man to his cabin. For several days the gallows in Richmond was in constant service, till the most humane said it is enough—stay your hands. Solomon, the brother of Gabriel, while standing under the gallows, looked around on the multitude, and defiantly said, "Well, you may hang Solomon, but let me tell you there are more Solomons in Old '*Firginia.*'"

Gabriel could not be found; but a high reward was offered for him. It seems he had boarded one of the river crafts commanded by a colored man, and fled to Norfolk, with an intention to put to sea as soon as arrangements could be made. The vessel lay at the wharf. After being confined some days to his contracted berth, he thought he would, in the twilight hour, put his head up the companionway, and breathe for a while a purer air. A little black boy, who had been acquainted with him in Richmond, in the innocence of his heart exclaimed:

"How-dy, Uncle Gabriel? when did you leave Richmond?" Fatal salutation! Some white men, who were standing by, rushed on board and seized him. His baggage was overhauled. He had a fine suit of uniform, splendid epaulets, and a costly sword. He was carried to Richmond, and thrown into prison. Some gentlemen, moved by curiosity, began to catechise him, but drawing himself up with a magisterial air, he said, "I will answer no impertinent questions, but will answer at the bar of my country." Every thing that might be made harmful was taken from his cell, but he found a large, rusty, crooked nail. This he swallowed with an intention of avoiding the gallows, but it became immovably fixed in his throat, and in this condition he was hanged. Years after this I heard an old negro playing on a bandore a lengthy song descriptive of the raid of General Gabriel. On a slight hearing, it seemed to be a burlesque on the defeat; but there were some sentiments in pensive air that drew tears from the African eye. No foot of power can crush national songs—even if they are African. Many a time, while a boy, I have stopped to hear the darkies, while working on the roads, sing—

> "Billy Gilliam kill a nigger;
>   O, boys! ye 'most done?
> He knock him down, and den he stomp him;
>   O, boys! ye 'most done?
> He drag him down to Sandy Bottom;
>   O, boys! ye 'most done?
> And den he swear he never toch him;
>   O, boys! ye 'most done?"

The relations of Billy Gilliam often had to drive their chariots under such serenading, and look as pleasant as they could.

5

III.

SEA·LIFE.

My father, having dissolved partnership with a firm in Philadelphia, was advised by some of his best friends to form a connection with two French gentlemen, who were in a large grocery business. These gentlemen were brothers, and were as distinct in their characters as any two men could be. Alexander, the elder, was very plain, and of an unusually-serious cast. He had emigrated with his father to the western wilds; and one morning, when he was seated at the breakfast-table, an Indian chief stepped behind his father, and drove a tomahawk into his skull. Alexander fled, and with much difficulty made his escape; but it was said he never smiled again. Francis had been brought up in the fashions and amusements of France. He was light and frivolous, a dandy who ran into the most ridiculous extreme of fashion. The business of the house was very promising. They sent a valuable cargo to France, and were looking for a rich return of merchandise. Francis was sent out as supercargo, and was charged to insure the goods. This he did not do—giving, afterward, the simple apology, that, as he was coming back in the ship, he thought if the ship was lost he would be lost, and all would go together. This, however, was not the case. The ship Neptune, returning, as it was said, with the richest cargo which had left that season, sprung a bad leak. With all hands employed at the pumps it still gained on them. When all hope had nearly fled, a sail hove in sight, but cruelly passed, and left her with all her signals of distress flying. Now they sank down in despair; the Protestants broke out in prayer, the Roman Catholic ladies began to count their beads, kiss their crosses, and to call on the blessed Mary. There were many passengers. Just then another sail appeared; hope revived; the pumps were again manned. Those who came to the rescue had barely time to transfer the crew and passengers, without baggage, when the old Neptune went down. I well remember the announcement of this misfortune to my mother. Late one afternoon, Aunt Milly, whom we have already introduced as the matron of the kitchen, stood in the door, with shawl and bonnet on, and said:

"Mistiss, I thought I would step in and ask you if you had heard any thing about this bad news."

"What bad news, Milly? O, do tell me! speak quick! Is my husband dead?"

"O no, mistiss!"

"What then—is my son Edwin?"

He was from home.

"O no, mistiss, it is nothing like that. I

thought I would tell you how, as I was coming up from town, I met Mr. Tucker's boy, and he asked me if I had heard of master's bad luck——"

"O, Milly, is he dangerously hurt?"

"No, ma'am. But he said the ship that was fetching all his goods across the sea is gone to the bottom—and it's printed in the papers."

"O, Milly! is that all—is that all? O, I am so relieved! I have my husband and my children yet, thank God! Is that all?"

"Indeed, ma'am, I thought that was enough; the ship and all dem fine goods gone to de bottom!"

In the evening my father approached the house with slow and measured steps. My mother was watching at the door, and with a smiling face said, "Come on; I have heard all. We are all here. We have resources within ourselves, and God will help us." And she so cheered him up, that he could give a deliberate account of the shipwreck, and all that had transpired. But this was only the beginning of the calamity. The brothers agreed to turn over to him the stock on hand, and an interest which they could command in Norfolk, to the amount of several thousand dollars, if he would take upon him the outstanding credits and debts. He felt he could at least weather the point on such terms. The elder brother left at once the country where he had drank so deeply of sorrow. Francis went down to Norfolk to carry out the contract, but was heard of no more. My father buffeted the adverse tide awhile, but finally broke—honorably broke—giving up all, without mental or pecuniary reservation. Many who were his friends in prosperity stood by the family to the last. My oldest brother completed his study of the law, under Mr. Wirt; and my decision was the sea, with an intention to become a sea-captain. This was common in that section of the country. There were few families who had not a representative on the seas. I laid by all other studies, and betook myself to the acquisition of navigation. I soon possessed a good understanding of it theoretically. The gentleman under whom I agreed to sail did not require indentures, but said he did not wish to retain me a moment after I might become dissatisfied. It was my intention not to make use of names in this work, unless absolutely necessary. I think it is wrong in an autobiography. Although many with whom my early history is connected are no more, yet they may have relations and connections still living, and they might not wish to see their names bandied about. Capt. C., or rather ex-Capt. C. was my temporary master. He had made a fortune on the seas, and now owned the beautiful ship "Sheffield." He had for years ceased to command, and always employed a captain proper to take charge. He would go as supercargo when there was a cargo, and when there was none, a gentleman at large. He was a great beau on land—and on sea when ladies were about—though he was a confirmed bachelor, and tidy but genteel in his dress. The front and top of his head was bald, and slick as a peeled onion. His hair, behind, was made up in a cue about as big as a pig's tail, with an abundance of pomatum and powder, which was daily dressed by black Tom the steward. When I would follow him to the naval store for some article, he would run me breathless; but when ladies were promenading on either side of the street, I would then gain on him; for he would stop and make a bow—an old-time bow. He would take his hat off his head, swing it down by his side, and give a lordly bend for every lady in the group, while his head would shine in the sun like a looking-glass; and then he would go on his way, talking to himself, but never distinctly enough for me to get into his secrets. It was to this man, whom I have described in advance, that I became a nominal apprentice.

Having rigged myself off, with jacket and trowsers, I proceeded down to the ship, about twelve miles distant, accompanied by a servant who was to bring the horses back. Arriving at the brink of a high hill overlooking the shipping, I suddenly stopped in amazement. I had never seen such a wide-spread sheet of water as the James River presented at that point. It was a sprinkling and windy day, and the water was considerably ruffled. Here I felt my faith giving way; but then I thought, if you falter at this, what will you do in the swellings

of the ocean? Ambition came to my aid, and I
went on board. The men were glad that a boy
had dropped among them, because he would do
many small jobs that they were glad to get rid of;
so I became a great favorite.

After we had passed the Capes, I can not describe with what extreme anxiety I watched the
dim continent, till the last streak of land disappeared. The sheep and pigs that had been placed
under my province were stowed away in the long-
boat, amidships, with the pinnace capsized over
them for a shelter, and all strongly lashed. I saw
the sheep putting out their heads between the boats,
and ranging with their eyes the horizon, as though
to catch the sight of one more verdant hill, or
flowery valley; and then they would bleat most
piteously. My whole mind was at once in partnership and sympathy with their sorrow, and I said
within myself, "What a strange and unnatural per-
version of things!" But I had not much leisure to
philosophize, for the sea began to swell more freely,
and all at once a strange class of feelings overwhelmed me. A deadly sickness which had no prototype aside of blue water, unless it be excessive
drunkenness, struck me, and I became the merrily
observed of all observers. The whole world became
topsy-turvy, and an utter carelessness of life and
death possessed me. A perpetual retching, without a possibility of discharging my stomach, was
my enduring torment. An alien from all human

sympathy, for the whole crew rejoiced, I had to endure as best I could,

"When my sorrows they saw, and smiled at the tears which I shed!"

Indeed, they labored to augment my affliction. I saw an old salt peeping round the foremast, and beckoning to me. I hastened to stagger toward him, for it was the only phiz that bore marks of commiseration. "My dear boy," said he, "you need not endure this nasty complaint for five minutes. I know a sovereign remedy."

"O, tell me what it is, do!"

"Well, if you will swallow this fat gob of pork, which is tied to this string, I will jerk it right up again, and you will be cured in a moment." The very idea of this operation increased my distress, and multiplied my gagging. When I had suffered a few days, the steward brought up from the cabin a keg which had contained cherry-bounce, and wished me to get the cherries out of the bung-hole, and give them to the pigs. The cherries looked pretty, and I thought I would taste them and see if they were fit for pigs. The first one brought back a little animation to my pallet, and I went on for quantity, till I was fearful of addling the remnant of brains that seemed to be left. Suddenly my stomach took a free somerset, and I had a profuse liberation. In a few days I was good for full allowance of fat pork.and ship biscuit. The captain would not let me be sent aloft during my

seasickness, and said, "Wait till he gets his sea-
legs aboard." But now I was sent up into the
maintop. To those who are unacquainted with ships,
we will say that the top is a platform of wood
which surrounds the head of the mast. The lower
shrouds extend from the sides of the vessel, inclin-
ing into the head of the lower mast, and with ratlins—like a ladder. When you get there you come
to the puttock-shrouds, their lower ends connecting
with the lower shrouds close into the mast; they
are fastened by their upper ends to the side of the
rim of the top, where they are in connection with
the topmast shrouds, giving you another slant to
the head of the topmast. The intermediate shrouds
slant over your head about forty-five degrees, till
you surmount the edge of the top and get hold of
the topmast shrouds; while climbing them, your
whole body hangs nearly horizontal with the deck.
When I saw men going up, with their whole body
hanging over the deck, I could not conceive how
they could keep their feet on the ratlins; and I
had many forebodings about my time to come. My
time had now come, and I ran up the lower shrouds
sailor-like, for I had been celebrated at home for
my agility. But when I looked overhead and saw
that I would now have to climb the other way for
a piece, with my head from the mast, and body
hanging over the deck, I trembled. But I saw
there was a short cut through the center of the
top, where the rigging came down, so wheeled

quickly, and was sliding through the friendly opening, when a simultaneous shouting arose from the deck fore and aft, "Ah! you lubber, you lubber, you soldier you! you are gliding through lubber's hole, are you?" I thought I would stop that music forever, if it were at the expense of my life; so I withdrew and ascended up the old way. And having passed the Rubicon, in a little while could run over the rigging like a squirrel.

But I had to learn the bend of the sailors as well as the rigging; for I was too trusty and confiding. The captain called me in the cabin to bottle off some Holland gin; and when I was done he presented me with a bottle of the stuff. I was so proud of it that I did not even cover it with my handkerchief, as the worst of drunkards do, but carried it, all sparkling as it was, to the forecastle, winking at the men as I passed, and deposited it in my chest, which I thought was impregnable when it was locked; not understanding at that time that all chest-keys were alike. My calculations about my bottle were very benevolent. I intended, at a proper season, to give a taste to every man before the mast. One chilly night I told the watch on deck, to which I belonged, that I would get out my bottle and treat them all. As I was going forward I heard a little tittering behind, but it might be in anticipation of a swig.

When I brought my bottle up I took a considerable pull at it myself—when, lo, I swallowed a draught of salt water! Yes, it was *salt*, but truth compels me to record it was something more than salt. Here followed an uproarious laugh on deck, and then came back a mighty echo from below; and I felt as if I did not care about owning another bottle of gin while I might live. The scamps had made a general conspiracy against my bottle.

We have not as great a variety in the scenery at sea as we have in traveling on the land—no towering mountains or wide-spread flowery valleys. Incidents are few and far between—still we have not a dull uniformity. The scene is considerably varied by the light winds that gently ruffle the glassy surface to the driving tempest which dashes the swelling billows to the skies, till all seems to be mingled in lawless but sublime confusion. Incidents seldom occur, but in proportion to their scarcity is their all-absorbing interest. When the cry of "Sail, ho!" is heard through the ship, all on board are aroused. When first seen, the stranger appears like a dark speck in the distant horizon—presently we raise her lower sails, then her hull; as we near her she comes pitching and rolling, and exposing half of her bottom by fits and starts, like some living monster of the great deep; and if the breeze is tolerably fresh we hardly have time to exchange the usual compliments—"whence came ye? whither are you bound?"—when she is gone, and we rush on to our destiny to meet no more.

The captain seemed much pleased when he found

I had studied navigation; and as he had a spare quadrant on board, he made me take the sun every day and keep a journal. I would sometimes be greatly annoyed by an antic sailor, who would stand partly concealed by the foremast so that the officers could not see him, while he could be seen by myself; and he would raise the jaw-bone of a hog to his eye, and twist himself about with the motions of the ship, and carry on his mockery, while I would be operating. The sailors did not seem to like it so well when they found I was getting qualified for the cabin. One, who was generally called growler, said, "I expect he will be a bully captain some of these days, and kick and cuff the poor sailors about." And then, instead of looking on me and weeping, as the prophet did before Hazael, he talked himself into a fury, grit his teeth, and clinched his fist, and cursed and swore what he would do with me if he ever fell under my jurisdiction. And so he battled against his man of straw. But I laughed and said, "No, Bill, you are wrong; I am going to be a very good captain to the sailors; I mean to give them their allowance of grog every day, besides splicing the main brace after every storm, and watch and watch, blow high or blow low." And thus I would talk till I got him into a good humor again.

The generality of landsmen, when they look at the rough exterior of a sea captain, and consider well his defiant carriage, conclude that he has very little of the milk of human kindness in him. So I thought

at first in regard to my captain, because he sometimes
made me shin up to the royal mast-head—a long,
slender pole, beyond all rigging, and well slashed
withal—to rig pendant halliards. But I made a
sudden discovery one day, and found that although
his tear-box was shallow, and his benevolence was
stowed away deep, and was not to be wasted on
every occasion, yet he was kind and feeling. One
day I was sent up to send down the top-gallant sail
yard. We had topped the yard, and I was standing
in the topmast shrouds, directing the yard in its
descent, when the ship brought a tremendous lee-
lurch and weather-roll, and the yard got loose from
me, and, returning with a powerful swing, knocked
me out of the shrouds. I caught with one hand on
a dubious ratlin, and my whole body swung to
leeward, suspended by the ratlin over the angry
billows. The captain on deck turned pale, wrung
his hands, and exclaimed in a shrill feminine voice,
which he always assumed when in distress, "O, my
boy, my boy! my boy is lost, lost!" He was unusually kind to me for some time after this. He
never knew how that outburst of concern riveted
me to him forever. My master was an out-and-out
epicure. Much of his time was taken up in considering what he would eat and what he would drink.
About one o'clock he would be about the caboose
inspecting and tasting the dishes. If they pleased
him he would smack his lips, and say to the old
negro cook, "David, David! I say, David, that's

nice, David—David, you deserve a dram for this, David!" This was David's only dish. I never saw him eat a meal in my life. He seemed to live on the flavor and steam of the caboose; but it was exhilarating to see him toss off a dram. The dinner was deferred till two o'clock, that the after-gang might become as ravenous as Polar bears. The captain would then sit for two hours, drinking wine with the passengers, and engaged in sundry talk. He would come upon deck about five o'clock, with a face as round and red as a full moon, take a round or two on the quarter-deck, and then slyly approach the bulwarks, and generously discharge his variegated cargo to the sharks.

When we made the white cliffs of Old England I was entranced. It was on a clear, sunshining morning; but every thing had to me a diminutive appearance. The farms seemed to be gardens with large beds, the shrub-fences — walks. Seeing a house near the shore, it appeared of the size of our dog-house on board. Here I first learned the relation of sight to distance. I said to an old sailor, "What are they doing with so many dog-houses ashore? Look at that little white dog-house on the beach!"

"Dog-house, indeed! I am acquainted with this part of the coast. That is one of the largest taverns on this part of England. How far do you think you are from land?"

"About a mile or a mile and a half."

"You barber's clerk, you! we are about eight miles off."

As soon as I understood the distance every thing appeared right. We are not going to afflict our readers with a regular log-book, but intend to take a running and general view of our sea-life. We made three voyages to London, and became better acquainted with the points and reaches of the Thames than with those of our own James River.

There is no small perplexity and fun in ascending the last five miles. Here the comers and goers became so thick often, that we had to drift up by the force of the tide, with very little sail, and sometimes got locked in with a raft of vessels of all sizes and nations. In that day American ships were highly ornamented and neat in their rigging. Our ship had a handsome figure-head, and a group of images as large as life reclining around her stern. There was a class of vessels called colliers, commanded by rough North-of-England men, with crews more uncouth and outlandish than themselves. It was one of their peculiar delights to smash a Yankee. They would rush into an American vessel, crying out in their rude brogue, "Take care of your gingerbread works there!" and away would fly an arm or leg from our stern-figures. Onward we would move amid thumping sides and snapping spars. The crews would sometimes get exasperated, and billets of wood and belaying pins would fly through the air. In the general row, if a negro should put his head up a scuttle, a general cry would rise, "Who dat? who dat?" This would be followed by a universal laugh, and the poor darkey would have to dodge back. We labored hard, but without success, to learn the origin of this. One thing is certain, it was not because they had any prejudice against Africans. Their currency in England is undisputed. It is no uncommon thing, in the atmosphere of shipping, to see fair ladies locked arm with the Africans, going to church, and their *beaux* carrying their Morocco prayer-books. Some of our officers got acquainted with a rich tobacconist. When the ship returned to London the young men of the family invited the mates to come and take tea with them, observing that their sister had got married, during their absence, to a Virginia gentleman. When the officers arrived they were invited into a splendid parlor, and introduced to the brother-in-law—a tall, double-jointed negro.

Sometimes our white men would get into a fight, on shore, with some of the colored cooks and stewards. Then the Cockneys would crowd around— "Give it to him, my African! Let him have it! You are not in America now. You are in the land of freedom—the land of liberty, my boy; plank it into him!"

One Sabbath I thought I would make the tour of London. I began by hunting a Methodist meeting-house, which could not be found; but as St. Paul's was looming up over all, thither my steps were bent. When close to it I was utterly disappointed. True, it was an enormous structure, and of its architecture I was not capable of judging; but standing, as it had done for generations, in the coal-smoke and moisture of London, many parts of it were as black as the back of a chimney. Having entered under the dome, I was astonished at the magnitude of the work, and the distance traveled in examining its monuments. Passing along the gangway that bordered the central space, the strokes of an organ struck my ear. I was bold enough to open, gently, a door, and found myself in an audience, and, from the splendor of their costume, I began to conclude that I had intruded into the nobility, if not into the royal family. I was afraid my sailor-dress would involve me in a dismissal, but they seemed to be so taken up with each other that I was hardly noticed. I observed that as often as the preacher or reader mentioned any of the Divine titles the organ struck.

Being dismissed from the ecclesiastical glory of England, we—you see we have found company—continued our explorations toward the court-end of the city, and in two hours got lost—as we believed, irrecoverably lost. If any one gets lost in London, let him ask the first genteel-looking person the way. He will stop, and, looking very wise, will say, "Find it out by your learning, as I did." Then turn next to a plain working-man, whose tanned skin appears impervious to mischief, and ask

him the direction to London bridge; he will say,
"With pleasure, sir. Take that street, and go one
mile, you will come to an open square, turn to the
right and that will lead you *right down to the
bridge.*" This will put you two miles more out of
the way. The Cockneys take sovereign pleasure in
putting strangers out of the way, and laying a
stumbling-block in the way of the blind. Happy
are the lost if they meet an American sailor, even
if he is two sheets in the wind, and the third shivering, he will put you in the right road, if he is
half-lost himself. The Londoners speak barbarous
English. Well may their literati hail with transports Webster's unabridged. Indeed, their orators
ought to finish their English studies in Philadelphia.

They—the common people—are, moreover, very
superstitious—full of fearful traditions, which they
hold next to Scripture. We might give one example:
"The time is coming when a blind man shall hold
the horses of three kings at the foot of London
bridge, while England shall be lost and won three
times in one day." Every one is disappointed in
London at first sight. Its principal prestige is its
overgrown qualities. The houses are generally
made of brick, which are the color of ours before
they are burned. This dingy hue, noways improved
by smoke and the almost continual moisture of the
atmosphere, has any thing but a pleasant appearance. The city is disgusting in comparison with
New York, Baltimore, or Boston. In all our trad-

ing with London, embracing all seasons, we never saw three bright, sunshiny days. It is not my purpose to dwell on this city. Travelers have, again and again, described its lions—I thought I would only turn up some of its substratum. I would hardly do justice, though, in passing by the Battle of the Bee-hive, which happened while we were there. There was a beer-house, not far from the Tower, called the "Bee-hive," which had been so long patronized by the Yankees, that the American flag waved over it perpetually. At that time there was an unusual number of Portuguese in port, and they came suddenly and unexpectedly upon the Americans, drove them out, and pulled down the flag. The next week the Americans mustered a considerable army, and undertook to dislodge the enemy. The battle was severe. In the midst of the fray, the Irish got to hear of it in their quarters, and they came pouring down like a hurricane. Some one hailed the leader, and asked him where he was rushing:

"There's a fight on hand, me darling! and we mean to have a finger in the pie."

"Which side will you take?"

"American, sure; for they say there is a little Ireland in America."

And they pitched in, knocking down, and dragging out. The fight became so serious that they had to order troops from the Tower to quell it; and several loads of the wounded were carried to the hospital.

The Bee-hive, however, was retaken, and the American flag, for aught we know, may be flying there to the present day.

According to our best observations, England is the most intemperate nation on earth. Often have we seen the lower class of females, with flushed cheeks, staggering along the city, taking both sides of the walk. Those in better circumstances drink their coffee laced, as they call it, with French brandy, or West India rum. But let us put out into blue water again.

IV.

VOYAGE UP THE NORTH SEA.

ONE of the most interesting voyages I ever made was up the North Sea. As it was in the days of the "Rambouillet decree," our ship joined a fleet of merchantmen of about seventy sail, under the convoy of a large English sloop-of-war, and a government vessel of inferior metal. When the weather is fine, with a tolerable breeze and smooth sea, there can be no scene more pleasant than a fleet under convoy. It always brings to the mind the idea of a hen with her numerous brood. The fleet was made up of vessels of different nations, order, and speed. Ships, brigs, schooners, sloops, and galliots composed the motley mixture. So various were they in respect to speed especially, that, while some were leisurely careering along under close-reefed top-sails, and sometimes one of them aback, others were groaning under a crowd of sail, top-gallant sails, studding sails, and all the canvas that they could show. Sometimes they seemed to lie almost gunwales under, and yet appeared to be stationary on the waves. Ours was a first-rate Virginia merchantman, and her speed had tried many a British frigate in the time of the Chesapeake

commotion.   Consequently, we walked among them
at our pleasure; and, backing and filing through
the fleet, we enjoyed the luxury of conversing freely
with persons from almost every part of the world.
This was vastly pleasant.   We had heretofore made
long and lonesome voyages across the Atlantic, and
we enjoyed but seldom the felicity of speaking a
ship at sea.   Under such circumstances, the cheering cry of "Sail ho! sail ho!" springs a flash of joy
in every bosom, from the captain to the cabin-boy.
The strange sail appears at first like a dark speck
in the distant horizon.   Presently we see her hovering like a dark bird in our wake.   We look
again, and she is gone.   We rush on to our respect-
ive destinies; but with renewed impressions of the
shortness of the voyage of life, and the rapid flight
of time.   The Bible student almost involuntarily
exclaims, with Job, "*They pass away like the fast-
sailing ships.*"   But on the North Sea we found ourselves in the midst of a floating, fugitive city, and
the solitude of ocean seemed to be driven away.
One night we were suddenly alarmed by a torrent
of blue flame, pouring over the stern of a distant
bark.   This was the signal of an enemy close
aboard.   It was at this particular time that the
analogy between the fleet and a brood of chickens
struck most forcibly.   Immediately the man-of-war
made signal lights for us to consolidate.   The vessels in advance hove to, or shortened sail; while
those which were laboring astern, and had been

straining a perpetual race from the beginning, crowded more. We soon huddled together like frightened chickens, while the sloop-of-war, wheeling round as an angry hen would do, to face the hawk, left us in charge of her consort, and crowded all sail in chase of the privateer.

And, while we are thus hove to, permit me to tell a story about an American merchantman that was taken at this time. The enemy proved to be a Danish privateer. She hastily threw a prize-master and crew on board, and ordered them into the first port. The Americans were not confined, and, as they had open intercourse with each other, the captain formed a plan to retake the vessel. He told his men to be always ready; that he would embrace the most favorable opportunity; and that the signal or watchword should be, *"The ship's our own."* Hours after hours rolled by, and no good opportunity seemed to present itself. At last the destined port hove in view. The ship was rapidly nearing the harbor. Orders were given to overhaul the cable and clear the anchor. The American ensign was hoisted under their national flag. The captive captain bit his lips. He cast a feverish glance around. He saw his hearts of oak at their stations, and their indignant sky-lights fastened upon him. He could stand no more, but bellowed out, in a voice that echoed from stem to tafferel, "THE SHIP'S OUR OWN." Some of the Danes, having an imperfect knowledge of the English, under-

stood him to say, "The ship's aground," and they
reiterated in their own tongue, "The ship's
aground—the ship's aground." These were luckless words; for every Dane ran to look over the
sides, to see if the ship's way was stopped. The
Americans had meditated a bloody rescue, and had
stationed a hand at the carpenter's chest, below, to
supply them with deadly tools. Not that they had
any particular spite against their foreign shipmates; but they were harrowed up by the thoughts
of a Danish prison. But when they saw them
standing so convenient to the blue water, they concluded to give them the most honorable quietus
that a conquered sailor could ask for; so they
tipped them over the sides, and gave them a
launch, as they expressed it, into "Davy Jones's
locker." A strong and active American brought
the man at the helm a kind of lee-lurch and
weather-roll, and sent him sprawling into the scuppers, dryly observing that, as the ship had changed
her papers, and it was necessary to relieve the
helm, he believed he would take the first trick at
the wheel. As he said this, he cocked his eye up
to the mizzen-peak, where the national flags were
taking a somersault extraordinary. Meantime the
captain spread himself as large as life on the quarter-deck, and once more cried out with an untram-
meled tongue, "*Hard a-lee, there! Foresheet, fore-
top-bowline, jib and staysail sheets, let go!*" The
saucy Eliza sprung at once into the wind's eye;

and in the next moment was heard, "*Maintop-sail haul! Board tacks, and gather aft!*" And, as they slewed their spanker to the shore, the astonished natives, who had crowded the wharf to see the prize enter, beheld the bright Stars and Stripes of the American Republic floating over the humbled bunting of Denmark. You may well suppose that the crew was not slow in obeying the command to muster aft and give three cheers, and then to break loose, in their hearty manner, and sing:

> "Stretch her off, my brave boys!
> For it never shall be said
> That the sons of America
> Were ever yet afraid.
> Stretch her off, my brave boys!"

The best of all is, we have no list of the killed and wounded, for this singular maneuver took place almost in the mouth of the harbor, and it was undoubtedly a bloodless victory. The discharged crew, of course, took to their flippers; and their active countrymen on shore would hardly let them perish. But the Eliza left them diving and floundering about like a Dutch galliot in the Bay of Biscay.

In returning to the fleet, we would observe, how often do we realize through life the folly of trusting in chariots or horses, or even in ships, however strong they may be! While we on board the Sheffield were felicitating ourselves on our advantages, both in regard to labor and safety — because the easy sail we carried was not too much for an ordi-

nary gale, and while others were continually making
or taking in sail, we had but little to do—a storm
came on, when we discovered that an unforeseen evil
was preparing to devour us. The ballast which we
had taken in, and which seemed sufficiently solid,
proved to be a species of quicksand. The pumps
became choked, and the bilge water, diffusing itself
through the ballast, liquefied the whole mass, and
the shifting boards were not sufficient for this
exigency. The ship could stand on neither tack
without capsizing. The hatches could not be safely
moved with the heavy sea that was going. The
scene, as viewed from the between-decks by the
light of our candles, was truly appalling. The ballast rolled in terrific waves fore and aft, and we
had in the hold a fearful miniature of the storm
that was raging without. Our captain was entirely
unmanned—he wept like a child; and as I· stooped
down by his side to hold the lamp, more than once
or twice I heard the half-smothered prayer, "Lord,
have mercy upon us!" We hoisted a signal of distress, when our noble convoy bore down, and threw
several boat-loads of hardy sailors on board. With
much labor we succeeded in establishing shifting-
boards, and securing the ballast, so as to go on
with some degree of safety. However, this gale
dissolved all our social compacts, and the fleet was
scattered to congregate no more.

In a few days we were standing in for Norway.
The prospect on approaching this coast was most

sublime. We do not say it was the most pleasing ever witnessed. The most enchanting scene we ever beheld of the kind was on a previous voyage, while making the coast of Holland. Hearing on that occasion the cheering cry of "Land ho!" I sprung from below, and looking over the weather bow, saw numerous stacks of chimneys, steeples, and spires rising apparently out of the sea, while the morning sun was playing upon them with his dazzling beams. All on board seemed to be perfectly entranced. It appeared to exceed all of witchcraft lore or fairy scenery that had ever been told. "What have we here?" exclaimed I. "A Dutch village," said one. "But where is the land?" "In the watch below; and never a needle-full will you see for an hour to come." And so it was. Presently we raised the roofs of the houses, then the windows, and, last of all, a dark pencil line, as it were, disclosing the bank or levee which protects the coast from the sea, and the whole country from inundation. On entering the river, we found that it was protected by a similar levee. All the meadows and pastures were separated by verdant banks of like construction; and to one aloft the whole face of the country wore the appearance of a vast honeycomb. The contrast between this and the coast of Norway was very striking. Here Nature presented herself in her most rugged sublimity. Lofty mountains, frightful cliffs, and flinty promontories stretched along the coast. We had a good pilot on board—but to be standing full on this iron-bound country, with all sail set, and not a bay, inlet, sandbank, or river's mouth, to indicate a harbor at hand, was truly terrific. Still she sailed on, and sailed on; and every knot she ran seemed to render the prospect more and more horrible. At last a narrow passage around a needle, that stood out of the sea, began to discover itself. We entered in, but it appeared to terminate against a perpendicular cliff, not far ahead, where it seemed we must of necessity come to the end of our rope. But just before we reached the frightful point, another passage presented, and another; and so we glided, as it were, among the enormous fragments of a ruined coast, till at last we shot into a tranquil basin, entirely shut in from the sea. The water here was smooth as a mirror, and clear and blue as the waves of the midway ocean. Even our very royal masts were protected from the storms that idly raged without; and in front of our anchorage stood the beautiful and romantic village of Christiansand. Were we writing the history of our travels in full, we would love to dwell on this Norwegian scenery; but we have brought our readers into this part merely to relate a circumstance which overshadowed our whole crew with mourning.

After the ship had taken in a cargo of lumber, and was prepared to depart on the next morning, it was the turn of one part of the crew to have a night's liberty on shore. When the evening came, the forecastle was lighted up; and there was a general overhauling of chests, in search of some favorite articles of dress, long togs, etc. An unusual glee pervaded the ship's company. There was a man on board named Charles. He was a Polander by birth. He was a man of more dignified bearing than generally falls to the lot of sailors, and, according to his own account, had held some important office in the army. He spoke English badly, but was so full of hilarity and good-humor, that he was a universal favorite. He was, moreover, the handsomest man on board; which, by the by, he might have been without being a prodigy, for we were a hard-favored collection of weather dogs. This last-mentioned quality was no let or hinderance to his popularity on board, as sailors think that beauty may do for soldiers or barbers' clerks. Charles had worn an uncommonly-gloomy appearance all this afternoon; and while the joke, the laugh, the repartee were going their usual rounds in the fore peak, a settled cloud rested on his brow. I have wished often since that I had taken him aside, and asked him seriously what was resting on his mind; for I have a curiosity to the present day to know whether some awful presentiment was gnawing on his spirits, or whether he was meditating some dark deed, unworthy of his general character. At last he made a powerful effort to shake off his reverie, and began to prepare for the shore. All things being adjusted, the company lightly tripped over the main deck,

and, passing out at the starboard gangway, entered
into a flat, which had been used in bringing off our
stores. There were no oars kept in her, as one good
shove would generally send her to the wharf.
Charles was the last who entered in. Some one
cried out, "Give her a good headway, Charley."
He took a very heavy set. The scow shot like an
arrow; but poor Charley, being either unable or
unwilling—God knows which—to recover himself,
fell with a tremendous plunge. The men in the flat
were receding from him, and having no means of
coming to his rescue, could only cry out with might
and main, "Man overboard!" The alarming cry
rang from ship to ship, from shore to shore, in all
the babbling languages of the harbor. "Man overboard! man overboard!" This, with the darkness
of the night, the plunging into boats, the rattling
of oars, the bursting forth of lights upon the water
and the land, formed a scene awfully terrific. At
the onset of alarm, those of us who were on board
searched diligently all around the ship for the pinnace, but no boat could we see; yet when he had
sunk to rise no more alive, we found the boat fastened to the larboard gangway, with all her oars in.
Our general belief in that day was, that "our eyes
were blinded that we could not perceive." And
many a fearful talk about that pinnace did we
have at sea, under the lee of the long-boat. Nearly
all night was spent in raking for the body, but to
no purpose. A deep gloom fell on the crew. The

next morning, with heavy hearts, we manned the windlass and got under way. After we arrived in England, we received a friendly letter, stating that the body of poor Charles was found on the day we sailed, and that he was buried with all the nautical honors that the port could afford.

V.

STORMS AND SHORT ALLOWANCE.

WE have been sometimes asked if we were ever shipwrecked. We never were, but we have encountered many dangerous and stripping storms. Once on the midway ocean we encountered a gale that continued for several days with increasing violence. It came on gradually, so that we could shorten sail as it increased. This we did continually, till we were under bare poles, hoping that this would suffice. But still the gale increased, so that we had to send down our top-sail yards, and even house the topmasts. But it raged on till we had to lower down our lower yards, and then it became a perfect hurricane. The seas broke over our decks, sweeping fore and aft, and we were apprehensive we would have to cut away our lower masts. The heavy thumps of conflicting surges so opened her seams as to cause profuse leaking, and we were under constant apprehension of the ship swamping under us. For several days we had no regular meals, and when we did eat it was raw provision; for it was impossible to cook. As tenacious as the captain was of his fine cabin, he had to take his crew into it, for the forecastle was necessarily battened down. Such was the laboring and pitching of the ship, that the men could not keep their feet while eating a morsel. One man had to sit on the floor with his feet pressed against the locker; another would get behind him, and press his feet against the back of the first, and so on till they formed a line across the cabin. Then a piece of fat raw pork was handed from one to another, and every man would out with his knife and cut off a hunk. The bread-bag was passed in the same way, and so we took our meals. When the gale subsided, it was like rigging a new ship, to get her in order to pursue her course. But we were once in a more dangerous position than this, as we thought. We were bound for Spain, and making for Cadiz—the land in view. After a beautiful morning the atmosphere became hazy. We were under a press of canvas, when we were suddenly struck by a levanter. I was at the helm at the time. The square mainsail flew from its bolt-ropes like a handkerchief. In clapping the helm aweather, it seemed to me as if my ribs were crushed. The captain called two men to the helm, and as soon as the ship was gotten under proper sail, we began to beat off; but it was a vain effort. We were partly land-locked, and in consequence of the reduction of sail, we made much leeway. It blew furiously. The levanter is supposed by some to be the euroclydon, which shipwrecked the apostle Paul. In the midst of all our trouble, night—dark, moonless, starless night—came on. When we tacked toward the shore, we would stand on till the surf could be dimly discerned like an enormous drift of snow, while its thunder would rise superior to all the howlings of the tempest. It was evident that with all our effort we were gradually nearing the shore. Although our topsails were close-reefed, the canvas new, and our spars strong, yet it seemed a miracle to all on board that she could carry any sail in such a driving tornado. The captain at last spoke out, "The gale is increasing, the sails and spars can not stand this much longer. If we take in any more sail it will only hasten our fate. Carpenter, get your ax; if a yard breaks, or a sail splits, we will have to cut away the masts and let her go—perhaps on an iron-bound coast, where all will be lost." A silent agony seemed to reign over the crew. The voice of cursing and swearing had long since been hushed. The boasting sailor stood as quiet as a lamb. When a spar would give an unusual creak, the sailors would squat almost to the deck, as though to receive with humble submission the final blow. O, what prayers silently ascended! What promises were made! The bitterness of death was almost passed, when it pleased God in his infinite mercy to haul the wind round six or seven points, so that, though the storm blew with greater violence, we were enabled to stand out to sea.

We are aware that some who are accustomed to

sea matters will regard this as incredible—incredible
that the ship should beat off as long as she did,
with such close sail—incredible that she could carry
sail at all. But we can add some things which will
give testimony to the violence of the blow. When
the weather moderated, we stood into the harbor,
and found that the vessels that outrode the storm
had housed their masts, and were pitching and
heaving, as if they would tear themselves away
from their moorings. Seventeen vessels in the harbor, mostly American, dragged anchors, during the
gale, and stranded on the side of the bay where
the French army was then encamped, and were
burned. A large Spanish prison ship, full of French
soldiers, was driven ashore, and saved by their own
countrymen. The inhabitants said there had not
been such a storm on that coast for twenty years.
The people saw us struggling without before night
came on, and they said, "That poor crew will be
rolling among the rocks before morning." When
we give these cases of narrow escape, we do not
mean that they were the only blows we had to encounter. We have had storms upon storms, and have
been frightened ways without number. But there
are other things we had to grapple with besides
storms. One of the evils incident to a sea-faring
life, is that of being put on short allowance.

True, it is not of frequent occurrence. We never
realized it but once. The captain had determined
to run down the trades on his return voyage, and

we soon got into a mild climate, where we had almost uninterrupted clear weather overhead — weather very similar to our Indian Summer of the West; but the great botheration was, we had no wind. Week after week, with an occasional parenthesis, our fine ship lay entirely becalmed. Some who have never been on the seas, regard a calm as being a season of desirable rest, notwithstanding it may be accompanied with the slight drawback of homesickness. But nothing is more annoying on the seas. Although at such a time the surface of the water is as smooth as a mirror, yet the long and heavy swells continue; and as there is not air enough to fill the sails, so as to steady the ship, there is a continual and irregular rolling and tumbling. The blocks and ropes are perpetually slamming against the standing rigging, and the sails flapping on the masts, and every thing above and below, fore and aft, jerking and surging, in spite of all the cleets and lashings that human ingenuity can devise. It seems as if all inanimate appurtenances on board have risen up in wild rebellion, as though to avenge themselves for all the straining and hauling they have endured from time to time. It is a perfect jubilee of misrule with blocks and tackles, and all their allies. The sailor-boy on the yard-arm, jerked and twisted as he is, sees the sail stealthily falling back toward him; he thinks he may control its gravity by a slight slue; but it gives a sudden rasp across his knuckles, the tears

spring from his eyes, he grinds his teeth, and while
he is in the act of shaping a ripsneezer—half curse,
half prayer — the leech sweeps back like lightning,
raking unmercifully the whole vertebral column,
and tossing his tarpaulin sportively on the blue
waves, with the cheers and laughter of the whole
crew, who are hungry for the slightest incident that
might break upon the monotony of the incessant
clattering; while poor Jack, clapping his hand to
his maintop, is right glad to find that his scalp is
left behind.   Sometimes, from the mast-head, we
would see a beautiful stripe of wind, far away to
the larboard or starboard, and some happy vessel
booming along with all sail set; but notwithstanding all our whistling, and all our wooing, not a
solitary puff would kiss our sails.   A sickening
ennui pervaded the crew, and all, from the captain
to the cook, unnaturally longed for a driving
tempest.

After we had been out more than a month, the
discontent of the crew was increased by their tobacco falling short.   Those of liberal build, who
had not been accustomed to chew their morsel
alone, first began to feel the pressure.   The foreign
sailors, whose standing-rule was to take care of
No. 1, held out longer, and speculated some on the
necessities of their shipmates; but as the prospect
became more dreary, they closed up their stocks
against love or money.   When we were called to
dinner, some would hide their quids in the most

secret places they could find; but one peculiar quality of starvation is the sharpening of sight, and others would find these "old soldiers," as they called them, and transfer them to a warmer berth. At last all was gone, and the crew, generally, substituted oakum, or rope-yarn, for the precious weed.

But after a while our provisions began to fail, and short allowance was proclaimed. Our water was not so much reduced; but as it was uncertain how long we might be detained, we were allowed a quart per day. This we thought would do; but we had not taken into consideration that a day was twenty-four hours, and that we would require as much drink in our long watches on deck at night as in the day-time. Well, as for our water, we would generally drink it all off before sunset, and then be tormented with a burning thirst till the next day at noon, when our rations would be distributed.

Our meat allowance was still more spare. At dinner-time the meat was taken into the forecastle. Some just salt was appointed to cut it up into twelve equal pieces. This was spread out on a board. One of the apprentices was sent upon deck, the lid of the scuttle was drawn over, and the carver putting his knife on a piece, would say, "Who shall have this?" The boy above would answer, "Long Jack."

"And who shall have this?"

"Tom—hog-face Tom."

And so they would go on to the end of the mess; and happy was he who got the fattest gob; for the share of one man, for twenty-four hours, was not larger than his thumb.

After being out three months from the Land's End of England, we made the coast of America off Savannah. As soon as the rope was thrown to the pilot-boat, the crew, as with the voice of one man, said, "Have you any tobacco?" "Plenty—plenty," said the pilot, and he soon handed up about a pound of nigger-heads, as they were called in those days. Then the pump was put into the water-cask, the kid well filled, the bread-bag replenished, and the songs and laughter of merry-hearted men were heard in the fore peak. So, we may imagine, felt the poor prodigal, after he had abandoned the hog-trough, and found himself seated with his parents and sisters around the fatted calf, while the old homestead shook with music and gladness. And happier—yea, almost infinitely — feels the poor sinner, when, redeemed from the husks and vanities of the world, he first tastes the celestial riches of redeeming grace and dying love.

Thank God, there is no need of short allowance in the old Ship of Zion; for she is laden with the bread and water of life, and the great Captain says, "Eat, O my friends, and drink abundantly, O my beloved! In my presence is fullness of joy, and at my right hand there are pleasures forever more." Yes, her breezes are gales of love, and her calms are *calms indeed.* Her spirit-rations are of the wine of the kingdom; and well may the poet say of that

> " New life it sheds through dying hearts,
> And cheers the drooping mind,
> Vigor and joy its juice imparts,
> Without a *sting behind.*"

Come on board, fellow-sinners, and eat, that you may live forever; and drink, that you may thirst no more. It is true, that while we are in this disordered world, we may suffer, physically, starvation, or even shipwreck; but our souls may feed and feast upon the promises of God; and as it regards our bodily sufferings, we may say—

> " Lord! what are all our sufferings here,
> If thou but count us meet
> With that enraptured host to appear,
> And worship at thy feet?"

VI.

SECOND MATE—PRIVATEERING.

HAVING spent several years in acquiring a knowledge of seamanship, under promising circumstances I went out second mate of a brig owned in Boston. The captain and the crew, with the exception of myself, were all New England men. I soon saw a great difference between them and Southern sailors. The sailors employed in the South are generally citizens of the world, with few local attachments—their home, if they have any, upon the sea. The Yankee crew is often an association of neighbors, having abiding habitations on the land, and sympathies clinging around institutions on shore; and their voyages are more like speculative enterprises than an unconditional lifetime business. They will talk about deacons and sextons, and never forget thanksgiving day, but distinguish it by large batches of sweetcake, and plenty of codfish. Each man must have a suit of long clothes to go ashore in. The Southern sailor glories in his sea-rigging. There is more familiarity between the officers and men on board our Northern ships than would be tolerated South. The captain of our brig was an elderly

man, and had seen much service in the West India
trade and coastwise, and was a good sailor; but he
was very deficient in education. He could scarcely
write so as to be understood, and I soon saw he was
very bungling in making his daily calculations. I
continued to keep my journal—indeed, it was now
my official duty to do so. When we were pretty
well on in our voyage, he said one evening, "Mr.
L., you have been looking over your reckoning.
How near do you suppose we are to land, and
what point would we reach standing on our present
course?" I answered, according to my reckoning,
we are near land, and keeping the course we are
now on, we ought to make Silly about twelve o'clock
to-night. At this he started up, and said contempt-
uously, "Silly! you must be a great navigator,
indeed, and you are out in your distance by two
hundred miles; and then on this course she would
run pretty well up the British channel." This was
said before the man at the helm, and I considered
it insulting, but there was no redress.

He retired into the cabin, and having the watch
on deck, I kept a bright look-out. Being a young
man, I did not expect to be very correct in my
reckoning; and I knew that some old captains were
sometimes as much as two hundred miles out in
their distance. While studying on these matters, a
bright light flashed up ahead, and in a moment it
vanished—returned—vanished. It was with tumult-
uous delight I stepped into the cabin and roused up

the captain. "What's the matter, Mr. L.?" "Silly light, sir." "Why will you persist in that, Mr. L.? How do you know it is Silly light, sir?" "Because it is a revolving light."

"What do you mean by a *revolving* light?"

"It revolves or turns, so as to appear and disappear alternately."

He bustled up on deck just as the light was in all its brilliancy; but when it disappeared he laughed and said, "Where is your Silly now? It's the light of a ship bobbing up and down in the seas." He had hardly said this before it flashed up again.

"Mr. L., have you ever seen this light before?"

"Yes, twice. There is no light like it on all the English coast. Look at the chart, and you will have to give it a wider berth, or be a wreck before morning." This awakened him. I have always believed if he had been alone in navigation the brig would have been laid a wreck. On his return he claimed to be the best sailor, but said, "Mr. L. is the best navigator."

As preparatory to the return-passage, the captain had all his empty beef-barrels filled with fresh water, as he supposed he was deficient in water-casks. We did not blame him for doing so, in case of emergency. But in open disregard of the old sailor-proverb, "Use the best first, and you will always have the best," he ordered that the beef-barrels should be broached first; and as the voyage was

short we used no other water. The consequence
was, the whole ship's company was afflicted with a
violent diarrhea. It fastened on me, without intermission, for three years. On our return the captain
was sick, and heavy duties rested on me. On making
the coast we had to beat and knock about in almost
constant snow-storms, till in a great measure exhausted. When we arrived I received the first sum
of money, of much account, which I had ever
earned.

When we returned, we found that our Government had passed the non-intercourse law, interdict-
ing commerce with both England and France.
Still some of our merchantmen would clear out, and
manage by spurious papers to evade the law. One
of our merchants sent for me, and proposed my
taking the command of one of his vessels. I told
him plainly that I would undertake nothing that
involved perjury, let consequences be what they
might. Immediately the war followed. There I
was like a fish out of water. I can not convey to
the reader, unless he has experienced it, the sickening ennui that takes possession of the sailor after
he has been a few weeks on shore. It is this which
principally continues the supply and unbroken succession. After dreadful disasters at sea, it is amus-
ing to hear the unalterable resolves of the forecastle.
One will say, "Bloody end to me, if I am ever
caught on sea again, if ever I put my foot on land.
Why should I be knocked about all my days, living

a dog's life, and no thanks for it? Why, look at
the farmer! if it storms, he can get under shelter
with his wife and cubs, and can look out of his
cabin and laugh at old Boreas—'blustering railer!'
What a happy life!"

"Farmer!" says another, "he's a gentleman, I
can tell you; and it's because we are his lackeys
to carry his produce at the expense of life and
limb. I would rather be his servant, and carry
guts to a bear, than to live this dog-life."

And thus they will growl on, and resolve and
re-resolve—the whole crew, going home—to dip
their feet in salt water no more. But, after they
have been ashore four weeks, the prettiest farm in
the country could not hold them, as a general
thing. "Come, boys—who's for blue water?"

I felt this longing for the sea again. Life
seemed stripped of all its charms. I could not,
just then, get a place in the navy that could meet
my aspirations, or do justice to the feelings of my
family connections. Then came in the well-timed
temptation, to seek a prize-master's berth in a
privateer. I saw plainly—with my religious education it could not be otherwise—that it was, morally speaking, a dirty business; and I shall ever
adore a merciful Providence that so strangely and
mercifully opened up for me a way of escape.
While waiting in a seaport, expecting a very successful privateer to come in from her cruise, with
the prospect of getting a prize-master's office, I

received a letter from home, stating that all my young friends were forming a volunteer company, and were urgent for me to join them. This touched a nobler chord in my heart; so I stuck a cockade in my hat, and returned home.

Have not Christian nations, at least, arrived at that point of moral science and international honesty, that should induce them to abandon the practice of authorizing the shameful enterprise of privateering during war—a mode of reprisal that brings neither profit nor glory to any government; but affliction, and ofttimes ruin, to thousands of private citizens, who have no more share in the injuries perpetrated by their nation than the birds that fly over their heads.

Privateering is robbery. No government can issue any kind of letters or parchments that can divest it of this character in the view of high Heaven.

When a privateer takes a prize, the captives, generally, are exposed to as much insult and outrage as is generally inflicted by a pirate; with the lone exception of being made to walk the plank— a thing which no civilized people would tolerate.

The victors generally strip their prisoners of their personal baggage, their change, their watches, their clothes, down to their shirts and pantaloons, and even if these strike their fancy, they will take them in exchange for some of their cast-off duds, if that may be called "*exchange*," where one party is bound to submission without any alternative.

It may be said, what can you expect of such un-
principled buccaneers as commonly man a privateer?
But the whole responsibility does not rest with
them. With all their natural and acquired taste
for plunder and carnage, they would be comparatively harmless, but for the impulse of those who
have fitted them out, and who claim the heft of
the plunder. And who are they? Most frequently
merchants, who embrace this opportunity of meanly
robbing on the high seas, those with whom they
formerly stood in friendly and commercial relations,
with whom they have for a series of years carried
on an honest and lucrative trade. They make no
other apologies for their infamous robberies than
that the Government has legalized them, and then
they laugh heartily at the fogy fanatics who mum-
ble about a higher law.

While privateering inflicts much suffering on the
unoffending citizens of the enemy, it has a very
disastrous reaction on the nation that institutes
and supports it.

It lessens the dignity of a government. What
civilized nation in this day would tolerate the practice of its army prosecuting the indiscriminate
plunder of the citizens of a country through which
they might be marching in triumph? When General Harrison landed on the shores of ·Canada, he
issued general orders forbidding his soldiers to
touch or destroy the property of the inhabitants.
The battalion of volunteers to which we belonged,

although they had been nearly twelve months in a wilderness, under great privations, marched every now and then under trees bending down with the most delicious peaches. As these would rattle against our helmets, we endured temptation; but a proud national glory swelled our bosoms, under the magnificence of the scene. But what right have we to plunder on the seas, more than on the land?

Patriotism is the most diminutive motive lurking in the bosom of a privateersman. He fights for himself, and not for his country. Indeed, he chooses not to fight at all, provided that unarmed and defenseless game can be found; and it is only when by fog or mishap he falls in with an armed enemy, that he is compelled to show his teeth, and *then* no longer than he can devise a way of escape.

We were acquainted with a captain, who in the war of 1812 commanded a privateer, which met with singular success. He was at one time unintentionally involved in a dreadful conflict, and obtained a bloody victory. After the heat of battle was over, and when he passed along the decks and saw them strewed with the dead and wounded, deep remorse seized his spirit. When he reflected that all this murder and waste of life was for the avowed purpose of accumulating spoil, he was filled with compunction, then repentance; and, happily for him, a repentance not to be repented of. He scudded for his native shores, abandoned the privateer, and became a humble follower of Christ.

While he had nothing to do but to rob the unarmed and unresisting, his eyes were closed to
the enormity of the crime; but this profusion of
blood and screaming agony awoke him to the guilt
and madness of his warfare.

The privateer is a school of robbery, a sink of
pollution to poison subjects and to scatter fire-
brands, incendiaries, and rottenness, through a whole
nation. It cost the United States more money to
sweep the Gulf Stream of pirates, in time of peace,
than all her privateers had taken during the war.

And when we see a government authorizing its
citizens to take, sink, burn, or destroy on the high
seas, we think of the advice given to the Philip-
pian jailer—"Do thyself no harm."

It would certainly be to the interest and glory
of all nations to unite in putting away this detest-
able practice.

9

VII.

SOLDIER·LIFE.

WHEN the news of Hull's surrender reached the patriotic town of Petersburg, in Virginia, it overwhelmed the whole population with indignation and sorrow. Some of the most popular young men, with martial music, and the American ensign, paraded the streets, and with impassioned appeals called on their youthful associates to march to the rescue. The scene that followed was soul-thrilling to the patriot. Promising young men sprung their counters, and fell into the ranks. Students of medicine and law shoved aside their volumes, sufficiently uninteresting before, but now made absolutely irksome by the ceaseless din of war, and rushed to the standard. The mechanic threw the uplifted hammer from his hand to swell the train. The placid farmer rode to town to behold the madness of the people, but took the epidemic, and fell in. And in a few days a company of one hundred and four, richly uniformed, offered themselves to the Government to serve twelve months under the banner of the brave Harrison. No married man was admitted into their ranks. There is no incident of merely a terrene nature that ever so swelled our bosom, as did our departure from that lovely town—the bright scene of all our juvenile joys.

At an early hour in the day the company marched to "Center Hill," which overlooked the town. There they were met by a procession of women; while two elect ladies, bearing a stand of colors, richly and tastefully ornamented, presented them to the company, with an appropriate address. Being now all ready, with our knapsacks on our backs, and all accoutered for the perilous campaign, we marched down through the town, to the plaintive tune of

"The girls we've left behind us."

The doors, windows, and side-walks were crowded with our friends, our parents, and our weeping sisters. But the severest cut of all was as we wheeled down into Bolingbrooke. At that corner the principal body of the inhabitants had assembled for the purpose, as it seemed, of giving us a few parting cheers. But they had not counted the conflict. It is true, they simultaneously lifted their hats; but their trembling lips grew pale, their arms fell powerless to their sides, and a silent shower of tears betrayed the true position of their souls. This was a season of deep sorrow; but there was a magnanimity in the affliction that seemed to bear us up. Many of our friends followed us several miles, in carriages, on horseback, and on foot; but it only served to spring our tears afresh by a second and more personal farewell.

The first night we encamped in a beautiful grove near Ware-Bottom Church. On the next day we made our entry into Richmond. As we drew nigh the city, all the troops turned out to escort us in. And, surrounded with prancing cavalry, the mingling music of conflicting bands, drums, and trumpets, covered with clouds of dust, and, as our simple hearts thought, with glory too, we entered the capital. We were soon marched to a neighboring grove, where we sat down, in military order, to the festive board. Among the first visitors at our quarters was the pious Jesse Lee, who, in almost every soldier, recognized the son of some highly-esteemed friend. He was solicited to give us a sermon. To this he readily agreed. On the appointed day we marched unarmed to the church, which was well filled with citizens and soldiers. After the preliminary services, he took for his text, "Shall your brethren go to war, and shall ye sit here?" To show how even religious minds are tinged with the prevailing contagion, in times of special excitement, we will slightly advert to his course. In the introduction he solemnly protested against the spirit of war—offensive war—such wars as were undertaken to aggrandize a throne, to acquire territory, or to satiate the thirst for military glory. But, first, he proved—of course very easily to us—that the present war was a rare exception. England had more

than once smitten us on the right cheek, and we
had as often turned unto her the left. Our Government had shown a singular example of Christian
forbearance, till forbearance had ceased to be a
virtue. The wellbeing, the very existence of our
nation depended on honorable resistance. Every
citizen was an integral part of the social confeder-
acy—he was a partaker of all the immunities and
blessings of civil government—he was protected in
his person, property, and character, and is religiously bound to afford his quota of support. The
powers that be are ordained of God, yea, they are
his ministers, appointed for this very thing, and
bear not the sword in vain. Therefore, "render
unto Cæsar the things that are Cæsar's." Secondly,
he showed the spirit in which war should be waged.
Here he descended to all the minutiæ of the soldier's duty and conduct; and he gave the boys
abundance of godly advice, and showed very clearly
that, as handsomely equipped as we were, we were
lacking in a very important article of defense—
"the armor of righteousness, on the right hand
and on the left." The application of his subject he
poured with scorching severity on the Richmond
youth. With all the sarcastic and biting expression
of which he was master—and he commanded a
legion of that matter—he turned upon them and
said, "Will ye sit here and see your brethren go to
war?" And he preached not as one that beateth
the air on that occasion; for they forthwith organ-

ized a volunteer company according to the same pattern.

We took up our line of march and pressed on. The rumor of our coming, and the knowledge of our daily progress, enabled the people to spread their hospitalities in our way; so that, as far as eating was concerned, we frequently had nothing to do but march up to the rural board and partake of the smoking barbecue. Thus we "sat down to eat, and rose up to play." The report of our history, as it rolled on before, became highly fabulous. "Here comes the flower of Old Virginia! every man splendidly equipped at his own expense! They find their own baggage-wagons, bear their own expense, and there is n't a man among them with less than five hundred dollars — pin-money! Hurrah for Petersburg! Old Virginia never tire!" The people flattered us, and cheered us, till we became as proud as Lucifer. Our vanity, however, received an occasional check. One day a wagoner had much ado to hold his horses in a narrow pass till the company got by. He, however, found time to give us a very quizzical examination in detail; and as soon as he got sufficient searoom in the rear to give us a raking fire, without fear of reprisal, he cried out at the top of his voice, "I have heard of you before, boys. They call you the flower of the land; but ye mind me of the old saying, 'Fine feathers make fine birds;' but if you an't as ugly a set of chaps as Old Virginia ever hatched, I 'll give you my head for a

football." We, however, consoled ourselves with
the surmise, that for this compliment we were more
indebted to the wrath into which his horses had
wrought him, than to his skill in physiognomy.
Indeed, the volunteers were generally handsome.
Petersburg was always celebrated for its beauties,
male and female. It is true we had some very
hard cases, almost enough to make the eyes of the
wagoner ache. Perhaps some comical lady reader,
who knows the author, may say, "Yes, and we will
plank you down with the proscribed remnant."
Well, be it so; but if so, we must, in justice to the
town in this particular, say, we were not exactly
born there; but those of the family who were, were
right—good-looking.

Monticello lay in our route, or rather we made it
so lie, that we might have a sight of Virginia's
favorite sage. We drew up, in military array, at
the base of the hill on which the great house was
erected. About half way down the hill stood a
very homely old man, dressed in plain Virginia
cloth, his head uncovered, and his venerable locks
flowing in the wind. Some of our quizzical clique
at once marked him as a fit subject of fun. "I
wonder," said one, "what old codger that is, with
his hair blowing nine ways for Easter Monday."
"Why, of course," said another, "it is the overseer,
and he seems to be scared out of a year's growth.
I suspect he never saw gentlemen volunteers
before." But how were we astonished when he

advanced to our officers and introduced himself as THOMAS JEFFERSON! The officers were invited in to a collation, while we were marched off to the town, where more abundant provision had been made.

The most interesting prospect we had was when we first came in view of the Blue Ridge. It appeared, in the distance, like a dark wall stretched along the horizon, and piled to the heavens. We could not but admire the scene; yet our pleasure in beholding it was considerably abated when we contemplated the Herculean task of scaling it on the morrow. At that distance it presented a uniform surface, and seemed to forebode an almost perpendicular ascent. Since that period we have been better qualified to estimate the value of the old proverb, "Do not climb the mountain till you get to it." When we arrived at its base our road wound up a dark ravine. True, when we would look ahead, an insurmountable barrier seemed to stretch athwart our way; but when arrived at the apparent difficulty our tortuous pathway presented a gentle ascent, sometimes a comfortable level, and occasionally a little valley. And when we supposed our troubles were merely beginning, we received the happy announcement that we had surmounted all, and were wending our way down into the valley of the West. So it is in our journey through life. How often does the pilgrim fret about troubles ahead, which loom higher than the Blue Ridge—

mountains which he may never reach; and even if he does, the Lord leads him by a way that he had not known! So the proverb is worthy of a binding in the Apocrypha at least.

We had not traveled a hundred miles before the whole corps were called after a new nomenclature, our proper names being current only on the muster-roll. One was "Old Hickory," another "Plantation Joe," another "Hog-face-Tom," "Sinbad," etc.

From our childhood, we had considered the Blue Ridge to be the grand scenery of all backwoods romance. So it was natural for our straggling men to expect a bear, or a tiger, or something else, to pounce upon them from every thicket. One day we came to an encampment, about a quarter of a mile below a plantation. One of the boys was left considerably in the rear. Pushing on through the dusk of the evening, he saw a hideous animal crouched up in the corner of the fence; and having no doubt concerning its genus, he blazed away with his musket, and running in full speed to the camp, he cried out, "Boys, I have killed a bear! I have *killed a bear!*" Some said, "How do you know it is a bear? have you ever seen one before?" "No, but, laws! did n't I see its bristles when it was all ready to spring upon me? and it was exactly like the pictures you 've seen in the primers. Certainly it is a bear, and we 'll go and get it as soon as it is daylight." Away he went from camp-fire to camp-fire, boasting of his exploit. But before he got through the lines an old farmer made his appearance at head-quarters, and claimed indemnity for an old black sow that one of the soldiers had shot.

Except when passing places of notoriety, the company proceeded in an informal march. On such occasions all the blunders and improprieties of the preceding day and night were canvassed in catechetical form. One, for instance, would cry out with a loud voice, "Who tried to kiss that girl last night, and was shoved over into the wash-tub?" The whole line would respond, "T. C." "Who shot the old sow, and said it was a bear?" "Why, C. W." From such popular decisions there was no appeal.

But the report, "They are coming! they are coming!" climbed the mountains, and rolled on before us; and the hospitality of our countrymen was prodigious. Pressing on by the way of the Springs, down the Kanawha, and crossing the Ohio at Mt. Pleasant, we at last arrived at Chillicothe. Here the Legislature, which was then in session, gave us a splendid dinner, which was quickly followed by one from the citizens. Here the festivals of Virginia were thrown entirely in the shade; for we had not only the substantials, the bacon and cabbage of the Old Dominion, but fowls and turkeys, pies, tarts, custards, and sweetmeats, and floating-islands, and all the luxurious variety that the generous daughters of the Buckeye State could devise. Surely, we thought, there was nothing like the glory and honor of war. But, alas! it was the lus-

cious finale of all our military glory! It is true,
we had fed, and feasted, and frolicked for a few
short weeks, and our march thus far had been like
a triumphal procession. But O, how short our triumph! how vulgar our happiness!

> "We ate—drank—slept. What then?
> We ate, and drank, and slept again."

And this was the total amount of all our joy; and
O, how dearly bought!

Our "Indian Summer" was now gone—our "paw-
wah" days were over. As we left Chillicothe the
bleak North-Wester began to blow, the rains descended, and the snows drove till the face of the
whole country was clothed with the white, cold
mantle of Winter. Through mud, and ice, and
storms, and swollen streams we forced our way to
Franklinton, which was then the head-quarters of
the army. For the twelve succeeding months our
tender volunteers, most of whom had not passed
their twentieth year, and in their fathers' houses
"had never waked but to a joyful morning," were
exposed to labors, dangers, deprivations, afflictions,
and deaths, of which their youthful minds had never
conceived. Often did they realize the prodigal
state—the prodigal recollections, "in my father's
house there is bread and to spare." But it was not
for them, but for Uncle Sam, to say when they
might arise and return to the fathers and mothers,
and brothers and sisters. O, these words were

precious in those days. But we now had no abiding city—no May-days and holydays. We moved on through the plat of Columbus, where there was, at that time, only one house erected—albeit, we left Franklinton in its meridian glory. Through most intolerable roads, and severe weather, we reached the town of Delaware,.which was even then a handsome village. But before reaching this desirable spot, we were frequently stalled, and our baggage-wagons broken down. Delaware was the *ultima thule* of American civilization, as far as our route was concerned. We passed only one cabin between it and Sandusky. The plains of Crawford presented nothing but a wild waste of crusted snow, through which we marched with excessive labor.

When we reached the embodied host, on the bank of the Sandusky, our little band seemed to mingle as an atom in the long-extended line. At day-break the whole force was mustered, in rank and file, on the high banks of the river. The united music of the army passed down the line; but truly it was "music of melancholy sort." It was not the lively tune of "Yankee Doodle," "The Soldier's Return," or any of those rapturous airs so sweetly played at the recruiting rendezvous, to lure the inebriate to his doom; but it was an inexplicable breathing of war and blood, which, in unison with the desolation around, forced us, in one moment, to realize all that we had ever read or listened to of Revolutionary lore. Our feast of "marrow and fat things" had also

fled; and "soldier's fare" was the order of the day.
When our rations were first issued, while every man
was hearty, and our appetites keen, our allowance
was beggarly enough. But after a few cases of
sickness and spells of hypo, our stores began to ac-
cumulate, and we had enough provision, such as it
was; but it was not the hams of Virginia, or the turkeys and tidbits of Ohio, but fresh beef and pork, and
that frequently without a dust of salt. The bread,
which was sometimes made of damaged flour, was
truly disgusting. This, however, was a small item
in the registry of our sufferings. While encamped
at Sandusky, it was issued in general orders that
the chaplain would preach on the Sabbath. Our
readers can scarcely imagine what interest this
waked up in our ranks. Even the most irreligious
have a kind of property or claim in the Gospel that
they are not sensible of till the privilege is apparently clean gone forever. At the appointed hour,
the entire army was marched into the hollow square,
the General and his staff in the center. The preacher took for his text, "And the Lord said unto
Moses, Speak unto the children of Israel that they
go forward." He first gave a historical account of
the Israelites, and held them up as a lucid example
of all that is martial, patriotic, and glorious. He
secondly made a most bombastic application of the
text to our militia, warmly exhorting them to cross,
not *Jordan*, but the *line*, and to take possession, not
of *Canaan*, but *Canada:* "The bones of the gal-

lant Crawford, which lie bleaching in yonder plain, cry out, move forward. The blood of the brave Montgomery from the walls of Quebec cries out, march forward." And thus he went on till his effusions were found to be hateful; for whatever merit his speech would have possessed, coming from a proper source, and on a proper occasion, as a Gospel sermon, it was monstrous. And this he might have perceived by the simultaneous artificial coughing that pervaded the whole square. The General appeared to be mortified. We were pleased to find, in after years, that he hated all such untimely and misplaced zeal. He has been heard to say that a chaplain is an indispensable officer in the army; but 'no post, no department requires a more exemplary and evangelical minister.

It was midnight, the ground covered with snow, the heavens profusely flaking down additional supplies, and our heavy-laden tents were rocked to and fro by the howling winds, when the troops were suddenly aroused by a call to arms. Orders were given for us to buckle on our knapsacks and blankets, and to be ready to march at a moment's warning. In a few minutes we were plunged into the dark and almost interminable forest, bound through the Black Swamp to reënforce Harrison, who, after Winchester's defeat, had fallen back on the Carrying River. It was a dark, dark night. An experienced pilot led the van, and the whole detachment followed in Indian-file, every man taking care to keep in feeling relation to his predecessor. We plunged and floundered on through brush and brier, deep creeks, and rising waters, mingled with drift and ragged fragments of ice. Like Paul and his shipmates, "we longed for the day;" but when light broke upon us, it seemed to augment our wretchedness by calling into painful exercise an additional sense, and greatly enlarging the scene of desolation. We had frequently to pass through what was called, in the provincialism of the frontiers, "swales"—standing ponds—through which the troops and packhorses which had preceded us had made a trail of shattered ice. Those swales were often a quarter of a mile long. They were, moreover, very unequal in their soundings. In common they were not more than half-leg deep; but sometimes, at a moment when we were not expecting it, we suddenly sank down to our cartridge-boxes. While fording such places our feet would get so benumbed that we seemed to be walking on bundles of rags; and it was really a luxury to come to a parenthesis of mud and mire, for then we could feel a returning glow of vitality. Occasionally a poor packhorse would fall down in his track — if tracks there were—to rise no more forever. It was heart-rending to see them roll their flashing eyes indignantly on the passing soldiers, as though to rebuke the madness of the people in driving to such an extremity of suffering. Droves of hogs, which had been abandoned to the wilds, grim, gaunt, and hun-

gry as the grave, were squealing through the
woods, and rooting up the snow; and under the
relentless scourge of war the whole creation seemed
to groan in pain. We passed one of our subaltern
officers, who was trembling like an aspen, and be-
seeching every soldier for a dram, declaring that he
would perish in a few minutes if not supplied.
Poor fellow! he had been in the habit of keeping
himself always under the influence of liquor, and
his supply had failed him in this day of affliction.
By draining several canteens, he obtained enough
to drag him through the horrors of the day. Some
may think that we are exaggerating, but several of
our young men afterward fell victims to diseases
which were engendered by the march through the
Black Swamp.

The reaching of Hull's road was a grand desider-
atum. It is true we had never heard it spoken of,
by those who had seen it, except in terms of unqual-
ified execration; but still it was a *road*, and there
was a kind of redeeming sound in the phrase that
struck pleasantly on the drum of our ear. At last
a triumphant peal in the van announced its appearance. We were not slow in rushing to the point of
observation. But, O! the burst of indignation that
followed! Sure enough the *Hull* was there, and an
occasional patch of corduroy, and there had evidently been an opening made through the dense
forest; but the road, if there ever had been any,
had been mostly washed away before our time.

The first night and day we traveled, through all
those disadvantages, thirty miles. At a late hour
we approached an arena which bore a strong resem-
blance to *terra firma;* and scraping away the snow,
we spread our blankets under the naked canopy of
heaven; for at the time of our departure from Sandusky we had left our tents standing, with all our
camp equipage. How long we lay that night in a
shivering condition before we fell asleep we could
never ascertain; but I awoke in the morning from
pleasant dreams, and in a profuse perspiration, and,
as I thought, under a heavy press of blankets; but
when I threw up my arm to take an observation,
and to see how the land lay, an avalanche of virgin
snow, which had silently ministered to my comfort
during the night, tumbled into my bosom, and
quickly roused me to a recollection of my proper
latitude and true bearings, and I found, by calculation, that I was bounded north, south, east, and
west, by the *Black Swamp.*

Reader, bear with me, but I begin to feel sick
about my heart at the mere recollection of such
scenes. And besides all this I am sensible that I
have written enough for one chapter; but it would
savor of impoliteness to leave the readers of this
narrative so abruptly in the quagmire. Perhaps I
might give a more ship-shape finish by setting
them to read a short annual written by my brother,
which I received in those troublous days, and which
lightened up my own spirits while committing it to

10

memory. It was in perfect tune with the times.
It runs thus:

Since now, my patrons, we have reason
T' exchange the best salutes of the season—
Since fate has granted that together
One year of wonders we should weather,
Mid comets, earthquakes, storms and all,
Along unhurt our course to roll;
And thereby hang some tales of humor,
But now, alas! put out of rumor,
By one continual din of war,
And heroes marching near and far,
To dress Montgomery's tomb;
And brigadiers of sorry doom!
Then Harrison, in awful might,
Boldly rushing to the fight,
Bent on purpose grand and glorious,
His banners move in course victorious.
Not so was he who led the van,
A route the muse could never scan.
Through many a street and many an alley—
Through many a wild, umhrageous valley,
His standard boastful threats conveyed,
And loud to arms the drumsticks played.
The sons of spunk obey the call,
And shoulder musket, one add all—
To Campus Martius bend their way,
And soon are formed in proud array,
And hail the mighty battle day!
Before the lines a curious creature,
With dappled shirt and hickory featnre,
And pipe of true Moravian mold,
Thus broke in accents big and bold:
"I am ——; believe me, 't is no rant—
I am your noble commandant.
'T is true, I 'm not in style of war,
But that is well accounted for:
I 've lent my coat—I 've lost my sash—
My epaulets are in the wash—
My sword I do not choose to trust
To run the hazard of a rnst;

For bright it is, and well you know,
That while it 's mine it shall be so.

.   .   .   .   .   .

These Indians look too nation red;
Our stomachs, too, are scarce of bread;
And, what is worse, we have forgot
To bring the powder and the shot.
So ground your arms, ye dirty pack!
Let Dr. Eustis get you back."
So spite of frown, and spite of pout,
The word 's given, "To the *sneak about!*"
Go seek your hero at his home—
Go seek him on the ocean foam;
There British guineas can not gull,
And there Columbia owns her Hull.

VIII.

SIEGE OF FORT MEIGS.

We were writing something about Hull's road. It was certainly an extraordinary structure. Here and there we found a fragment of rail-road, not of the modern, but Gothic order. But for the most of the way the rails had been routed in disorder by the swales, and scattered in every direction and various forms, angular and triangular, vertical and horizontal, visible and invisible, so that our ankles at times appeared to be extremely loth to acknowledge our footsteps. At other times we were scraped, and snagged, and railed. And then we would get our temper up and rail back again; and it was railing against railing. Then old General Hull came in for his share of blessings, and Winchester was not forgotten. But our only hope was in progress; and after a forced march, which could find no prototype—as we believed—in the American Revolution, we joined the army on the banks of the Portage. As we marched in every man was presented with a small glass of *"high wine."* When I drank my allowance, it produced an indescribable titillation, reaching to the ends of my toes and fingers, and appeared to spread a new world upon my vision.

I have for many years been a strenuous advocate
of the temperance cause; but whenever I hear a
lecturer say that spirits have never done good under
any circumstances, I deliberately enroll the dogma
with clairvoyance, witchcraft, and similar delusions.
It is true that strong drink has seldom done good.
And of all the drams that moistened my lips, before
I embraced religion, that alone can I remember
with complacency, because it was Scripturally
administered—"*to him who was ready to perish.*"
This is no argument for intemperance; for what
was that transient benefit in comparison with the
wide-spread ruin which overwhelmed many of our
company in after-life? It was in the service that
some were initiated into, and others confirmed in
the habit of intemperance, which rapidly hurried
them on to the most deplorable destiny. And we
do most devoutly pray that the day may speedily
come, when Temperance will evaporate the last
intoxicating drop from earth by the brightness of
her shining.

It will be recollected that we had left all our
private stores behind, and had to commence on a
new issue of rations. Although the United States
owed us several successive back meals, yet these
were silently repudiated, and our allowance by no
means satisfied the demands of appetite. However,
we had ground to lie on, and rousing fires to cheer
us through the night. About midnight a sudden .
volley of cries, wailings, and unearthly howlings

broke from every quarter of the dense forest around
us. The raw troops, who had never experienced
any thing analogous, "in the void waste or in the
city full," took it for granted that all the northern
tribes were charging upon us, front, flank, and rear,
and they sprung to their feet. Pop! pop! pop!
went the sentinels. "To arms! to arms!" cried the
officers; and in a few minutes all the brave reënforcement was found in battle array. Just then an
old veteran came snickering along the lines with
his forefinger on his nose: *"Boys, did you never
hear the wolves howl before?"* It is wonderful how
those false alarms, frequently repeated, strengthen
the courage and improve the prudence of the soldier! This, the first, was perhaps the greatest
alarm we had. It showed us how careless and how
unprepared we were. The scrambling and scuffling
in the dark, for our arms and accouterments, were
truly ludicrous. The interruption of rest added
keenness to our hunger, so that we were more than
prepared for our scanty allowance next morning.
The flour which each man received made a very
respectable biscuit when kneaded. The great difficulty seemed to be as to the *modus operandi* of
cooking. Our culinary utensils were left behind,
and we had not as yet been let into the Indian
mode of twisting the dough around a stake, and
setting it up before the fire to roast. After a brief
consultation, we settled on the African method, and
concluded that we could get our cakes through in

the ash-pone style. So covering them cleverly with ashes and embers, we were about to broil our pittance of meat, when the drum suddenly beat to arms. We buckled on our armor, hoping it was some new-fashioned morning drill, or that some general order was about to be promulged. It was in vain for the subalterns to pass down the line and say, "Dress—dress—dress by the right!" for we could not keep our eyes from glancing askance toward our smoking cakes, which we were fearful were dressing too fast for the occasion. But what was our extreme disappointment when the luckless word came, and from high authority, "Right face! forward march!" Our legs, being as practiced as stage-horses', began to beat time; but our eyes, although carried away, still had independence enough to cast "many a longing, lingering look behind." Some of our boys, who seemed to be of that class who have a free pass through the world, "blow high, or blow low," dodged into the bush, as we cleared the encampment, and returning to the fires, gathered a rich harvest of ash-pone and spare-ribs, and thus profited by the general calamity. The majority, however, had a very afflicting march, without tasting any food the whole day. The next point of importance which we reached was the Maumee, or the Miami of the Lakes. Here the army was halted awhile, as though to view the desolate prospect around. On the opposite bank stood the ruins of the post that had lately been abandoned. After a short consultation among the officers, we were marched down upon the frozen river, in solid order, with all our heavy ordnance and baggage, to proceed to the Foot of the Rapids. Here we were presented with a lovely road, that human ingenuity could not imitate. But we were somewhat in the condition of old Bob Armstead, who used to say, "When I was a young man, and was poor, and had nothing to eat, I had a beautiful set of teeth; but now I am old and rolling in plenty, not a tooth have I got." So when we were strong, and had sufficient elasticity to march, we had no roads to march on. But now, when we were exhausted and starved, and could hardly drag one foot after the other, we had as beautiful a turnpike as Jack Frost could make. We were, however, helped by the philosophy of a good man, who, when he had the rheumatism, thanked the Lord it was not the gout; and when he had the gout, he was thankful that it was not the gout and rheumatism together. Late in the day our route lay through a rich bottom, where there were about fifteen hundred bushels of corn standing. As soon as we entered this inviting field the army broke in every direction, like a drove of frightened cattle. Deaf to the commands of our officers, and regardless of all military order, we tore down the precious ears, and filled our pockets and our bosoms till we were richly laden with the spoils of the field. With the musket in one hand, and an ear of corn in the other, we marched on, greedily devouring the unstinted supply of a merciful Providence. No pound-cake ever tasted half so delicious, till the wire-edge of our starvation was worn off. We were amazed that we had lived so long in the world, and had never discovered before the transcendent luxury of raw corn. Toward evening, we arrived at the Foot of the Rapids, as it was then called. Here we were met by an appalling object. Our rangers had brought in the body of one who had a few days before left our camp for Detroit, in company with Doctor M'Heehan, under the protection of a white flag. It seems they had stopped the first night on the banks of the Maumee, and taken up their lodging in an old cellar, which was all that remained of an improvement which once occupied the site. Here they were surprised by a party of Indians, the Doctor taken prisoner, and his companion shot and scalped. When we came up, we saw Major L., of the Virginia militia, spreading himself over the corpse, and with all the fervor and pathos of Mark Antony, addressing his men, and calling upon them to behold the cruelty of the savage foe, and to hate their red-coat allies who had prompted them to the revolting deed: "Drink in—drink in the spirit of noble revenge! stiffen your sinews, summon up your joints, and nerve your vengeful arms for deeds of mighty daring!" Seeing several men turn away sufficiently infuriated, I marched up to see if I could be inspired with the same desirable ardor;

11

for it seemed to be in horrid harmony with the
dreariness of the surrounding scenery. I looked
down upon the corpse, which wore all the freshness
and bloom of life, and contracted my muscles, and
clinched my teeth, and held my breath, and put
forth every device, mental and physical, in courting
the furies, but all to no purpose. I felt no fell
spirit of vengeance gnawing at my heart. Despite
of my late supply of provender, the sensation of
hunger was the dominant distress within. I saw
that it was sad butchery that had been perpetrated
by naked savages, who had been goaded and hunted
down themselves, like beasts of the forest. But the
sight neither augmented nor diminished the principle with which I set out—the *amor patriæ* which I
had drank in at my mother's breast—nor did it
rouse me to emulate the barbarous example. And
this patriotism sustained us long after Major L. had
grounded his fury at his own peaceful fireside.

Here it was determined to take up our Winter
quarters. We formed a hollow square in a thick
grove, on the most commanding hill. We then had
to fell trees, and throw a breastwork around the
whole army, before we were permitted to retire to
rest. As it regards regular meals, they were fast
going out of fashion; and that night supper was
postponed. After we were suffered to see to ourselves, each mess kindled a princely fire; for whatever else might betide, we always had an enviable
supply of wood. We then sat down, in doleful

plight, to parch corn; and we comforted each other by talking martially about Tupper's men, who had occupied that ground before us, and who had been driven to such straits as to eat roasted hickory roots. Our ambition rose no higher than parched corn, till a luckless epicure exclaimed, "Boys, did you ever hear of hog-meat and hominy?" "O! don't mention hominy; you will make us squeal right out." "Well, sirs, it is not only mentionable, but it is highly feasible. Now, if you will only cast in a generous contribution of corn, we'll borrow a camp-kettle, and make a royal mess of hominy." Having been partly raiséd on hominy, we all understood very well how to dispose of the good dish when cooked, but we had brought out no recipe concerning the preparation. However, it was decided, without a dissenting voice, that it must be boiled. Moreover, we knew that we had taken the first step right, according to Mrs. Glass — we had "caught" the corn. So at it we went. All other business was suspended, and we laid as close siege to the camp-kettle as ever Edward, King of England, did to Calais. Every hour or sô we would dip up a spoonful to try it; but it really appeared that the longer we boiled it the harder it got. Wo persevered till day dawned upon us, and then, to our great mortification, found that we had not only lost our corn, but our night's rest.

Our distressing march had closed; and for several subsequent weeks we tasted the labors and fatigues

of a soldier's life. The troops were employed daily
in digging trenches, felling trees, splitting logs,
setting up picketing, raising block-houses, and doing
every kind of work that was necessary to fortify
our post, which embraced nine acres, and which,
when finished, was called "*Fort Meigs.*" This season of fatigue was replete with hardships, especially
as it was in the depth of Winter, and accompanied
with many privations. However, our bodies and
minds were actively employed, which rendered our
condition far preferable to that which immediately
followed; for having finished the public and private
work which was necessary to make our quarters
tolerable, if not comfortable, a state of indolence
and inactivity succeeded that was highly deleterious
to the army. The Winter was unusually severe,
even on the frontiers. One unfortunate sentinel
froze at his post in less than two hours. We here
had an opportunity of testing the mistaken policy
of some fond parents, who think that they have
accomplished a stroke of generalship, when they
hide their children from the contagious disorders
which occasionally visit their neighborhood. Numbers were swept off by the mumps, measles, hoop-
ing-cough, and other distempers, which came upon
them at this unpropitious time and place, where
there was little remedy and less medical skill, and
where the soft hand of the warm-hearted mother,
and the sleepless solicitude of the affectionate sister
could not reach them. They died daily. The

mournful air of "Roslin Castle" became the prevailing music of the day, while the sharp rifle-cracks
of the platoon told how many were borne to their
long home. A deadly homesickness overwhelmed
our troops, and we believe a repentance of war was
kindled in every bosom, from the highest to the
lowest.

Some stirring incident would occasionally occur,
as a kind of ennui-breaker, and rouse us from our
torpor. At one time our spies brought intelligence
that a party of about seven hundred Indians were
diverting themselves with a war-dance on the ice,
near the mouth of the river. In the dusk of the
evening, General Harrison, at the head of fifteen
hundred troops, started for the party, although not
particularly invited. At a late hour in the night
the blazing fires of the enemy appeared on the bank
of the river. We were now wide awake. The day
of battle, about which so much had been said, was
now right before us. The detachment, thrown into
a crescent, with the artillery in the center, cautiously approached. We found the fires burning
bright with recent fuel; but the Indians had fled.
This disappointment was probably owing to our imprudence in marching on the river. It is said that
an Indian, by laying his ear flat on the ice, can
discover the approach of a large force five miles
distant.

It was now announced that those who were sick
or exhausted might tarry by the fires till morning.

Some were so completely worn out that they not only accepted the boon, but threw themselves down by the fires, and, without a sentinel to guard the camp, fell into a profound sleep. For my own part, I felt that my strength was almost gone; but some very forcible questions presented themselves to my mind; such as, how far had the wily enemy retreated? Might they not now be lurking in the dark forest before us, watching all our movements? Again I rubbed the crown of my head, and concluded to value my scalp at a higher price of suffering than had yet been realized. It also occurred that I was not made of softer clay than my fellows, and that there was a point of endurance beyond which none could go—a point at which the officers themselves must succumb. So I would not report myself among either the sick, the lame, or the lazy. The General, being disappointed in the matter of the dance, concluded to proceed on to the River Raisin, and to bury our dead, who had been inhumanly left on the field, and were now "bleaching in the northern blast." He, therefore, sent back to Meigs for sleds, pickaxes, spades, etc., and the main body moved on. The frozen face of the river was an unbroken level. It had been put into excellent order by a previous sprinkle of snow. There was no impediment in our way to call for vigilance. The companies marched in very compact order, each man being partially sustained by his comrades. These circumstances, together with the uniform and monotonous tread of the troops, acting on men so enervated, induced an unconquerable drowsiness. Numbers slept as they marched along. Some platoons, thus dozing, so far diverged from their course as to lose their companies, and mix with strange columns. I not only slept myself, but had short, distinct dreams. In this way we marched all night. About day-break we began to approach the lake. The ice had evidently become softer. We pressed on till our way became quite sloppy. We persevered, however, till the wheels of our six-pounder broke through the ice. The expedition was then abandoned. The troops were marched to a projecting point of land, where we had a short intermission. About thirty minutes were spent in dozing or eating, as drowsiness or hunger prevailed, when we were again beat to arms, and marched back to our fort, where we arrived late in the evening, having marched sixty-four miles in twenty-two consecutive hours. The detachment was so prostrated, that it was exonerated from all military duty for several days.

The cheerless and wearisome· months of Winter rolled heavily along. At last some faint indications of Spring began to appear. One afternoon, as numbers were gathered together on the "parade," two strangers, finely mounted, appeared on the western bank of the river, and seemed to be taking a very calm and deliberate survey of our works. It was a strange thing to see travelers in that wild country, and we commonly held such to be enemies, till they proved themselves to be friends. So one of our batteries was cleared forthwith, and the gentlemen were saluted with a shot that tore up the earth about them, and put them to a hasty flight. If that ball had struck its mark much bloodshed might have been prevented; for we learned subsequently that our illustrious visitors were Proctor and Tecumseh. The garrison was immediately employed in cutting deep traverses through the fort, taking down the tents, and preparing for a siege. The work accomplished in a few hours, under the excitement of the occasion, was prodigious. The grand traverse being completed, each mess was ordered to excavate, under the embankment, suitable lodgings, as substitutes for our tents. Those rooms were shot-proof, and bomb-proof, except in the event of a shell falling in the traverse, and at the mouth of a cave. This gave occasion, in the course of the siege, for an English officer, who had been taken prisoner, and returned on parole, to say to his general, "It is powder and shot thrown away to fire at that fort. I can compare the Americans to nothing but an army of ground-hogs. As soon as a sentinel cries, 'Shot,' every man dodges under ground; and the ball has scarcely swept over the ground before they are on their feet again, inquiring into the damage." This observation of our prisoner was true, as it regarded that portion of our men who were not on duty for the time being. But the shot did consid-

erable damage to those who were necessarily at
their posts.

The above works were scarcely completed before
it was discovered that the enemy, under cover of
night, had constructed batteries, on a commanding
hill, west of the river. There their artillery-men
were posted; but the principal part of their army
occupied the old English fort below. Their Indian
allies appeared to have a roving commission; for
they beset us on every side. The cannonading commenced in good earnest on both sides. It was,
however, more constant on the British side, because
they had a more extensive mark to batter. We
had nothing to fire at but their batteries; but they
were coolly and deliberately attended to; and it was
believed that more than one of their guns were dismounted during the siege. One of our militia-men
took his station on the embankment, and gratuitously forewarned us of every shot. In this he became so skillful that he could, in almost every case,
predict the destination of the ball. As soon as the
smoke issued from the muzzle of the gun he would
cry out "shot," or "bomb," as the case might be.
Sometimes he would exclaim, "Block-house No. 1,"
or, "Look out, main battery;" "Now for the meat-
house;" "Good-by, if you will pass." In spite of
all the expostulations of his friends, he maintained
his post. One day there came a shot that seemed
to defy all his calculations. He stood silent—mo-
tionless—perplexed. In the same instant he was

swept into eternity. Poor man! he should have considered that when there was no obliquity in the issue of the smoke, either to the right or left, above or below, the fatal messenger would travel in the direct line of his vision. He reminded me of the peasant, in the siege of Jerusalem, who cried out, "Woe to the city! woe to the temple! woe to myself!" On the most active day of the investment there was as many as five hundred cannon-balls and bombs thrown at our fort. Meantime, the Indians, climbing up into the trees, fired incessantly upon us. Such was their distance, that many of their balls barely reached us, and fell harmless to the ground. Occasionally they inflicted dangerous and even fatal wounds. The number killed in the fort was small, considering the profusion of powder and ball expended on us. About eighty were slain, many wounded, and several had to suffer the amputation of limbs. The most dangerous duty which we performed within the precincts of the fort was in covering the magazine. Previous to this the powder had been deposited in wagons, and these stationed in the traverse. Here there was no security against bombs. It was therefore thought to be prudent to remove the powder into a small block-house, and cover it with earth. The enemy, judging our design from our movements, now directed all their shot to this point. Many of their balls were red-hot. Wherever they struck they raised a cloud of smoke, and made a frightful hissing. An officer passing our quarters, said, "Boys, who will volunteer to cover the magazine?" Fool-like, away several of us went. As soon as we reached the spot, there came a ball and took off one man's head. The spades and dirt flew faster than any of us had before witnessed. In the midst of our job a bomb-shell fell on the roof, and lodging on one of the braces, it spun round for a moment. Every soldier fell prostrate on his face, and with breathless horror awaited the vast explosion, which we expected would crown all our earthly sufferings. Only one of all the gang presumed to reason on the case. He silently argued that, as the shell had not bursted as quick as usual, there might be something wrong in its arrangement. If it bursted where it was, and the magazine exploded, there could be no escape: it was death anyhow; so he sprung to his feet, seized a boat-hook, and pulling the hissing missile to the ground, and jerking the smoking match from its socket, discovered that the shell was filled with inflammable matter, which, if once ignited, would have wrapped the whole building in a sheet of flame. This circumstance added wings to our shovels; and we were right glad when the officer said, "That will do: go to your lines." When retired to my cool subterranean lodge, I called a meeting of the whole cabinet of "Mansoul;" in which, after considerable discussion, the following preamble and resolution were unanimously adopted:

" *Whereas*, Volunteering is a mere work of super-

erogation, and commonly founded on animal passions, and, moreover, brings no revenue of respect
to our judgment; therefore,

"*Resolved*, That this shall be the last volunteer
service with us, come what will."

To this I have strictly adhered, both in State and
Church. Indeed, in our Church, where there is
such stupendous locomotive power, volunteering is
truly ridiculous. Although I have generally gone
where the determinate council have sent me, yet
I still cherish an abiding and habitual diffidence
about flourishing in a "*forlorn hope.*"

The siege still went on with various success on
both sides, the enemy becoming more formidable
by experience and practice, till the fifth of May.
We will begin with that day by saying it was set
apart by the authorities of the State of Ohio, as a
day of fasting, humiliation, and prayer. The infidel may say, "Pshaw! that was only accidental."
But if that said infidel will take the pains to examine the papers and journals of the times, he
will find that nearly all the victories which were
gained in the last war, by the American arms, were
gained on fast-days. On the fifth of May, a reënforcement, under General Clay, was descending the
Maumee. The previous evening Harrison had sent
a confidential officer to meet the force, and give
them the plan of operation. A division of the body
was to land on the western shore, and by a rapid
and secret march come down upon the enemy's bat-

teries, spike their cannons, and then retreat down
to the river under cover of our guns, till they could
be transported to the fort. The other division was
to make their way down the river, in their boats,
to the garrison. As soon as this last division came
in sight on the rapids, they attracted the sole attention of the armies on both sides of the river. Meeting with some obstructions in the river, they were
obliged to land. This they did under a heavy fire
from the Indians on the eastern shore. A detachment, embracing our company, was marched out of
the fort, to cover the Kentuckians who were coming
in. With little loss they entered the fort.

As soon as we had retired to the garrison, the
Petersburg, the Pittsburg, and Greensburg volunteers, with some companies of regulars, and Captain
Sebree's brave militia, numbering, in all, four hundred men, were drawn up in a deep ravine outside
of the picketing, preparatory to a sortie. The object was to destroy a battery which had been constructed on our side of the river, which had done
us much harm, and which was supported by fifteen
hundred Indians. The sally was also to be so timed
as to divert the attention of the enemy from the
approach of Dudley's command, that was slyly stealing upon them. The few moments immediately
preceding the battle are, of all others, the most
awful. Then the soldier is capable of reflection,
and the mental vessel, under the high pressure,
moves fast. To counteract this, our first lieuten-

ant, who had been nicknamed "Old Sluefoot," passed up and down our line, encouraging the men. He was a wicked man, but had so many good traits withal, that he was very popular. "Boys," said he, "when they give the word, do you all rush with a tremendous shout." And then he exclaimed with an awful oath, that there was nothing under heaven like a shout. At last the word was given—the charge made. As we cleared the ravine the whole forest was in a blaze. The continuous roar of the rifles was like the long roll of the drum—no intermission. The balls flew like hailstones—*pish—pish—pish;* now and then *rap—rap.* In our passage to the woods we became exposed to the British battery on the other side of the river. They were not slow in playing their artillery on us; but we heard it not—we felt it not—we saw it not. With a blazing line before us, and a crowd of anxious witnesses in the fort behind, we had no time for way-side chitchat and lateral sallies. Those who were in the fort said it was amazing to see how the balls plowed up the earth about our heels, and with what little effect. But while the foe were engaged in this very act, Dudley's Kentuckians rushed down upon their rear, took their batteries, and spiked their guns. If they had then retreated to the river, according to orders, happy would it have been for them. But, unfortunately, the Indian yell was raised in the forest. That was more than a Kentucky ear could bear. Our victors rushed to meet their mortal foe, and a general slaughter ensued. After the siege, while gathering up the dead, in several places were found the white and red man, as they had fallen in single combat, locked in deadly strife. This imprudence was not confined to raw troops. There was too much of it on our side of the river; for when our sortie was crowned with success, the eastern battery destroyed, and thirty artillery-men, with two officers, taken prisoners, our soldiers continued to drive the Indians till we were beguiled about three-quarters of a mile into the woods, and the enemy began to outflank, and get between us and our works. In this move Sebree's company became surrounded; but they fought desperately at close quarters, muzzle to muzzle, and hatchet to hatchet, till a regular company cut a passage through. This militia company suffered more than all the rest of the detachment. We, however, considered that victory was on our side; for we retreated into a fort that was now comparatively safe. The enemy's guns were all silenced, and if they continued the siege, their only hope could be in storming, and this was most ardently desired on our side. We were afterward informed by deserters that this was their intention. The English general had engaged the Indians to assist him in this work at the breaking of the day. Some barrels of whisky, as part and parcel of the contract, were issued to the savages that evening, and they spent the night in drinking and torturing

the unhappy prisoners who had fallen into their
hands.   At the same time the company of Irishmen
that we carried into Meigs, were treated with
American hospitality, and regularly drew their rations, even to their whisky.   They were profuse in
their expressions of gratitude, and their tongues
moved as on a pivot.   Just before day-break Proctor
sent for the Indian chiefs, and asked them if they
were all ready for the storm.   They answered, "All
ready! S'pose you take your braves and go before,
and drive your nails into the big guns, as Kantuc
serve you; then we come—Indian much—strong!"
This the English were not disposed to do.   The
next morning the dissatisfied Indians began to file
off by companies and tribes; and the English general becoming alarmed, hastily raised the siege, and
retreated, leaving much of his baggage behind.

When None of our company were left on the field.
About twenty-five were wounded — some of them
dangerously—who recovered; and six died of their
wounds.   These added to the sixteen, whose deaths
might be traced to their exposure in the Black
Swamp, made our total loss twenty-two.

When I look back at all through which we
passed, it seems to me a mystery of God's goodness
that I was spared.   But this mystery, reader, is
partially solved by the reflection, that I had a pious
and praying mother, who pleaded for the prodigal,
day and night, with strong cries and tears.   When
the news reached P——, that there had been an

engagement at Fort Meigs, and that many of the volunteers were wounded, and some killed, my mother was sorely afflicted. The sound of every footstep on the threshold harrowed up her soul. She could not think of stepping out for fear of evil tidings. And what made it still more distressing was, that it was her regular class day. From the means of grace she was not to be driven by the smiles of friends or frowns of enemies. To her closet she fled, and while wrapped up in a conflict of prayer, *she said*, and *I believed her*, that God gave her a comfortable assurance that all was well. She now went forth to her class meeting. As she passed down the street, the postmaster, who had been a schoolmate of mine, ran to the door, with tears in his eyes, and said, "Mrs. L., I have just heard from the army; my poor brother John is killed; but, thank God! Alfred is safe." Under the mingling emotions of sympathy and gratitude, she burst into tears, and as soon as utterance was given, answered, "Mr. S., truly I feel with you the loss of your excellent brother; but the Lord had before given me the most satisfactory assurances in regard to my son." So she hastened on to her class, and in the bosom of an affectionate and praying Church buried all her sorrows. And I do believe that if I could live to be as old as Methusalah, I should still be childish enough—if childish it be—to say, blessed be God for a praying mother!

12

IX.

THE SEQUEL AT FORT MEIGS.

OUR readers will perceive that, to the raising of
the siege of Fort Meigs, our campaign was nothing
but a scene of suffering and toil, with the exception
of our gala promenade to Chillicothe. We have yet
to speak of the slain, the wounded, and the dying,
as these must be taken into the account in reckoning the cost. After the sortie, we visited the hospital. Reclining on a bed in one corner lay a gal-
lant officer, who was attached to the engineer department. He had rendered much service from the
beginning of the war, and his courage was unquestionable. But now, in consequence of the irritation
of his nerves by the roar of artillery, the bursting
of bombs, the pain of his wounds, and his feverish
condition, he had become as timid and as peevish as
a child, and was constantly apprehensive of being
torn to pieces by a cannon-ball.

> "Lord, what is man! poor, feeble man!
> Formed of the dust at first."

Stretched on a pallet lay Captain Jack Shore, "the
darling of our crew." He had formerly commanded
a merchantman; and although only a private in our

company, and a sailor withal, he was better qualified for a military officer than any man in our
corps. But he *was a sailor;* and that, in the land-
lubber's vocabulary, implies every thing that is
awkward and back-handed, on horse or foot. He
was related to General Harrison, and had more
than once taken tea with his distinguished cousin,
"*sub rosa,*" in the grand marquee. At the commencement of the cannonading, he had solicited a
station in one of the principal batteries, and han-
dled the big guns to admiration. One of the guns
was dismounted by a shot from the enemy, and an
iron splinter pierced his leg. It was immediately
extracted. The wound was considered unimportant,
and was slightly bandaged. However, in a few
hours it became distressingly painful, and he retired
to the hospital. He was now suffering in the last
stage of lock-jaw. In his spasmodic agony, the
smoke of his torment literally rose in a mist from
his blanket. We gave him a hot bath, but to no
purpose; he sank in death, lamented by all.

In another corner lay the handsome and delicate
Cluff, mortally wounded. He was earnestly begging
a messmate to read to him. In this he was grati-
fied. We can not recollect the book that was used,
but remember well noticing at the time that it was
not a religious work. His comrade would read a
few lines, and then ask him how he liked it. With
a vacant stare he would shake his head, but immediately repeat, "Read, read." The thought struck

me at the time that it was the Word of life which he wished to hear from, in that trying hour, but that he had not yet reached that point of contrition which would embolden him to express the humiliating request. And, alas! alas! I had not moral courage to direct him to a source of comfort which had been so shamefully neglected by myself.

In a tent, surrounded by his affectionate mess, was nursed the brave, intelligent, and well-educated Booker. He spoke of death, not only with composure, but sometimes with exultation. His hope was cheering; but it soon appeared, from his conversation, that it rested on the common opiate of dying soldiers: he was dying for his country. Although my stock of theological lore was very scant, yet it showed me that this would not do; but I durst not point him to a better foundation, lest he might say, ironically, but justly, "Physician, heal thyself." Precious young man! he was, doubtless, less faulty than myself. He felt that he was consummating the work which God had given him to do, by sacrificing himself on the altar of his country, while "I knew my duty, but I did it not." We have not time to speak particularly of our fallen comrades. There they lie, each in his dusty bed, deep in the cold banks of the Maumee, awaiting the grand reveille that will usher in the day-break of immortality, "which shall their flesh restore." But, in seeing all this, the impression fastened on my mind, and revolving years have not erased it, that if there is any situation which calls loudly for a pious, industrious, and self-denying minister of Christ, it is the army.

We have before us a communication, lately received from the Peace Society. We cordially agree with it, that the spirit of Christianity is the spirit of peace. We are, moreover, highly delighted with the project of a grand court of arbitration, governed by well-defined international laws, to settle differences that may arise between governments. We believe that the common safety and interests of all nations may yet prompt them to establish such a tribunal. And if the Peace Society stood upon the high resolve, 1. To do all that we righteously and consistently can to prevent war; 2. To do all that we possibly can to mitigate its evils, when it does come, and labor by all justifiable means to restore peace; we see no cause why the whole Christian community might not advocate it. But we really fear, from a perusal of its documents, that it leans to ultraism:

1. Because it claims too much—to be the *summum bonum*—the "land's-end" of all conservative virtue. It boasts of controlling the press. "It has waked up the pulpit." Waked up the pulpit, indeed! Were it not for the pulpit, and its associate means of grace, all divinely instituted, we doubt whether a Peace Society would have ever been mentioned on the continent of America. This is the first emanation we have received from the

said society, and yet our conscience bears us witness
that we have, according to the grace given, preached
peace by Jesus Christ for, lo! these twenty years
and more.

2. Because its morality outstrips the Bible, and
even leaves its Divine Author in the dark distance.
The Peace Advocate holds that the time is coming
when no conscientious minister can officiate as a
chaplain in the army. Surely that will be a day
of high lustration! a day when mortal man will be
too conscientious to preach for Christ at all; for he
requires *his ministers* to preach the Gospel to *every
creature*—to the civilized and the barbarian—to the
master and the servant—to the sailor and the soldier. Did our Lord's commission embrace the soldier? We judge so from his practice. When a
centurion sent for him to minister to his family,
our Savior promptly answered the call. And when
the centurion, on second thought, feared he had
ventured too much, and sent a messenger to modify
the request, our Lord turned to his followers and
said, "Verily, I have not found so great faith; no,
not in Israel;" not even in his own apostles. Again,
the first Gospel sermon that was preached to the
Gentiles was particularly addressed to Cornelius, a
centurion of the band, called the Italian band, and
his devout soldiers. And this by the special command of Heaven. In all probability it was preached
in the barracks. It is true, all this was before the
Peace Advocate had waked up the pulpit. We hope

the time will *never* come when ministers of the Gospel will be so tender in conscience as not to go any where this side of hell to save souls from perdition.

3. Because it claims affinity, or seeks partnership with every one who will in any wise promote its design. The flowers of Pettit are quoted to prove the inconsistency of acting as a chaplain in the army. We wonder that the Peace Society could not see that Mr. Pettit was more intent on degrading the Christian religion than promoting peace. He was trying to show what a poor, weak, pusillanimous thing Christianity is—how it creates a superstitious conscience, that "makes cowards of us all." This was just what we might expect infidelity to throw out in her pangs of expiration. But the Peace Society will not soon swell its ranks with Christian men and women, if it expects them to enlist at the enormous expense of underwriting the Pettit parole. Christianity make cowards of soldiers! Time and experience have each placed a foot on that gross libel. Did religion make cowards of the Methodist soldiers in the battle of Fontenoy? No. One of the society cried out with holy joy, as he marched into the field of battle, "I am going to rest in the bosom of Jesus." Others, when they fell, covered with wounds, exclaimed, "I am going to my beloved." Others, "Come, Lord Jesus, come quickly!" When William Clements had his arm broken by a musket-ball, they would have carried

him out of the battle; but he said, "No, I have an arm left yet to hold a sword; I will not go." When a second shot broke his other arm, he said, "I am as happy as I can be out.of paradise." John Evans, having both his legs taken off by a cannon-ball, was laid across a cannon to die, where, as long as he could speak, he was praising God with joyful lips. John Haine, of the cavalry, filled with an assurance of Divine protection, cried out, "The French have no' ball molded and billeted to touch my life this day." After seven hours' hard fighting, a cannon-ball struck his horse from under him, and down he tumbled in the dust. An officer cried at the top of his voice, "Haine, where is your God now?" Springing again to his feet, he replied, "Sir, he is here with me, and he will bring me out of this battle." Presently there came a ball and took the officer's head off. O! these simple-hearted Christians carried their Bibles in their knapsacks. Their conscience was not shaped by lectures, and preambles, and resolutions, all tending to canonize and deify one Christian grace at the expense of all others, or to exalt one Bible duty as a commutation for the rest. They *feared God* and *honored the king*. They rendered unto *Cæsar* the things that are Cæsar's, and unto *God* the things that are God's. And yet, even in the army, they were a peculiar people; for while the soldiers were gathering watches and jewels on the battle-field, and said to them, "Come, will ye not fly upon the spoil?" their' noble answer was, "We have Christ in our hearts; we desire no plunder." They believed that, in their peculiar place, it was their duty to fight for their king and country; but they knew that it was no duty to God or their country to plunder the dead. But to resume:

After the hasty retreat of the enemy, a detachment was sent out to scour the woods, and gather up the dead. They brought in a great number, and spread them out before one of the gates. They had been abused and mutilated in a most shocking manner. About midnight it fell to my lot to stand a lonely sentinel over this ghastly, silent congregation. The stars shone sufficiently bright to give effect to the scene. As I looked down upon them, I became more astonished at myself than any other part of the creation. I felt truly like an apostate from human nature. A few months before I could not feel comfortable in the idea of sleeping alone. The sight of a corpse could once afford me subject-matter of trembling for weeks to come. Even in the Black Swamp I had a tear to spare to the expiring pack-horse. But now, at this lonely hour, while all the army were wrapped in sleep, except a few widely-scattered sentinels, I could look down on this ghastly, disfigured group, without even a tremor stealing over my nerves. I found that my heart had become wretchedly hardened by the scenes, sufferings, and conflicts of war. What particularly afflicted me was, I thought that all the

13

social feelings and sympathies of my soul were clean gone forever; that I should no more feel with those who feel, or weep with those who weep. But I found subsequently that in this I was mistaken. After I returned to the pacific relations of life, the kindred streams gushed back, I was restored to the fellowship of humanity, and more—glory be to God! through whose mercy the day-star from on high hath visited my soul—admitted to the communion of saints, and the household of faith.

The next day, after laying out the dead as decently as circumstances would admit, we committed them to the earth. Then all the cannon around the fort were fired in slow and solemn succession, while the wild and unpeopled banks of the Maumee echoed and reëchoed the funeral honors to the distant lake.

Our army was now restrained from further operations by the War Department, till the contemplated battle on the Lake. As Perry stood in need of men, there was another beat for volunteers in the fort. This matter was not without its temptations. But I rigidly declined for the following reasons:

1. I remembered burying the magazine, and the subsequent pledge. It was said, a bad promise is better broken than kept. Yes, but there lay "the rub;" I was not yet convinced that it was a *bad* promise.

2. I rather suspected that there would be hotter times on the lake than we had seen yet; and I had

never vaunted myself on a surplus of courage. It is true, I had heretofore felt a kind of fear—I will not call it cowardice, lest it should involve too many—a fear of public opinion—a fear of disgracing myself, my family, my country, etc., which had answered as an excellent substitute for courage, and had borne me up in all our sufferings and dangers thus far; but I had not sounded all its depth and shoal; and how it would work when we came to be grappled yard-arm and yard-arm, I could not tell.

3. I could not bear the idea of being recognized by some old salt, perhaps some shipmate, under a soldier's coat, as I knew the standing antipathy of a sailor to my temporary profession. If they had held out, on a pole, a suit of blue, jacket and trowsers, with a neat tarpaulin, it is probable that all the other scruples of this soldier might have fled, and he might have snapped at the bait. But, avast! As I had started on a land cruise, I thought it was best to end it before engaging in new enterprises.

Soon after this the fort was broken up, or reduced to an inconsiderable post, and the army was concentrated at Camp Seneca. Here a poor deserter was brought in. He was a young man of agreeable appearance. The court-martial condemned him to be shot. The sad day arrived. The whole army was paraded and formed into a semi-square. The executive platoon was marched out. The unhappy culprit was blindfolded and seated with his back against a stump. A deadly silence pervaded the whole host. Harrison, in full uniform, towered in the midst. I was near enough to the condemned to observe that he trembled like an aspen, and writhed in all the bitterness of hopeless death. The thrilling word was given, "Make ready! take aim!" Here the General waved his hand to the officer, and announced to the trembling deserter that his sin was forgiven. He then solemnly raised his right hand to heaven, and pledged himself, before the Lord of hosts, and God of the armies of heaven, that the next deserter who should be condemned by a court-martial should die. Harrison was always beloved by his men, but never did he appear more majestic or more lovely than he did on that occasion. The poor young man seemed for a while petrified, and utterly incapable of comprehending the sum of benevolence; but when restored to his quarters he gave loose to the most unbounded joy. The next day he was employed on fatigue, in driving an ox cart. As he went, he leaped, and danced, and sung, and squealed, and seemed to be seeking, in every member, every faculty, every sense, for some vital testimony that he was alive, and not dead.

X.

ENEMY PURSUED–DISCHARGED– HOME.

THE news of Perry's victory set every thing in motion again. The army was marched down to Sandusky Bay, and thence transported by boats to Put-in Bay, a beautiful harbor formed on the bosom of the lake by the position of some islands. In this bay lay the American squadron, with its captured fleet, entirely land-locked. It was distressing, in the dark watches of the night, to hear the agonizing groans of the wounded and dying on board the hospital-ship, who had suffered in the late conflict. On these islands we rested a few days. While here, another deserter was brought in. He was condemned. The usual solemn preliminaries were attended to—the word given; but there was no Harrison on the field to wave the signal of mercy, and the poor criminal fell.

At last the important day came, which was to land us on the shores of our enemies. The army embarked in the fleet and a great multitude of boats which had been gathered together. The General, with the Petersburg, Virginia, volunteers, sailed on board the Ariel, with Commodore Perry. The morning was beautiful beyond description. The sun shone with refulgent splendor on our polished arms. The martial waving of the snow-white plumes of the officers, the various uniforms of regulars and volunteers, the solemn silence, interrupted only by the regular movement of springing oars, altogether formed a scene awfully grand. But the scene became still more imposing, when, arriving within a few rods of the shore, every soldier expecting to breast the fury of an ambushed foe, all at once the flapping banner of our host was unfurled to the whistling wind, the concentrated music of the whole army burst, in a national air, on the ears of a feeling soldiery, and the whole atmosphere around us was filled with the shouts of freemen. It was terrible, even to ourselves, although our bosoms swelled high with the expectation of victory, and every heart throbbed with national pride at the sublimity of the scene. In one moment the extended line of boats struck the shore, and in the next the whole embattled host stood on the bank. We took up our line of march for Malden. But we soon learned that the fort had been fired, and that the English had retreated. All had fled but the brave Tecumseh. The citizens told us that he sat on his faithful charger, at the head of the street, and looked till he saw the van of our army entering the suburbs below. He then turned his horse with a sigh, and as the Americans entered one end of the town, he slowly rode out of the other. He had exhausted all his eloquence in trying to persuade the British general to leave him and his braves in possession of the fort. Those who had an opportunity of knowing him, said he was as much superior to Proctor in humanity as he was in courage. To finish his history at once, we will add, that he fell in the battle that followed, in the midst of his people, that were stationed in·the swamp, and, as they say, pierced with many balls; and was buried four miles in the rear. There we suspect he remains to the present day. And the razor-strops, and other precious relics, that will be handed down to future generations, as samples of his hide, are all, as the old chief himself would express it, "*ec-shaw.*" And we believe if his resurrection should take place to-morrow, it would interrupt nobody's shaving utensils in Kentucky or elsewhere.

As soon as possible we went in pursuit of the enemy. It was my fortune to go by way of the lake. We soon found that we had not yet passed through all the shades of military starvation. Before we crossed the lake, we had our rations issued for several days, and were ordered to jerk our beef, to the end that it might be better preserved, and made more convenient to carry. And it was, indeed, made much more convenient to carry, because, by that process, it became so depreciated in size and weight, that it did not last more than half the time contemplated. And now we had to embark destitute of sea stores. It is true, we had the privilege, three times in each day, of ranging our noses around the caboose, while the jolly tars served up their allowance in almost all the variety of culinary science. This was the more aggravating to me, as among their dishes I recognized many an old acquaintance, which I had not tasted since I last entered Cape Henry. There was the "duff," the "chowder," the smoking "lobschouse," and that, too, served up in the very *fac-simile* of my old smoked tin-pot, out of which I had quaffed many a gallon of tea, and other good things, in by-gone days. Meantime, the sailors looked carelessly among us, as if they thought gentlemen of the army lived upon the wind. I had a great mind to reveal myself to them, and fall upon their sympathies; but as I had taken it upon myself to sustain the character of a soldier, for the time being, I concluded to endure hardness as a good soldier. We went on board hungry—we were hungry through the whole cruise, and were at last landed at the mouth of the Thames as ravenous as wolves. For several miles we marched through a mixed population of French and Yankees, and gathered up enough scraps to keep soul and body together. At last we encamped in a beautiful neighborhood that was settled by Scotchmen, who were more loyal than the Englishmen. They would neither give nor sell to His Majesty's enemies. They acknowledged that we had ample power to take; that was one thing; but to collude with the enemy was another. It was against general orders to plunder, and our battalion had strictly obeyed. But now we had come to our wit's end. At last our commander said, "Boys, you see your case: we can get nothing from these farms for love or money: there is no alternative but to help yourselves." One of every mess took his tomahawk, and walking about the fields, brought in an abundance of pigs, turkeys, geese, etc.; and there was great feasting in the camp.

At last our van came up with the enemy. It is unnecessary to give a particular account of the battle, as it has been so often described. Indeed, there is but little to be said about it. The Kentucky mounted men rushed down upon their lines like a hurricane, and swept all before them. It was a momentary conflict. The whole army surrendered. The Indians on the flank prolonged the fight for a while, but soon fled. Our battalion, which constituted the rear guard, could not get up in time to stop a ball; and I for one was right glad of it; for our time of service was now expired, and the word "home, sweet home," seemed to gather additional charms every day. We returned to Detroit by the lake. The weather was unusually squally. The vessel that I was in carried an enormous gun amidships. It was lashed fore and aft. The militia becoming very seasick, crowded down the main hatchway into the hold. We were suddenly struck by a squall, when the Long Tom breaking the lash-

ing at the muzzle, slued down to leeward, and the
schooner was struck down on her beam-end. The
water gushed into the hatchway — the soldiers
gushed out by platoons. Those who were on deck
held on for their lives, and every soul expected in a
few minutes to be in eternity. A sailor who was
down in the scuppers, had the presence of mind to
let fly the fore-sheet, when she partially righted,
and the gun was secured, and the sail shortened.
It was, however, a very narrow escape. Though
alarmed, I recollect, in the midst of the danger, a
mortification—a kind of cheapness seemed to creep
over me at the thought, that after I had traversed
over so many mountain swells, and had escaped so
many dangers, on the wide Atlantic, I was about to
be cast away in a mill-pond, comparatively. We
safely arrived at Detroit, where, shortly after, we
were discharged on the public parade, the General
pronouncing over us a high encomium, and declaring
that we had set an example of military subordina-
tion to the whole army.

After our discharge we were landed in Cleveland,
and left at perfect liberty to follow our own course.
The citizens of Cleveland and vicinity showed us no
little kindness the few days we rested among them.
We diverted ourselves much with one little circumstance; and that was, the citizens, from the lordly
dome to the log-cabin, were mostly either generals, or
colonels, or majors, or captains, or—squires, any how.
We could scarce find a man without some kind of

handle to his name. Here I stood on the shore
of the lake, high and dry, and said in my heart;
"One woe is passed! I shall no more travel that
ugly, muddy road from Chillicothe to Columbus!
I shall no more flounder over the snow-drifted
plains of Crawford! I shall no more shiver on the
bleak banks of the Sandusky! I will hie me home
to my own sunny Appomattox, and perhaps live
and die on its verdant banks." But there is a
book, a blessed but mystic book, which says, *"It is
not in man to direct his steps."* Little did I then
think that, in less than twelve years, it would be
my allotted duty to stand in the city of Columbus,
and preach to listening congregations the Gospel of
the Son of God. Little did I think that, in a few
years more, the house, the very house in Delaware
that sheltered the benumbed and weather-beaten
soldier, should be his parsonage, while he should
travel over the length and breadth of the plains of
Crawford, not an unpeopled solitude, but beautifully
spotted with farms and dwellings — in Summer a
boundless prospect of undulating grass, and fragrant
flowers of almost every form and shade—in Winter
a sea of crusted snow, over which the sailor might
glide at large in his bounding jumper, and, in his
high-wrought imagination, live over his Atlantic
rambles. Little did I think that there, even there,
I should mingle with the congregated saints, hear
the shout of heaven-born souls, and, least of all,
that I even—even the *sinner*, *I*—should rejoice in

the sound with a joy unspeakable and full of glory.
But all this came to pass. While laboring in that
section of our work, I was strongly solicited by
Russel Bigelow, the superintendent of the mission,
to visit the "Reserve." I did so on a quarterly
meeting occasion. While preaching to the Indians,
through an Indian interpreter, I mentioned that I
had once earnestly sought them before, with my
body clothed in hostile armor, and murder in my
heart; but that, in examining my soul, I found that
God had gotten to himself a greater victory there;
for now the weapons of my warfare were no longer
carnal, and the theme that I most delighted in was
peace on earth, good-will toward men. To give
them a clearer understanding of my position in the
last war, I told them that I belonged to that company which the Indians used to call, "*The men
with the silver birds in their caps.*" As I mentioned
this, significant glances were thrown round the
assembly, and my interpreter faltered as he gave it
out. As soon as the service was over, he declared
that he was with the hostile Indians that defended
the British battery against the sally from Fort
Meigs, and that he fought against that very company. He said the Indians were particularly anxious to kill our men; for they thought that the
silver-leaf spread eagles on our helmets were made
of the solid stuff. Brother Bigelow took advantage
of this circumstance while administering the sacrament next morning. He laid one hand on my head,

and the other on the interpreter, and said, "Brethren, these two, during the last war, were arrayed in hateful strife against each other; but behold the victories of the Cross! they are now kneeling, in Christian fellowship and communion, at this table, to show forth the death of their common Lord and Savior." The effect on the white part of the congregation was powerful; but as the interpreter gave it in excited and broken accents to the nation, it was overwhelming.

Our company being broke up at Cleveland, we scattered in little social bands, in different routes, to seek our homes. I traveled in company with three of my most intimate friends. Our reception, or treatment, on the way, was various, according to the religious and political views of the people. One of our company became lame at the commencement of the journey, which retarded us considerably. In this dilemma we saw a very starch-looking Quaker overtaking us with a led horse. At this sight our comrade's limping evidently increased, and his pain became almost insupportable. We each made a very low and handsome bow to the stranger as he approached; but no response did we receive. We, however, surrounded him, and with the most moving eloquence that we could command, began to intercede for our lame friend. He very roughly refused us, declaring that he had nothing to do with war or any who were concerned in it. This exasperated our invalid, and he began to be abusive. I told him this was wrong. Perhaps the Quaker was conscientious in this matter. No doubt he thought he would be doing the devil service by giving him a seat in the vacant saddle. This was like throwing oil on the flame. "Conscientious, indeed! What, too conscientious to give a lift to a poor lame soldier, who has been fighting the battles of his country?" "Yes, it is even so, and you may just as well coil down, and take the world as it is, and not as it ought to be." O, give us forever that religion

"Which hates the sin, but still the sinner loves"—

which hates war, but is ever ready to mitigate the evils and heal the wounds which war has made!

We sometimes met with those who were politically opposed to the war. They also answered us roughly. At other times we had to do with real patriots — true blues. Among these were women, not a few, who, with moistened eyes, blessed us, as we passed, in the name of the Lord. When we were well advanced in our journey, we fell in with a company of loafers, a kind of people who, as soon as they see any person or new thing, begin to cast about in their minds what they can make of it. They chose to look upon us as deserters, and set about to arrest us. We labored with many arguments, to prove that we were true men; but all to no purpose. When we found that they were meditating to carry us to Washington, we concluded, on consultation, that such a ride, at their expense, would advance us considerably toward home, and it was more than probable that when Uncle Sam recognized us as his old fast friends, he would lift us still farther by way of indemnity. So we concluded to be deserters, if they would have it so. But when they found that we had become so well reconciled to a jaunt, they began to conclude we were Virginians, and possibly Virginia volunteers.

We now walked rapidly, sometimes as many as forty-five miles in a day. Our money also went rapidly, and our purse began to wrinkle with age. On the evening of a beautiful day, we were entering the romantic town of Winchester. A gentleman rode hastily by, making a profound bow. He quickly turned his horse, and inquired if we were of the Virginia volunteers. Being answered in the affirmative, he put whip and spurs to his horse, and was soon hid from our view by the houses in the suburbs. At the head of the main street, we were met by several young men, who conducted us to the hotel, and ordered a splendid supper. Their number continually increased; and we found that they were members of a volunteer company that had served a tour on the sea-board, and were, therefore, tenderly alive to our sufferings. We sat up to a late hour, indulging in a social interchange of our adventures. One of their company was truly a singular genius. He was famous for his extemporaneous effusions in the way of song. The company requested us to propose some topic of national

interest. This we did twice or thrice, but he sung
them off in such a masterly manner, that we could
not help surmising that he had previously exercised
his pen on almost every subject of public notoriety.
The company then proposed that we would relate
some incident that had transpired in the western
army, which was not generally known, provided it
was sufficiently stirring to elicit his zeal. This we
did. And after clearing his throat, and attending
to all the preliminaries that good singers always
observe by note, he caroled forth a beautiful versi-
fication of the whole matter. When the company
broke they paid off the bill, including in the settlement a warm and early breakfast for the poor
soldiers. Such a windfall as this would have been
considered only as a circumstance in our jolly *debut*
into the military life; but coming to disbanded
soldiers, displumed of all martial attractions, it was
truly grateful.

The day before we entered Fredericksburg we
had spent our all. And although it was a lovely
day overhead, yet our hearts were sad, as we
deliberated on our situation. We were far from
home. We had not time to dig, and to beg we
were ashamed. When we entered into the town,
we naturally stepped into the first tavern, as stage-
horses would stop at a post-office. We had hardly
seated ourselves, when a schoolmate of mine entered. He immediately recognized me; and, after
a few friendly remarks, requested me to step out

with him. He took me into a retired part of the yard, and looking round, as if to see whether any fowls of the air were hovering about, and as if he meditated some grand outrage on fallen human nature, he asked me, in a subdued tone, how I was off for funds. I plainly and honestly replied that the "last shot in the locker" was expended. A flush of humanity suffused his benevolent brow, and he put his hand in his pocket. I knew that his family was of Virginia's noblest stock. And from all that I had seen in our school-boy days, I believed that he had inherited all the nobility of his house. Therefore I could not accuse my eyes of presumption, when I felt that they were anticipating the circumference of a full *"shiner"*—a *Dei Gratia*, a *Spanish dollar*—for which I would have been truly thankful. But the reader may guess how my soul was flooded with joy and gratitude, when he presented me with a twenty-dollar note, and a handsome apology, that he was on a journey, and knew not how long he would be gone, otherwise he would give me more. He then fled from my overflowing soul and eyes, as if he had perpetrated willful murder. I know not whether he is still living; but, *dead* or *alive*, I still pray for him, as the old negro said, "at a venture." I may be in the same fix that the pious sister P., of Xenia, once was. When we moved to this State, more than twenty years ago, she inquired about an old Methodist preacher, whom she had highly esteemed. We told

14

her he had been dead about six years. "Dear, dear me!" said the old lady, "why did they not send me word? I have been praying for him faithfully, night and day, six years, and he all the time safely landed in heaven!" I went into the tavern, and gave my comrades a pluck; but they seemed to be fast moored. Poor fellows, they still had a faint hope that some liberal loafer would offer them a drink, or luncheon, or something of the kind. But at last they weighed anchor, though I could hardly tow them along. Every step they took seemed to indicate that they looked for nothing but ruin and starvation beyond the corporation of Fredericksburg. But when we had got beyond the public gaze, I said, "Cheer up, boys; Providence has sent me a breeze. I am now able to take the stage, and reel it off at the rate of eight knots an hour, homeward bound; but for your sakes I forbear. If you will be economical, leave off this tavern fare, and let me be your purser, I will take you all home." I then stepped into a grocery, and stored our knapsacks well with cheese and crackers, and we moved on with fresh life.

At last we arrived at Richmond. Here, at the commencement of our career, every door was open to us. But now the returning soldier passed along unheeded, unrecognized. At last a poor man—I believe a pious man—invited us to his home, to take *pot-luck*. And this he did, not through ostentation or vainglory, but sheer benevolence. We found that girding on the armor was one thing, and taking it off was another; and we were well convinced that a young man of fruitful imagination might reap all the honor and glory of war in the domestic muster-field, without suffering any of its evils. Here our little platoon scattered again. I had twenty-five miles to go to reach home. This distance was measured leisurely, soberly, thoughtfully, with an intention to make my return after nightfall. In all my returns home, by land or water, I loved to come in under the cover of night. About dusk I crossed the Appomattox, on Pocahontas bridge—trod lightly over Sandy beach—entered Bolingbrooke-street. It was now dark. I was closely scrutinized by every passenger, but had drawn my helmet down. I can not describe my feelings as the familiar scenes of my bright boyhood came up in quick succession. At last I stood, with almost breathless agitation, at my home's door. A few faint raps—raised the latch, and stood in the presence of my mother. She lifted her eyes, gave one shrill scream, and exclaimed, "O Alfred! Alfred! my son Alfred!" A pious lady, who lived in the next tenement, and whose soul was, religiously speaking, on the hair-spring order, and who, moreover, always levied a contribution of honey, more or less, on the most poisonous bitters of life, as they passed, heard the exclamation. It reminded her of David, "weeping as he went, and saying, O Absalom, Absalom, my son Absalom!" This sprung a class of reflections that instantaneously exploded in a shout. My little sisters, and neighbors, and acquaintances crowded round. And here my pen would paint a domestic scene; but perhaps my fair readers might drop a tear or two, inflame their eyes, and put their lips out of "prim;" and this might anger you, and ye might say, as a certain lady, who takes more liberties with me than any other, sometimes says, "Pshaw! Mr. L., you certainly are the *childishest* man that ever was."

XI.

THE CAPTURED BUGLE.

IT is not generally known that after the long siege of Fort Meigs the enemy invested that post the second time. Although this is but slightly or incidentally mentioned in some accounts of the last war, yet it was an expedition that was largely presumed on by the English. The intention was to carry out a stratagem which had been conceived and principally planned by the celebrated Indian chieftain Tecumseh. It is spoken of to the present day, by the veterans of the Rapids, as "Tecumseh's sham battle." After the first repulse of the British, measures of very strict precaution were adopted. One improvement was the establishment of a picket guard in the edge of the clearing, to prevent a surprise. This guard was generally marched out at the rising, and remanded into the fort at the setting of the sun. The post was occupied at first with true military vigilance. But as no enemy appeared for some time, the soldiers became very careless. They would sometimes stack their arms, kindle a fire, and spend the whole day in telling stories, playing cards, etc. One lovely morning, as the

guard was marching out, not strictly in the order
of battle, and were within a few yards of their post,
as many as eight or ten rifles blazed away from
the thicket, and not more than two men made good
their retreat. It was soon evident that we were
again surrounded by an English and Indian force.
They lay round our fortress for several days. As
no batteries were constructed, and no besieging en-
gines or apparatus could be discovered, the general
belief was that they meditated a storm. Indeed,
constant efforts were made to deepen this impression.
Every morning before daylight, they marched round
the fort—at a respectable distance, of course—playing
on a single instrument, which poured forth the most
perfect and lovely music of the kind which we had
ever heard. Mullen, who was one of the volunteer-
band, and who was passionately fond of instrumental
music, would listen with the most profound but
quizzical attention, presenting either ear alternately,
blinking significantly, like a magpie, till the close
of the air, and then would exclaim, with the
strongest assurance imaginable, "Boys, I will never
see Petersburg again till I blow a blast with that
same sweet bugle." This always provoked a burst
of incredulous laughter; but as often as the music
came round, he would repeat his unreasonable
prophecy, to the no small diversion of his comrades.
After the enemy had made their pompous and
harmless promenades, till they had lost both their
novelty and terror, they aimed to carry into execu-

tion the scheme of their grand ambuscade. About 10, A. M., on a sultry morning, a distant, continuous roar of small arms was heard on the Sandusky road, but heard very indistinctly. The sound, however, rapidly increased. It seemed as if a reënforcement was fighting its way to the camp. Hark! hark! Now they rush on with an impetuosity that bears down all opposition. Louder and louder — nigher and nigher! Well done, old Kentuck! Now they will cut their way through, in spite of redcoats or red skins.

But now, alas! alas! they retreat, they fly! They are making back for Sandusky. The din of the battle recedes toward the settlement. No, no; they rally to the charge. Onward the human tempest comes — "enlarging, deepening, mingling peal on peal." Now they have almost gained the clearing — columns of smoke are seen rolling up among the branches of the trees — the roar of rifles and musketry, the shrieks of the wounded and dying, the shouts of the soldiers, the brutal yells of the savages are heard. All the horrors of the battle-field are about to burst upon our sight. The soldiers in the garrison are standing at their posts in almost breathless anxiety, with their strained and aching eyes fastened on the underbrush, expecting every moment to see our victorious band make their debut, amid the cheers and huzzas of the whole fortress. But O, sad reverse! A general flight commences. The British and Indians seem to drive

the retreating forces like sheep to the slaughter.
At this juncture the troops in the fort became
almost unmanageable. "There," said some, "see
how they are driving and cutting up our men, our
friends, our BRETHREN, who have pressed to relieve
us, and that right under our guns! Here we are
with our hands in our pockets—where is the General? O, if Harrison was only in the fort!" Some
could scarcely be restrained by the officers from
springing over the picketing, while some wept like
children. Messengers were dispatched through the
lines with the information that the commander had
received, the evening before, an express from Harrison, stating that he would send on *no reënforce-
ments*. While the running fight was raging in all
its fury, an unusually black cloud, which had been
gathering over our heads for some time, began to
discharge its magazines of forked lightning and
deafening thunder. In a few minutes the rain fell
in mighty torrents. The martial flame of ardent
warriors became quenched, and in one moment the
clamor of battle ceased.

We were told by prisoners, that several of Tecumseh's men realized, by fatal experience, that the
battle, so far as they were concerned, was *no sham*
at all. The Irish soldiers cherished such a mortal
hatred to their red allies, that they occasionally
dropped in a bullet, and laid some of their finest
braves on the ground. We were subsequently informed that, pending the engagement, the English

cavalry were posted both above and below the fort, under cover of the forest. Their orders were to rush between the garrison and combatants, as soon as a sortie might be made. It was also contemplated to make a sudden assault, by choice troops, on the most defenseless quarter of the camp at the same time. In all this our enemies were disappointed. Being much chagrined by their entire failure, and believing the old proverb, that "a half of a loaf is better than no loaf," they confidently filed off to Fort Stevenson, to take that "for certain." But here they met a very disgraceful defeat. Soon after, the army at Meigs marched for Camp Seneca, to await the battle that was expected on the lake. There were the prisoners who had been taken at Fort Stevenson, and among them the little trumpeter who had so often and so untimely partly charmed and partly frightened us to our quarters. And Mullen — yes, Mullen — had the inexpressible satisfaction of giving us his best flourish on the captured BUGLE. But as slavery debases all subjected to its malign touch, the sweet instrument was stripped of all that interest and melody with which peculiar circumstances had graced it. It no longer threw its wild notes over the nocturnal solitude of the Maumee, and told a startled enemy that it was followed by "an army with banners." Indeed, its legitimate owner, like the captive Israelite, could no longer breathe with complacency the loyal airs of old England "in a strange land."

15

XII.

RELIGIOUS EXPERIENCE—LORENZO DOW.

IN entering on this subject we need not go back to that sweet and timely introduction which I had to the power of Divine grace in early childhood, of which we have written. Like many of the children of our people, for several years I felt that vacillating conflict so closely described by an inspired apostle—"the flesh warring against the Spirit, and the Spirit warring against the flesh"—now careless or reckless; now repenting and weeping.

But suddenly there was a report in our land that a wild man—a preacher diverse from all others—was making his way into Lower Virginia. He had a solemn presentiment that his days were numbered, and he was drawing nigh to his terminus. In after-life he insisted that this decree was reversed by his going to preach the Gospel in England and Ireland. He slept on the floor, and was very abstemious. He received no money unless it was clear to him that it was to meet some pressing want — such as ferriage or hire of conveyance. It was reported that, at times, he possessed the spirit of prophecy, and occasionally the discernment of spirits. We

were daily looking for his advent; but wondered
how it would be. One.day a stranger was seen
walking down the street with hasty strides and
noiseless tread, with a wonderful train of children
of all colors—at least, white, black, and yellow.
Some preceded in double-quick time, and announced
with great satisfaction—"The wild man is coming!"
Indeed, he looked wild enough. He had a sailor
tarpaulin on his head, a green military coatee, half-
worn and displumed of its party-colored ornaments,
a pair of kneebreeches, with straps and buckles
dangling about, and his shins "*sans* every thing,"
as Shakespeare would say. He carried a bundle of
handbills, which he distributed freely; they were
headed with large letters—"HUSH! and HARK!
This afternoon at three o'clock, LORENZO DOW will
preach under the FEDERAL OAKS." He carried
besides a package of tracts. These were sparingly
delivered. In passing one man he would suddenly
stop, and look as if he were searching into the
inner chamber of his soul, and he would hand him
a tract. He would then pass by several as if they
belonged to another planet. Sometimes he would
pass a store several yards, and then, as if arrested
by a sudden impulse, he would wheel round and
throw in a paper messenger. Sometimes he would
dart across the street to give a tract to a man—the
whole current of little ones pouring after him as
though they expected every moment some grand
development of which they were determined to lose

nothing. Who could blame them when all the doors, windows, and entries were crowded with adult gazers as excited as themselves? Children always take hold on religious novelties. In the days of our Savior they followed on and cried out, "Hosanna to the Son of David that cometh in the name of the Lord; hosanna in the highest!" The Pharisees here saw that their cause was gone, and they said among themselves, "Perceive ye how ye prevail nothing? Behold, the world has gone after him." Yes, the rising generation has caught the sound. But Jesus said, "Have ye never read, Out of the mouth of babes and sucklings thou hast perfected praise?" The triumph would not have been perfect without those juvenile praises. The Lord bless the children! as bad as they are. We have been accustomed—I mean my chief mate and myself—at every removal to say, "Surely, the children of this place are the worst we have ever seen;" but Christ said, "*Let them alone.*" Many that paddled after Lorenzo Dow, at last rolled "right side up;" and some will, doubtless, walk the gold-paved streets of the New Jerusalem.

At the hour appointed nearly all the stores were closed, and the whole population was afloat—some on foot, some on horse, some in their chariots, and some from the country in wagons, and an immense congregation was found under the wide-spread branches of the Federal Oaks. Presently the preacher appears. He looked round for a convenient stand, and seeing an old-fashioned chariot, almost unvarnished by the brush of time, that had a large platform behind for a footman, and a small window in the rear, he leaped up, and faced the most of the congregation. Lorenzo was, even then, eccentric, but seriously so. He had not attained to that humorous and laughter-rousing vein that marked his discourses after he believed that God had added more than fifteen years to his probation. In the course of his remarks he spoke of family difficulties; of children who had eaten at the same table, slept in the same bed, and had gone to the same school, yet in after-life engaged in lawsuits with each other; and of some who would even bring lawsuits against their own mother who bore them. He then stopped short, as by a sudden surge, and stooping down, he put his mouth to the window of the carriage, and said, "Ah, old mammy, *you* know what I am talking about!" This startled the whole congregation. The talk was applicable to her, and her only. She was the richest matron in the town. Her sons had been lawing with each other, and one had been so unnatural as to sue his mother.

After he had preached, he proposed to enter into a covenant with the people. The covenant was, that he would pray daily for three weeks for every one who would pray in like manner for themselves. Their agreement to this was to be manifested by their shaking hands with him while singing the concluding hymn. The congregation flocked around him weeping and trying to sing. I felt almost as if my salvation depended on entering into said covenant. My father was standing by me, and this was a great cross. But I looked up in his face, and saw that he looked uncommonly mellow. I felt as if my heart would burst outright. I reached up my hand, but would not let the preacher catch my eye, for fear he would tell all the people what a bad boy I had been. As well as my memory will serve me, I believe I kept my promise. Some days I might have forgotten it, but then on other days I would pray double; for I was a great believer in the doctrine of commutation. The preacher had his next appointment some miles in the country. He was trudging along on foot, when one Mr. R., who had heard him under the oaks, came along in his chaise, and kindly gave him a lift to his appointment. After he had preached, Mr. R. took leave of him, saying he had some business to do, but he would see him again at his next appointment at P. Lorenzo looked at him sorrowfully, and said, "No, I feel there is a blow coming; where it will strike the Lord knows—whether on you or me—but I have a strong impression we will not see each other again in time." Mr. R. left, but had not gone far on his way, when his horse took fright and ran away; Mr. R. was flung out and killed.

Lorenzo did not seem to aim at prophesying. He told some of the preachers who inquired of him in regard to this matter, that when he first started, sometimes in the midst of his discourse, an idea altogether foreign to his arrangement would be presented, and he would reject it. In doing so he would plunge into darkness, mental and spiritual, so that at last he determined to follow such impulse, and then he had freedom. While we are writing of him, I will say that many years after, when I was living in New Orleans, I saw him again. When I entered the room where he was, and before any introduction, he said to me, "What do you think of Bonny?"

"What Bonny?"

"Why, Bonaparte."

"He seems to be laying waste."

Here he began to unfold to me the important niche that he occupied in the Apocalypse. And his mind seemed to be mostly occupied with Bonaparte and the prophets, and he seemed to forget the vices of Napoleon in his victories.

Several years after I saw him down in Ohio, and heard him preach in my own pulpit. Then he discoursed in a funny way of courtship and matrimony, to the great amusement of old and young. Wisdom might be justified in all these changes, and I hope his life of labor was crowned with a triumphant end. Many were laid under conviction in his earliest labors, and in many this conviction resulted in bright conversions. Not so in my case. He laid me under contribution for some time, but my seriousness passed away "like the early cloud." In my last voyage home as mate of a brig, as already observed, with a heavy charge, beating about, and making and taking in sail continually, on the coast, and driven by a long succession of snow-storms, I again became serious, and spent much of the short rest allowed me in my state-room, in prayer. On this occasion I attained to the condition which our Discipline accords to a mourner or seeker; but I was without the Church. In after years I have felt very thankful that the Methodist Episcopal Church *"receiveth sinners,"* penitent sinners. In this she is most apostolic. This shines out in the Gospel. One apostle in writing to the Church, addresses members in various conditions: *" babes, young men, old men,"* or sages, and this not in reference to their natural ages, but to their attainment. For the time is come when the *child* dies a hundred years old, but the *sinner* dying a hundred years old is accursed.

An inspired apostle addresses some in the Church who were still carnal to a considerable extent. Again there were some who had been religious, but were fallen from grace. " Ye are fallen from grace." Our Savior in his message to the angel of the Church of Ephesus says, "Thou hast left thy first love." Does he excommunicate? No, but says, "Repent and do thy first works, or else I will come unto thee quickly and remove thy candlestick out of his place, *except thou repent.*" He bore "with him for a season." And why? Because if backsliders can not be reclaimed in the Church, with all her means of grace, they may be irrecoverably lost when cast out. The whole world has no remedy for the lost. We regard the Church of Christ as a divinely-instituted hospital, a blessed asylum for all who are oppressed of the devil. But while it is a hospital, and strains every means for a recovery, when patients become incurable, she casts them out—"*except they repent.*" In these gracious times of refreshing which come from the presence of the Lord, ·we have seen those who have been in the Church seeking salvation for one, two, sometimes three years, brightly converted. During their probation, their membership has shielded them from outbreaking sins, and when they see the bush all divinely fired, they begin to cast their shoes from off their feet, and cry in mighty anguish, "Speak, Lord, for thy servant heareth."

We have seen, with pain, our ministers, in some sections, insisting on unquestionable regeneration, as a term of Church membership.* If this should become general, it would destroy one of our distinct features as a Church, and would work ruinously. Moreover, it would hurt our Church only. The Calvinistic Churches receive those who are evangelically convicted, and who truly repent; because they sincerely

---

* It seems to us that, as a condition of full membership in the Church, it is not too much to require that the candidate shall be a new creature in Christ Jesus.—ED.

believe that regeneration is before repentance; and that when the Holy Spirit truly convicts, He will carry on the work to full redemption. They call true penitents "babes in Christ," but although babes, they have the promise of a full growth. We do not stop to contend whether they or we are right in doctrine. We are both right in receiving such characters into the Church. But if we go to receive only regenerated persons, according to *our standard* of regeneration, we will turn away many who in future years would be an ornament to our Church. We are well persuaded, if the question could be put· to our whole Church, it would be found that a majority of our members experienced religion in the Church.. But unfortunately for myself, I did not join the Church on my return; but having received full wages as an officer, I strutted about in a suit of "long togs," which I had purchased in London, and neglected the high concerns of my soul. This will appear by my seeking a place in a privateer. I feel thankful to this day that I was led to the war; because it was a higher principle that urged me on; and in comparison with the floating hell from which I escaped, war itself was a minister of grace. It did not, however, add one cubit to my moral stature.

When I returned from the war, the whole world looked gloomy and sad. I was sensible that the beauties of nature were in no way impaired, and that the wrong was in myself. I determined to seek a higher life. With this in view, I retired, at stated periods, into a garret, and prayed and meditated, and became very serious.

XIII.

CAMP MEETING—DAWNING OF LIGHT.

ONE day my mother told me that she and some Methodist ladies were very anxious to go to a camp meeting that was to be held soon; but they could not go without some male person to assist them. I had never been to a camp meeting, and cheerfully consented to take the supervision of things. I intended not to remit my private religious exercises. On the day appointed, we started in the wagon, with our tent and baggage. When we drew nigh to the encampment, and made a sudden turn in the way, a large portion of the camp broke upon our vision. The tents were made mostly of the old bleached sails of sloops and schooners, and sheets and coverlets, and contrasted beautifully with the dark-green pine forest in which they were pitched. When this scene suddenly broke upon us, this idea flashed upon my mind, "How goodly are thy tents, O Jacob! and thy tabernacles, O Israel! Let me die the death of the righteous, and let my last end be like his." This almost overwhelmed me. After we had established ourselves, I walked about the encampment, attended on the services, and did not forget my own religious arrangements.

One dark, rainy night, our young stationed preacher held a prayer meeting in a tent, and after exhorting invited those who were seeking religion to kneel at some chairs that were set out. I went with the rest. Straw was strewed over the floor, and although the tent did not leak much, yet the water, unperceived, had run under it, so that when we kneeled our knees plunged down in the straw and mud, and before midnight it became somewhat of an annoyance; but still I thought I gave myself up, altogether, to God, for time and eternity. Still the meeting broke without affording any comfort. The next day brought no relief. In the afternoon, while lying alone in our tent, bemoaning my state, with tears in my eyes, a beautiful girl, about twelve or thirteen, a daughter of one of our Methodist neighbors, came in, and scornfully turning up her nose, said, "Ar'n't you ashamed, seeking religion? If you do n't quit this, I will never have you in the world," and with indignation burning on her cheeks, she left. This was the first that I knew that such a thought had ever mingled with the whimseys of the little innocent. This was a personification of the gay world—the scorn and contempt that awaited me. Still I thought, if I can only have salvation, I can surely afford that loss.

The next morning, feeling cold and somewhat indisposed, I saw Charles, a mulatto that my father had raised, and who was now a hackman. He was much attached to me, for I had taught him to read.

He beckoned me to his hack, and said in a confiding whisper, "I have brought a little spirit along with me, and I think a little dram might do you some good." Well, I truly believed with Charles that it would do me good, physically. I had been in the habit of meeting with other young men, when we would go to market for our mothers, in the dram-shop of a widow, where we would treat each other, and we did not apprehend any danger; but I had found out, before the camp meeting, that I had got so as to have no appetite for my breakfast till I had taken my mint sling; and I had abandoned the practice. It seemed to me that it would amount to a serious sin to take a dram in my present state. I refused, and opened my mind freely to Charles. It was not long before he got to see things in the same light, and became a pious Baptist minister, and finally a citizen of Liberia. I mention these small things to show to what mean shifts the enemy will resort, through his various agencies, to turn aside one who is learning to do right. I wandered about the camp, and was almost driven to infidelity. The argument in my mind was, the Lord has said, "Whosoever cometh unto me, I will in no wise cast out." But you have come to the Lord—come sin-cerely, as your own heart tells you, but he has not received you. Where is the promise of the Lord? Then this came to my mind—others have come, have found mercy, and are now rejoicing; therefore, there must be something wrong in your case. Be-

sides, it does not become a mortal sinner, who has
been so often called, and who has so often rejected
the calls of God, to expect him to come promptly
at your call. If you should call all your life long,
and the Lord should then save you, what a great
mercy it would be! This thought struck me with
great force, and seemed highly reasonable. Then I
said, I will still pray, and avoid all sin, as I have
been striving to do, and if mercy comes at last my
fortune will be made for all eternity.

In this frame we got into the wagon to return
home. After we had proceeded several miles, while
some of the sisters were singing one of the songs of
Zion, strange and supernatural fire seemed to glow
within my breast; new views, new motives, new
purposes arose within me. I requested the wagoner to stop his team awhile. I got down, walked
ahead, and sometimes felt like leaping for joy. My
sorrow was gone, and sweet tranquillity reigned
within. But still I did not take this for conversion; I was looking for something more miraculous,
not considering how great a miracle it was for
peace to take possession of a sinner's soul. My testimony was very fluctuating. When a religious
friend would meet me, and express the joy he felt
on hearing of my conversion, if I was in a happy
frame, I would say, yes, I believe I have been converted. If another would question me, while dif-
ferently exercised, I would say, I feel there has
been some change, but I hardly know whether it is

conversion. I have since believed it was justification without a clear evidence.

It was not very long after this that I received two bright manifestations of the mercy of God, as I believe. The first was while I was meditating on Christ as a babe in the manger. All at once I was overwhelmed with a most unearthly transport of joy and peace. The second was just as I had prayed, laid aside my dress, and was laying my head upon my pillow. It seemed as if a flock of happy and invisible spirits were all around me and over me. I was as sensible of their presence as if I had seen them with my eyes, or touched them with my hands, and this was accompanied with a bliss that was all celestial. Then this came to my mind with a definition and clearness that I had never felt before, and may add, have never fully realized since—*"A joy unspeakable and full of glory."* And I said, "Lord, what is this?" And there came a voice to my soul—bear with me, reader—a voice that did not traverse my auditory nerve, and which my ear had nothing to do with—a voice as clear and as distinct to my soul as that of earthly sound to my ear—"The Spirit of the Lord, bearing witness with your spirit, that you are a child of God." Some will say, "enthusiasm!" Well, if it is found so at the last, it has ever been my safeguard from disbelief in the spiritual world. It has established in me the doctrine—not independent of the Scriptures—that the soul possesses senses of itself, to which our outward senses are only mediums — mediums between the outward world and the inner man. But God, who is a pure and unmixed spirit, can operate on our inward senses, independently of our bodily organs.

At this time I did not know that others had been so exercised; but I soon found, by reading and hearing the experience of the pious, that the Lord has manifested himself to others in similar ways. Some have had a representation of Christ to their spiritual sight, as Colonel Gardner; some to their hearing; and the Lord reveals himself to all Christians through their *spiritual* feeling. We feel, not physically, but spiritually, the Spirit of God bearing witness with our spirit that we are born of God. We do not believe that these extra manifestations exalt those who receive them, in point of Christian distinction, above the youngest child of grace; nor do we believe that it adds any force to their justification. I believe I was as much accepted when I first felt the free grace of God, in the camp meeting wagon, homeward bound, as I was under these extra manifestations. I give them as circumstances in my experience. I had united myself with the Church by giving my hand to the venerable John Potts, in the absence of the preacher in charge. There were, now, only three young men in the Church in P.—Louis Lasart, Henry Tatum, A. M. Lorrain. We concluded that we might gain much by forming ourselves into a band. We met

16

first on one Sunday morning, in the meeting-house. Louis was a Frenchman, but could talk tolerable English. He had been raised a Roman Catholic, and understood something about confession before he was converted. And he understood, from our Discipline, that, to be faithful to the band, we must turn our hearts wrong side out. He began to tell his experience, and presently came to a place where he received a backset, while courting a young lady. He must needs enter upon this narrative; and he did it with so much sincerity and earnestness—the tears streaming down his cheeks—while he entered into particulars, laboring on in his broken English, that Tatum and myself began to shake like aspen-leaves. We found this would not do; and I told them I thought we would do better in the classes among the old folks. Ever since this I have been opposed to young men's prayer meetings, or young ladies' meetings. Old Christians, when they get right happy, are simple and childish enough for any thing.

I now lived a life of faith. My peace was like a river. I had full confidence in the Church, and esteemed all the brethren better than myself. I looked upon the female members as sisters in all purity; I can not express the celestial chastity with which I regarded them—so diverse from all I had experienced before. Here let me ask, has any soul ever walked in the light and power of their first love for forty or fifty years without wavering? I do not ask if it can be done. The Bible, to me, is clear on this point: "The path of the just is as the shining light, that shineth more and more unto the perfect day." This is God's provision, but who realizes it? Well may we say, "What troubles have we seen, what trials have we passed!" The preacher, having prepared to attend Conference, proposed for me to lead his class in the middle of the week. From this I shrunk back dismayed. But he urged it so vehemently that I got alarmed at my own obstinacy, and finally consented. As the day advanced, the cross loomed up heavier and heavier. I made it a matter of prayer, telling the Lord that he knew I was not sufficient for that work, and that I hoped no one would come. At the appointed time I attended, and found the sexton brushing the benches. We waited there a long time, and, although it was a beautiful day, not one member came. This filled me with gratitude; for I verily believed my prayer was heard—and I think so still. Many a colt has been spoiled by premature harnessing.

XIV.

NEW ORLEANS—FIRST SERMON.

I HAD now to look around for something to do. I had been in a great measure weaned from the sea, and determined to abandon it. No business presented itself where I was. My oldest brother, who was a counselor at law, in New Orleans, invited me to come there; and I concluded to go. Brother Potts, who received me into the Church, told my mother he was sorry I had made that decision. He did not see how a young Christian could stand the seductions of New Orleans. He wished I could continue on the sea. He thought that the power of God, as displayed on the great deep, was calculated to cherish religious emotions in a soul already under the influence of Divine grace. His views influenced me considerably; so that, while on my way to Norfolk to embark for New Orleans, I became undecided and distressed. As soon as I arrived at the hotel, some of my young sea-friends crowded around, and one said in a loud voice, "Why, L., we have heard that you have been converted, and have joined the Methodists; is it so?" I answered in a dignified tone, but as loud, "What you have heard is certainly true."

"Well, that is curious, for a sailor to join the Methodists!"

This gave me an opportunity to "show cause;" and in a little while they began to slip away. The gentlemen around looked at me as a curiosity, smiling—some, as I thought, with scorn—some, with approbation. I was still undecided in my course. I attended the Methodist Church in the evening. The introductory hymn was,

> "God moves in a mysterious way,
>   His wonders to perform."

As they were singing,

> "Ye fearful souls, fresh courage take,
>   The clouds ye so much dread
> Are big with mercy, and shall break
>   In blessings on your head,"

light, joy, and comfort came down, and my pathway to New Orleans shone bright. An intelligent and genteel young man, who belonged to the same volunteer company that I did during the war, took passage with me. I soon made known to him my views and determinations; and although we sometimes disputed on doctrine, yet he always treated me with great respect and consideration; and, as we had the cabin to ourselves, we had an agreeable voyage. When we arrived at the city, and looked around, it seemed to be given up, to a great extent, to idolatry. The holy Sabbath was generally unheeded, or made a day of merriment; and, so far from being drawn into the vortex, my soul shrunk

back from the gulf of immorality. I first got a
place under my brother, who had been appointed
naval-officer of the port. As he still attended to
his law business, he made me his deputy in the
revenue business, and the principal weight of that
concern rested upon me. This at once brought me
into business acquaintance with the merchants—
French and English—of that city; and happily, as
I thought, this was mostly the principal social connection of that people. It was often said by strangers, that, when they would inquire of a man if his
partner was a married man, he could not tell.
After the business of the day was over, I would
retire to my room, where I could read, meditate,
and pray, and enjoy the company of a very amiable
family that boarded me.

About this time Clarke's Notes were published in
pamphlet form, and I became a subscriber. It was
a great advantage that it came out periodically, so
that I could study each number in course. But I
longed for the preaching of the Word. When I
saw my friends buying tickets for the theater once
or twice in the week, I felt how glad I would be
to hear sermons at the same price! We were not
entirely destitute of preaching; there was a gentleman of learning, who had been employed by some
to preach on the Sabbath, or rather to read. But
he was not regarded as an experimental Christian.
One Sunday in reading the morning service he
came nigh tilting over two or three times. This

startled the congregation. But when he ascended
the pulpit and spread out his manuscript, he began
to read; but after a while he looked very quizzi-
cally at his writing, and began to talk nonsense.
The people, who seemed to have some idea about
ministerial decorum, poured out of the house in a
stream. A committee was appointed to investigate
the affair. They reported that the parson was not
intoxicated, as some had supposed, but had always
been in the habit of taking a little opium to improve his elocution; but as he had a particular subject on hand, he had that morning taken an over-
dose. A sea captain who was present, exclaimed,
"Worse and worse! we thought he had got drunk
on brandy or wine, like a Christian; but it seems
he got drunk on opium, like a Turk!" We, however, attended his ministry to set an example of
Church-going. One evening as I was going to my
lodging, I heard in the upper faubourg a Methodist
tune. It thrilled through my soul and body. And
although it was raining and the roads muddy, I
was determined to find it out. The sound brought
me to an old cabin. There was hardly a whole
pane in the windows; it was filled with Africans,
and a colored man who had come down in a flat-
boat was telling the simple story of the Cross. His
congregation rolled their eyes as if a new dispensation had opened upon them. I stood at the window
in the rain; and while the preacher was happy
within, my soul was happy without. Surely that

was one of the richest evenings I had in the South. Brethren who smile at this, may have never known what it is to feel a famine of the Word of God.

I had been two or three months in Orleans, before I discovered a Methodist in the place. It was announced one Sunday that a Baptist missionary would preach in the afternoon. He seemed to be a plain, pious man, but only a slender preacher. After dismissal I spoke to him, and he invited me to take tea with him. The gentleman with whom he stopped earnestly backed the invitation, and it was accepted. In the course of the evening it appeared that this gentleman was also a Baptist. I was acquainted with him in business transactions, but did not know that he was a professor of religion. He informed me that he knew two very worthy Methodists in the city, and directed me where to find them. I lost no time in hunting them up. These were old brother Nabb and his wife. Brother Nabb and myself had often passed and repassed each other, with mutual suspicious glances, but neither had courage to challenge. He was a plain German, had been there fourteen years before me, and had been twice put in the calaboose for exhorting the negroes on the levee to turn from the wrath to come. By the means of this couple I found out another Methodist. Now we began to muster our forces. There were four Methodists, three or four Baptists, and a few Presbyterians. We agreed to establish a prayer meeting on one night in the week, and to labor to gather up any religious persons who might visit the city from time to time. This prayer meeting was very singular, wavering with the seasons and commerce. Sometimes the large room was nearly filled; at other times we were reduced to our original number. Presently we had an addition to the Methodists — brother Hyde, of New York, and Captain Pray, of Brooklyn, and their families. We now made a class, and appointed Captain Pray leader. And the brethren of other Churches attended; for, in the absence of all preachers, we were firmly united.

After a while brother Pray said, "Brother L., I have been deeply exercised about our condition here. We are in no Conference, no district, no circuit; indeed, we are without the jurisdiction of Methodism. We have called for help, and have received none. It has lately struck me that the Lord has placed some recourse within ourselves. There is surely some one among us who ought to feed these poor sheep."

To this I readily assented, and urged him to take this matter in hand, as I knew, from his manner in leading the class, that he would be acceptable. This, he said, was not what he was aiming at by any means; but in looking over the society, he concluded I was the man. I told him he was certainly mistaken, as I was not sufficient for that thing. He, however, renewed this kind of talk from time

17

to time, till one Sunday morning, when the class
was met, and our friends of other Churches were
present, he took me out into the back porch, and
said he would decide my case on the answer of a
single question: "Knowing you to be a man of
truth, answer me before God if you have had no
impressions on your mind that it is your duty to
preach?" Here he drove me into a corner. I acknowledged that this was the case, but argued that
the American population of that city was uncommonly intelligent, considering their number; and I
had thought, if my impression was Divine, that the
providence of God would open a way to some people
who might be benefited by my talents, poor as they
were. Now he became urgent for me to go into
the class-room, and preach a short sermon. Supposing that, after hearing me, he would be better
satisfied with letting me alone, I promised on condition of his taking it up in case of failure. So,
after getting my mind somewhat composed, I took
the Book and gave out as a text, "What I say
unto you, I say unto all, watch." I spoke about
thirty minutes, and then slunk back into my seat,
supposing he would stop all leaks, and clap on a
few backstays or bobstays; but he rose up, and
very coolly observed, "Next Sunday evening,
brother L. will preach in my large upper
room." I expostulated with him, after meeting,
but he said, "It's all right." I told him, as the
appointment was out, I would try to meet it, but

he really must not rush me on in that way.   Our
people told all their acquaintances, and next Sunday evening there was a large congregation.   We
had hardly closed before *"Next Sunday evening"*
was again heard.   And so it went on till the house
became crowded.   But now we received the joyful
intelligence that a Methodist missionary, for New
Orleans, had left Baltimore.   Our little society was
glad, but none so glad as myself.   He got there
late one Saturday afternoon.   On Sunday evening our usual place of worship was crowded.   I
held back till late, and then slipped into the back
of the congregation, where I might hear without let or hinderance.   The missionary was at the
stand, frequently looking at his watch.   At last he
stretched forward his head, and said, "Is brother
L. in the congregation?"   "Yes," said one, "here
he is, back here."   "I wish to see him."   Supposing he only wanted me to close the service, I
walked forward.

"Brother, it is high time to begin."

"I think it is."

"Well, you had better go at it."

This astonished me, and I very decidedly declined, telling him that the whole congregation was
expecting to hear him; that they had been for
years without any regular ministry, and it would
be a great disappointment if he did not preach.

"Well, if you don't intend to preach, get up and
tell them so, and dismiss them, or I will do it for

you. It is your appointment, and I assure you I shall not preach this night."

I reflected a moment, and saw clearly that such a course would greatly injure him at the commencement. And I preached, but fully resolved that no more such pranks should be played with me, and that my sermons should be few and far between during his administrations. Happy was I in the consideration that I had no more appointments out. But I knew not my man.

XV.

LAND-OFFICE RECEIVER—DIVERS LABORS.

BROTHER Mark Moore was considerably advanced in years. He was a classical man, deeply pious, generally a good preacher, and sometimes overwhelming. He was, however, subject to a very troublous disease—the hypo. He did not at all recognize it, but in all good conscience pronounced it sickness. He held a theory that the earthquake, like the comet, had its appointed race; that in former ages it trampled furiously across our continent, as may be seen by the deep dells, precipices, and scattered rocks that abound in our country; that it was now playing its game beyond seas, but would very soon visit this part of its orbit again. Then he would start, look wildly, woe-begone, and say, "Brother L., do you feel *that?*"

"What?"

"Why, the trembling of the earth. I feel it every few days, and just now distinctly. I am surprised that you can not feel such a sensible move."

"Brother Moore, you are certainly mistaken; the earth never was more solid."

"It is you who are mistaken. I have a peculiar

discernment of earthquakes." When he was in this
mood all was over with him; he was sick, and man
Friday had to stand up.

Our little society now began to stir. A gentleman who was friendly to our Church, and whose
wife was a Methodist, offered us the upper part of
a large tobacco warehouse, on condition of our fit-
ting it up, as a preaching-place, with the privilege
of our removing our improvements, if the property
had to pass from his hands. The room was 100
by 80. We purchased heavy cotton, and nailed
it to the posts that supported the rafters on both
sides, put up a pulpit draped in baize, and then put
up stairs, outside of the building, by which our congregation might ascend. The returned captives
were not more pestered in putting up the temple
at Jerusalem than we were. Some said one thing,
and some said another; but the majority thought
it was an immense object. No respectable person
would attend, and what lady would climb up the
steep, open stairway. All we could say was, "Not
many great, not many noble, not many mighty are
called." But when worship was opened, they came
crowding from north, south, east, and west. The
ladies tripped up stairs right gracefully; for there
were no hoops worn in that day. Mr. M——n, bless
you, the king merchant of New Orleans, came bust-
ling up with all his family, and looked right glad
to get a seat; and brother Moore laid the vast congregation under contribution of tears. I should

not have blamed him if he had felt the earth quake that day. I had not been long in New Orleans, when the commission of "Receiver of public moneys for lands of the United States in the Eastern District of Louisiana" was sent me by Mr. Madison. I had to get security to the amount of thirty thousand dollars.

"Now," said my brother, "where will you get that?"

"I am acquainted with a Baptist gentleman who is very wealthy, and professes strong friendship for me."

"If that is all your dependence, I am sorry for you; but go and try."

I called on my friend, and told him I was appointed to the Land-Office.

"O, how glad I am! you will now be permanently fixed among us."

"Yes, but I have to give security in thirty thousand dollars; and I have called to see if you could accommodate me. It is only a nominal thing, the security, as the lands in this district will not be sold for many years, and we will only receive our regular salary."

Here his countenance fell, and he said he could not go my security in whole or in part.

"But if I do not get this security, brother, I will lose this fine office."

"I shall be very sorry indeed for that, but I can not accommodate you."

When I returned, my brother laughed heartily at me. "Now," said he, "I will go out and try my luck. It is certainly a very heavy security." As he passed down the street, he met a very distinguished lawyer, who hooked arms with him, and wished him to go with him. My brother told him he would like to do so, but he had set out to procure security for his brother, who had just been appointed to the Land-Office. "Why, I did not know you had a brother. Come along; I'll go his security." This afforded my brother great amusement, and myself some mortification. When my friend asked me if I had got that security, and I told him yes, a gentleman who had never yet seen me kindly offered to go my security, he looked comical too.

Mr. Larned, a young Presbyterian minister from the East, preached a few times in the city, and was employed by the Presbyterians and their adherents. He was a very amiable young man, highly polished, and of popular manners. He went home to prepare for a permanent residence. He returned in the ship on a Sabbath, and the people generally expected he would occupy our tabernacle. This was not known to brother Moore, and he, of course, prepared to preach. Here was saddled on me, perhaps, the heaviest cross I had to bear in the morning of my experience. Just before brother Moore began, here came in Mr. Larned and all his staff, and the house was well filled. Our preacher had asked him in the pulpit, and a considerable conversation passed between them. Presently the preacher requested that brother L. would come in the stand. I had got to understand some of his facial expressions, and moved up with some considerable timidity.

"Here, ·brother L., you will have to preach this afternoon."

"O, not at all, brother! Here is brother Larned. All the congregation expects *him* to preach."

"No, brother L., I have been several weeks knocking about at sea, and I have nothing in the world to preach."

I could not comprehend this reason — how these several weeks of perfect leisure on the solitude of the ocean should incapacitate him. I looked up to brother Moore, and saw that his "sickness" was upon him, and the prospect hopeless. In the mean time, Larned seized me by the arm, and pulled me up. I will not say, reader, that there was nothing like natural spunk creeping over my nerves. I rose up and preached; yes, through mercy, I ·*preached*. There are times when men may speak honestly of themselves. When our Lord said of Nathaniel, and to his face, "Behold an Israelite, indeed, iu whom there is no guile," Nathaniel asked with childish innocence, "How knowest thou me?" He felt himself that he was without guile; but the curiosity with him was—how the Savior knew it. So, laying aside all voluntary humility, I carried the rag off from the bush that day.

Some, who were not in the habit of going to church, said, "Does the Deputy preach?" Others said, "Well, if we can raise up preachers from among us, where is the necessity of importation?" Brother Moore was well pleased for more than one reason; and he lectured me severely on my diffidence, and finally said I was a greater preacher than Mr. Larned.

"Why, what do you mean?"

"I mean that, although you are not so flowery, and so well drilled in elocution, yet if each of you were required to preach on a text you had never thought of, you would beat him."

This made me feel cheap, under a consciousness that my sermon was not the impulse of the moment. I had been plowing with Adam Clarke, and had learned that it was a shame for a minister to say, "I am not prepared." And as I was liable to so many traps, I had concluded always to have at least a frame-work standing in my mind ready for clapboarding and shingling; and I thought that Mr. Larned could almost shake sermons out of his coat sleeve. A little while after I was speaking to a lady of a beautiful sermon he had preached on the Sabbath. She smiled, and said, "It was very pretty, but you had the advantage of me in hearing it." "Why?" "You know his office adjoins my room, and I heard it preached six times last week—once a day—as audibly as I heard it on Sabbath." This labor of love did not lessen my esteem for him, but it disabused me of the idea of his preaching without labor. One Sabbath he preached on the unconditional perseverance of the saints. His argument was—a Christian might commit any crime in the catalogue of human vices—"he may steal, get drunk, yea, murder, if he will; but here is our stronghold—no child of God *can will* to do such things." On going home I saw him seated in the open parlor of a Presbyterian lady; he hailed me, and asked me to step in.

"How did you like my doctrine to-day?"

"You know, of course, we Methodists don't believe a word of it."

"Where was it deficient?"

"You said a child of God might get drunk or even murder."

"Yes, but observe—'*if he will;*' but it is morally impossible for him to *will*."

"Do you not believe David was a child of God?"

"Yes."

"But David sinned—"

Here the Presbyterian sister rushed out of the other room, and said, "Yes, brother L., you have him there; for David did actually commit adultery with Uriah's wife." This raised a laugh and blush from both of us, and lest the lady, in her vehemence, should enter into particulars, I fled—quite pleased with handling him in this "*shorter way.*"

Mr. Larned was of a handsome exterior, and had

he lived a few years would have been the brightest shaft in the ministerial quiver of the Presbyterian Church. But, alas! he finished his course in two years, lamented by all.

To finish this sketch. At the General Conference in Boston, being sent to assist a Presbyterian minister, in one of the suburban villages, as we were sitting in his study I saw a small picture hanging over the mantle-piece; approaching closer, I exclaimed, "My friend Larned!" There he was, in all the bloom and beauty of youth, though nearly fifty years had intervened.

We were getting rich in preachers now. The Baptist minister still labored among us. He heard me preach one day, and afterward called to see me—no doubt with the kindest intention, for he was a good man—and in a very delicate way began to show me wherein I had perpetrated heresy. And as our Churches were just organized, it became us to watch over each other in love.

"Wherein have I erred from the truth?"

"Why, we have judged, from your sermon, that you do not believe in the preëxistence of Jesus Christ."

"We believe firmly in his divinity."

"Yes; but you do not believe in the eternal existence of his humanity."

"Certainly not."

He labored hard to recover me; and finally, waxing warm, he notified me that he would make known his discovery to my minister: "He will correct it, and put an end to this error."

He laid in his charge to brother Moore: "Brother L. does not believe that the humanity of Christ is from all eternity."

"Do you believe it?"

"Yes."

"Well, my dear brother, *you* are in error. And if you were charged before the Baptist Church, and would not recant, they would expel you."

He took considerable pains to put him right, and the Baptist minister, before he left, requested to let it "fall in the water," as the French say.

There were some colored people in the city who used to be Methodists, and they applied to our Church to give them a leader, as they were not permitted to meet without a white man of character. No one among our white members was willing to take up this cross. After considering the thing in all its bearings, although the most public man among them, I consented to lead them. This class grew fast. The masters generally would give them a certificate that they were willing to put them under my religious instruction. They were as pious a band of Africans as ever assembled together. Religion seemed to be their all. They hired an indifferent building at a very extravagant rate. When the day would come to raise their quarterly rent, after meeting they would march up to the stand, and almost cover it with notes and silver—money they had earned on Saturday, or by privileges their owners had accorded them. Some, from their appearance, needed the money themselves; but they seemed to plank it down with great glee. I never saw the like among whites or blacks, except in Honnold's settlement, on the Zanesville circuit. When they would come up, on the day appointed for the collection of quarterage, and almost cover the table with their money, it would always carry my mind back to my Orleans Blues. It was rather a fearful work to lead this class. Many would stop and eavesdrop during the exercises. One day a powerful-built man seemed to get very happy, and wound up in a voice that might have been heard half through the square, "Glory be to God! we will *take New Orleans yet.*" This made me tremble, and I peeped out of the window.

One of our class was a preacher, and quite popular among his fellow-servants; and when he joined the Baptists they were greatly aggrieved. The Baptist missionary had an immense crowd to see the immersion. But Hawkins shook off the muddy water of the Mississippi, and returned to his own company, and said he was all Methodist, only he wanted to be dipped. Our colored class became very large before I left the place.

XVI.

LICENSED TO PREACH—LIFE IN NEW ORLEANS.

HEARING that the Mississippi Conference was to sit, about thirty miles beyond the lake, the society delegated me to attend it, and, if possible, to persuade the Bishop to come over to our city and see the society. My brother wishing to cross the lake, we rigged up one of our revenue boats, and sailed over. When I arrived at the house where the Conference was to assemble, it was found that we had mistaken the time by one week. But the brother who owned the farm insisted on my staying. The farm was surrounded by a dense forest, as far as I could see, of several miles, and seemed to me a dreary solitude; but while walking down the lane, in the evening hour, meditating like Isaac, but not under the same expectation, Bishop M'Kendree and his traveling companions hove in view. He was much surprised at finding me in that region, as the last time he saw me was in old Virginia, and not grown. When the Conference assembled, there were about seventeen preachers. The most of them were entertained by our farmer-brother with princely kindness; and, as the session was held in his house, we had not far to walk. I had never encountered Methodist ministers in a body. As they had met me singly they appeared of very solemn aspect. I was not prepared to appreciate the high key to which their nerves were strung by a joyful meeting, after twelve months of excessive labor, and long good behavior, and their spicy wit and jovial jokes almost gave me offense, and I came very near concluding that I was about the best man there except the Bishop. A number of us slept in one room, and, while I was saying my prayers, one raised up his head and said, "Brother, if you do n't hurry on that prayer, you will be left in the dark, for your candle is 'most out;" and he really kept his ear up, as if he expected an answer. The Bishop finally concluded he could not go with me to New Orleans, nor could he tell when we would have a visitation. A few days after our return, he, in company with brother Winans, suddenly appeared among us. One day, while seated in a private house—among several members, male and female—he said, with his own peculiar smile, "Brethren, I pronounce this a quarterly conference. You are in no Conference, no district, no circuit. I say this is a quarterly conference; and, if any object, or dispute my authority, show your objections."

"No objections. Well, if you have any business, bring it forward."

One said, "We have not much business, but we

wish brother L. licensed. I immediately rose up and said, "I had made no such request." "Well, brother, you will not set up your judgment against the Church." The vote was put, and the Bishop wrote my first license. This was the way they made me a preacher; but I have always contended that I was a preacher before they touched me.

My eldest brother, Edwin, was residing in the city before I went there. The brother next younger than myself, Thomas, soon moved there, and published a popular paper, which kept a strict oversight of the city fathers and sanitary officers — mostly French—who cared very little about the cleanliness of the place, because they knew that what would poison Americans would fatten themselves. They, however, subscribed liberally to the paper, to learn what was said about them; and our labor was not in vain. My third and youngest brother, John, who was an artist, came out last, and got a profitable place in the custom-house. My manner of living was on the bachelor order, which was pretty much the ruling order in those days. We might give a specimen of our fixings and rambles.

In order to secure an occasional retreat from the busy scenes of life, I fitted up a small building, which stood in a retired situation, behind my brother's printing-office. It was so surrounded by loftier tenements, as to throw the incessant rattling of drays and noisy hum of men in the dull distance. We have nothing romantic to record concerning the

house of our pilgrimage. There was no spreading
beech, with "old fantastic roots"—no cooling fount-
ains—no well-dressed garden, breathing rich per-
fumes; but, contrariwise, Jamestown weed and dog-
fennel, of luxurious growth. It was, however, a
place of comparative quietude; and that was all to
me. It was no light task to establish a closet in
the Crescent City; and, moreover, to make a full confession—"my public shame—my solitary pride!"—
I made poetry in those days. A novice would say,
"The cloud-capped mountains, the flowery vale, the
embowered garden, perspiring celestial fragrance"—
these are the scenes where the Muses love to frolic,
and dispense their richest favors. But sour experience says, Nay. The somber and unfurnished
room, where no "woodbines flaunt—no roses shed a
couch"—where sweat and ink ooze in close affinity—
where, indeed, there is no production of nature or
art to rival, in beauty, Webster's Dictionary—there
is the palace of song, the factory of poesy. Well,
here we wrought till we found that all the best
rhyming words were used up, and there was no
new jingle under the sun. This will, by and by, be
the case in regard to prose. The only advantage it
has now, is, that the rhymeless words are in the
majority, and, consequently, can run more changes
and transpositions. But as the words are finite,
and men and women will talk and write perpetually,
there must come a time when they will have to stop,
not only for "lack of argument," but lack of sound,

unless they go on, as our poets now do, not knowing they are mere echoes. This is our comfort in regard to the novelists. When they have made all the lies that can be shaped in the English language, then will their end come.

But, if this is the case, it behooves us, also, to "make hay while the sun shines." So to return to our narrative. A high board-fence separated my homestead from a building of similar structure. Who lived there — whether they were English or Irish — whites or quadroons, were questions which did not concern us. We used, then, to live strictly up to the good rule, "Let not your left hand know what your right hand doeth." We Southerners were not busy-bodies in other men's matters. A certain new-comer, in remarking on this singularity, said that, in questioning a merchant closely, in regard to the domestic matters of his partner, he could not tell him whether he was a single or married man. We suspect, however, that he would not, for this simple reason—it was nobody's business, and the unmannerly stranger was breaking in upon our order of things. This habit might seem unsocial in some; but it is abundantly better than the gossiping and backbiting of some folks, who attend to every body's business better than they do to their own.

On one occasion, however, I was compelled to pry into my neighbor's matters. On Christmas eve I had retired earlier than usual, and had begun to doze comfortably, when I was disturbed by a low, murmuring sound of distress, occasionally mingled with groans and sobs. The little gate was ever and anon swinging on its hinges; and every new visitor seemed to swell the tide of woe. This did not make me unhappy; it only roused my sympathy, and turned the tide of thought into a more serious and mournful channel; for, in those days of youthful piety, whether I wept with those who wept, or smiled with those who smiled, still my God was with me, and I had peace within. It is true, even then, I had heard of the "hypo" with the hearing of the ear; but I had placed it in the catalogue of "Old Wives' Fables." I said to myself, "Can this be a wake?" Stealing softly from my bed, and peeping through the fence, I saw the house was brilliantly lit up, the doors and windows spread wide open, and there was a corpse, surrounded by relatives and friends, who had come to weep with the household. My heart was touched; for never had I witnessed grief more sincere—more natural. Having again retired, I soon fell asleep; but not so soundly as to be wholly unconscious of what was passing around. The weeping and the wailing mingled with my dreaming fancies: the earth seemed to be floating in a sea of tears, and charity and faith were still in wild disordered exercise.

About midnight the clock began to strike. At every stroke the tempest of sorrow rose higher and higher. "Nine, ten, eleven, *twelve !*" Just then the afflicted crowd broke loose in one united, and, as I felt, infernal laugh. They sprang to their feet, and danced, and fiddled, and romped, and laughed again, louder and still louder. My mind, in the mean time, took a complete somerset, and I exclaimed, "Surely the devil's abroad in the land!" I felt that he was rummaging in every corner of my room, rolling and tittering under my bed, trying to scramble up into my soul, whether I would or not. My flesh crawled—the hair of my head seemed to rise. I sprang from my bed, with my eyes shut, of course, for I strangely felt that the testimony of sight was all that was lacking in bringing me in open and manifest contact with the *"wicked one."* I hastily threw on my clothes, and rushed into the street, slamming the door behind me, and hastened to leave the unnatural merriment. The cool and bracing air of midnight, so peculiar to Orleans, pressed my throbbing temples with its friendly breath, and seemed to whisper, "How mean, how niggardly mean, that the devil could not allow one poor Christian, and he 'less than the least,' the small space of six feet by three, within the bounds of his nocturnal range!" The enemy might have had more to do with my heart on other occasions; but never before had I realized such an experimental verity of his presence — in proper person.

I passed on to a region of quietude; for there is commonly an hour or two of silence, out of twenty-

four, even in that babbling city — that conventicle
of every language and every faith. As I passed
down by the great church, the door being ajar, I
. discovered that there was a light within. Prompted by curiosity, I slipped in, and beheld an unusual
sight.   In one corner of the church had been
erected a manger—a rough temporary shed, such as
we find connected with almost every cabin in new
settlements. About a cart-load of straw was piled
in the center. Two animals, of the size of a New-
foundland dog, in carved work, were stationed on
the right and left. It would have saved strangers
an abundance of perplexity, if the artist had
printed on one, "The ox," and on the other, "The
ass."   But, as I had some idea of the drift of it, it
was made out. Joseph and Mary were as large as
life, and dressed in royal robes, richly spangled
with gold and silver, and sparkling jewels, sufficiently imposing—as we thought—to have secured
a reception at the inn, if the Roman emperor and
all his tetrarchs had been guests. The blessed Virgin was placed, according to our Protestant notions,
in a very improper attitude, and the babe presented
a strange appearance. Two angels were perched
upon the eaves of the shed, and gazing on the
group below. I was soon satisfied with the poorly-
contrived fixment, and would have retired; but
thinking it was more tolerable than the loud Satanic
"ha! ha!" that had dispossessed me of my lodgings,
I concluded to sit down to see the end of the mat-

ter. As the day began to dawn, the entry and aisles became vocal with the prattling of infantile devotees—groups of smiling children, bearing their offerings to the consecrated manger. It was diverting to see their buoyant and exulting joy when they first saw the babe. Candies, raisins, kisses, cakes, and other sacrifices, all costly, no doubt, in their young imagination, were freely thrown into the manger, till the straw was almost hid under the profusion of "good things" that had been showered upon it. That morning's exhibition lightened my mind of one mystery which had been hanging about it. At other religious festivals we had seen some of our fellow-citizens, who were evidently men of strong minds, liberal education, and polished manners, who nevertheless succumbed to the most disgusting idolatry. How they could, allowing them to be sincere—which of necessity we did—be so grossly imposed on, we could not conceive. But here it was all revealed. This manifest idolatry was planted in infancy. It had grown with their growth, strengthened with their strength. It had been entwined with all the associations of their younger, brighter, and happier days. If error, which has no countenance in reason or revelation, by an early lodgment in the human breast, becomes so immovable, that even high attainments in science can not displace it, how industrious ought parents to be in fixing in the infant's mind the omnipotent truths of the everlasting Gospel! These

juvenile exercises continued till after sunrise, when,
I suppose, they melted away "like the morning
cloud;" for I found, about noon, that the manger of
Bethlehem, with the ox and the ass, and all its inmates and appurtenances, had fled, and made room
for other idols and older worshipers. I retired to
my lowly domicile, found the atmosphere more pure,
the malign influence all gone, and spent there many
an hour of piety and peace—"prayer being my
chief business—all my pleasure praise." Some may
smile at my sore wrestling with powers and princi-
palities; but, hark ye, I do not say the devil was
actually in my hermitage. I only state my feelings
pending that sudden and inhuman transition from
what I conceived to be the most sincere and heart-
felt sorrow, to a revelry unparalleled, as I thought,
in all the fiendish orgies on mercy's side of hell.
Neither dare I deny that *he was* there. It might
please a class; but what should I gain thereby?
The boon which the dying fox would have inherited
by the kind interference of his friends—*a fresh
swarm of bees and flies*. There are still many, who,
with the open Bible in their hands, would dispute
with me the very personality of the devil. Moreover, I like to anger infidelity by exercising every
kind of credulity that can be possibly fastened on
the Scriptures.

As my place in the naval office made it necessary
for me to sign the clearance of every vessel, the
secretary of the Bible Society kept me supplied

with a large stock of Bibles, in every modern lan-
·guage, for gratuitous distribution to such captains
who were destitute. I enjoyed much in this work,
and also some persecution. One day I presented a
copy to a lake captain. His face at once flushed
up, and he cursed heartily, and said,

"If you would give me a volume of Shakspeare,
or something of that kind, I would read it."

I felt hurt, and I suppose he saw it. Before he
reached the city again an awful storm of intense
coldness swept the coast and lakes. Several of
the lake craft went ashore, and some crews were
found frozen to their posts. When my thundering
skipper came into the office again, after his papers
were signed, he stood silent with his eyes fixed on
my pile of Bibles. At last he said in a subdued tone,

"When I was here last, you kindly presented me
a Bible, and I roughly and wickedly rejected it;
but I have been brought to feel the need of such a
book on board, and if you will be so kind as to
make me the offer again, I would gladly accept it."

But in most cases the Bible was gratefully received. A German captain, who commanded a large
merchantman, came to clear one day. I held out to
him a fine family Bible, in German, and asked him
if he would accept of it. He understood English
very imperfectly. "Why, that is the very thing I
have long been wanting." Seeing that he misun-
derstood me, and expected to pay, I told him we
charged him nothing.

19

He jumped back, and exclaimed, "O, no, you can not afford that." I explained to him that there was a large society that supplied us with them to give away. He pressed the book to him, and said,

"Is it possible that in a world like this, there can be found so many generous men—generous even to foreigners that they have never seen? Pray, sir, let me express my gratitude to you. I have two or three cases of my costly Holland gin on board, put up in highly-finished bottles. I will send a case down to your office."

"O, no, captain, I am only the distributer; they cost me nothing, and, besides, there are a great many men in this country who never drink spirit-uous liquor."

At this he stretched his eyes still wider, exclaiming, "What a country!"

It is a matter of sincere regret that even in this enlightened age of Christianity, while the Gospel of Christ, the kingdom of the Babe of Bethlehem, is spreading its victorious march, and waving its blood-stained banner over almost every nation, there should be found men—professedly religious—who not only neglect the Sacred Volume themselves, but would prevent others from receiving its saving teachings. The Popes of Rome, in their imaginary holiness, have denounced the Bible Society as an enemy who is sowing tares among wheat. When we think of the awful consequences these unhappy men are drawing down upon their guilty heads, our souls tremble for those consequences; but when we reflect how fragile and nugatory are all their attempts to impede the progress of Divine truth, or to prevent the glory of the Gospel, we are led to laugh at all their fruitless efforts. Jehovah himself will hold such characters in derision, and if they repent not of their folly, he will laugh at their calamity, and mock when their fear cometh. Blessed be God, the age of unsanctified profession has passed away. The kingdom of God is still advancing, lengthening its cord and strengthening its stake. The temple of the Lord Jesus is rising upon the ruins of demolished idolatry, and will rise till its holy steeple will pierce the heavens, and the topstone itself be brought forth with shouting, crying grace unto it!

XVII.

LEAVE NEW ORLEANS—SCHOOL-TEACH-ING—CAMP MEETING.

As I was so favorably situated at New Orleans, both as it regarded my spiritual and temporal interests, it might be proper to say something about the circumstances that led to my removal. My oldest brother, the only one of us who was married, in returning from a visit to Virginia, brought a sister along with him as far as Lexington, in Kentucky, when finding the Ohio River so low that he was obliged to take to a skiff, he left her there. When he got home, it was determined that I should go up for her, hoping that before my arrival the river would be up. The steamboat on which I embarked could get no higher than the mouth of the Ohio, and I was under the necessity of walking up to Louisville, in order to take the stage for Lexington.

It was a very singular Fall. The woods in Kentucky, Virginia, and as far as we could hear from, were all on fire. Although Indian Summer, the sun was not seen for several weeks. In traveling through the forests, we would often have fire on both sides of the road, and sometimes we had to

wait till a tree, nearly severed by fire, had fallen.
At other times, after nice calculation, we would
venture to run past, just in time to hear the crash
behind. Sometimes we would get out of the fiery,
stifling region, but be waked up in the night by
the cry of "Turn out to fight the fire!" And here
it would be coming like a mighty army, crackling,
roaring, and spitting, as it were, tongues of fire,
far ahead. In some parts it enveloped fences, barns,
stacks, and even dwelling-houses. It was a hard
matter for several miles to get a drink of water.
Some had to haul it eight miles. When I arrived
at Louisville, the whole atmosphere was filled with
smoke and dark ashes. I brought my sister from
Lexington, to wait the rise of the river. As we
came out of a Methodist prayer meeting in the
evening, my sister said,

"Brother, the man who closed the meeting is a
tailor."

"How do you know he is a tailor, Angelina?"

"Why, did you not hear him say, in giving out
his appointments, 'We must *cut* our *pattern* according to our *cloth?*'"

"Well," said I, "whether he is a tailor or not,
I'll go and see him to-morrow, and see if he can
board us, for the river may not rise this Winter,
and I like his looks very much."

We found out his name, and set out in the morning to find his house. When we came to his door,
and saw the style of the house, we at once despaired

of getting board, but thought he might recommend us to some pious family. We rang, and brother Overstreet appeared. We made known to him our circumstances, and he kindly smiled, and said,

"I have never taken boarders yet, but I think I will have to take you two."

We found this family to be the kindest we ever found away from home.

The river did not rise before Spring. Brother Overstreet was a man of great sociability, and would often invite young company to spend the evening with the strangers. One thing that struck me particularly was the size of the Kentucky girls. In one large room full there was not one but what was far above medium hight. They plagued my little sister a great deal, by saying that Virginia did not produce as large corn as Kentucky, and they reckoned the reason why she did not come up to the mark was, she was raised on dodgers made out of nubbins. I preached but seldom here. The Church at that time was ranged into two parties. The females had separate prayer meetings; but they would attend both—the party "*out*" seated in the rear. When the party "*in*" would pray, "O Lord, we have sinned, and done evil in thy sight," there would be a response behind, with provoking emphasis, "True e-*nough*, Lord!" When the prayer was, "Forgive us, O Lord, and enable us to live soberly, righteously, and truthfully," the response was, "Amen, and *amen*." And yet, to take the parties separately, they were all as sweet as sugar.

Toward the Spring of the year, as I was coming out of the meeting-house, brother Bascom took me aside, and asked me if I had left any brothers in New Orleans.

" Yes, three."

" Because," said he, " I saw, in a paper, to-day, that a gentleman of your name—I have forgotten his first name—fell lately in a duel."

This went like a dagger to my heart. I requested him to get fuller information, and, hunting up my sister, we passed on rapidly to our home—for it seemed to me that I would drop before we could reach it. As soon as we entered the door, I informed my sister of the awful tidings, and we were plunged into grief inexpressible. The extreme anguish that possessed us is, even in this day, a mystery to me. Brother Overstreet and his kind family bent over us with all the sympathy of close relations. Brother Bascom took a fraternal interest in our sufferings.

The tide of affliction was abundantly swelled by hearing that my youngest brother, John, had fallen, and that my oldest brother died immediately after, with a natural disease. The practice of dueling had kept me uneasy all the time I was in New Orleans. Public opinion there, in that day, was such that no man, unless he was a member of some Church, could refuse a challenge—or, if manifestly

insulted, omit to give one—without ruining all his
temporal prospects. On this account I often conversed with my brothers on this subject, and tried
to inspire them with a proper abhorrence of the
practice. But they contended that it was easy
enough for me to talk, as every body knew my
profession bound my hands. But hardly any official
or political man there had escaped being called into
the field. The case, as far as I could learn, was
this: It was my oldest brother who first became
involved in the affair. My youngest brother insisted on taking his place, as he had left his family
in Virginia for a while; and he was, moreover, the
principal stay of our widowed mother and her family. My oldest brother would not consent to this;
but John so managed it as to get in between him
and his antagonist, and fell. My brother Thomas
was called out into the same field, at the same
time, but the seconds brought about a reconcilia-
tion. This brother I had saved from a duel before
I left New Orleans. An officer of the army, up
the river, called on him one day to give an account
for some little observation that had appeared in the
paper. He talked so insolently that my brother
struck him; a scuffle ensued, and the hands in the
office put him out. The next thing was a challenge.
I asked my brother if he was going to accept it.
He said, "Certainly; he is an officer, and I must
of necessity accept it right off, according to general
opinion." I told him I only requested him to do

one thing, as I knew he would fight, and that was, to return as an answer, that, as the gentleman was an entire stranger, he would hold the matter in consideration, in order to make some inquiry. It was hard work to get him to consent to this. But I urged that, although the youth was in military costume, he might nevertheless be in disgrace. He took the course that was advised, and, before the time had expired, he found that the fellow had been cashiered, and driven from the camp—so that he was pronounced by all the *"honorables"* to be unworthy of his notice.

Now our family in Orleans was broken up, and when these sad tidings reached my mother, they almost killed her. We concluded to return to old Virginia in the first place; and we could only do so on horseback. As we were about to start, I was fearful my board would nearly strap me, as they say in these times; but when I asked brother Overstreet for the bill, he pleasantly answered, "Not a cent. I never intended to charge you from the beginning." And he pressed me to move my mother's family out. When we thought of the love and kindness of this family, we departed in tears. When we arrived home, I concluded that, after all that had passed, I never could reconcile it to my feelings to live again in New Orleans. I sent my resignation to Washington, sold one of my horses, and departed on the other for the West, with an intention to seek a living in some place where I might move my mother's family, and live at less expense. In all subsequent years occasional doubts would arise in my mind of having done the best, by yielding so far to my feelings, as to abandon that place—Orleans. My temporal prospects were very fair; fields of usefulness were opening before me. I preached, visited the hospitals, carrying them the Holy Bible, besides distributing it to all the ends of the earth, prayed with those who were dying with the yellow fever, and I enjoyed a Savior's love; but now I see the hand of Providence in giving me a timely removal from the great evil that was coming—before my hands were stained with the institution, or my tongue steeped in rebellion toward God and man. Our white society there had increased to about thirty members, and our colored class to about forty. The Church there has extended greatly, and if the members possess the spirit that moved their predecessors, many of them are mourning over the desolation of the land. There is scarcely any part of our Church for which I have cherished a more lively interest than the society in New Orleans.

"What crosses have we borne, what trials have we passed," since the Crescent City faded away in the dim distance!

Traveling westward, with a half-formed intention of making for Louisville, I came to the pleasant-looking village of Wythe. Here I preached, and some of the citizens beset me to stop, and open a school. They said they had not had a male school for some time, and the last master would sometimes get drunk, go to sleep on a bench, and the children would run rampant. I consented to stay for a while, and got such a crowded school that I thought it best to adopt, to some extent, the Lancasterian plan. We would commence in the morning by hearing the first class read; then, at the signal given, all the inferior classes would rise up, and the boys of the first would take their places as monitors. Standing in the midst of the whole, I acquired great adroitness in detecting the smallest blunder. When this was over, the monitors would all take their seats at the writing-desk, where every thing was previously prepared. Then I would commence with the lower classes, and hear them all myself. By this time the writing would be finished, and the boys would have time to look over their grammars. After the grammar exercises were over, at the signal given, all the classes would be heard by the monitors. In the afternoon, arithmetic would be attended to. In this way the classes of young scholars would have six lessons in the day. No time, except play-time, was unoccupied. The school moved on like a factory; and the large scholars were highly elated by the idea of taking a game at teaching, and being themselves masters—some. In writing my history, my teaching enterprise must not be slighted—so bear with me. One little girl, the daughter of a notorious infidel, had been almost frightened out of all growth by the despotism of the school-discipline of that day. She could hardly spell in one syllable; and when she would make a mistake she would tremble like a criminal. I saw she had something to learn before she could learn to read. I sat down by her and talked kindly, told her she should be my girl, and that I would never whip her; then took her on my knee, whenever she said her lesson. At last she had all confidence in me, discarded her fears, and. progressed astonishingly. She soon could read well.

Her father heard that my school was opened every day with prayer, and he became exceedingly angry. He came down one evening to vent his wrath—indeed to whip me. I was boarding at the house of one of the merchants, an Irish gentleman. He came into the dwelling-house, swearing that if I did not quit this whining and praying in school that he would thrash me and break up my establishment. I talked calmly with him; told him it was one of the rules of my school. The parents generally had no objection, and the children now looked for it; and if the President sent his child to my school I would not alter the rule to please him; but if it was so disagreeable to him he could withdraw his child, and he would be charged nothing. Here he broke out afresh with his curses, and swore he would not take her away, for she had learned more in one quarter than she had learned in other schools in twelve months. I suggested that, perhaps, the reason was God had helped me because I called daily on him for help. This made him furious. He would not take her away, but he would come to the court-house on Sabbath, drag me out of the stand, and do my business for me.

By this time my Irish landlady got her nap up, and, rising majestically from her seat, said,

"Mister ——, if you have no other business here but to abuse the master, I will advertise you that when the carpenter built this house, he left a hole in it; and you may take that advantage, and walk out."

On this he cursed at her, and reminded her that they had bought the house from him.

"Yes, but we bought it with that hole in it, and I tell you to walk out."

On this he looked sneeringly at her, and said,

"Yes, you are at their gatherings, too, and I ex-pect it will not be long before you will be talking about being 'born again.'"

She bridled herself up, and said,

"I thank you, sir, I have not put off this im-portant business to this late day. I was baptized into Christ when I was a baby in my mother's arms, and was confirmed long before I saw the likes of you."

And she put at him in good earnest, and cleared her castle. It is singular that he never interrupted me again, but still continued to send his daughter to school; and when I wound up my business, I concluded not to send my bill, because I hated strife and debate. But some who knew him best, said that would make him desperately mad; so I called on him. He politely invited me in, and said,

"Mr. L., I am sorry to hear that you are going to leave us. My child has improved amazingly. under you. And I am sorry also that I gave you that rough talk; but your religion recommends forgiveness, and I hope you will extend it to me. I assure you I never paid a debt more cheerfully."

While teaching here, the circuit preachers invited me to come out and help them hold a two days' meeting. We preached all Saturday and Sunday. A Presbyterian tavern-keeper invited the preachers to close the meeting at night in his tavern. They concluded, if I would exhort, they would close it with a prayer meeting. While exhorting, the power of the Lord seemed to come down; some shouted, some cried for mercy, and a revival commenced and ran through the neighborhood, especially among the Presbyterian children. The tavern-keeper walked about the house clapping his hands and praising God, because he had condescended to bless his tavern with the shout of heaven-born souls. But his daughter, who had been a vain, fashionable girl, was converted, and she threw off all her jewels and finery. This so exasperated the old man that he declared no Methodist preacher should ever enter his house again, with the exception of the young man from Wythe—he was a gentleman.

The Presbyterians generally forbid their children

to unite with our Church, and were very anxious to receive them into their own; but the young people said they would join no Church but the Methodist, and this they would do as soon as they were of age. I have understood since that some of them did so, and others backslid, as might be expected. A young man professed to get religion there, who claimed me as his spiritual father. He was very zealous, and could pray well from the onset. In after years he became a popular minister in the South, and filled some important stations. A few years more, we heard he had removed to the extreme South, and had backslidden and become a gambler. A few years more, and he turned up in Congress—still an orator. One of his opponents in debate threw in his face that he had been a Methodist preacher. He replied that in the days of his youth and indiscretion he had taken that chute, but it was irrelevant to throw it up now. When I heard this I trembled. But on a subsequent occasion, when an infidel member of Congress was declaiming against chaplains and Christianity, he stood up in his place — as if the latent embers of grace were stirred within—and gave him a scorching rebuke, and made a masterly defense of Christianity. Then I hoped. But where he is now, whether in time or eternity, we know not. If in time, may he be reclaimed from his wanderings, and find mercy at the hand of the Lord! Some of our old members did not believe in him at the start, because he prayed with his eyes open; but I told them not to stumble at this, as it was our duty both to *watch* and pray.

We had a camp meeting soon after this—a very singular one. As I was riding to it, a gentleman overtook me, and asked where I was from. "Wythe." He said they had heard strange news from Wythe, that the folks had permitted a Methodist preacher to live among them. He then went on to recount some of their wicked doings in former years, and how a gang of them followed a Methodist preacher who came through the place, and forced him to dance to the sound of a fiddle. On subsequent inquiry this was found to be true, and my old infidel friend was at the head of the gang.

We had only two or three sermons on the campground, when there came on a rain which precluded all public exercises to the close of the meeting. There were only eight or nine tents. Happily, some of them were very large—and we betook ourselves to singing and praying. The fashionable people, who came out on Saturday, crowded into the tents to save their finery, and a wonderful time followed. While the exercises were going on, they would drop like shot blackbirds, tear off their ruffles and ornaments, and cry for mercy. I would look on, and ask myself who told them to do this. Nothing had been said about dress; and some of them had never heard the Methodist preachers before. It was the Spirit of God writing on their truly-awakened hearts. It was a singular scene to see converted young men standing up, their wet, torn ruffles flapping in the wind, while with all their power they exhorted their companions to flee from the wrath to come. On Monday morning the white members were completely exhausted. The little colored camp was marched up. They rushed into the battle like a reserved corps, and the very heavens resounded with prayer, praise, and the shouts of regenerated men and women. The gentleman who had just been elected as their representative was converted. A family was justified, all but one son. He was roused up from the mourners' bench to go home and bring the horses. He did so—harnessed them up; and, returning to the tent, flung himself on his knees, and never rose till he stood up to praise God for his redeeming grace. It was said that more than one hundred were converted on the ground. And how many more after, who can tell? As we rode home, shouting, prayer, and praise seemed to ascend from almost every farm-house on both sides of the road. Taking into consideration the number of people assembled, the paucity of the means, the apparently-unfavorable weather, and other circumstances, I hold it to be the greatest camp meeting I ever attended—and I have been at many truly great.

XVIII.

SETTLE IN XENIA—THE MINISTRY.

I now concluded to move farther west, having Kentucky principally in view. I procured a small wagon and two horses, and, with my mother and three single sisters, took up my pilgrimage. For lack of experience, we were nearly a month in traveling a distance we ought to have made in two weeks. After we had entered Kentucky we came to a fork in the road, where we stopped and held a council. I told them my feelings were all for Kentucky; but it was a slave State, and, as we would have to depend on our own resources, we might be subject to occasional mortifications; whereas Ohio was a free State, and although it might have some disadvantages, yet I believed that, in the long run, it would be more suitable to us. After considerable deliberation, we took the direct road to Cincinnati. Although this at the outset had not been contemplated, yet it was certainly the better course. We finally settled in Xenia, and found there and in its vicinity many old Virginians, and a few acquaintances. Here I opened a school, and when it increased considerably my mother took charge of the female department. She was well qualified to teach, especially in arithmetic.

While in Louisiana I trembled at the intelligence of the people, and longed for "a lodge in some vast wilderness," where my talents, slim as they were, might be more needed; and especially where I might not be buried by superior ministerial lights. Vain hope! About the first man I heard preach was Dr. Taylor, who was an extra minister. He was profoundly doctrinal and argumentative. He had, however, a considerable drawback. He had an incurable devotion to all the obsolete words of our dictionary, and was inclined to verbosity. On one occasion he changed appointments with a preacher in an obscure region. When the regular preacher came back, the people told him that they hoped when he sent another man in his place, he would send one who could preach English, not Latin. After I had entered the traveling connection, I came on a bitter cold day to a large meeting-house. As the door opened, a blast struck me which almost capsized me. Leaving the door open, and advancing, I saw a large brick platform, and on it a glowing charcoal fire, surrounded by a large congregation. I stopped short, and as the people had never seen me before, every eye was fixed upon me. Stretching forth my hand toward the glowing pile, "Brethren, that is precisely the way we used to kill rats on board our ship. When we had got into port and discharged our cargo, we filled an old pot with a charcoal fire, placed it on the keelson, battened down all the hatches for twenty-four hours, and when we would open them, every rat in the ship would be lying dead about the pot. Is it possible that no preacher has ever told you of the danger of sitting over such a fire?"

One brother said, "No preacher ever said any thing about our fire excepting Dr. Taylor. He stood over it once, and made a speech, but none of us could understand it. I only remember two words of it which he often repeated, 'hydrogen and nitrogen;' but you speak plain, and say *it will kill rats*, and we 'll put it away. Our women have often fainted when we had large congregations, but we never blamed the fire."

Nevertheless, Dr. Taylor was an instructive preacher. The next I heard was John Strange, his colleague. He was universally popular, even at that time. When the quarterly meeting came on, the elder, James B. Finley, preached in his most successful style. I had to acknowledge that the whole Virginia Conference at that time had no three men that could match them.

. Brother Sale lived in the neighborhood. A more pleasant and upright man I never knew. He was my fast friend, and I enjoyed his counsel and example for many years. He was remarkably conscientious. On one occasion, he related that before he embraced religion he was in company with two or three wild young men, who concluded to lash something to the tail of an old horse, belonging to a neighbor, to stir up a little fun. He did not approve of the sport, and tried to prevent it. The horse ran off in a terrible fright, and was killed. Although he had no hand in thus depriving a poor man of his horse, yet he felt somewhat guilty in keeping the secret. But after he obtained mercy of the Lord, in the forgiveness of his sins, he returned to the place, and having understood of the owner the full value of his horse, acknowledged the part he had in the transaction, and paid his full share of the assessment. When he was traveling out westward as a young preacher, he was under the necessity of putting up at a tavern. Every thing around him appeared so irreligious, that he had no encouragement to speak of prayer—it was only a tavern. When the landlord lighted him to bed, he asked him what was the object of his journey. He said in a tremulous voice, "I am going out to preach the Gospel." The tavern-keeper fastened his piercing eyes upon him, and said, "Young man, you will not be of much force. The preachers out here will hold family prayer if they are in the very gates of hell." He said he never neglected it again. There was considerable controversy abroad when we moved to Ohio. Some of the young preachers were riding along the road and telling some of the smart and pungent turns they had taken in this line; brother Sale turned in his saddle and said, "Boys, I want you to take one idea along with you—you can catch more bees with honey than you can with vinegar." This word spoken in season was of immense importance to myself.

Dr. Joshua Martin, of Xenia, proposed to me to study medicine; at the same time offering me his office, books, and instructions gratuitously. This offer I embraced, and spent all my leisure time in reading medical works, according to his arrangement. After I was employed to teach a Methodist school in Lebanon, he still supplied me with books and periodical instruction. While residing in Xenia, Bishop M'Kendree came along and insisted on starting a Sabbath school there. At that time there had been no Sunday school, that I knew of, in Southern Ohio, outside of Cincinnati. He selected me for the superintendent. I objected on the score of my preaching almost every Sabbath. He said this could be done in the afternoon; and even if I did not preach so often, I might, in the long run, do more good with the school. We started the school; and a first-rate school it was. We had about one hundred and eighty scholars; many of the children coming from one to three miles around. Out of that original school came five or six traveling ministers, several local ministers and officials; and, indeed, there were very few of those scholars that did not become acceptable members of the Methodist Episcopal Church. Now, I do not, reader, monopolize the praise of this work; for we had pious and efficient teachers; but it is meet to show that, in entering on the great work, I did "in the morning sow my seed," and "my labor is with my God," and if he approved it, the "record is on high."

When I had advanced considerably in the study of medicine, I became uneasy about what would be my best course. The first inquiry was, can a man be an efficient preacher, and at the same time attend to the duties of a physician, allowing that he has only a tolerable practice? The answer was, no. Can he be a useful doctor, and attend to the whole duty of a minister? No more than a man can serve two masters. And the decision was that I should prefer the most important call. Another thing that lay heavy on my mind was this: in removing from New Orleans I had, of necessity, to forego many special privileges — regular and stated periods of devotion, reading, and meditation; this, with continual moving, and mixing with young company, considerably impaired my enjoyments in religion. Indeed, although I have not set out, after the example of Rousseau, to write my confessions, which would benefit no one, yet I can not, on the other hand, like a simple biographer, pass by my sins altogether. I felt that I was going back considerably. Sometimes I thought it was wrong for me to profess to be a Christian at all; then I would be filled with bitter contrition; then peace and comfort would return, and I would feel the Lord had not cast me off. I felt that I dare not give up any of my duties—praying, preaching, and meditating. It seemed to me that my own safety would be in letting go the world altogether, and giving myself entirely up to the work of the ministry. I was recommended to the Conference and received. As far as the itinerancy is concerned, it has been with me a standing cross for nearly forty years. It was with great trepidation that I first mounted into the saddle to take a circuit. I went to sea before I had learned to ride. I took for my motto,

> "Some trust in chariots made for war,
> And some of horses make their boast;
> My surest expectations are
> In Thee, the Lord, the God of hosts!"

Time would fail me to tell of the many dangers and frightful hair-breadth escapes through which I passed—the ground and lofty tumblings that befell me. But the Lord was very gracious to me; for as often as my honor was laid low in the dust or mud, horse and all, I always rolled *"right side up."* Again, my leaning was for a settled ministry. My experience has taught me that the longer I preach to a congregation the better I know how to serve them. And I never enjoy myself better than when I preach two new sermons every Sabbath. It may be asked, then, why I did not join some religious connection where a settled ministry was the order. Such a proposal was made to me, in the morning of my ministry, by an authorized agent. But,

First. I saw no Church that I considered so

orthodox, in doctrine and practice, as the Methodist Episcopal Church.

Secondly. I believe that the itinerancy—whether it suited me best or not—was, as a general thing, the best plan for the salvation of souls.

Thirdly. And all-sufficient; it was the plan laid down by our Savior. ·He sent them forth, two by two, into all the world.

When we speak of the itinerancy, of course we mean as it is laid in the Discipline, without guile and without partiality. As it regards any deviation it rests on broader shoulders.

I went forth believing I was called to the work. As the call to the ministry is regarded by some as somewhat mythical, I will express my views in regard to this matter.

We believe that the man who is called of God to preach his Word, has a deep, solemn, and abiding impression resting on his soul, that it is his duty to hold forth the Word of life to his fallen race—that it is an all-absorbing impression, strongly checking all his natural aspirations after wealth, honor, worldly settlement, as though he were by no means his own, but constantly awaiting the disposition of Almighty God. It may be asked here if a man may not be deceived at this very point—taking the fervid workings of his own fancy for a Divine call. Certainly men may be deceived. We have seen some who, in our opinion, were deceived in regard to their having religion. But this impression is

not the whole call. There is in connection a provi-
dential call. The God of grace is the God of providence. It would be unreasonable to suppose the
Lord would call a man by his grace, and forbid
him by his providence. If he has called him by his
Spirit, he will assuredly open his way. Some have
insisted they are divinely called, but when the
matter is investigated by a godly Church, that
Church kindly, but firmly, dissents. A pious
Church is a good judge. The ox knoweth his
owner, and the ass his master's crib, and true
Christians know who is instrumental in feeding
them with the bread of life, and building them up.
It is seldom that the Church is mistaken. They
might be for a season, but if the individual exercises Christian charity and patience the Lord will
open his way, if he is called; but in too many
cases they fly off, and show by their subsequent
conduct that their cases are doubtful. Again, one
who believes he is called should examine closely his
motives. Particularly should he search his own
heart in regard to being moved by pecuniary considerations. This inquest with some is not elaborate, for in many cases it will be found that, as far
as money is concerned, the step will be a sacrifice.
But he should inquire whether he is moved by a
love of fame, also; for this would be as sinful a
motive as filthy lucre. And when he feels that he
is clear in all these things, and the ruling impression of his mind is, "For Zion's sake I will not rest,

for Jerusalem's sake I will not hold my peace, till her righteousness goes forth as brightness, and her salvation as a lamp that burneth;" then, we think, he has a comfortable evidence that he is called to the work. It was by these rules that I judged my own case. I had an abiding impression that it was my duty to preach.

XIX.

ITINERANT LIFE—COLUMBUS CIRCUIT.

1824. IN entering on this, my first circuit, I had two especial crosses to face:

1. My colleague—Charles Waddle—was, without exception, the most popular preacher in the Conference. I felt no envy, and never had any, in regard to any colleague; but I was afraid that the congregations were so accustomed to such extra preaching, that my efforts might not be as serviceable as they might be under other circumstances. I was soon relieved of this fear by the urbanity and fraternal attentions of the whole Church. I suppose there never was a society of Methodists, in Ohio, more experienced, more pious, more forbearing than the Church of Columbus in that day.

2. The Legislature was much in my way. It was indeed a venerable body, and would compare favorably with any that has occupied the State-House since. I regarded them at first as the collected wisdom of the State.

But I soon learned that they were mostly men of circumstances—that intellectual worth was seldom the qualification of popularity. Indeed, that year one of our counties had sent an idiot, by way of sport, to represent them. At first I preached *to* them, with fear and trembling; but before I was done I preached *at* them, with much assurance. I was very awkward in my circuit duties, of which I might give one instance: After preaching at Columbus, I asked some member if he could tell me where my next appointment was, as I had no plan. He said the Monday appointment was at Dublin; that I must cross over to Franklinton, and any one would put me in the road. "All right," I thought, as I mounted my horse—"*a chief city in Ireland.*" As soon as I crossed the river, I asked a man if he could tell me the way to *Belfast.*

"Belfast? No, sir. I know of no such town in these regions."

"Why, it is not more than seven or eight miles from this place."

"Then it must be some new town."

Then I inquired of another, and another, and so on. Some said it was not in that county; some said they did not believe there was such a place in all the country. Then I took what seemed to be the most probable road, thinking that the nearer I approached the place the better the people would know it. Having proceeded about eight miles, I again inquired. One put me on one road, and one on another; but nobody knew exactly where Belfast was. It was all surmise. Thus I rode all day, and got into a forest, where I expected night would overtake me. But about dusk I came to a cabin; and I asked if I could stay all night.

"You have come to preach to us to-morrow."

"Is my appointment here, to-morrow?"

"It is, I suppose."

"Well, do tell me where Belfast is. Is it the appointment for to-day?"

"No. If they have not altered the plan, you should have preached at *Dublin* to-day."

"O yes, Dublin! Dublin! that's it!"

I did not hear the last of this for twelve months. I was now like a young bear—my troubles just beginning. I was weighed at the penitentiary, and found that in two rounds I had gained thirteen pounds. My mare also took advantage of the change, and began to cover her bones, and to lay aside her meekness, and sometimes get into awful frights. We hardly know whether it would be more proper to say we rode, or walked, our first circuit. When she would commence a great fright, in the self-same moment I would step on the ground—for I yet retained my sailor agility—and then it would take all my strength to hold her. I would then take her by the bit, and walk a mile or two, till she got calm. The brute got so used to this that, when she intended to take a fright, she would cock one ear and look back to see if I was getting down. Sometimes I would not, but would pat her and talk to her, and persuade her not to scare just then. This was a source of much mortification to me, for all the awkwardness that was ever recorded in horse-jockey lore was fastened on me; and I had sometimes to hear grave ministers recounting awful mishaps in my traveling that I had never heard of before. For this reason I would run great risks in the saddle when in company. When about to start, one day, from town, in the presence of several who, I knew, were watching me, I thought I would cut something extra, so as to reduce my slanderers, and I undertook to spring from the ground into my saddle. That I might not come short, I gathered up all the force necessary—yea, rather more—for I landed on the other side of my nag, to the great amusement of my brethren. For about forty years I have been seeking for a perfect horse, but have never found him. In that time I have owned thirty-two—all of them possessing some good qualities and many bad ones. If one did not scare, he would stumble, and occasionally fall, at most inauspicious times and in most inconvenient places; some would scare and fall, too, simultaneously. As it regarded my support, I had little or no forethought about it. This was not my object. The school which I taught afforded me almost four hundred dollars annually. My quarterage, the first year, was from eighty to ninety; but it was the most beautiful money I had ever received; it looked pure and holy—the wages of the Lord.

But although quarterage—if the term is not

obsolete—never troubled me much on my own account, yet it troubled me greatly in connection
with others. I found scores of Methodists who
bore without murmuring the whole pecuniary
weight of their circuits, paying regularly the fare
of hundreds toward Mount Zion. I say *toward*.
Men who would indignantly forbid their neighbors
to pay their fare to Cincinnati, would quietly sub-
mit to their paying their expenses all the way to
heaven. Now, the difficulty with me was to have
any confidence in their profession. "But could you
not quietly pass them by?" No, I had to meet
them in the classes, and to listen to their thunder
in rooms they had not warmed any farther than
the animal heat of their own bodies extended, and
by lamps that they had never oiled, and to exhort
them with words which were without money and
without price—they had a religion which cost them
nothing, and, as Dr. Clarke says, was good for
nothing. These observations do not apply particularly to my first circuit. I only throw them in as
preliminary to the long conflict. The Columbians
did well in that generation. On the circuit my
saddle-bags were stuffed with socks, gloves, and
other necessaries, and all these were pure demon-
strations of friendship, inasmuch as I was pretty
well rigged from the beginning.

In that day we had no protracted meetings. The
term was not then coined even among the Presbyterians, where it originated. We made, however, a

steady draw on sinners through the year—Winter
and Summer. Faith came by hearing, and hearing
by the preaching of-the Word. Persons would get
impressed under our ministry, and having to preach
again in the afternoon or next day, we would leave;
but the local preachers and leaders would get up
neighborhood meetings, and the convicted would
find relief in the ordinary means of grace. When
the preacher would come round, he would take in
two or three, sometimes as many as five or ten at
the different appointments. These coming in gradually and understandingly, and being consigned to
large classes, were cared for, and they generally
persevered.

Having now retired from charge, I feel it to be a
duty, which I can not neglect, to protest solemnly
against the practice into which we have fallen in
this day. Our people, generally, do not look to the
ordinary means which God has established in his
Word. It would be wonderful now for a soul to be
converted in a prayer meeting. Our faith and hope
stretch forward to the protracted meeting. The
people and sometimes the minister pray mightily
for God to meet them at the approaching big meeting. Speak to sinners about seeking religion, and
they will say, "We have been thinking about it,
and we have concluded to try when that big meeting comes off." Some will say, "But we take in
large numbers on such occasions." True, and aside
from the great drought and apathy which intervenes

through the whole year, it might seem as well to take them in at one sweep as to be receiving them the whole year. But what becomes of them? In most cases the majority of them are laid aside in twelve months. Some have been converted by the Gospel, but many have been pressed into the Church by exciting circumstances, youthful sympathies, and novel measures unknown in apostolic times. They have not embraced the truth in the love of it. The meeting is run to such an extreme, that when the members fall back on their ordinary services, they are cold, spiritless, and surfeited; and the young members begin to feel the reaction too strong for them. So the neighborhood is filled with people who have once been in the Church, but not long enough to form an attachment to it, and it is doubly difficult to catch them again.

This is not all. It is destroying our ministers. This extraordinary strain, long continued, on young preachers produces bronchitis and diseases in their vocal organs, so that we can find very few, even among those on probation, who are not as shattered trumpets. In a modern protracted meeting they preach and exhort day and night, and in some places they have to pray, sing, and shout, and do all, till the members begin to think that the meeting has been protracted to that point that it is proper for them to dash in; custom has fixed that point on the third or fourth week. The reader must not think that we are croaking merely against others. We old men have followed suit simply because we know that unless we get members according to this programme, we can not get them at all—and it must be done in the Winter, too. The old preachers have this advantage—and we call on the whole Church to remark it by audible attention to the few who are still among us—they have in their youth, by constant preaching, acquired a volume of voice, enlarging with their growth, that can ring, distinct and loud, through all the phases of the most protracted meeting, as far as the natural infirmities of age may allow. They are generally sound in their throats.

On my first circuit, in addition to those we might receive on our regular rounds, we received a considerable number at two-days' meetings. Sometimes we would continue these meetings at the expense of our rest days, or by procuring ministerial help. These we regarded as special revivals. We had two such on Columbus circuit; one on the Scioto. Here the New Lights had borne sway for some time; and it did seem, then, as if they would take the whole community into the river. My colleague preached much against their errors; and I always felt I was doing the Lord's own service when preaching against Arianism. Here we had a great work, and we had to make two societies along the banks of the Scioto. The New Light preacher's daughter came to our meetings, and joined the Church. One of his people went to his house to bear the intelligence to him. He bowed his head awhile, and lifted it up, and raised his eyes to heaven, and said, *"Thy will be done!"*

We had another extraordinary meeting in a village at one extremity of the circuit, where there was a small Baptist Church. Seeing that the grace of God was with us, they requested to unite with us in the work. To this we cordially assented, and we had a powerful revival. As the Sabbath drew nigh we proposed a love-feast; and, as the Baptists knew nothing about that means of grace, we invited them all to come. When we opened the meeting we explained its character—how that the eating of bread and drinking the water was only an outward expression of our Christian friendship; but the exchange of our experience and Christian communion was the spiritual banquet to which we were looking. We then told the Baptists to do as they would see us do, one not waiting for another. As soon as the Methodists had started the speaking exercises, the Baptist minister arose, and gave a clear and feeling account of his experience—his convictions, his conflict, his bright conversion, the time when and place where he received the remission of sins. The power of God seemed to fall upon the assembly like a sweeping shower. Now a Methodist would rise—now a Baptist; and a stranger, coming in, could not have known who was a Methodist or who was a Baptist, for we all felt that there was one Lord, one faith, one baptism—the baptism of the Holy Ghost and of fire. When the meeting was about to close, we hardly knew how to house our sheaves, for my colleague was away at General Conference, and a local preacher and myself had conducted the meeting. However, with the consent of the Baptist minister, we stated that it was always our custom, when we closed a large meeting, to open the door of our Church to see who were candidates for membership; but, as we had worked together, there might be some who might wish to join us, and there might be some whose leanings and associations might be for the Baptist Church. We only wanted those—if any—who thought they could serve God best in the Methodist Church. If there were any who thought they could get more good and do more good in the Baptist Church, we hoped they would not, through the impulse of the moment, join us—because they would afterward be dissatisfied. When we opened the door, nearly the whole school rushed into our net. The Churches then fell back to their own work—the Baptists crying out, "Water! water!" and the Methodists, "Fire! fire!" and all the young converts, "Glory! glory!" We had, also, a very good work in Columbus; and it was a reviving year to the membership.

There was a blacksmith in the city who was much given to intoxication. His story was: While sitting in his shop, about twilight, his attention was roused by an extraordinary light springing up suddenly in his shop. He raised his eyes, and saw a brilliant personage standing before him, with a look of anger, mingled with compassion. He upbraided him with his past misconduct, but concluded by telling him there was room in heaven for him if he would reform. He was found stretched on the floor. He was dreadfully alarmed, and for some time was afraid to be alone. He went further, and quit using spirits for a while; he went further, and came once to our church—but hid behind the door. We did not believe that this man had any supernatural visitant; but all the people in the place could not persuade him otherwise — and, as it regarded *him*, it was the same as if it had been real. We only refer to it as a remarkable illustration of Abraham's doctrine, "Neither would they be persuaded if one should arise from the dead." The same blacksmith had a very amiable daughter, who attended our revival, and in hearing Moses and the prophets, and the holy evangelists, was *"persuaded,"* and powerfully converted. She returned home, threw her arms around her father's neck, and told him what great things the Lord had done for her. He wept, and commended her step, and said he hoped she would be faithful, for there was no character so hateful as a backslider. He went out, resumed his dissipated habits, and pressed on with renewed thirst the downward way to ruin.

The close of the Conference year, and departure of the minister to a new field of labor, presses hard upon the feelings of the preacher. Nearly forty

years of travel and wandering has not blunted my
sensibility of the parting pang. It is made endur-
able only by the solemn promise which God has
given, that we shall be gathered together again.
We have sometimes almost envied those who have
administered for a long lifetime to the same congregation and its succession, and when they die
leave behind a Church that has been baptized in
infancy by their own hand; but when we remember
how many Churches we have been allied to, and
look forward to the day when they shall be flying
home from the north and from the south, from the
east and from the west, to take their places in the
kingdom of God, and while we cherish the hope that
the acquaintances we have made on earth shall be
perpetuated through a blissful immortality, we say,
it is enough. The children of God, in this world,
are necessarily a scattered people in many respects.

1. They are scattered by the distance of time.
Abel, that eminent servant of God, stands at a
great distance, in point of time, from the saints of
this generation. Still there is a gracious alliance
of fellowship binding him to the Church now mili-
tant. We realize how much we love him, when we
regard him in comparison with that wicked one
who slew him.

When we come down to the history of the apostles, the distance diminishes, and we feel a more intimate union. Again, when we descend to those

Christians who have just preceded us, the tide of Christian sympathy swells delightfully, and we run after them to the very banks of the river, and stretch out our hands to catch their falling mantles, while we exclaim, "The chariots of Israel, and the horsemen thereof!"

> "So seemed the prophet, when to mount on high,
> His master took the chariot of the sky;
> The fiery pomp, ascending, left his view,
> The prophet gazed, and wished to follow too."

But we are separated. We must abide the times.

2. The saints of God are separated or scattered by geographical lines. Even those who are cotemporary with us, are not all present. We hear of them, we read of them, and of their trials, their labors, their success, and sometimes we may correspond with them; and, O, how we long, in the bowels of Christian communion, to embrace them, to converse with them, to weep with them, if need be! O, ye ministers and children of our God! may we not flow together, and break bread, and drink wine in our common Father's house? Hush, O, my soul, and be quiet! Not *now*. Alas, how seldom do the children of God, in any one family, gather together! I look back to the days of childhood, and see myself as a little white-headed boy—a smiling item in a wide and joyful household. I comprehended that Death would come, sometimes, like a sparrow lighting on an ant-hill; but I thought his visits might be far between, and that the survivors would

close up the chasms from time to time, and that even when the last fell, one social graveyard would hold the band. But, years gone by, "that once fair spreading family is dissolved;" the majority have crossed the flood, and no two lie beneath the same green sod. Never more shall we be gathered together in this wayward world.

3. The saints of God are sometimes scattered here by Church polity. We do not all subscribe to the same ecclesiastical government, to the same forms; but this is nothing, provided we are not cursed "with a want of love." There is variety in the inner as well as in the outer man. Still this separates. It is a separation of convenience. Indeed, convenience sometimes calls for the separation of members of the same denomination. Can all the Methodists, in a large city, meet in one house? Can all the Presbyterians gather themselves together under one pastor? Not *now*, my beloved. But of all the saints of God, who sacrifice on earth, none are more separated than the Bethel saints—the true saints of God, who are scattered abroad over the wide seas, and lakes, and rivers, as well as many who are laid up in dry dock, and others who are water-logged all along the coast of life, scattered and peeled, and as Sterne would say, "and that to the quick."

Some of these, in their short stay on land, have made their confession to Almighty God, meekly presenting a crucified Savior, as their only sacrifice, their only argument, their only lamb. God has

heard in heaven, answered on earth, and, as father
Taylor has said, "before the tears of penitence have
dried on their cheeks, they have weighed anchor,
and are again facing the chilling north-wester."
By and by, like a bird of passage, alighting, they
drop into port, hie away to the Bethel, have a song
and a prayer, with shipmates dear, break bread and
drink wine, with a floating brotherhood, shake
hands, and shout and sing,

"Farewell, dear friends, time rolls along,
    We have no home, no stay with you;
We hoist our sails, and travel on,
    Till we a fairer world do view."

What would the Christian sailors be, in this tem-
pestuous world, but as feathers driven to and fro,
were it not for the hope,

"The blissful hope!
The hope by Jesus given;
The hope, when days and years are passed,
We all shall meet in heaven?"

But there is a day of gathering coming. We are
taught that a period is coming, when the God of all
spirits shall arise out of his holy place, and call
upon the heavens above, and the earth below, and
on all his mighty angels, saying, "Gather together
my saints, those who have made a covenant with
me, by sacrifice!" Alleluiah! At that sound all
the stays and stanchions, and props, and shores of
time will give way, the ages of earth will sink
into the bright eternal now, and martyred Abel

will embrace the last elect of Adam's ruined family.

> "Abraham and Isaac, there,
> And Jacob shall receive,
> The followers of their faith and prayer,
> Who now in bodies live."

At that sound, the earth with all its wearisome miles, and deep seas, and rivers, and mighty mountains, will shrivel as a parchment-scroll, and all the saints of the Most High will come flocking home from the north and the south, and the east and the west, and, O, what a gathering of the waters! What multitudes will flow together into the everlasting kingdom of God's dear Son! At that sound, Church polity will be no more — there will be one fold, one shepherd, one temple; "for the Lord God Almighty and the Lamb are the temple" of the New Jerusalem, and the will of God will be the will of his people, from thenceforth, and forever more. Come, shipmate, will you set sail for this gathering? Then bring your sacrifice. Bring one that God will accept. Bring the Lamb, slain, in the Divine Mind, from the foundation of the world. Bring Christ, for him hath God the Father sealed. And he has said, "This is my beloved son, in whom *I am well pleased.*" Now present your offering. "Here, Lord, am I, a poor, wretched sinner, lost, undone; but here is my sacrifice, my ransom, my only plea. I have sinned—O, how grievously!—but Christ has died, the just for the unjust, to bring us to God."

Pray on, wrestle on, believe on, penitent soul, and God will enter into an everlasting covenant with you, for life and salvation, for time and for eternity.

Having passed the morning of my life on the seas it is not strange that the habitudes of the sailor followed me into the ministry. This gave rise to many questions, and I could not, without rudeness, avoid satisfying the social firesides by relating some things which had fallen under my observation in my ramblings on the sea. They seemed to be so deeply interested in every thing of a nautical nature, that I conceived the idea of explaining several passages in the Bible where marine figures are very happily used; and I often illustrated them by what I had seen and experienced on land and flood. I soon discovered that this kind of preaching was effective; but it was not long before I found it was peculiarly so under certain circumstances. When the devotional feeling of the congregations had taken a spring tide, and the soul of the preacher in unison, then have we received extraordinary power, and the revivals have been mightily advanced. We had the most satisfactory evidence of the utility of this course, of which we may give illustrations hereafter.

The use of technical language in discoursing on religious and solemn subjects, by no means implies an absence of veneration or want of piety. A presiding elder, who is now in heaven we trust, once told us he would like to hear us preach a sea-sermon at any other time but on the Sabbath. This we received, but did not resent, as an insult, because it implied that we would dare speak, as a minister of God, on a week-day, what would be unsuitable to the Sabbath. The revelations of God are clothed in language suited to the common professions in life. It is true that nautical phrases might appear singular, yea, ridiculous to a novice, but to the sailor they are natural, indeed oftentimes unavoidable. We felt a religious swell in our soul, a few weeks since, when a gentleman from the East was telling us of the death of a pious sailor.

A religious shipmate, who was solicitous of his welfare, approached his berth and said, "It seems, messmate, that your glass is well-nigh out; we would like to know your prospects—how do you head?"

"O, all is well—I see land just ahead."

Some hours after, when his eyes were almost set in death, the question was repeated, when, with a smile that revealed more than mortal tongue could utter, he whispered, "Glory be to God! I am just *doubling the cape!* Alleluiah!" Was there any thing irreverent in this? No; it was the spontaneous and, therefore, sincere language of a sanctified seaman. And if our vocabulary should extend into eternity, we will doubtless hear again of the "steadfast anchor," the "blissful haven," the "sailor's home," in a world of light and glory, "with God eternally shut in."

Some people think it is all right to preach on the parable of the sower, and to illustrate the sermon with all the technical phrases of a farmer, or to preach on the Christian temple, all "fitly framed together," using the square, line, and plummet, as a skillful carpenter, or on the "balm of Gilead," exhausting all the pharmacology of materia medica, but it is awful to come down into the ship, and "sit in the sea," and preach to those on the land, as our Savior unquestionably did.

We are not among the number of those who contend that sincerity will save a man. God has his ordained plan of salvation. But we are willing to admit that sincerity is a very necessary ingredient in that peculiar frame of mind which prepares the sinner to receive with meekness the ingrafted Word that is able to save.

It was sincerity that nerved the arm of Saul of Tarsus, when he was laying waste the Church of Christ, but it was a sincerity powerless to save.

A gentleman went on board a ship to invite the crew to a temperance lecture, which was to be delivered in the evening. The men with one accord began to make excuses. At last they agreed if one of the crew, pointing him out to the gentleman, would go, they all would. This sailor was the bully of the ship, the ringleader in all mischief, and they had no idea that he could be towed into a temperance meeting. He was kindly approached, and by one of those eccentric whims often found in man, he declared solemnly that he would be on hand. In the evening the crew refused to go, but steady to his purpose he went alone. It happened that a pious lady presented him a New Testament, which he thankfully received. When he returned on board his shipmates asked him what he had got by going to the temperance meeting.

"I got that," said he, holding up his book.

"And what's that?" asked some of the crew.

"Why, it's the New Testament."

"It's all a pack of lies," said one.

"Avast heaving, and let me read a bit."

He then solemnly read a very impressive portion of the book, and when he had finished, he flashed his eyes around and said,

"Do ye see, if any man now says that's 'a pack of lies,' I'm bound to thrash him."

As many as three, who were ambitious of a fuss, at once exclaimed, "It's all lies." Whereupon he unbuttoned his collar, and laid the whole triumvirate on their beam ends, and suffered them not to rise till they acknowledged that what they had heard was truth, and nothing but the truth.

Believing himself that his book was the truth of God, he continued to read it, and it was not long before this violent defender of the Word of God was found peaceably sitting at the feet of Jesus, and clothed, and in his right mind. He was sincere in fighting for the truth, but God had mercy upon him, for he did it ignorantly—in unbelief.

XX.

FIRST CONFERENCE—BRUSH CREEK CIRCUIT.

ZANESVILLE was the first Conference I attended after my reception. In attending the camp meeting, I was invited by the preacher in charge to preach the night before the Conference met. I consented, in my simplicity, not knowing the preachers would come in till the morning of the Conference. I now began to consider what I should preach about. There was one text that I had used just before I left my circuit—somewhere in the woods—and it seemed to be unusually successful. That was fixed upon. When we got into the meeting-house we found it full, and about one-third were preachers. The bishops were in the altar, and a cold shiver ran over me. This was somewhat allayed by my good friend, James B. Finley, taking his seat in the pulpit to follow me. My text was, "Therefore he said unto his servants, See, Joab's field is near mine, and he hath barley there; go and set it on fire. And Absalom's servants set the field on fire." In the first place, we set forth the narrative, paying a strong compliment to Joab, and somewhat disapproving David's constant prejudice against a servant so brave, so devoted. Then we showed that people in modern times cultivated opinions and doxies with as much care and industry as Joab did his barley-field—to instance:

1. The barley-field of Arianism. But God in great mercy sent his servants to set that notion on fire. And then how we did it. Then they would come to God to inquire.

2. The great barley-field of Calvinism. It was our duty to set that on fire. We here stated how we had heard some, in our class meetings and love-feasts, tell how they were once devoted to this ism, and how the preachers set all their bigotry on fire, and drove them to God.

3. The barley-field of Universalism. This we set on fire; and, in connection with it, the field of infidelity.

4. Idolatrous barley-fields. Here we showed how parents would sometimes love their children with undue affection, and how God would send his angels to take them away; how merchants would become too much engrossed in commerce, and the Lord would set their ships on fire, or sink them; how strongly sinners were wedded to their sins; but in all these cases God—not in wrath, but in mercy— sent his servants to set their fields on fire, as a means of their seeing the reconciled face of their father, as Absalom did. We had hardly got half-way through, when we felt the pulpit waving and

23

shaking as if we had been at the royal-masthead, and, casting a glance behind, saw brother Finley with his head down between his knees, and his sides rising and falling like a blacksmith's bellows. This damped my ardor a little; but I made out my points. Still there were too many Joabs there of different denominations, and too many of Absalom's servants—too heavy a press of black cloth. So I sat down considerably mortified, and determined to hang up that text, with all its appurtenances, like a ham of venison to dry. When meeting was over, brother Finley said, "Brother L., you have been six months making that sermon." But I assured him I had never preached on the text but a week before. We record this as an error, hoping all young preachers may take warning, and not undertake singular texts, or hastily believe that they were originally intended to apply to things spiritual. Were I a bishop, I would embrace this advice in every charge: "Let your text be as plain as, 'Repent ye, for the kingdom of heaven is at hand.'"

In that Conference I saw a man who seemed to be a pillar, and who delivered several speeches. I asked brother Sale who he was. He told me, and said,

"He is one of our great men."

"Yes," said I, "but he is not religious."

"O, brother L., you must not talk so. What evidence have you got that he is not religious?"

"None; only I feel that he is not sincere."

Here brother Sale, with pleasant smiles, gave me a lecture, showing that preachers would often be obliged to deal with men according to their profession in the Church, although their own minds are not clear in their characters. Still the observation seemed to strike him, coming as it did from one who was an entire stranger to the man; and I believe he thought I had not come far short of striking the nail on the head. Before two years had passed, the subject of our conversation suddenly turned his back on religion, and gave ample evidence of previous unsoundness.

While speaking on the subject of Conference I will say, that many at this time think that the young men take too much on themselves in debate. This is a consequential reaction; about the time my class, and, indeed, several preceding classes came on the roll, the Conference was oppressed by a strong seniority. Although these classes embrace some of our strong preachers, yet there is not to be found a Conference-speaker among them. There were a number of old men in the Conference—pious and wise, and very able to do the business of the body. When a young man—as they would call him, though stiffly bearded—would rise up to speak, some of them would roll something in his way— some parliamentary omission or something else. I remember one saying, "Mr. President, I think it becomes *young men* modestly to refrain from speak-

ing on such an important subject." The preachers
would talk a great deal about this in the lobby.
One would say, "Brethren, who will know how to
do Conference business when our elder brethren are
removed? We are not permitted to learn." Another would say, "Well, they will go to heaven
soon, and leave you the field." This last one,
though a preacher, was not a prophet; for they
lived on till the boys became gray-headed, and
had by reverential silence lost the animus of controversy. Then the later classes—Young America—took the floor, and some of us are glad they
did; because they tolerate old folks rather more
than old folks tolerated them. So, all can have
their "*say*." He who is now the lion of the Cincinnati Conference floor, had·many a hard tack to
get the weather-gage of seniority, and he could not
have done it unless the Lord had laid his keel and
head of adamant. Our English brethren try hard
to guard their seniority to the present day; but,
now and then, an adventurous cutter runs the
blockade. We believe that a Conference is a place
where "*every person may speak freely whatever is
in his heart.*" If this is heresy let us be tried by
the Discipline.

Some might say, "Well, the young men wanted
to make showy speeches, and so become popular."
This was not always the case. We sometimes saw
the very gist of the question—the mystery hidden
from the beginning of the argument in the heat of

debate, and could have placed it in lucid position, but our "lot forbade." It would have required an effort beyond the power of modest clay, even to get the floor; an effort that would have knocked all the wind out of our sails.

One thing more in regard to Conferences, and that is the practice of making the question of appointments the last question, contrary to the Discipline; or, in other words, making it the question after Conference has been closed with singing and prayer, and leaving *some ministers* ignorant of their destination till read out publicly. A minister who can bear this without extreme laceration of feeling is unworthy to bear the vessels of the Lord. It is also a very impolitic course. An appointment which under *some circumstances* might be almost ruinous to one, might, under other circumstances, be very acceptable to another.

BRUSH CREEK.

1825. The next circuit to which I was appointed was Brush Creek. My colleague was William Simmons. We were both young men, and had a very agreeable year. This circuit, in some of its appointments, was considerably tainted with witchcraft and conjuration. In working on the camp-ground, I was telling a local preacher of some standing how I had just lost a horse. He expressed much regret that he had not heard of the hurt of the animal in time, as he could have most certainly saved his life.

He spoke so confidently that it struck me that the receipt might serve me on some future emergency. But I was astonished when he unfolded the course of conjuration through which he would have cured my horse. When he had got through I laughed. This horrified him, and he denounced me on the spot as an infidel. We had a very interesting trial founded on witchcraft at one point of the circuit. There was a very amiable widow and her daughters living in the neighborhood, who were reported as witches by a member of the Church. It was some time before the slander reached their ears. They had shown many acts of kindness toward the afflicted member who had for a long time suspected them. As he was poor and not able to work much, the widow carried to his family a large package of sugar. She had hardly got out of the gate before he threw the sugar on the fire, and observed to some of the neighbors present, that the witch could not come over him in that way. When the widow heard the report she was greatly afflicted, and was advised by her friends to bring the slanderer before the Church. At the trial there was abundant testimony that the slander had been widely spread through the country. When the defendant undertook to prove the malpractices of the lady, it became a question with the committee whether such an attempt might be suffered in such an age of light; but one of the committee, who was a little tainted with the belief of witchcraft himself, insisted on hearing the defense. The most of the testimony was what we call "*hearsay.*" Still the preacher, like a good fisherman, slacked off the line for a season, and the auditors were astounded at the romance. A German doctor, somewhere in the woods, had averred that the witch had several times dragged him from his bed, at midnight, and had sent him up among the rocky branches of the hills and dales, in search of hens' nests. Another had said, not having heard his cow-bell in the evening, he had walked over all the forest seeking her; but when he got back in sight of his house, there was the cow, and the said woman was on her back, holding the clapper of the bell. The defense was going on for quantity, when the member of the committee, for whose sake it was allowed, looked at his peers, and said, "Must we sit here listening to such abominable stuff? I'm satisfied."

He was expelled. When I came round to my appointment the expelled man took me to one side, and said,

"I am now put out of the Church, and do not intend to make any fuss; but I will ask one little favor which you can easily grant, that is, let that sister, that has prosecuted me, come and lay her hand upon my head before the congregation, and say, '*God bless you.*'"

"No, sir."

"Then I hope before twelve months have rolled round, you yourself will become bewitched."

Whether his hope ever reached its fruition, I leave the readers to judge. It would, however, be doing nothing more than justice to them to say that, before the twelve months were out, I got married to a pious young lady, that I considered very bewitching, and she has been my mate for many years over life's rough sea, and has endured as much in the itinerancy as any other woman. This same witchcraft, under the dress of "spirit-rappings," has molested some of our charges in later years.

The Minutes give us this year an increase of ninety-five members. This does not seem to fill my recollection of things; but my colleague held the reins of discipline with "a mild but firm hand." In those days members could not stay in two or three years, and not attend class, unless prevented by infirmities, or wicked parents or husbands.

I learned a good deal under brother Simmons, in regard to Western Methodism and administration; and if he learned any good from me, he is welcome to it.

I lacked, especially, one thing, the talent of singing. At first I thought I would at any moment dismount, and give up my horse, saddle, and bridle, for the ability to sing. Then again I have thought I was so fond of music, that, if the Lord had made me a singer, I would have broken down long ago. I can join, in some sort, with the congregation; but can lead in only one tune. If you ask, reader, what tune is that, you are too hard for me. I put it forth in emergencies.

In one obscure appointment, on a new circuit, I found no one to start the tune. I invited the brethren, but no response. I turned an imploring look to the sisters; one gave a woe-begone shake of the head, as much as to say, vain hope! I fell on my own resource, and the congregation joined in. After the meeting was over, a smiling sister came forward and said, "Brother, I must shake hands with you. Thank God! the Ohio Conference has sent us a preacher at last who can sing!" I sighed and thought, "Alas, sister, you know not how slender my capital is."

SCIOTO.

1826. I rode this circuit in connection with brother Absalom Fox; Russel Bigelow presiding elder. We had a good year, and a fine revival about the Forge. Several young married people were converted, and came to their leader to inquire about baptism. This struck him with conviction on that subject. He had been about thirty years in the Church, and some years class-leader, was convinced that he ought to be baptized, but had all that time been studying about the mode. The converts wished to be immersed. We gave out an appointment to baptize them. When the hour arrived, no house could hold the multitude. I preached on the subject, with all the candidates seated before me. The view held out was the difference between baptism and the different modes by which it was exhibited; that the *mode* was not *baptism;* it was a sacrament not more holy than the Lord's Supper. This was administered by the Churches in different modes; but the Churches did not unship each other on this account, or think that a mode could vitiate the ordinance. Therefore, we as ministers were willing to perform the service in that mode which would be most agreeable to the recipients. Still, if they could patiently bear, I would give my own understanding of the subject. Among other good things which had been mentioned, it was a sign or representation of that all-essential baptism of the Holy Ghost. How was this performed? The Scriptures most definitely declare by affusion. The grace of God is represented as coming down as the early and the latter rain, like dew on the mown grass. On the day of Pentecost, all that was visible in that baptism were cloven tongues of fire, falling on the heads of the disciples. All that was audible was a sound *from heaven*, like the rushing of a mighty wind. Now, when the Lord commissioned the apostles to put the sign of this baptism on their converts, whether is it the most reasonable to suppose that they represented it, as they had experienced it as coming down from heaven, and falling upon their heads, or that in exhibiting it they reversed the whole order of things, and immersed the subjects beneath the water? With many other words did we reason on this subject; but finally observed we had fully prepared for every mode; that

no mere mode could destroy the validity of the consecration. Baptism was the sincere dedication of
the soul to God with water. The matter was purely
between them and their God; and if the Lord saw
they were sincere he would accept them.

I then came down, and asked each candidate separately, and in a whisper, What mode? To my
astonishment, every one but the leader said he—or
she, as the case was—would be fully satisfied with
affusion at the altar. We had a good time, and
this discharge of duty gave a fresh impulse to the
work. Some, though, were almost, not quite, *disappointed;* for some people, who seldom go to meeting in their own neighborhood, will walk five miles
to see a man or woman put under the water. I
said *not quite.* The leader rose up, and said he had
long studied this matter, and read the Bible, and
he had found that it would carry him *into the water,*
but no further.

"Philip," said he, "went down with the eunuch
into the water; but that was not baptism, for it is
said afterward, '*and he baptized him;*' after this
they came up '*out of the water,*' but this was no
part of baptism. The baptism was between their
going into the water and their coming *out of the
water.* So I wish the preacher to go down with
me, knee-deep—then I will kneel down, and he will
pour the water upon my head, and then we'll come
up out of the water." The whole congregation
marched down to see this new kind of baptism.

So I got my feet wet any how. But all the while I did not believe that Philip and the eunuch did more than to go to a certain water—perhaps a spring. Even the Baptists understand the word "into" as covering no more in many places in the Bible where it is not in connection with baptism— then it means "*under*."

We had a fine camp meeting toward the close of the year. As it was in the neighborhood of a Presbyterian charge, and as the minister had to be absent that Sabbath, he recommended his congregation to attend the camp meeting. Many of them came. In those days, we thought we were doing a small business on Sunday morning if we did not have two or three sermons, one after another. Rest to the ashes of that habit! After the eight-o'clock and noon services, the Presbyterians retired to a convenient spot to take their lunch, and a Methodist heard something like the following dialogue:

A. Well, brethren, what do you think of the sermons?

B. Why, my opinion is they were truly orthodox; but I have been trying to reconcile it with what I have been taught from childhood, and that is, that the Methodists preached salvation by works. Have you ever heard the doctrines of grace set forth in a clearer light?

C. Well, they did *at first* preach dead works; but their theology is improving. In fact, they have altered their Discipline. I have been informed that their present Discipline is widely different from the original.

D. There can be no objection to the doctrine we have heard this day; and their preaching talents, on an average, are superior to those of our ministers. We have a great man here and there, but where will you find so many at one meeting?

E. Well, the reason is, we are so stingy about theological schools. It is evident to every observing man that all these men have been highly educated. We will have to be doing in the way of education, or we will certainly be left behind.

This year I was married to Miss Mary Mitchell, daughter of George and Ann Mitchell. My wife's father was a local minister in the Methodist Church. Mary is so well known, and so well beloved by all the sisterhood, where our lot has been cast, that it would be out of place for me to get up any eulogy. It will not soon be forgotten with what zeal and promptness she gave in her testimony in our love-feasts and classes, and with what fervor and modesty she labored and prayed about the mourners' bench. Her father's house was a preaching-place in Kentucky for many years. Under William Holman and Samuel West a great revival broke out in that house, and all the family that had come to years of understanding were converted, with about one hundred of the neighbors. Mary claims that brother West was the instrumentality of her conversion. This was when she was fifteen years of age. The day that this revival broke out, Holman said he prayed, at every step his horse took, all the way to his appointment—and prayed especially for the family.

Brother Fox, my colleague, was an old acquaintance. When I was teaching school in Lebanon he was working on his bench. He had been authorized to preach, but through diffidence and temptations he had almost ceased to work when I invited him to accompany me to my country appointments. Believing he was of the pure material, I exhorted him not to become faint, but to double his diligence. He soon after joined the Conference, and on this his first year I enjoyed the pleasure of his partnership. He became one of our most useful ministers, and filled several important appointments; but he sank down at noon, or rather rose to a higher orbit, as we trust, to shine with brighter luster, world without end. O, Absalom, Absalom, my friend Absalom! Sweet is the remembrance of thy many virtues and labors.

One day, while riding my circuit near Chillicothe, I passed a distillery. My attention was arrested by a dog raising water with a tread-wheel. I paused to watch his maneuvers. The principal came to the door, and viewing me as a greenhorn, said,

"Did you ever see the like before?"

"No, sir, I never did; but I think it very appropriate. It always struck me that this business of yours is extremely doggish."

His face gathered up, like a storm off Cape Hatteras. I touched my horse, and was off.

With all our losses by removals and otherwise, we had an increase of seventy-seven members. I can not remember the exact number we took in, but there was one singular circumstance connected. At the opening of the year we ruled lines in our memorandum for the record of such as might join. I ruled till I thought, surely if all these lines are filled we will do well; so I ceased ruling. The last member I took in filled the last line. Then I thought of what the dying prophet told the king— if he had smitten five or six times with his arrows he would have consumed Syria.

The following circumstance transpired on this circuit. A well-bred young man, apparently under much religious concern, united himself with an excellent religious society. Although he had formerly been rather wayward and inconstant in his life, yet by his steady attendance on all the means of grace, and the rapid improvement which he seemed to make in his religious course, he had gained largely on the affections of his classmates; and some of the most pious and discerning had already begun to regard him as a youth of some promise. In the same neighborhood resided a comely and, in many respects, a very amiable girl. Heaven had, in mercy, granted her one of the greatest of all earthly blessings, a pious parentage. But she was of an unusually-volatile disposition, and passionately fond of the world, its fashions and amusements. Our young 'friend saw her, loved her, and finally made proposals of marriage. Eliza acknowledged that she was pleased with him. "But, William," said she, "there is one insuperable barrier to our union. You profess religion, and I have no reason to doubt your sincerity. You see what a giddy, vain, and heedless sinner I am. What domestic happiness do you suppose will arise from our marriage? You, as a man of God, would feel it to be your duty to erect a family altar; I am illy qualified to participate in holy exercises. You would love to see every thing clothed in the somber aspect of Christianity; I might love to shine out with my fashionable friends. Consider the great gulf that lies between us. It is true, it is not impassable. But I am not prepared to come over to you, at present. It remains for you to consider whether you can forego your religious associations to accommodate me." William, with a sorrowful countenance and heavy sigh, observed that he would consider the matter. A few days after, in a heartless and reluctant manner, he requested the leader to have his name erased from the class-book when the preacher came round. The leader, supposing he was laboring under some cruel temptation of the enemy, urged him to confide in his integrity, and unbosom all his sorrows. The more solicitous the leader was to dissuade him from his purpose, the more earnestly he pressed his suit. The preacher, judging from the vehemency of his manner, that all was not right, and that it might be more creditable to the Church to let him go, granted his request.

It was not long before he stood before Eliza, and renewed his suit. She observed,

"You are aware of the only difficulty that lies in the way——"

Before she finished the sentence, he exclaimed, with a smile,

"O, that is removed—my name is taken from the book—I am no longer a Church member."

The young lady fell back in her chair. A deadly paleness overspread her face, and with quivering lips she said,

"I will never consent to marry you while the world stands. It is true I am wild and irreligious; but the pious instructions of my parents, the religious opportunities which I have had, the many heart-searching sermons which I have heard, have for a long time disturbed my peace, and have determined me not to choose death. In view of my natural proneness to ruin, I had determined to marry none but a man who would help me to save my soul. I had flattered myself that you were such a character, but thought it would be safe to try your steadfastness. When the proposal to leave your class was first made, if you had rejected it with a manly and holy indignation, you would have received my hand on the spot. When you promised to consider the matter, I saw an indecision of char-

acter that made me tremble. But even after so
many days' deliberation, if you had returned and said
that you loved Zion above your chief joy—above
father and mother and wife and all, then I could
have confided my life in your hands. But the die
is cast. You will please never mention the subject
again—forever."

We hope the reader will never realize the anguish
of the rejected suitor. The Church avoided him as
an insincere and dangerous character. The world,
more cruel, reserved him as a standing target of
ridicule. Some think that a compromising course,
in religious matters, is most likely to win over their
irreligious friends and connections. Hence they
have relaxed their fervor in the services of the
sanctuary. They have even admitted the propriety
of things which were doubtful, and shaped their
profession too much in conformity with the views of
the world. This, we will admit, has often warded
off persecution, and has sometimes restored peace in
families; but it is a peace that impoverishes piety,
enervates the soul, and is always bought at the expense of the Cross and kingdom of Jesus Christ.
We doubt whether this vacillating policy has ever
saved a soul. Steadfastness and decision of faith
have, and always will, where salvation is possible.

XXI.

MIAMI AND MAD RIVER CIRCUITS.

WE were appointed to Miami circuit, with Andrew M'Clain in charge, and John Collins presiding elder. We deem it unnecessary to give the boundaries of every circuit and the history of every appointment. This would fill a volume; for every society has an interesting record, and the remembrance of events very pleasant to its own circle. But, as an example of the circuits of the time, we will say that this circuit had twenty-eight appointments, and the reader can judge of the rest days, or account, if he please, for the absence of bronchitis. The circuit approached within five miles of Lebanon, embracing Hamilton, Blue Rock, Cheviot, neighborhood of Clevestown, through Cincinnati to Fulton, Columbia, Helltown, Carthage, Madisonville, Indian Hill, and Germantown, within two miles of Milford, with minor intervening places. The ground now comprises seven stations, and five circuits, and part of two districts. This was, in that day, a very religious country. People would come from all parts to our quarterly or two-days' meetings; and generally they would not come in vain, but carry the hallowed fire to their homes and to their classes. We had not been settled here long, before the brethren sent to us a wagon-load of provisions, of divers kinds, from Indian Hill, about ten miles distant.

We rode this circuit again, in 1845 and 1846. It was then very much curtailed in extent. I was associated, these two years, with J. W. Steele, another noble-hearted colleague not soon to be forgotten; and we had for our presiding elder, Zachariah Connell. Again I was returned to this circuit, in 1858, with brother Levi White — William Herr presiding elder. So we have been well acquainted with the most of the old members for many years, and can testify that some of the excellent of the earth are found among them. On my last year there, we had much affliction in our family, and my wife's sister died. Dr. John Cox attended us night and day. I expected the bill to be high—justly so—and would have met it cheerfully if it had taken my horse; but he generously refused any compensation. I feel under everlasting obligations to him. In my travel of forty years, I have found the doctors uniformly kind, and have wondered that the preachers do not make more of them stewards. They understand our frame. On one circuit, where a doctor might have brought a heavy bill against me, he was urged by some of the stewards to do so, as it would so nicely foot the quarterage, but he indignantly rejected the proposal. So it is;

there are some stewards who do n't care how the minister is paid—whether in money, or pumpkins, or calomel and jalap; whereas, if they were of the spirit of Christ, they would pay the physician— inasmuch as physic is not allowed with fuel and table expenses.

MAD RIVER CIRCUIT.

1828–29. This circuit was considered, at this time, as the garden of the Lord in Ohio, and Urbana as the midst of the garden, where waved the Tree of Life. Burroughs Westlake was the preacher in charge. He was a good preacher, an honest man, and guileless almost to a fault. He just spoke what he thought of every man; but he spoke it to *him* rather than to *another*. This, of course, frequently gave offense. We often expostulated with him, arguing that it was not necessary that we should speak out all our mind, and that there was no deceit in holding back what might raise a squall.

One day, after a tiresome ride, he stopped at the house of a prominent member—not on the Urbana circuit—and the brother was not at home, but the family invited him in. According to his description the house was disgustingly filthy, and the floor fearfully slippery. He withdrew immediately, and rode on to the next house. This cottage was as clean as a new pin, the coverlets like driven snow. Although a stranger, he was warmly solicited to stay all night. This he did, although the inmates were clothed in a skin not the color of his own. The brother whose house he had left had him arraigned for quitting his house so abruptly and lodging with a negro man. He insisted that the preacher had some hidden prejudice against him, and he had a right to demand what it was before the quarterly conference. Westlake arose and said, as the brother demanded of him the reason of his conduct, he would, with Christian candor, give it. He then went on to describe very closely the filthy condition of the brother's house, the appearance of his wife and children, the unwholesome odor of the atmosphere around, and concluded by saying he would not feel easy if his horse had to pass a night under the brother's roof. True, he did stop with an African family, but they were distinguished for their Christian cleanliness. He had nothing against the brother, as he was an entire stranger. The brother, finding he had nothing criminal against him, as he supposed, but only a matter of taste, sat quietly down, and pushed the investigation no further.

At one of his appointments there was a member of another Church who always staid in class meeting, and would sometimes speak disrespectfully of the proceedings. After leading class one day, Westlake observed him, and said, "Stranger, you are at liberty to speak." The stranger arose, and was eloquent in praise of the means of grace, and told how he enjoyed the privilege, etc., and sat down. Burroughs looked on him, and said, "Brother, we are willing that you should call *occasionally*, and partake of our sweetmeats and tidbits; but mind you, we do not want you to take up your lodging with us, unless you become one of the family." This gave everlasting offense to many of our old members.

My colleague was the strongest man I ever knew in a running conversational argument, and he was full of the most spicy wit. Late one night, I was lying in the preachers' tent, at a camp meeting, awaiting sleep; but a noisy, verbose, jolly, and irresponsible Universalist was seated in a crowd on the camp-ground, and playing, as he might suppose, the piano-forte on them with his silvery tongue. Presently I heard the voice of Westlake among them, asking him some very simple questions in the tone and manner of a hopeless greenhorn. I looked out; there he was seated among them, so disguised that his friends could not know him except by his voice. The orator, at first, was very gracious in instructing his unknown disciple, and we felt impatient with the round-about approaches of the inquirer. At last the teacher began to ridicule Solomon, and made many vulgar remarks about his wives and concubines. Here Westlake, with great simplicity, said,

"But don't you think Solomon said some wise things?"

"When? I want to know, when?"

"Why, he said, 'Though thou shouldst bray a fool in a mortar, among wheat, with a pestle, yet will not his foolishness depart from him.'"

Here the battle commenced amid repeated roars of laughter. The Universalist showed considerable *low* wit for a while, till he had exhausted the meager dogmas and stereotyped arguments of his profession. Then Westlake played upon him, cheered by the applause of the surrounding group, which every moment became larger and larger. His antagonist at last inquired in a respectful tone, "Are you not a Methodist preacher?" A horse on the outskirts was heard to neigh very impressively, and an eloquent voice in the crowd exclaimed, "Yes, yes, I hear you, and will be there in a minute."

Westlake was eccentric, though religiously so. Sometimes when preaching delightfully, if he heard no *Amen!* it all went for little with him. One time, while preaching in the evening, at Urbana, to a large congregation, he suddenly stopped, and said, "Can I get no Amen? I would give a fi'pennybit to any one that would say Amen! You do n't know how it would help me." A drunkard, who was rocking to and fro in the crowd, cried as loud as he was able, "Amen, and Amen!" The preacher, making no question of the author, sprung his luff, and had a good time. Early the next morning one of those who are accused in the Bible of rising early, appeared at the parsonage, and told my brother that he was the man who helped him out of his scrape last night, when none of his brethren would give him a lift, and he called for his fip.

"What do you want with it?"

"Why, to get a dram this morning to wash down the cobwebs, to be sure."

"I can't give you money to buy drams, certainly."

"Can a minister of the Gospel break a promise given before three or four hundred people?"

Westlake found himself outgeneraled, and had to fork over to feed the groggery. He had reached a knot that he could neither loosen nor cut.

Toward the close of the first year I strongly urged my colleague to let me take up a collection for the Missionary Society. This was rather a new thing. There were societies, here and there, who sent up contributions, and some were gathered from individuals. Westlake was at first opposed to this.

"Why, brother L., this will prevent our pay. We had better give a liberal donation ourselves; for it will come out of us."

My argument was, that the more a Christian gave the more liberal he would become. Still I felt that my stand was somewhat problematical. So we did not do it. At the end of the year we did not get all our pay. The next year I urged the matter so as to get his consent. What was the result? The Urbana circuit paid Westlake and his children and myself our quarterage and table expenses, and bought a nice parsonage, and gave us

25

fifty dollars missionary money to carry to Conference. When we made the report there was silence
in Conference for the space of some seconds, when
our elder, brother J. B. Finley, arose and begged
us to inform the Conference how we got *so much*.
Since that day we have done what we could for the
Missionary Society. But many of us who set the
ball in motion, and have increased its impetus ever
since, are never detailed to present its claims at
Conference. It is a subject which affords a fine
opportunity for those who are eloquent of speech.
One of our brethren was once eulogizing the missionary enterprise and the itinerant power on the
Conference floor, and presently he broke out' in the
impassioned quotation,

> "Should fate command me to the farthest verge
> Of the green earth, to——"

"Stop there, brother," said a preacher from
Michigan, "we want just such men as you in *our*
green '*verge*.'"

This cut off the speech at once, like the negro
who prayed that the Lord would curtail the devil
"*smack smoove*." The brother had never straddled
a pair of saddle-bags, and, perhaps, never intended
to. Let it·not be supposed that we are hinting
after such jobs now. The time has gone by, and if
we could not expatiate on this theme which our
soul loved in the ardor and prime of noon, we will
hardly dishonor it before a Conference with the
snuff of our eloquence.

This year we attended a large camp meeting on the road between Urbana and Troy. I preached on the Sabbath, before a crowded congregation, a sea-sermon. Toward the close a melting influence descended on the congregation. Many of the members were walking the aisles, shaking hands, and their faces seemed to shine, while shouts and rejoicing rolled over the ground. That was a good meeting throughout. Some years after this, while the Conference was sitting in Cincinnati, my landlady told me there was a gentleman in the parlor wishing to see me. When I went in I saw a very genteel and intelligent person, who said, we were both strangers to each other, in a certain sense, but he had come some distance principally to see me. He asked if I did not, some years ago, preach at a camp meeting near Troy, and preach from a certain text. I answered in the affirmative. "Well," said he, "I was a thoughtless, irreligious young man, making a tour through Ohio, and that camp meeting being near my road, I thought I would stop and rest a little while; so I tied up. I seated myself in the crowd. Till that time I had never heard preaching; that is, I never paid enough attention to a discourse throughout so as to derive any benefit. Some of your phraseology being singular, fixed my attention till you had finished, when I pursued my journey, but under convictions which have eventuated in my conversion, and I have, for several years, been a preacher in another Conference. I wished for a long time to know who the minister was that had been instrumental in reaching my case. Lately I saw a preacher whom I recognized as one who was at that camp meeting, and asked him if he could tell me who it was that preached that sermon. I got your name, and thought it was my duty to report to you." When he told me his name, I recollected seeing it frequently in the Advocate in connection with good works.

When he had left, my soul was overwhelmed with gratitude to God. It is said, "he who turns *a* sinner [one sinner] from the error of his way, shall save a soul from death, and hide a multitude of sins." Then I thought, "And if that sinner should become a minister, and save others, and so on to the end of time, till the enlarging circles shall strike the shores of eternity, who can tell the eternal consequences of a word spoken in season?" Then I thought that the Savior said to his elated disciples, "Rejoice not in this, that the devils are subject to your power; but rejoice in that your names are written in the book of life." Yes, our reward is pendent on that.

> "Lord, what are all my sufferings here,
> If thou but count me meet
> With that enraptured host to appear,
> And worship at thy feet!"

May the Lord save that brother, whether North or South! What is Mason and Dixon's line to Almighty Power?

It was on this circuit that we first received the outlines of the rules of the Radical Church, drawn up and issued by the collected wisdom of that organization. I do not mean *all* the wisdom, for we had a considerable embodiment of it in the person of one of their leading agitators, who held his membership on our circuit, and who had not attended the conclave. This was brother Joseph Mitchell, commonly called "Yankee Mitchell," not out of disrespect, but to distinguish him from the numerous family of Mitchells then ranging *our camp*. He was an acute, fluent minister; but not an orator in the common acceptation of the word, neither did he pretend to be. But all that Calvinist or Arminian knew of controversy's vast art, was to this Mitchell known. In his youthful days he was, doubtless, instrumental in turning hundreds, if not thousands, in New England, to the doctrines of Methodism. He was terrible too on baptism. When preaching controversy — and, what else did he preach?—his delivery was as rapid, as cutting, as interesting as that of a smart, racy old woman when scolding. Every body who held to the truth loved to hear him. He was the presiding elder of Lorenzo Dow at his *debut*. Lorenzo, every now and then, taken with a sudden impression, would shoot off from his circuit like a wandering star, and Mitchell would have to push after him and bring him back to his moorings. Lorenzo would cry and promise to do better, but complained of his galling harness. Now,

whether the youth had caught this wandering infec-
tion from his elder, or the elder was overpowered
by the logic of his pupil, we can not say; but certain it is that Mitchell fell into the same cosmopo-
litish habits; and at the time we knew him he
was in the habit of making an annual tour of all
the States, if not the Territories also, of the Union;
any how, he was at home when the Reformed Discipline appeared. We crowded to him to know
what he thought of the missive. He looked it over
and rubbed his eyes; he looked it over again and
scratched his head, and then exclaimed something
like this, "As the Lord liveth! I could go to sleep
and dream a better discipline than this."

About this time the ministers of that connection
were making heavy efforts on our circuit. There
was one place where we had taken in a number of
young people. While they were rejoicing in their
first love, they were told that they had taken shelter under an unmixed despotism. As they had
been lately converted, and knew but little about the
constitution of Methodism, they became alarmed.
What rendered their situation more perilous was,
there were a few of the old members who looked
favorably on the innovation. Brother Westlake took
considerable pains to show the matter in its proper
light, and succeeded to some extent. Some of our
best men urged that it was better to say nothing
about it, and quietly let things take their course.
But there was a higher voice, saying, "Son of man,

I have made thee a watchman unto the house of
Israel; therefore, hear the word at my mouth and
give them warning from me." When I came again
to that appointment I was supplied with the new
Discipline. I understood that notice had been given
that a Reformed Methodist Church would be organized next Sabbath. Some of our old members feared
that there would be a large split. The congregation was large. As it was my regular time to read
and explain the Discipline, I preached very short;
then read the rules without comment; then, to
the surprise of many, pulled out the rules of the
Radical Church, showed the contrast in several important points—not forgetting the clause that threw
a sanctity over all property acknowledged by the
laws of the States, and which Joseph Mitchell himself had denounced as a covert for slavery. I knew
where I was standing, and I understood their cue.
I exhorted them not to suppose that I was meddling
unnecessarily with the rules of another Church, as
they all knew that the last time a Radical preacher
was there, he had done us the kindness to preach
on *our rules*, and one good turn deserves another.
The day of "organization" came, but our ranks
were unbroken.

Brother James B. Finley was, without exception,
the most useful man of our connection in the West.
He had not a polished education. This, we believe,
was his own fault. His father superintended a
most excellent school, in which some of the first

men of Kentucky received a liberal education. When we say it was his own fault, we mean he did not lack the opportunity of a teacher, or the acuteness necessary to comprehend; but his disposition was adventurous and enterprising, and his physical and mental energy corresponded, and it was a mercy that he learned any English, with so many wild deer and turkeys peeping at him in his walks.

His father said John could preach, but James was a tolerable exhorter. All we might draw from this was that James was impatient of the old school systematizing, yet he would set his congregation on fire before his father would lay down his introduction. Still his father was an excellent specimen of the Presbyterian type, and justly popular, in the strength of his manhood. He excelled in sermonizing with his pen, and preached well extemporaneously. James, sometimes in the impetuosity of zeal, might speak or act unadvisedly, but when convinced, no man, in my knowledge, was more ready to make humble confession.

In examining the character of a certain minister who had been suspended, our elder, having received wrong impressions of the case, left his seat to advocate the cause of the defendant; and being wrongly posted in the matter, his reasoning and conclusions were all defective in the estimation of the quarterly conference. Brother Westlake, in his quaint but good-natured way, said, "Brother Finley, may not some of us sit in that chair? Our conference is without a president while you are pleading." He quickly resumed his seat, saying, "This conference acts like a parcel of little children." We adjourned awhile to return to the camp-ground and dine. After dinner Westlake met the elder on the ground, and said, "Brother Finley, do you think you did well in saying that such a venerable body of men acted like children?" He turned away, not in anger, but apparently afflicted. When the conference reassembled, brother Finley occupied the chair in silence, and seemed to be absorbed in serious reflections, till we became impatient. He then arose, with tears in his eyes, and said, "Brethren, I am unfitted to perform the duties of my office till I make suitable amends. When I look around on this assembly my eyes light on old venerable Methodists, who were humbly serving God while I was a wicked sinner, and some may have been official members before I was a preacher; but before we adjourned I said, 'you did business like little children.' I hope you will forgive me, one and all." We all fell on our knees, and, O, what a prayer! It seemed as if all the bottles of heaven were opened, and were pouring on our assembly. When he came to understand the case correctly, he seemed to be more than ever afflicted at his course. No man ever discharged the duties of a presiding elder better than he; and we could write a chapter in his praise, but his life is before the world.

About this time the disaffected members withdrew from our Church, and caused considerable decrease.

XXII.

ZANESVILLE CIRCUIT.

1830. THE Conference was held this year in Urbana. Some of the friends from Chillicothe told me I would be sent there. I did not place much confidence in this till some of higher authority confirmed the rumor. The last morning of the Conference, the appointments were to be read out, and I thought as my calling and election was sure, and as I had been run down in attending on the session, there was no necessity for my going to hear my appointment. Then again it occurred to my mind that this would be mean and selfish. I ought to go, and hear, and sympathize. I felt as calm as Summer evenings are, till the bishop came to Chillicothe district; he read Chillicothe, but said nothing about A. M. L., and he kept silence about him till he had gone through that and another district or two, and I was looking out for New Virginia, when it came out Zanesville. Some who had strongly assured me my name was down for Chillicothe, came to apologize. They said on the last evening some brother, who had found out where he was appointed, had broke traces; and this caused several removals on the chess-board, and threw me off more than one hundred miles. Here was a ship to pay, and no pitch hot. But we addressed ourselves to the journey. On arriving on the field of labor we stopped with a pious brother. While sitting by his blazing fire in the evening, he said,

"Brother, where have you been traveling?"

"On the Miamis and the Mad River."

"O, yes, you have been down in the *back parts*, but the Conference has highly favored you *now*. They have sent you to the *garden* of Ohio."

"Which end of the State did you come in at, brother?"

"Why, I came in at this end—why?"

"Because if you had come through the Miami and Mad River country, you would never have seen these hills."

There was no parsonage on the circuit, no place to put my goods. In this dilemma we were laid under lasting obligations by Dr. E. D. Roe, now of the Cincinnati Conference, and his amiable lady. They took care of us till, with the assistance of some of the brethren, we purchased a lot with a log-house on it in the town of Norwich. It was a tolerably new building, and we thought it would answer for a kitchen when the circuit had time and means to improve it.

One of my successors gave me an awful tongue-lashing about purchasing the property. I told him if he had hung as long by the eyelids as I had, he would be glad to get in a manger, and it was his province to improve-it. Dr. Roe was, at that time, a merchant in very brisk business. I believe I licensed him to exhort. At first he did not attend much to this. When expostulated with, he said he was so busy from morning till night through the week, that he had but little time to study, and but little heart to hold meetings. I then told him to examine his case closely. If he was not clearly convinced that it was his duty to preach, to give it up, for he was in good business, and might get rich and do much good, and serve God acceptably; but if, on the other hand, he was confident in his call, then he should give up his business, however promising it might be, and devote himself altogether to his work. Soon after I left the circuit he was announced in the Minutes.

This was the year of the organization of the Radical Church in this part of the State. In reading the appointments of that Church, I was astounded to find that they had embraced several of our classes, and had hardly left me root or branch. In making out their numbers, they had counted up whole classes that had been returned to me. Still I thought I would go to these classes and bid them "good-by." But I found them generally steadfast and immovable, and glad to see their own preacher. The disaffected ministers had visited them several times, and because they had treated them hospitably, and did not quarrel with them, they thought they might count the chickens before the eggs were hatched. However, there were some individuals at all these appointments who joined them subsequently. It is astonishing what frivolous excuses some made for leaving in this split. The work had begun before we left Urbana circuit. A very grave and sour-looking old member told brother Westlake before a large class, that he wished to withdraw; that he had no fault to find with bishops, or government, or any such thing; but that our Discipline forbids us to sing "songs which did not tend to the knowledge or love of God."

Westlake rose up very solemnly and said,

"Well, brethren, this brother wants to withdraw from us because our Church does not approve of his singing 'dump de diddle' and 'congu mingo.' We will have to let him go."

The old man laughed, and the class gave a sympathizing echo.

One, after he had left us, was applied to for some quarterage.

"What, do you want quarterage? This was what I left the old side for—money, money! I might as well have staid where I was."

No doubt, many left for good reasons, as they supposed; a number left because they had lost their taste for class meetings, a sure sign of their decadence in grace. We could not see how any warm-hearted Christian could object to class meetings or love-feasts. We know it is said they are not Gospel ordinances; neither are the Bible and missionary societies. The Lord has revealed the elements of salvation, but has left much for Christian ingenuity to accomplish, suitable to different ages and countries. In regard to our physical wellbeing, the Lord did not create houses and agricultural implements; but he gave us forests and ore, and endowed man with powers of perpetual progress, so that he might have something to do. Man progressed in invention and discovery — the bamboo tent, the log-cabin, the stately mansion rose up in succession; the rude blade, the reap-hook, the cradle, the mowing machine, corn-planter, etc.; so that the time may come when the once laborious work of the farmer may become a diversion of unbounded amusement and delight. The Lord never intended man to be physically idle—why should we be spiritually lazy? We have a right to institute prudential means that are of evident utility, and in their spirit Scriptural. We then inquired, are our love-feasts and class meetings Scriptural in their features and ingredients? Let us analyze them. They, for they are twin means, are constituted of three Scriptural duties—prayer, praise, communion. Can any Christian object to prayer? "Pray without ceasing." "Ask and you shall receive." "Men ought always to pray." "Pray for one another."

Can any object to praise? "Praise God — sing praises unto God." "Speak to one another in psalms, and hymns, and spiritual songs, making melody in your hearts." And who will object to the communion of saints? This exercise has been dear to all the distinguished saints of God in all ages. The Christian does not love to eat his morsel alone. In sister Churches now they have their "conversational meetings," "conferences," and "inquiry meetings." These meetings, under different names, are constituted of the three simple ingredients — *prayer, praise, Christian communion.* It seems to be the prevailing opinion of the pious that this communion or interchange of religious sentiment will constitute a delightful exercise in heaven. We can not tell what will be the way of human interlocution in the new creation—whether by the present slow communication of speech, word by word, or whether we will intuitively understand the body of the communication in a flash. But it is highly reasonable that the most beloved theme of Christians on earth will enter deeply into their celestial converse. And if this sweet communion will enter into the celestial enjoyments of the saints in light, how jealous of ourselves we should be, if we love not such gracious opportunities on earth!

As our field had been especially cultivated by the Reformers—so called—we suffered a declension in number—quite a number left.

XXIII.

DELAWARE CIRCUIT.

1831–32. MY first year on this circuit was in connection with brother Samuel Shaw, a rather eccentric but very upright man. It was a successful year, and we had a good time. The next year, brother David Cadwallader was my colleague on the same circuit. He was, in my opinion, the most simple-hearted, holy man ever connected with the Ohio Conference in my day. When he first came to this country from Wales, he settled down among some of his own countrymen, some of whom he had known on the other side of the Atlantic. He had not been long among them before he heard some of them shout in their meetings. He had never heard the like before, and he was filled with indignation. He reproved them sharply, telling them that God was a God of order, and not of confusion. He was afraid that the Methodism, which he loved so ardently on the other side of the water, was gradually depreciating into fanaticism. After a while, he heard some who were of undoubted piety and sound minds indulging in the same practice. This led him to doubt whether he might not be wrong. He passed through a season of deep affliction, strong

26

cries, and tears on this very account; and he implored the Lord, if he was wrong in opposing his
brethren, that he would manifest it to him in some
way. On one occasion a resistless gale of love
swept over his soul, and before he knew what he
was doing, he was shouting at the top of his voice.
This convinced him it was no sin; but, as if to
keep him convinced, he was made to shout on all
interesting religious occasions ever after.

On one occasion he had received at Conference an
appointment to a Welsh mission in one of the Eastern States. Subsequently he fell into doubt whether
it was in the order of Providence. He was returning from Conference, in company with several young
ministers—but he was in poor company. They were
elated with the prospects opening before them, and
indulged in innocent mirth. He lagged behind, in
agonizing prayer, under a thick cloud. In the evening they put up at a village tavern. The house was
crowded with men who were employed in cutting
the canal. The preachers slept in a long, upper
room, which was well occupied. Under the circumstances they were very restless, and indulged some
in talk. Cadwallader still prayed. About midnight
one of the brethren drew the curtain of a window,
and, looking out on the bright moonlight, said,
"Surely, it is day." At that moment Cadwallader
got supremely blessed, and he sprang on the floor,
and exclaimed, "Yes, glory to God, it *is day!* daylight through all my soul!" And he shouted on,

without limitation. A man and his wife, who slept in one corner, arose and gathered on their clothes, and the man cried out, "Brethren, pray for us. Some time ago I came to work on the canal. A pious young man, a member of my class, came with me. When he had worked a little while, he said he would go home again, because, if he staid here, he would certainly lose his soul. I laughed at him, and I staid—and now all my religion is clean gone. O, pray for us!" The brethren prayed and sung. Cadwallader started down stairs, shouting. The bar-room floor was covered with Irish laborers, packed close like a box of smoked herrings. They rose in great fright, and scattered every-where; the family came pouring down, and two young ladies were converted. There was no more sleeping that night. Cadwallader's horse was brought out last, and the young brethren pushed on. On their way, they began to discuss their bills, thinking they were unusually high; and they turned round, and said, "Brother Cad., what did that old tavern-keeper charge you?" With an innocent smile, he said, "Just nothing at all. He said he would not charge such a man as I was, and he invited me to call and see him again." As innocent as my colleague was, he would sometimes join with the brethren in re-marking on my horsemanship. In the Spring of the year, he came home one day in a wretched plight. We inquired what was the matter. He said, in coming over Crawford's plains, he saw a

most beautiful plat of young grass not far from the
road; and it looked so smooth and inviting, he
thought he would ride over it; but his horse had
hardly got his length on it, before both horse and
rider were almost swallowed up in it; but he scuf-
fled out, with the loss of his hat. I told him he
had often remarked on my riding; but I had passed
that same beautiful oasis, and was tempted to ride
over it; but, seeing that the cattle grazed every-
where but on that strip of tender grass, I thought
if they were dubious I might well beware—so I
kept the homely road. "Well, brother, I will say
no more about your riding. I saw the cattle, too,
but did not follow out the argument." Our circuit
took in three county seats—Delaware, Marion, and
Bucyrus—embracing the plains of Crawford, almost
to the Wyandott reservation. The snow covered
the ground for nearly three months. In my little
jumper I sailed over the undulating surface, and
almost imagined I was at sea again. We had a
blessed revival—almost universal—taking in upward of four hundred members; so that the circuit
had to be divided for the next year. The revival
at Bucyrus was great. We could not then hold
what we now call protracted meetings. We would
have to leave the work, to fill other appointments,
in charge of responsible brethren, who would carry
on a prayer meeting till we returned. Having thus
left Bucyrus one Sabbath evening, a crowded congregation came out to prayer meeting. Just before

the time to begin, a preacher came in, with a pair of saddle-bags on his arm, ascended the pulpit, and without invitation or license, sung, prayed, and preached—preached bitterly against the whole economy of Methodism, and took peculiar pains to warn seekers of religion to keep aloof from our tyrannical institution. He concluded by saying some would wish to know who he was. He was an old Methodist preacher, and knew what he had stated was correct, and that he had been acquainted with their preacher in charge for many years. He also added that he was a missionary to the Wyandott Indians, whither he was going. When we came back, we found the old members indignant at the deception. The young members, and those who were thinking of joining, were anxious to know how far his declarations were correct; and I had to travel over ground which I had fondly hoped it would not be necessary to travel over in that latitude, and at that late day. I was anxious to find out who he was, for he told no one his name. But, in describing his personality, they mentioned one physical defect, that led me to suppose he was one of the awful fathers of Radicalism. This supposition was afterward found to be correct. But we survived the blow.

The Church of Christ is a working Church, and there are few in it who can not do some good. There was, in Bucyrus, a very pious member, but he had no education. As he stood at the altar, looking at the members engaged in the work, he

thought, in himself, can I do nothing in this good
work? He saw a young man who was rather de-
riding the work. He said something seemed to say,
"Go and talk with that young man." Then he
thought again, that young man knows more than I
do; he is learned. Still something seemed to say,
"Go, go!" He approached him—took his hand—
his soul was too big for utterance—he burst into
tears—and the tall and proud young man fell prostrate among the mourners.

Brother Cadwallader has passed into the heavens.
I know not whether any marble covers his remains;
but I believe that he was, in God's sight, a great
man. I do not say he was the most useful man
among us. Some men may be very useful—yes, a
necessity of the Church—and yet not be the most
sanctified. Peter was one of the most useful of
Christ's disciples—he was bold, daring, and a real
business man. Yet the compliment which our Lord
paid to Nathaniel was the most that was said of
him in all the history of the Gospel, but it speaks
volumes: "Behold an Israelite, indeed, in whom
there is no guile!"

Brother Bigelow was our presiding elder, and
was deservedly popular. His oratory consisted
principally in earnestness of spirit combined with
physical energy. His introduction would be generally about thirty minutes long. It was a kind of
fireside talk, and sometimes tiresome, and some of
his hearers would begin to feel fearful forebodings

about the length of his sermon. When he had fairly entered upon his subject, he became very entertaining for about an hour. Then he would rise—rise—rise, higher and higher, for another hour, till soul and body would seem to be rapt in a mighty conflict of emulation. It would be useless to describe his gestures; they were of all kinds, and indiscriminately applied. When the tempest culminated it came down on the congregation with a mighty shout, leaving a shower of tears, and all the congregation on their feet. They were not raised to their feet altogether by the power of his eloquence, as some of his friends have said; but while the minds of the congregation were all deeply absorbed by the preacher's eloquence, tired nature would seek relief in a change of posture, and our poor bodies which had been cramped up for three hours, till almost entirely benumbed, would, despite all human volition, rise on their feet.

No man could imitate Russel Bigelow for want of physical endurance, and he could not have commanded this for any length of time were it not he was endowed with an extraordinary appetite and digestive power which seldom fall to the lot of man. It would have proved fatal to any common preacher to have competed with him in eating—pound for pound—in a very little time. We do not mean that he was gluttonous. His constitution and excessive labors imperiously called for it, and what would have been intemperate eating in another, was in him a necessary supply and no more. Truly the young preachers on the district did—whether unconsciously or not—imitate him in *some things;* his voice, his provincialisms, his exuberant and inexpressive gestures; but these were only the hinder part of the orator. They would fag out in one hour in the wake of his fervor. Brother Bigelow was a humble man, considering his business tact and official duties; and I believe he desired to be more so, and labored to habituate himself to a lowly carriage. He would frequently say to the young preachers, "You see, brethren, I make free to speak of your faults and advise you; but this is the common duty of Christians. If you see any thing wrong in me, tell me of it." He once said,

"Brother L., if you see any thing wrong in me, tell me of it, and I will try to mend."

"Well, brother B., there is one thing in you which is wrong in my opinion, and I think it is wrong in the sight of the Lord, and that is your treatment of your horse. You ride him furiously in all seasons, and he has always a sore on his back as big as my fist; you throw a piece of rag-carpet on it, and you will go as far as fifteen or twenty miles as fast as the animal can move; you then deliver him over to any body when you stop. The Bible says a righteous man is merciful to his beast. You ride so much like Jehu, that when the young preachers wish to ride fast, they will whip up their horses, and say, 'Come, let us *Russel it.*'"

While I was delivering my lecture, I saw him screw up one corner of his mouth, and when I was done he smiled, and seemed to regard it as one of the most trifling reproofs that had ever been uttered. The business he was on — preaching the Gospel — he thought, overtopped the horse and every thing else. The king's business required haste.

Bigelow was scrupulously exact in regard to every point of Discipline, great or small. He met me once on the plains, and broke loose upon me, because he had heard that I had admitted a certain lady to love-feast.

"Brother B., you know that she is the wife of one of our leaders, and that she is very pious, although not of our Church. No woman on the circuit treats the preachers better. She has been particularly kind in nursing you when you were sick. Would you have received her husband, and driven her from the door?"

"Yes, I would have kept her out."

"I do not believe Mr. Wesley ever intended no exceptions. Indeed, I read otherwise in his Journal. Any how, the Methodist Discipline or any other power on earth shall not compel me to act in an unchristian or brutal manner."

If brother Bigelow had lived till now he would be borne down by the progress of this generation, for he would never yield a piece of old-fashioned Methodism as big as his thumb nail. He held the

27

most orderly camp meetings ever seen in Ohio; and
he possessed the courage necessary to do it. At our
camp meeting, a citizen of Marion took his seat
among the ladies. Our elder very politely observed
that the gentleman perhaps was not present when
the rules were read. He then mildly gave the
reasons for the rule, and said he hoped he would
oblige us by sitting on the other side. The man's
face turned red with anger, but he kept his seat.
The elder added he had hoped that a mild request
would be complied with by any gentleman, but he
had force sufficient to remove him, and that should
be attended to before proceeding to any other business. Seeing he was preparing for this move, the
man went off very angry, declaring he would whip
B. if he ever saw him in Marion. When our camp
meeting broke, the brethren of Marion strongly
urged Bigelow to take a by-road; but he laughed
and said he had determined to go back on the usual
road. As he passed by the man's shop, he was
hailed and invited to come in. Although he had
been warned that he was a notorious bully, and
always was equal to his threatenings, yet he answered, "Certainly." He dismounted and went in.
The bully said, "You have had your time, and now
I have mine. I am determined to thrash you, and
I will do it." B. observed that he would of course
be manly enough to give his reasons and a chance
for explanation. He ran over his principal griev-
ance, and B. asked him if he did not have his rules

to govern his family and shop, and if any one came in to bear down his authority if he would be such a coward as to suffer it. He said he would not; and taking this as his platform, he continued to talk till the lion was pacified. They shook hands, and the preacher was invited to call again. In one word, Bigelow was one of the most useful ministers in our Western country. The people would crowd from every point of our circuit, and many points on the neighboring circuits, to hear him at our quarterly meetings. We traveled under him many years, and he lodged with us as often as he could.

I exercised the strictest discipline upon this circuit, catechising the classes on the General Rules. One member would be examined on one rule, and one on another, and a short exhortation addressed to the rest on the rules under consideration; but all were examined simply and singularly on the rule regarding spirituous liquor. At the onset a sister in one class flew into a passion, and said she held it to be her privilege to drink when she pleased, and what she pleased. "Well, sister, the rules provide that we must bear, for a season, with those who break them. This day four weeks we will be round, if the Lord permit, and in the mean time I will pray for you every day. I beseech you to do the same, understanding that, 'if you repent not,' we will be compelled to drop you." At another class we found a brother who had once been a Universalist, and was high-spirited by nature, but was pious and intelligent. He rose up against the rule. We gave him the same advice; but I feared he would prove a hard case. At the extremity of the circuit I found another Amazon inebriate or user of liquor as a beverage. She flew into high opposition to the rule on drinking, and also that on private prayer. When I got to the capital of the circuit, I anticipated trouble. There was a venerable man who was leader, exhorter, and steward, who used liquor habitually, and especially in harvest and log-rolling. He had told me that before he embraced religion he could not drink enough to intoxicate him. He used to take especial delight in getting his companions together and drinking with them, glass for glass, till he had them all down—dead drunk—and then he would stand over them and laugh. On one occasion, after drinking his usual portion through the day, he bet a man five dollars that he could drink a quart of brandy, measured from the pipe, without taking it from his mouth. He clapped the measure to his lips and tossed it off at one draught. He said in one moment he was, as it were, all on fire, inside and out. Death seemed to clasp him, and hell opened before him. In the next moment his stomach revolted, and he threw it all up. He would tell this with tears of gratitude; for he said if it had not been for this instantaneous discharge he would have dropped quickly into hell. He still used spirits, and it was publicly known. To deal with others, and pass by him, would have been wicked partiality.

So I put the same question to him, and he gave an unfavorable answer.

On the next round, when we met in class the first delinquent, she rose up, all subdued, and said she had taken the advice given her; that she found herself well-nigh gone, and had requested the class to appoint a day of fasting and prayer. This they did. Her soul was recovered out of the snare, and there was a revival in the class. When I came to the member who had been a Universalist, to my surprise, he said he had thought the matter over, and found that liquor did him no good, and he had determined to keep all our good rules. The woman, who said she was opposed to my examining her on family prayer and drinking, was also cured. She said, after she had so misbehaved in class, she went home, and set about getting dinner. Her husband went to his plow. When she had set the table she went out and called her husband to dinner. He turned round, and said, "My dear, you gave me enough in class for breakfast, dinner, and supper;" and he drove on. This reached her heart; she felt she had offended her pious husband; she had offended the preacher; but, what was more than all, she had offended the Lord. She went to her closet and to her knees, and was now as humble as a lamb. Now remained my old rich friend, one who had been particularly kind to me. But I determined to know no one according to the flesh; for my labor was not fruitless. I had hard work here.

I appealed to him as a steward who was appointed to see that I did my duty. I told him how other members had renounced liquor, and the good that followed; and assured him that I would be driven to the painful necessity of bringing him to trial if he did not comply. I got his consent within about five minutes before the time for preaching—and my whole circuit was cleansed of this iniquity, and all the rules observed.

In the first years of my itinerancy, I always found that a strict adherence to Discipline always revived the Church. No man can administer it now, *in all points*, without being regarded as a tyrant, a bloody Bishop Bonner. Then it is reported he is not acceptable to the people; and then the very power that has pledged him, when entering into holy orders, to administer the Discipline "with a firm but mild hand," has to put him where they can get him. Now, if we have come to the day when all the obsolete requirements of the Discipline *can not* be administered, the General Conference ought to do them away, so that the new ministers ought not to be required to promise to do what the old men know they can not do. If the rule on class meetings should be enforced now, as in ancient days, it would cut off one-third of our membership and disaffect another. We know that there are some exceptions. For this cause we have of late years sought to be excused from the charge.

XXIV.

MOUNT VERNON CIRCUIT.

1833–34. WILLIAM WESTLAKE rode with me on this circuit the first year, and Charles Lovell the last. When we arrived at Mount Vernon, there was great excitement about the cholera, which was reported to be advancing in different directions. While preaching in a crowded school-house, on Sunday evening, it was announced in the congregation, that one of the doctors, who had been out to attend a case of the cholera, had returned home in the last stage of the disease. This caused almost a general stampede. We had no place to accommodate our congregation here till our meeting-house was finished.

We had on our plan "Martinsburg;" and we were a little puzzled, in seeing no society and no official names in connection. I could get but little information in regard to the road, and got out of the way. About two o'clock I entered the town, and inquired of the first man seen, if there were any Methodists living in the place. After considerable study, he said there was not one; but, pointing to a certain house, he said there was an old woman living there who might lean that way. I

entered the house, and asked if she knew of any
Methodists living in Martinsburg.

"Laws! no, sir. There were some here once;
but they have moved, died, or backslidden. There
is not one here now."

I sat a little while, hoping she would ask me to
put up my horse, and take a bite myself; but this
she did not think of. After a while she said,

"I can tell you one thing for your comfort; if
you are a Methodist preacher, as I suppose, the
people here, generally, love to hear a Methodist
minister better than any other."

"Well, madam, can you tell me of any Methodists who live within a short distance of this place?"

"Yes, I have a son who is the leader of a class
about three miles off."

She gave me directions, and I got to her son's in
the evening — man and horse sufficiently tired and
hungry. While we were sitting around the table,
there came a messenger, express from town, saying,
if the ministers would give them regular preaching,
two of the merchants and a cabinet-maker would
pledge themselves to keep them and their horses.

"Then tell them we will begin with them to-
morrow evening by early candle-lighting."

When I went, I found that the Presbyterians
were holding a sacramental meeting. I told my
friends that I had no knowledge of that, and was
ready to postpone. They said this would make no
material difference, as we could get a large school-

house crowded with persons who would not be likely to attend the other meeting. We faced a crowded congregation at night, and felt that we had struck the right vein. The work of God revived, gradually, but gloriously; and before we left the circuit, ninety persons, embracing the bone and sinew of the village, embraced religion. The two merchants and the cabinet-maker were converted, and that brightly. At one meeting a couple of brethren went to brother M'Claughlin, and asked him if he would not join the mourners at the altar. He said, "Friends, I would, but can not. I am unstrung in all my limbs." They raised him, and brought him up. At a subsequent meeting he was converted, and went home shouting through the street. The other merchant was a brother-in-law to the Presbyterian minister. His people tried hard to keep him from joining us. He told them he could not indorse their doctrine, and expressly referred to its bearing on infants. One of the elders utterly denied that it had any such bearing, and he looked to the minister for confirmation; but the preacher was silent. Then the gentleman opened his library, took out a volume, and read the quotation he had made. The elder's look of astonishment showed that his contradiction was entirely innocent. The brother told them he would not be hasty. He wished to examine all the ground before taking another step. He went eastward for goods, purchased a Methodist Discipline and some other works, and read them on his way home, like the Ethiopian, and joined our Church. The brethren built a handsome meeting-house, plastered it in the midst of Winter, keeping their stoves in full blast night and day.

Before I left them they gave me one of the most costly coats I ever wore, even in the days of my brightest prosperity; and it was made in a finished style by a tailor who was expelled from the Church. Without self-flattery, this was owing to my just manner of administration. I always endeavored to secure to the defendant every facility in his defense, and that even when I had prescience enough to know he *would be* expelled. In doing this I have had sometimes to try the patience of an indignant committee. They would think certain round-about statements were entirely irrelevant in the defense. I thought so myself, but could always bear with a dying man, and let him have a fair swing. So the expelled seldom abused me. I once had to pronounce a brother expelled, and from the excitable disposition of himself and wife, I expected no mercy. Still, God blessed them with an heir in a few weeks, and they named him A. M. L. I always thought it a most solemn thing to cut off a soul from the congregation of the Lord, for if we do it *justly, mind ye,* it will be done in heaven.

There was an appointment a few miles from Martinsburg, up a rocky run. It was one of your old, staid societies, in number truly apostolic. If one member died or removed, another would move in and make up the round dozen. When I went there, some said,

"Brother L., we have heard of revivals, and sometimes not far from us, but we have never had one in this society. Can you tell us what to do in order to a revival?"

"Brethren, do you truly desire a revival, and pray for it?"

"We always pray for it."

"Have you ever added fasting to prayer?"

"No, we never thought of that."

"Well, try it; but don't try it till you hold a conference on the subject, and get the consent of every member; then appoint a day, leave off all work, come together, and pray for a revival."

The brethren did so, and the Lord heard on earth, and answered from heaven. They had a precious work. Our appointments were in the evening. The house was crowded, and sometimes the porch and part of the yard, although the weather was disagreeable. The Campbellites infested this region, and withstood us greatly. When a member would come out of the house they would beset him in this way:

"Why are you always dunning the Lord? Suppose you owed me a few dollars, and I should be always dunning you for them, would you not despise me? But you dun the Lord in the morning, at noon, and then all night. You must know it is displeasing to him."

Methodist. "I pray to God because I am needy, and none but him can help me. Do you not pray to God in time of need?"

Campbellite. "I allow a man may get into a strait, once or twice in his life, when he may pray; but what's the use of always dunning?"

The Campbellites had so incessantly preached immersion, as to influence the neighborhood on that point, so our converts all wished to be baptized by immersion. We gave out an appointment to attend to that matter. In the mean time it turned unusually cold, and the run was partially frozen. The class-leader met me on the road, and said,

"Brother L., will you baptize our new members to-day?"

"Certainly, if they wish it. Did I not set apart this day to that purpose?"

"You did; but the Campbellites have been troubling our new members, and asking them if they are so simple as to suppose that a Methodist preacher would put his foot into water such weather as this."

"Let them mind their own business."

When we marched down to the water, the whole country crowded the banks. I first walked in alone, sounding every depth and shoal with my staff. As I descended into the water and ice, it seemed as if my legs were cut off; but I walked about with a countenance as serene as a basket of chips, stopped and compared places, and splashed the water like a canvas-backed duck. This was no hypocrisy. I felt joyful in the prospect of putting the mark of the covenant on our young converts, by whatever mode. I then took the candidates in one by one, and felt the bottom with every one of them, and the Campbellites acknowledged it was done *secundum artem.* But this was the beginning. As fast as they came in they wished to be immersed. We made only one blunder—that was with a large African. Before going in he said he wanted to be baptized like the colored people in old Virginia—that was to tie his handkerchief around his head, so as to leave a tail for the preacher to take hold of. I told him I was raised in old Virginia, and had seen that operation often, but he had better let me do my own way, assuring him I had never failed; but he insisted on his own way, and he tied his cotton handkerchief around his head; but the misfortune was he had little or no forehead. His head appeared to be as flat as a turnip. When I undertook to lay him down he threw his head back, and the handkerchief slipped off. There was considerable floundering, but I put him under. He seemed somewhat mortified that his chosen mode did not take.

William Westlake had a sprinkle of eccentricity. At a distant point of his circuit his host told him a Campbellite was going to preach at night in the school-house, and that it was a new occurrence. He asked him if he would not go. Westlake said he believed he would. When they got there, the house was so crowded they barely got inside.

The preacher, in illustrating his system, used much "bargain and trade" figures. He said when men got title-bonds for any thing they felt legally safe, knowing that, at the time and place specified, they would certainly receive the consideration. So it was in salvation. Baptism was God's title-bond of eternal life given to the sinner. All who would receive this would be certain of salvation. This was the backbone of his discourse. When he was done preaching he said if there were any in the congregation who had not understood his doctrine—new to the most of them—he was willing to answer any questions which might be asked. They professed to be teachers rather than preachers.

Westlake. "I would not mind asking you a question or two, sir, if I could be simply answered without any controversy."

Preacher. "Controversy, indeed! We wish to *teach* in the most simple manner, and are willing to answer all objections in meekness and love."

Westlake. "If I did not misunderstand you, sir, you hold that immersion is a title-bond to eternal life, and he who is immersed has a right to heaven?"

Preacher. "Exactly, you understand me right; and pray, what do you think of it?"

Westlake. "Why, it drummed up curious thoughts in my mind. I thought that if your doctrine is true, there must be many hogs in heaven."

Preacher. "What do you mean, sir?"

Westlake. "When our Lord cast a legion of devils

out of one who was possessed, they went into a great herd of swine, and they ran violently down a steep place into the sea and were *immersed*. They received your title-bond and a legion of devils with them. Good-night, sir."

The gravest in the congregation could not restrain themselves.

Preacher. "Stop, sir—O, don't go—now see that, he is off. I do hate a man who will not wait for explanations."

Westlake. (Putting his head into the doorway.) "You proposed, simply, questions and answers, without controversy. Good-night."

That Campbellite sermon, in that neighborhood, was—*solus*. Six days' controversy could not have effected as much.

Charles R. Lovell was in his first itinerant year. He was a young man of pleasing appearance, talented, and popular. When I had an interview with him last year, at Conference, and listened to the melting recital of his loss, in the death of his amiable daughter—and when I looked up, and saw how care and anxiety had begun to sprinkle his locks—and when my mind went back to the day when he, and I might say his bride, for they were lately married, lived together with us, blithe, cheerful, and religiously happy—I said, in the depth of my heart,

> "What trials have we seen!
> What conflicts have we passed!"

May his last days be his best days, and may he get safely home, bringing his sheaves with him!

Brother Christie was our presiding elder, and his fame spread all through that region and the country round about, drawing great congregations from all parts and all denominations. He always put up with us when he could; and I always blacked his boots—not to curry favor, for I never eat post-hay for any man, but because I loved him. When I went to assist him with a big meeting, at his home, he would clean my shoes in spite of all my scuffling. He was determined the sailor should not outdo him in hospitality. I was acquainted with his wife from her girlhood. We may have occasion to speak of Christie again; but, lest it might be forgotten, I will say he was an extraordinary man. He had an uncommon memory. He could read one of Watson's sermons, and get up and preach it much better, as I thought, than the author ever did. He was not given to this, for he had an energy and power in himself sufficient for all cases, elaborate or extemporaneous. He beat Bigelow on the Canadian question—not only confuting the arguments he had brought, but continued on, in anticipation, to answer every one that he might possibly bring, till he left his opponent high and dry at flood-tide; and, like the ass between two stacks of hay, we knew not which to sympathize with.

XXV.

UNION AND MADISONVILLE CIRCUITS.

1835. On the Union circuit, embracing Xenia, I had with me Alexander Morrow and Stephen Holland. Morrow was a very correct speaker, and a good sermonizer, justly esteemed. Holland was above mediocrity, and although not possessing the advantages of a liberal education, this want could seldom be detected by a stranger. He was naturally impulsive, and graciously filled with the blessed Spirit, and with power. Affectionate in his intercourse, he could not be otherwise than popular. This was a six-weeks' circuit—and we humbly think there can not be an arrangement more unfortunate. The people could hardly get acquainted with their preachers. When the quarterly meeting took a preacher from a certain appointment, that appointment would not have his services for three months. If the preacher should be taken from the same appointment by every quarterly meeting, then he would not be at that appointment the whole year. But this was not suffered to happen. This arrangement gave much trouble to the preacher in charge, and he had to do much by delegation to his colleagues. Nevertheless, we had some good times, and quite a revival at Centerville.

There had been a general revival the two preceding years, under Latta and Laws, and this was necessarily a year of pruning and confirmation. The reader will recollect that I started from Xenia. It was there, while a local preacher, that I had the honor of drawing up the heading of the first missionary subscription that was started in the West— and, for aught I know, in the Union—that is, in the Methodist Episcopal Church. It was when the Wyandott mission was yet in the hands of the local ministers. Subscriptions had been raised in the congregations; but now the missionary friends began to assume the form of a society—every subscriber a member.

We were very well situated on the Union circuit, surrounded by old, tried friends—friends who, when they recommended me to the Conference, told the elder they did not recommend to others one whom they would be unwilling to receive themselves. ˙

But at the last quarterly meeting a circumstance occurred, which led to my voluntary removal. The elder, brother Raper, told me his manner of conducting the last quarterly meeting in the year. He said, among other things, he examined the stewards in regard to the performance of their duties, one by one. I begged he would not do this, as I had never unto that day known it to be done, and as there was no doubt about our getting our quarterage, it seemed unnecessary; that our stewards were like the stewards on all other circuits—some very faithful, and some who did not concern themselves with their office at all. But if he inquired about each man, as a Christian I would have to tell the truth, and that, in the very nature of things, would raise a smoke, as it always does. But he held me to it. Some of the stewards I praised highly—they were worthy; but of others I had to say that they never came to quarterly conference only when it came to them. They never spoke of financial matters even in their own classes; and they never entered the parsonage to inquire whether we were dead or alive. This raised a warm conversation, for it was necessarily personal. Some said brother L. should have his quarterage if no other man had. This cut me, as I was one whose standing rule was never to utter a word about the quarterage. I observed that there was no anxiety about that. My motive was altogether moral. The elder had pointedly asked me if such a brother performed all the duties of a steward. The brother himself knew that he had not. His colleagues knew that he had not. His own class knew that he had not. The Lord knew that he had not; and how could I, a professed minister, lie, and say that he had? I had never been asked the question before, and tried to stave it off, and was obliged to answer as I did. After quarterly conference I told the elder he must move me. He thought there was no occasion. He consulted with the brethren, and assured me I was not yet done over. This I believe, for the brethren who were most nettled were afterward remarkably kind. But still I held to my request, and it was granted.

We might say a great deal in praise of this circuit, but it is unnecessary, because it is so well known by many of our ministers. Xenia always seemed like my home, and while that generation lasted, I never stopped there without being surrounded and taken by storm. It was like Auburn—"loveliest village of the plain."

MADISONVILLE.

1836. We rode this circuit in 1836 and 1837, having traveled it before while connected with the Miami circuit. The first year we labored with brother Cheney, and the second, with brother Parish. They were both very pious and pleasant. We had some very encouraging meetings, and the societies were lively.

1856. As it is my design to keep every appointment under one heading, I will add that I rode the circuit again in 1856 and 1857. So I labored five years on this charge, and from time to time renewed my acquaintance with members that I had taken in—long time ago. Having endured thus far, we hope they will continue till eternal life. I feel thankful to the brethren there that they bore so long with me, and especially for the kind reception they gave me on my last coming. The parsonage being already occupied by my colleague, brother Glasscock, who labored on the circuit the previous year, I settled in Columbia, a beautiful village on the bank of the Ohio.

On my second year we had an extraordinary wet season in the Fall, and mud in abundance. On one of the most dreary and showery evenings of that season, about nightfall, the parsonage was stormed at all available points by horse and foot, ladies and gentlemen, who poured down upon us a profusion of the necessaries and comforts of this life. Colonel Holmes, on the part of the company, made a humorous but chaste speech, observing that he hoped the visit would be more grateful to me, when he assured me that it was not on account of any murmuring or complaining on the part of the preacher or his family, for no such thing had been heard. Neither was it because they had heard of any pressing want, but it was simply as an expression of their good feeling toward us. We might also see that it was not simply a Church matter, but the citizens generally had joined in the visitation, and if the night had been clear, the yard, instead of the house, would have been full, and he had heard no one in or out of the Church object. This is only an outline of his speech, and before he was done I was pretty much used up. I have been accustomed to make speeches in and out of the pulpit, and if any one should rouse my anger, I suppose I could talk *some;* but when one knocks out the bung of gratitude I'm "done over." I made some kind of reply, but it was very unworthy of the occasion. The doctor presented Mrs. Lorrain with some coffee, under the notion of a specific medicine, and began to give a verbal recipe, if we might so speak, and directions how to mix and prepare it. I saw this gave her considerable diversion, and I said, "Doctor, you need not be very precise, she can mix that medicine better than any one in this community. She is famous in that decoction throughout the Conference."

I can not express my affection for the brethren of this circuit, with many of whom I have taken sweet counsel for so many years. The principal strength of the Church in Columbia was the female members. They were well qualified by gifts and grace, and although duly modest in all social relations, yet they were

> "Bold to take up, firm to sustain
> The consecrated cross."

Brother Murphy rode with me during the last year on this circuit. It pleased God to take away the wife of his youth in the midst of the year. I preached the funeral sermon, and must say that I have seldom seen a congregation sympathize so deeply with the bereaved. She was an extraordinary good woman, and was fully prepared for her great change. She lies in the same graveyard with my own mother, who died in the same parsonage in 1837.

In this circuit live some of our most choice members: Langdon, of Columbia, Green, of Carthage, Buckingham, of Miamisville, and—; but here I must stop, or give a list of worthies who live there and will live forever. Ever since we have had charge of societies we have held firmly to the ministerial right to receive into the Church *on trial* such as give evidence of true contrition. We have held to this key with an unconquerable grip. We have sometimes met with opposition from the officiary on this point. An instance of this kind occurred, during one of our terms on this circuit. There appeared in our community a strange female who earned a bare support by washing. It was reported that she had been seen intoxicated several times by the wayside. Several temperance lecturers came out of Cincinnati, and held a series of meetings in quick succession. This woman came up, among others, and took the pledge. She then began to attend our religious meetings, and during a refreshing season sought and obtained religion. She applied for admission into the Church. The difficulty was, there was not a leader that would have her name on his paper. I went privately to a young leader, and told him if he would let me put her name on the bottom of his class-book, I would pledge myself to take it off whenever she violated the rules. To this he agreed, supposing he would not be burdened with it long. She had heard the Church was unwilling to receive her, and the first time she attended class she meekly observed that she was not surprised or hurt by the Church being unwilling to receive her. She felt deeply that she was unworthy, but if they would only suffer her to come inside the door, where she could hear them sing, pray, and talk of the Savior, it was all she craved.

From that day she was an example of piety, attending all her meetings, through all weathers, and she gradually drew on the respect of all, inside and outside the Church. After she had fully established her character as a humble Christian, she came down one day to the parsonage, with a bright countenance, and gave me a full account of her case, from which I gathered the following: She was brought up in Kentucky, and was a happy member of a pious, happy family. There was regular preaching in her father's house; but when her mother died her father married a woman who scattered the family like a tigress. She came to Ohio in order to get a living if possible; but exiled from all she loved, she felt lonely and abandoned. In that condition she had indulged in spirits, but the temperance lectures had fully opened her eyes to the unfathomable gulf to which she was tending; and having learned in her father's house where there was rest for her soul, she sought and found salvation. She then informed me she had just received a letter from her father, to whom she had written after she was converted, and he informed her that her step-mother was dead, all his children were gone, he was old and infirm, and that she must return and take care of him in his old age, and his property should be hers when he died. She felt it was her duty to go, but thought, as she had been a stranger among us, it would be best to leave these particulars with the preacher. We gave her a letter, and was happy to hear, some time after, that she was with her father, and growing in grace and the knowledge of the Lord. Now, if I had taken the advice of the officiary, had rejected this penitent, and driven her back to perdition, what board of leaders could have answered for the violation of my commission? When any have had a trial, and proved delinquent, then it is time to consult with others about laying them aside. Some think it is scandalous for the Church to try to save one whose former life has been shameful. We think it is the proper work of the Church below, and we believe the Church triumphant will embrace in her happy belt too many reformed prodigals, to blush at her past mercy. "But the world! but the world!" Well, to many of these it may still be said, the publicans and harlots enter into the kingdom of heaven before you. The children of this world would do well to "keep their breath to cool their own porridge."

We are aware that as a Church declines in apostolic grace, she will gradually be driven from apostolic practice. No Church ever went down with a surge. We will make no noise against lay delegation, but when it comes we do hope that the preachers will fence in, stronger than ever, what is purely ministerial right.

We had, while under the superintendence of brother Christie, the most singular meeting we ever saw or heard of before or since. It was in Bates's settlement. The meeting-house on Saturday night was crowded. Brother Parish had sung and prayed, and was just about to read his text, when a simultaneous shout from nearly all the Church — men, women, and children—broke loose like a tornado, and continued for nearly two hours by the elder's watch. It was deafening. Some eight or ten sinners came tumbling over the benches and fell at the altar crying for mercy; but several fled out of the house and cursed like privateersmen, declaring it was a concerted scheme of the Methodists to scare them. There might be a division of this question. It was no concerted plan; but that they were badly scared there can be no doubt. In the midst of this human storm the elder requested brother Parish, who had a powerful voice, to slip down into the altar and try to exhort them. This he attempted, but although we were leaning over him, it was only now and then that we could understand a word. He soon sunk exhausted. As soon as the shouting subsided in a measure we opened the door of the Church and received a number. Some thought this would be followed by a general revival; but the whole Ohio Conference would not have raised such another shout, for it was a Church remarkably orderly.

XXVI.

WEST UNION CIRCUIT.

1838. THIS circuit was a part of the old Brush Creek circuit, and as such was an old acquaintance. Brother J. W. Weakley was my appointed colleague. He had preached but one sermon before he came on, but he improved rapidly. There was evidently a good feeling getting up in Ripley, and we built much hope on our first quarterly meeting. Brother Christie came on in bad health, so that he had to preach sitting in a chair. We made several efforts to get mourners to the altar, but not one would come forward. It at last struck us to invite sinners to join the Church. In a few moments the altar was surrounded. At every succeeding meeting we would try to prevail on them to come to the mourners' bench; but all in vain. As soon as we would open the door of the Church they would come in. We went on working in this way till we had received several scores. Although I had always believed in convicted persons joining the Church, I was a little alarmed at seeing so many unconverted members coming in at one time. But as soon as we began to hold social prayer meetings around town, persons began to obtain forgiveness, and we received something over one hundred and fifty. We were considerably opposed in a private way. One minister, even, went into Methodist families, and tried to proselyte. A lady belonging to our Church said,

"Sir, why take so much pains to turn a person from one Church to another—seeing, if we get to heaven, there will be no Methodists, no Presbyterians?"

"Indeed, madam, you are mistaken. There will be Presbyterians there—and we can prove it."

"I would like to know how."

"Saint John, in the Isle of Patmos, had a clear view of heaven, and he saw four-and-twenty elders around the Throne. Now you know the Presbyterian Church has elders."

"Bless my soul! and has not the Methodist Church got a plenty of elders—and *presiding* elders, in the bargain?"

The same minister seemed to be exceedingly uneasy at the continuance of the meeting; and, while we were preaching to crowded houses, he sent a note to be read, that there would be a meeting of the Temperance Society, at the other church, on the next night. This society had been lately organized, and the Methodists had taken great interest in it.

When I received this notice in the pulpit, I handed it to the brother who was going to preach, and requested him to read it distinctly, before he took his text. While he was preaching, I remembered that some of brother William Armstrong's children had requested me to preach a sailor sermon; and then I thought, "Be ye wise as serpents." Perhaps the minister who sent the notice had been digesting the same command. When brother Gaddis, who was on a visit, had finished preaching to the children, he caught several young folks. This gave occasion to some, next day, to say, "The Methodists are 'most done, they caught nothing last night but minnows." Before the meeting closed, we arose and observed, that some of the young people had requested me to preach a sea sermon. I concluded that I would, as in the morning of my life I had followed the seas, and it was pleasant for me to take a cruise now and then. I then opened the Bible and read, as my text for the next evening, "They that go down to the seas in ships, and do business in the great deep," etc. The next day, one would say to another,

"Where will you go, to-night?"

"O, I will go to hear about those who go down into the seas."

At night our house was crowded, and the secretary of the Temperance Society was there. Our people were not indifferent about temperance; but they did not like it as a cloak for bigotry; and they knew, moreover, that the Temperance Society was always with them, but times of refreshing were transient.

We called up the mourners, after preaching, and

had an amazing haul. It seemed to me that some of the tallest and most bare-boned folks in the town rushed forward. One Methodist rose up on a bench, and, turning to the congregation, said, "See here! Are these minnows? No. We love minnows. But, look here: monsters! whales! sea-serpents! Glory be to God!" And the work still went. on.

The next thrust at me was infamous. A country minister told a large congregation, on a Sabbath, that the preacher in charge of West Union circuit, hearing that the trustees of the meeting-house in Decatur had given leave to an abolition lecturer to use the house, had violently taken the key and put it in his pocket, declaring that the preachers had a sovereign right to all the churches. When told of this announcement, and that the story was going the rounds, I had never heard that any one had applied to the trustees for the house. When we inquired of the trustees, they said that they had promised a gentleman the use of the house; but that a report had gone abroad, that the friends of the lecturer intended to carry private arms, and this report, whether true or false, had exasperated a certain class, and they were determined to attend under similar circumstances. So, fearing the meeting-house would become a place of slaughter, they had stopped the proceedings. The trustees could be qualified that this was done in my absence, and, as far as they knew, I was innocent of the whole matter. The town preacher made a great blow about this matter, and I authorized a friend to give him the right version. He said, "Then, why does not Mr. L. appoint a time, and fully explain himself on this matter, from the pulpit, and define his position?" I knew he would rather hear this than the Gospel, particularly if it would get us all by the ears, and stop our revival.

But I requested the friend in answer to this to say, that I regarded the pulpit sacred to the Gospel, and the Lord had called me to preach not *myself*, but Christ Jesus the Lord, and myself his servant for Jesus' sake. And as the Lord and myself knew that the report was false, they were welcome to handle it as much as they pleased, provided they would do themselves no harm. Still the work of God went on. I felt it to be my duty, in the light of the golden rule, to visit the minister who was circulating this whole-cloth slander through the country. A member of brother Meek's family was present on one occasion when he entertained his congregation with the interesting narrative. Still I charitably hoped that he had been imposed on, and that he would like to be disabused, if it was false. He had invited me some time before to visit him, in virtue of our former acquaintance when I was traveling Brush Creek. So I went to see him, but not without much prayer. He invited me into his study, and I soon opened my business by telling him that I had understood that he had used my name in connection with the trustees of Decatur meeting-house, and whatever might have been the source of his information, the story he had told was without any foundation. I had never heard it till it came to me from his pulpit. He promptly denied the whole matter. I then asked him if brother Meek did not stop him as he passed his house, coming from that meeting, and advise him not to repeat the story, as he knew that brother L. was too well acquainted with the Discipline to assume such authority over the trustees; and although he had not mentioned it to him as yet, he knew that such a procedure was entirely contrary to his whole character. At the mention of Meek's name he began a eulogy on him, and allowed if *he* said so, there must have been something of it. Then his face grew red, and he said,

"If you did not do *that*, you have done *worse*, sir, and I have no apology to make."

"Well, what have I done worse? If I have stolen or murdered let me answer to my crimes; but clear me of what I have not done."

"You have oppressed the African. You have no mercy for him. You rivet his chains. You take away his Bible. You are the man who roused up the citizens to pelt me with rotten eggs, as I passed through the other day. You are the man who slips threatening letters under my door, saying you will burn up me and my house if I do not renounce my principles, or if I do not lodge money in certain places, and—"

"Stop, stop, sir. I am the man who would rejoice if every slave in the nation had a Bible and
could read it, obey it, and get to heaven. This is
the first intelligence I have had of your being
egged in passing through Decatur. I should have
certainly heard of such a remarkable circumstance
if it had happened. And take care how you talk
of me and secret missives."

Then he flew into a fury, and cried in a loud but
tremulous voice, stamping his feet, at every repe-
tition, "Begone! begone! begone! Leave me! leave
me!" I coolly retired toward the door of the room.
He waddled round the table, following me through
the passage with "Begone! leave my house." I
still kept my eye a little quartering, expecting a
poop. What I would have done if he had kicked
me, the Lord knows; but I reached the street in
safety, and he slammed the door with a noise that
resounded through the whole castle. It was something singular that although till this time I had all
the tranquillity that I had prayed for, yet I had
not walked fifty yards before I felt my fists coiling
up, and my feet in stays, and something seemed to
say, why did you not knock the lubber over? You
could have slapped him to the floor. Then I found
that prayer after meat was necessary as well as before. When I told my adventure to some of our
leading men, they wondered that I went to see him
at all. They said he had some sense on ordinary
subjects, but we have found him perfectly insane

on his favorite theme. One of our stewards, a plain, serious man, told me he had carried a cowhide under his skirts during a whole day to give him a thrashing wherever he might find him; but when he got a little cool, he said, "Why should I whip a crazy man?" His conduct to me was unaccountable, as I had never interfered with his "*Jinny Quockisan*" while on the circuit. The secret "*letters*" I understood were written by one of his own household for fun—a kind of "Monsieur Tonson" affair. One day a genteel-looking negro approached some of us, craving help to purchase his wife. He had letters from well-known citizens of Maysville, and we judged from his documents and his honest carriage that he was worthy. We pointed to the stately mansion of our zealous minister, and advised him to apply there, for the owner was a great friend of the African.

"O, massa, he too conscientious!"

"What do you mean?"

"Why, I done gone to see him."

"What did he say?"

"Why, he argufy that if he give me a dime to buy my wife, den, y'see, he trade in human flesh and blood, and dat is de thing he preaches against— he conscience entirely too tender, massa."

Years upon years rolled away, even unto green old age, when being stationed in a town on the Ohio, as I was about to cross the muddy street on a narrow gangway, there appeared at the opposite end a stately, venerable gentleman, coming from the other side. There had been a report for several days that the President was coming down the river on a Western tour, and as the gentleman approaching was not of our river-eel type, I said to myself, "Surely, here he is as large as life;" and I stepped aside in the mud, as in duty bound—rendering unto Cæsar the things that are Cæsar's. And I was determined to take a good look, as it was my only chance. As he came up, he rolled his large eyes on me, committed a smile, and said,

"Surely, this is my old friend, L. My name is B."

So it was, and we entered into a pleasant conversation; but in the most interesting part, conscience stirred up in her lair, and he said,

"Look here, L.! did n't we once have some kind of a stir round—he—it seems almost like a dream; but I came across a humorous piece in the Advocate, written by you, and it so pleased me that I forgave all—so we 'll let old matters pass."

Amen! Pass on, brother B.; may we meet in heaven!

The Methodists got up a school in Indiana, and solicited my colleague to take charge of it. To this I was opposed. I believed it would be better for him and the Church for him to continue in the itinerancy. I believe he thought so too; but by the force of circumstances he was taken away. I know that he has since filled his vocation with honor and credit; but what is it to what he might have done?

Brother Oliver Williams was put in his place. He was one of the most innocent and devoted young ministers of that day. He rode a few years in the work when alarming symptoms of derangement began to appear. His friends hoping that by a scientific treatment of the disease by physicians practiced in such complaints, he might be restored, carried him to Columbus. But vain was the help of man. The Lord took him to his people's rest. Some think it strange that a child of God should be suffered to lose his reason. But when we reflect that insanity comes by natural or accidental causes that are common to all men, so that the Lord, in preventing it in special cases, would have to exercise miraculous power; and when we consider, moreover, that he has pledged himself to his people to save them *in* their afflictions, and not to preserve them from the natural ills of this life; that although he may suffer them to *pass through the waters*, the waves shall not overwhelm them, or to pass through *the fire*, the flame shall not destroy them, we may well have hope for the pious amid all the ravings of insanity.

In almost all cases where Christians have been demented and subsequently restored, they awake as out of an unconscious state. I read a beautiful illustration of this: A young man became serious, and was diligently seeking religion. He suddenly lost his reason. His pious parents were deeply afflicted, and especially afflicted because they had no evidence of his justification before this misfortune. The doctor, however, told them he thought it was a case arising out of malconformation of the cranium, which caused a pressure on the brain; and if this was the case he might be restored at the period of life when the fullness of youth began to decline. The parents anxiously watched him for years, and when the period that the physician spoke of arrived, he gradually recovered his senses. It was noticed that he was of a new disposition, full of meekness and love to God and all mankind. When he sufficiently recovered his recollection he stated that the last thing which he knew before the unconscious parenthesis through which he had passed was, that while struggling for mercy he was powerfully blessed — overwhelmed — and knew no more. How strangely did the Lord preserve him! Christ has said, "My grace is sufficient." Sufficient for what? For the most stupendous ills that sin has made. We never had any uneasy thoughts about the eternal state of our beloved brother Oliver. Viewing the subject in the above light, we have a most potent argument why every man should make his peace with God, lest that awful day of darkness should suddenly overtake him in his sins.

This was the only appointment, as far as I know, that the devil or any of his agents procured for me. In saying this we do not call in question the purity of the bishops or my presiding elder. They made the appointment in good faith, and, as we learned, under the impression of a request; and I paid for it in current money. Neither do we cast any reflection on the circuit. We were old friends, but I objected to the fraud that an outsider played. We mention the circumstance for the consideration of young preachers. In the morning of my ministry I received my appointments with both hands, as though sliding right down from heaven. In later years I allowed some appointments were only by the *permissive will* of Heaven, and some through the secret treachery of wicked men. Still, the Lord will cause all things to work together for good to those who are the called according to his purpose. This year we received more than two hundred members, according to our account; and after assorting the fish for twelve months, and mending the *old net*, the Minutes gave us an increase of one hundred and fifteen. The devil sent John to the Isle of Patmos, where it was supposed he could do nothing; but in that dreary solitude he exposed his whole programme through succeeding ages—down to the bottomless pit. So let us go to all our appointments, come whence they may; we are not accountable for the making of them. Still, long-suffering itself has its periods and stops, and lest the devil should take an advantage of me, I determined not to return. So at the last quarterly meeting I raised a breeze among the trustees of the parsonage.

I showed Christie and the conference that they held a little log-house, with one room and a garret, which they called a parsonage in order to meet the letter of the Discipline. If the preacher said it was a miserable shanty, they said "no, it is *our parsonage,* and if you are too proud to go into it, you can rent, at your own expense, as the Discipline directs." A warm debate followed, which resulted in some of them acknowledging that it was a piece of barbarism that they were ashamed of; and my successors got a place "where to lay their heads."

XXVII.

FRANKLINTON AND CIRCLEVILLE CIRCUITS.

1839. THIS circuit was somewhat diverse from any that I had traveled, both in its geographical and social characters. It embraced a wide range of barrens, and was eminently suited for cattle. We would often ride along a fence two or three miles in extent, and some of the graziers possessed several thousand acres of land in a body. This made the country extremely inconvenient for schools and churches. A stranger would judge the land to be poor, from the scrubby character of the oaks. But this, it is said, has been produced by the annual fires which swept over these plains before the settlement. The land is good. We had no revival on this appointment; and we doubt whether there has ever been one of much note. The materials are rather obdurate. One part—the wealthy graziers—are genteel, polite, and generous; they will give largely for building meeting-houses, and supporting the preachers; they will attend meetings regularly, and behave with as much decorum in the house of God as members of the Church—and the preacher thinks he will get them before the year is up. But he is mistaken. He will get some nice hams, butter, flour, coffee, and sometimes money—as much as five dollars at the time—as presents; but their souls are their own, and they are confirmed infidels. I attended a wedding one evening, at one of their houses. The old gentleman invited me into his private room, and conversed freely with me about the affairs of the Church. About supper-time there was a considerable buzz among the large company of young folks below; but when the patriarch made his appearance they were all as still as mice. And, later in the evening, when much hilarity prevailed in the hall, when the old man appeared, and gave the signal for prayer, all was still. Every one rose and joined in singing, and every one kneeled in prayer. When we retired again, I looked at the gentleman. His external appearance was so venerable—the order of his household so correct—I began to think that he might be a Christian, or that he might be partially sanctified by his Methodist wife; but he broke my reverie by saying:

"Mr. L., why does your Church make such efforts to send missionary preachers to the Indians?"

"To Christianize them, sir."

"But there is no necessity for this. I was in this country in Indian times, and I assure you that their morals are superior even to ours. They are men of truth. I could depend on their verbal promise with more confidence than I can on the bond of a white man; and I think their religion is of a superior order."·

I directed him to certain passages of the Bible— ·but I found that he did not believe in the Bible, and that he was an immovable infidel.

These rich graziers are called, by way of distinction, "*Short-Horns.*" The gentleman to whom I refer, would attend our meeting, like others of his class, and would not venture to breathe any doubt of Christianity before his hands or tenants. Whatever they may think of Christianity, they admit that the preaching of it is calculated to keep the lower class in bounds. The Short-Horns fare, like the rich man, sumptuously every day—for they say they know not when company may come upon them. They are very hospitable; but it is considered a miracle of miracles for one of them to get converted. Some of their children, however, joined us. The next class, the tenants, generally have no fear of God before their eyes, and very few of them are ever found at meeting. The tradesmen, and owners of agricultural farms, are, many of them, in the Church, and accessible to the Gospel; but all are a scattered people, and it is with difficulty they can attend church in bad weather.

The population is very light-spirited, and even the girls are given to horse-racing, fox-hunting, and daring horsemanship, leaping fences, and swimming creeks and rivers. It is true, the Methodist girls are easily distinguished from the mass, having sacrificed these pleasures; but when they come to the quarterly meetings, you may see, by the way they hold their loaded horsewhips, and give them an occasional smack, as they pass along, that they have known something of the turf. They are Christians, but very blithe and buoyant Christians.

The best appointment on this circuit was on the Scioto, above Franklinton, on the very ground where we had that revival on the Columbus circuit, where Arianism once prevailed. The most of the members with whom we had met, in the beginning of our ministry, had passed into their rest. A number of members from the East had settled in that region, and built up a large and respectable meeting-house. They were intelligent and liberal. Some paid from five to ten dollars, annually, to the Missionary Society, but their peculiar strength in supporting the Gospel was in every one giving *something*. The last time I preached to them, they presented me a very generous bonus. Perhaps we may never meet them again in this world. May we all meet in heaven!

My colleague was Jeremiah Hill, a young man of very promising talents, both as a preacher and a writer. We had a remarkably-pleasant time in working together. At one of our quarterly meetings brother Jacob Young, in preaching on "Come, let us go up to the house of the Lord, to the house of the God of Jacob," became quite fanciful. in explaining by faith the missionary fields of futurity. Yes, he saw, in his imagination, Alfred M. Lorrain in Arabia, walking among the tents of the Arabians, with his Bible in one hand and his hymn-book in the other, saying, "Come, let us go up to the house of the Lord." Then he saw Jeremiah Hill in Africa, among the krawls of the Hottentots, saying, "Come, let us go up to the house of the Lord." I looked at Jeremiah and saw his face unusually red, and I found out that, although an ultra abolitionist, he did not like at all to be stationed among the Hottentots. But the elder rose higher and higher at the thought, and the congregation looked as though on the verge of the millennium. This pious, gifted colleague of mine soon passed away to brighter worlds on high. I never knew age with grace to do so much for any man as they did for our highly-esteemed elder, Jacob Young. He was my elder when I started, and he was in the prime of life. Then he was a doctrinal, argumentative, and instructive minister, but as dry as a chip. In his latter days his ministrations were melodiously melting, and full of grace and love. I am glad he lived so long. Still he was sometimes a little short. While he was a widower he often stopped with us, and was a great favorite in the family. On one occasion several of the members called to see him, and he was giving his opinion on a favorite subject. After a while he made a long pause, and thinking he had ended his "say," I began to take up the parable. He turned round, and said, "Brother L., just hush—stop talking—is it come to this, that old folks can not talk without being interrupted by the young?" As this was before some of my parishioners, I felt a blush flash over my face, and gave a very polite apology, stating that I supposed he had ceased speaking. I saw that his hasty remark troubled him. As he rode home he went several miles to see my colleague. When brother Hill saw me again, he said, "What did you do to our elder when he was last with you, that you are placed up so high in his estimation? He came several miles to see me, and staid only a little while, but all his talk was a eulogy on A. M. L., and he finally concluded you were the greatest gentleman in the Ohio Conference." I told him the good brother had—hastily—insulted me, and I suppose he thought it would be too much to make amends in person, and had taken that opportunity to do it by proxy. He grew more and more devoted to his favorite calling, and has gone up on high, like a ripe ear, to swell the garner of his Lord. O, may I be a partaker of that bliss!

CIRCLEVILLE CIRCUIT.

1840–1. On this circuit I was in connection with brother T. A. G. Phillips. Although each of us had our own share in the variety that marks the Methodist ministry, yet we were happily yoked together. Soon after we commenced our labors a

Divine influence seemed to pervade the circuit; and although we sent messengers to crave help of each other, yet we both had our hands full. We, however, sometimes got together. My colleague had been carrying on a good work in Kingston when I came to his assistance. One night, supposing the times favorable, I hoisted all sail and took a cruise. Our meeting-house doors were each side of the pulpit, and what some called the devil's half acre was abaft the congregation. As we began to make land under cheering circumstances, I exhorted the mourners to come on while I was yet preaching, and began to portray the awful shipwreck of the soul on the iron-bound shores of eternal damnation; and in the midst of the bursting of timber, the crash of masts, the thunder of parting bolts and sweeping breakers, the sinners made almost a general rush toward us. One stream down each aisle shot through the door, like thunder, and the other stream dropped around the altar, and cried for mercy. My colleague braced right up to the wind, till he saw what was the nature of the coming hosts, and then he sprang into the altar, opening an awful broadside that seemed to make the moral atmosphere shake. In going round he saw a wicked tavern-keeper down on his beam ends, and he cried out, "Salvation! here's the devil's own major-general down on his bends!" We made a great haul before we were done. One thing is worthy of remark: this work was in the midst of the most exciting political canvass we ever had; and although we both avoided the stump, through grace, yet every man, who came through, came out on the right political side. The two parties, which then were, are dissolved, and it might be no offense to say which was the right side; but lest we might turn up some latent spark, we simply say *the right side;* and if you, reader, were on the right side, then they came out on *your side.* A wicked politician, hearing this, said, he would to God all the world would get converted.

But whether we worked together or singly, the Word of the Lord had free course. A society at one end of the circuit requested me to give them preaching for one week. I began Monday night, and continued through the next Sunday without any ministerial help, excepting one sermon on the Sabbath. We took in about fifty members. There was one singular circumstance connected with this; I did not preach at all to my own satisfaction, and sometimes found it hard work. When I looked at the effects I was astonished. I was astonished at the work in connection with the paucity of the means. While on this subject I will add, that on a certain occasion I was traveling to Cincinnati in company with a preacher; we concluded to stop at a camp meeting on the road, and feed. While there they put me up to preach. I felt greatly in the brush, and thought my sermon entirely out of place. It was on sanctification. About fifteen years after, I fell in company with a brother who asked if I was not at that camp meeting, and if· I did not preach on such a text. I told him I·did, but thought it was poor preaching. "Well," added he, "I wanted to tell you that that sermon was salvation to me." Another singularity to offset this is, I have sometimes preached when there was no sign of external good, when my own soul was overwhelmed with the subject; when it has appeared to me as if grace and peace have flowed out in a circle and returned into my own bosom, in good measure, pressed down and running over. Almost four hundred souls on this circuit professed religion that year. Numbers of them belonged to the Church, as seekers, for years, but this revival brought them through. I continued on the circuit another year, and our societies were blessed and edified. On the last year I had two very severe spells of_ sickness, and it was reported in some places that I had died. Dr. Brown waited on me with all the tender solicitude of a brother, and when I called upon him for my bill, which I expected would be heavy, and justly so in view of his untiring services, he smiled, and said, "*Nothing at all.*" Some of our leading members said he should lose nothing, for they would promote his practice as much as was in their power. A few months after I left I was rejoiced to hear he had embraced religion, and joined the Presbyterian Church. All the doctors called to see me in my illness, and said, if at any time Dr. Brown was absent, it would give them pleasure to wait on me. The apothecary was equally generous in his department. I can never forget the tender care with which I was watched over by the young brethren in the Church by night and day. When my last spell of sickness was arrested I could not hold a pen in my fingers so firmly as to write. My mind was enfeebled as much as my body, and in the utter absence of all appetite, I concluded I would never engage again in the useless and dirty work of eating. I argued that there was substance enough in water to sustain life, and thought if I could be only settled down by a clear spring, I would ask no more. I continued in this way till my wife had serious apprehensions that I would die with starvation. One day some of the brethren brought a large fish they had caught in the Scioto. When I saw this a kind of recollection of past agreeable acquaintance induced me to taste a piece, then my appetite returned at once, like a cataract. Three weeks embraces the amount of time that I have been detained from my work by sickness in the course of forty years. I have had considerable sickness, but not of such a nature as to lay me up.

About this time Bishop Hamline, who was then editor of the Repository, solicited me to write for that monthly. I was surprised that he should make such a request of me, but in explanation he said that none of those on whom he had principally relied would come to his help, and he was almost alone in the work. I complied with his request, and contributed to that magazine for several years, and till the literati came to its succor, and I found the editors were furnished with more material than they could manage.

The great centenary celebration came on while we were on this circuit. On that day I preached to an overflowing congregation, in Circleville, on "The weapons of our warfare are not carnal, but mighty through God to the pulling down of strong-holds." And my colleague and myself raised a subscription of about thirteen hundred dollars, in cash, land, etc., on the circuit. The enthusiasm of the Methodists on that occasion was grand; indeed, the Church there was in that day called, faithful, and chosen; and we hope they have not degenerated.

XXVIII.

URBANA STATION.

1842. My next circuit was London. The first part of the year the weather was open, and the long roads were very muddy. I had a little horse that was as active as a deer, and it would have puzzled the ingenuity of man to trip him. However, the creature had a hard gait, and splashed the mud about like a beaver, so that, often, on my return home, horse and man would look as if they were lathed and plastered.

About this time I was taken with an affliction in my loins, which has been like a thorn in my flesh ever since, and has compelled me finally to cease riding. While it has been wasting me away, my external appearance has been robust and healthy.

I was now so worn out that it appeared I could ride no longer. In my distress I wept, and called on the Lord. One cold, rainy day, as I was riding home through the mud, after hard labor, I saw a person riding toward me, with his head braced against the storm. As he passed he handed me a letter. It was from my presiding elder, and directed me to remove, as soon as I could, to Urbana. This I gladly received as an express call from above. I was not glad because I was going to exchange my circuit for a station merely. The London circuit at that time was a good circuit for any one in perfect health. The brethren had liberally supplied my table, stable, and wood-yard, and it was not necessary to lay out much money. Still, in my gloomy moments, it seemed to me that the people cared but little about me. They were a prudent people, and were not given to flattery. It is said, in order to get a good name a man should die; and I would have never known the estimate that the Church in London had placed on me, had not my ministerial term so suddenly expired. As soon as my orders were known, there was almost a general insurrection against my elder. Some of the leading men said they would not let me go, unless I would promise, as soon as I could, to come and ride their circuit again. I told them I did not choose my places, for that was contrary to Methodism; but if the bishops should appoint me there again, I would cheerfully come—so I would. Again, I was not glad of the providence that led to my removal. The health of brother Christie, which had been waning for some time, was about exhausted. With tottering steps he would ascend the pulpit in Urbana, against the expostulations of his best friends. He would begin his services in a feeble voice; but, gathering interest and animation in his subject, his eyes would flash up, his nerves tighten, and he would pour forth his eloquence in his wonted volume of voice, as in days gone by. Having the consumption, he appeared to be entirely insensible of the nearness of his death. A Presbyterian brother visited him in the parsonage, and spoke of his rapid decline, and made some religious remarks on his removal, very soon, to the spirit-land. When he retired, Christie looked round with a smile, and said, "That good brother thinks he knows all about my complaint." When he determined to visit his friends in Cincinnati, he was so feeble that the brethren had made arrangements to send a friend to drive. This he would not listen to; he felt all-sufficient for the journey. He could not drive far, and his wife, who had never been accustomed to horses, had to take the reins, although she had a young child. When told by his brother-in-law, an experienced physician, that death was upon him, he seemed to be surprised—but in a few moments observed that he was ready, and thanked God that he had not preached an unfelt Savior. He died calmly, resigned, happy.

It was something of a cross to follow immediately this seraphic minister; and the people, doubtless, felt the change, but they were too good to let me know it; and I preached here nearly two years more with improving congregations. Brother Christie had a most extraordinary revival, both as it regarded numbers and its singular type. We hardly know whether the word revival is suitable, as the work was almost altogether among the irreligious, while the Church was comparatively in a lifeless state, and receiving so many converts into the Church was like putting a live child into the arms of a dead mother. We often heard the members conversing about that work, and wondering at it. When mourners were called to the altar, they would come promptly and in crowds. The members would stand back amazed, and the heaviest work of the preacher was to persuade them to the work. Although they had generally been a working Church, yet they had to be almost compelled to come up. One of the leaders—about the best leader in our Conference—when brought up almost by compulsion, told me that he could hardly find a word to say to the mourners. They would frequently say to each other, "When will this meeting close?" and some of them expressed a wish that it might close. The backsliding that followed this work was also singular. A great number had gone back before I came to the station, and many went after.

Another difficulty that met me at my coming was a division of opinion in regard to the music. A preacher who preceded Christie had put a choir in the gallery. When Christie came he put it down. The singers thought they were too lightly esteemed, and refrained from taking any part in the singing. Many who were opposed to choirs could not sing. There was one very pious brother who could not sing much better than myself, who was our only dependence. Some of the young men said if he did not quit singing "John Grimes" they would whip him. And we evidently needed some improvement in this department. I was waited on by persons on both sides of the question, and I listened complacently to their reasons and arguments, and told them that I required some little time to examine the subject. After examining the Discipline I waited on one of our principal singers, and told him that the gallery was only a question of place, and if he would assist me I would revive the singing in the center of the congregation. He spoke to other singers, and they agreed to this. I told two of them to take their stations under the main lamp the next Sunday, and to invite some females to do so on their side, as leaders; and to invite other good singers to sit by them, and all to be in place before public service. On the Sabbath v? arose with the Discipline in my hand and observed, that we had had some difficulty about singing, and all would admit that there was room for improvement; that it was well known that a difference of opinion existed in that Church on the subject, but as a minister there was but one course for me. When I entered into orders I promised to adminster the Discipline with a mild but *firm* hand. Now, what says the Discipline on this very subject? "If you can not sing yourself choose a person or two, at each place, to pitch the tune for you. Exhort every person in the congregation to sing." This is the order of the Discipline, and I am sure I am in the path of duty. I appoint these two brethren to pitch the tune—mentioning their names. I have stationed them under the large lamps, where they will, on evenings, have the greatest body of light, and where their voices will reach all the walls of this spacious building at once, and where they will not displace the old members. Every one in the house is exhorted to sing with them. We struck off delightfully, and the singing increased in purity and melody every Sabbath, till it was enchanting; and strangers from the eastward said they had heard no better singing in the Atlantic cities.

I mention this because difficulties often arise about singing, and the devil is never better pleased than when he can turn this part of divine worship into contention and strife. It has been my rule never to put up a choir ¬here there has never been one, and not to pull down a choir where it is. In either case it will raise a smoke in the wigwam. I believe in improving in singing as well as in other matters. The people of Urbana deserve great credit. At the time we are reviewing, they had spent fifteen hundred dollars in the acquisition of vocal music, and they had then a most accomplished teacher. During my short stay on London circuit I was associated with brother John Steele, with whom I renewed fellowship in travel in subsequent years. Brother Zachariah Connell was our presiding elder. It is doubtful whether the Ohio Conference, in all its history, ever had a better. He was clad in pure Methodism, in doctrine, discipline, and usage. He was a strong preacher, argumentative and forcible; and with the professing congregation, on Monday mornings, tender, melting, and experimental. I never heard him preach without wishing I could have his sermon written as it fell from his lips. He only wanted the voice and delivery to make him perfect in preaching.

We had a revival in Urbana. The work was not so great among the irreligious—we only received about fifty new members—but the Church was very lively, and some professed to receive sanctification. We suppose there is not a more pleasant station in the Conference than Urbana. Many of the old members have passed into their rest. May the smiles of Heaven rest upon their offspring!

XXIX.

HAMILTON STATION—MONROE CIRCUIT.

HAMILTON STATION.

1843. HAMILTON is one of the most pleasant places in our State; and, in our day, we had flush congregations. But we received the charge with a great drawback; Millerism was then in its zenith—perhaps a little beyond. It had infected the Church, not in the extremities, but it had disordered its head by getting hold of some of the officiary. We say *some;* the larger part of that department was sound. We saw clearly that we could not get *round* it, still we fully comprehended the delicacy of laying a hand upon it, and saw the propriety of the caution of the Discipline—"*mild but firm.*" As it was the all-absorbing subject, we so far took to the current as to give our views on the subject.

We have always believed that where a charge is endangered by any besetting evil, it is the duty of the preacher to pay attention to that evil in a prudent manner. Under this impression we have sometimes had to make almost a new set of sermons. To preach sermons that would suit equally New York, Cincinnati, or any other place, when a deadly evil is eating up our charge, is nothing more than stage-horse monotony. In Hamilton we undertook to show that however startling the figures of Mr. Miller might appear to some, he was wrong in their application. The *end* that the vision of Daniel referred to was not the end of the world. What did such a good man as Daniel care about the end of the world? One who could sleep all night with a lion for his pillow and a tiger for his footboard, had no effeminate tremors about the end of the world. As a captive Jew he did mourn over the prostration of the Church of the living God. Jerusalem was in ruins, and all the pleasant things of Mount Zion laid waste. He fasted, wept, and prayed, and desired to see an *end* to the desolation of the Church, and he cried out "how long? how long? O Lord!" The vision itself was not to gratify the curiosity of an individual, but to comfort the Church for ages to come.

We endeavored also to show that the end—the restitution of Israel—would be the birthday of the kingdom of Christ, the universal reign of grace; that this glorious reign would last more than three hundred thousand years; that the very structure of the earth seemed to favor this doctrine, inasmuch as we had barely lifted the crust and entered on the thresholds of immense beds of minerals suited to the wants of a civilized and Christianized world for ages to come; and our earth was supplied with a cargo and all necessary small stores for the eventful voyage. We showed them that the vision of John, in the Isle of Patmos, agreed with this view, putting the millennium before the day of general judgment. We argued that their doctrine was wrong because it troubled the Churches. The same doctrine was broached in the apostles' day, and one of them wrote to the Churches *"Be not troubled."* It troubles the Churches now. We did not at first think it would. We said, Supposing it is false, if Christians believe the judgment is immediately impending, surely they will live more holy, have more love for God and man. Vain thought! The errors of man can not work the righteousness of God. The Church is troubled now; separate prayer meetings are established, in which old and faithful members are regarded as infidels, however bright their experience or holy their lives; they lack the *sine qua non*, faith in the doctrines of Millerism. The preachers are publicly denounced as blind leaders of the blind. And does all this look like being prepared for the coming of the Lord?

Again, the argument of Miller is in direct opposition to that of Christ. Millerism says, "Because we know the day, we will watch and pray." Christ says, "Because you *know not* the day, watch and pray." Here the *"knowing not* the day" is the argument why we should watch and pray; and the argument is natural as well as evangelical. Suppose a man should receive a letter from his father, that he has not seen for many years, stating that he would spend a particular day—say Friday—at his house; that man would not watch for his father on any other day. If pressing business should call him away on Monday, Tuesday, or Wednesday, he would go. But, suppose the letter should state that his father would be at his house some time next week; then he would watch for him all the time. If business or pleasure should call, he would say, I can not go, I must watch for my father, for I *know not* the day he will come; he watches *all the time.*

But we had something to do besides preaching. Our Church was in a bad way. At our official meeting, one leader complained that his class had ceased to meet him, but still he seemed to have no notion of resigning. I told him I would take his book, and visit the whole class immediately. The class was made up mostly of females. Their testimony was generally to this amount: "We love class meeting; but our leader, of late, asks each of us if we are just ready to go to judgment. We answer, we can not say that we are. We love God, and are trying to serve him; and we believe that he will give us grace for that day when it comes. He then denounces us as in the gall of bitterness—lost, and undone. Such class meetings do us no good." At the next official meeting we made a faithful report, without censuring the leader.

Some of the members said they believed, if their class should abandon them thus, they would at once resign. Such talk went round, without any reflections on the leader, till at last he grasped the idea, and threw up. Thus one of the latter-day saints was eased off without violence.

Two of our exhorters were propagating Miller's doctrine, especially the annihilation of the wicked. We had a calm interview with one, and, after hearing his statement, asked him if he was well assured that the doctrine was Scriptural. He said he was not as well satisfied as he wished to be on the subject. He read many passages that seemed to favor it, and then he saw some Scriptures that seemed to be against it, and his own mind was not settled. Then, brother, do you think it safe and right to preach to others doctrines concerning which you yourself are doubtful? He said it did not seem right; and he would promise to desist till, after a longer investigation, he might be convinced the doctrine was of God. Thinking that, if he would do this, we might be able to manage the case, we went to see the other brother. He obstinately held to his views, and was zealous to convert us. We told him that many of the brethren were dissatisfied, and perhaps some of them would call for an explanation at the quarterly conference, which was soon to be held, and then he would have an opportunity of defining his position. At that conference, some of the officiary stated that there were unfavorable reports concerning that brother's orthodoxy, and he rose up, and gave an honest exposition of his faith, and his license was withdrawn. Then the first-mentioned exhorter took fire, rose to defend his colleague, and in so doing committed himself, and lost his license. They still continued in the Church, but stripped of their power to do harm.

Another man, who had exercised considerable influence in the Church, read, in the Advocate, a communication under the caption of "The Setting Goose." He found out, somehow, that I was the author. And, although there was nothing personal or local in it, but merely an exhibition of the deathless "hang-on" of Millerism, it afforded an opportunity, and he came to withdraw from the Church. We expostulated, and showed the unreasonableness of his forsaking God and the Church, merely because a brother, in a free country, had expressed an opinion contrary to his own. O, he was not going to forsake God; he was more devoted than ever—loved his Bible better, because he understood it better.

"Brother, you may think so now; but let me tell you, you are driving fast toward the whirlpool of infidelity, and it will not be long before your Bible will be covered with dust, and you will lay it aside like a loathsome thing. Your family altar, too, will be cast down; and when you find that the Lord will not burn up our world at your beck and call, you will spurn his service."

He smiled at my simplicity, and took his departure. Nevertheless, all these things came to pass.
About three weeks before the world was to be
burned up, the said man, supposing he saw a speculation, traded off his property in Rossville for a
place in Hamilton. We saw another distinguished
disciple, about the same time, setting out fruit trees
not much larger than a rattan-cane. We looked
over his fence, and said, "Brother, how long will it
be before these trees will bear fruit?" He appeared
to be considerably nettled by the question. It is
astonishing how people will torment a whole Church
with something that they themselves can not believe!

They finally brought up from Cincinnati the great
tabernacle. The people went to see it through the
week as a curiosity, and its priests expected on the
Sabbath to empty all the churches. But Israel
abode in their tents, and the vast proportions of the
tabernacle served to display more fully its discouraging emptiness. The people of Hamilton were
denounced as irreclaimable, and the tabernacle
returned to its rest. In answer to one of our arguments the preacher said he frankly admitted that
in the Apocalypse the millennium was placed before
the day of judgment, but he could easily account
for that. The apostles wrote on separate slips, and
the fathers, in binding the book, had got the day of
judgment shuffled out of its place. This was received with a broad grin of approbation. And who

32

could withstand such intimacy with the blunders of the fathers?

Through the mercy of God we got rid of this pestilence, and without a single expulsion. Still, those who were involved in this error had their relations or connection in the Church; and although they did not participate in their views, and sometimes ridiculed them in the family circle, yet they were their kin, and they did not wish others to touch them. So, although my congregation was as large as it ever was before, and, perhaps, has been since, yet I concluded that I had done a good work, and laid a smooth platform for a successor; so I earnestly entreated the presiding elder to procure me a circuit next year. This he did, but declared I should not have been removed, only on my own solicitation. My brother's daughter, that we had raised from a child—Ellen—was married and settled in Hamilton. We feel very much attached to the place, for we had many kind friends there. We regard Hamilton as one of the best stations. May the Lord have the people in his holy keeping!

MONROE.

1844. This year we removed to Monroe, a small but very pleasant charge, abounding with loyal Methodists. Here we had the satisfaction of residing with brother Connell, our presiding elder; and we became more and more attached to him as we became better and better acquainted. On one circuit, where I labored, the people did not like him at first sight, especially when he undertook to reform their order in quarterly conference, which, by the by, was no order at all. But when his term expired they voluntarily passed resolutions highly eulogizing his character, and thanking him for the reformation he had made in their councils, and for what he had taught them of law, order, and Methodism. Connell never suffered himself to kick back, but left all to God, conscience, and time, and he always triumphed.

We had large congregations on this circuit, good meetings, great peace, but no extra revival. Monroe has lately become a station, and of the first order, we are told. It is situated in a beautiful part of our State. In our day they had a large Presbyterian connection around.

XXX.

PUTNAM STATION.

1848. IT was by hard traveling that I reached this station on Saturday evening — my goods all lying topsy-turvy, and my preaching tacks not on board. I do not know but that the people thought it was a slim chance. One intelligent brother said, "Why, you don't look like I thought you would. I have read your communications in the Repository and Advocate, and I had painted to myself a tall, slim, scholastic-looking man; but, but—"

An old veteran, who knew me in years gone by on the Zanesville circuit, passed among them, and said, "Be still! I'll go his security."

What a prestige! a thin man and a pair of green spectacles! In a few weeks the brethren began to draw nigh to me, and I drew nigh to them; and in process of time I became entirely too popular. Some of them, supposing I was impervious to temptation, would praise me to my face, and I got alarmed, and pressed closer to my closet and my knees, and hoped the Lord would not kill me or do me any harm, because the members were so imprudent. When my year was out they expressed a wish for me to come

back. On this point I have always expressed myself as uncertain, and as being at the disposal of the
bishops. This perhaps made them suspicious of me;
so two of the stewards attended Conference, and
watched the bishops and watched me till my appointment was fixed. When my second year was
expiring, and in one of our last official meetings,
one, speaking for all, said,

"Brother L., if our Discipline would admit it, we
would agree with the bishops to take you for five
years to come. You preach the Gospel in every
sermon, and yet you have never preached two sermons alike."

When I first came on this circuit the leading
members said they had heard I was a great disci-
plinarian, and they wished that I would prune their
Church, for there was great delinquency in regard
to attending class and other matters. I told them
this would depend in a great measure on themselves;
that discipline must begin with them; charges must
originate with them. If members could not be persuaded by them to attend class, they must hand me
their names; then it would be my duty to see
them, and if they would not reform, I would have
to bring them to trial. They took me at my word,
and I had enough to do. We had to lay aside
some forty or fifty from time to time. The next
year I read in the Advocate of a revival there. At
this my heart rejoiced, and after a while we visited
them. I was congratulating some of the brethren

on the work they had had. They smiled, and said, "Yes, brother, we have taken in again all you cast overboard, without any promise of doing better, and they don't attend their classes any better than they did before they were put out. This is the revival, with the addition of a few who never belonged."

I felt in my heart, "I have labored in vain, and spent my strength for naught."

The two years spent in Putnam were unusually pleasant. Brother Dustin had the old charge, and brother Warnock the new, in Zanesville during that time; and we were truly a threefold cord. We had a social, happy time with our families. When the Zanesville friends invited their preachers to break bread, they would frequently invite us, and the Putnam friends would return the compliment. The upper room of Warnock's church being finished, it was determined to have a dedication. One of our bishops was to preach the sermon; but he sent word after a while that he could not come. They then tried to get a distinguished preacher from the city, but he could not come; time rolling on. So I supposed one of their own ministers would preach it. True, *they* had been joking, as I thought, me about it. A few days before—perhaps the Friday before—the set time, a member from Zanesville came over, and opening his hymn-book, pointed out two hymns, and said,

"Brother Lorrain, the sisters have selected these two hymns to be given out at the dedication."

"But stop, brother," said I, "you should carry them to brother Warnock or Dustin, as the case may be."

"Why? It has been given out for you to preach the dedication."

I was confounded, if I know what *confounded* means. At first I was tempted to think the preachers, in view of an expected disappointment, had concluded to lay the burden on Jonah, as a scape-goat. But I had to say, "Down, down, busy devil, try it again;" for they were too good to play this game. So, at the time appointed, we gathered up our good singers to add to the choir, and all our praying folks followed. The music was extra, and I felt something like Saul, the son of Kish, under the melody of David's harp, and preached to the crowded congregation. We had a mellow time, and when I closed, brother Brush and the trustees pitched in, and before the benediction was given they wiped off the whole debt as clean as a woman would wipe a dish, turning it upside down. Hush! Let me tell it, for I never dedicated but three houses in all my travel.

Let not the reader suppose that because we magnify the kindness of the people of Putnam, that we never were popular before or since. We only give this as an example of sunshine, we have sometimes had our clouds and conflicts, met with oppositions and inflictions from members, that would make a pious Chinese blush; but we lay all our wrongs before the throne, firmly settled in the decree, "*Vengeance is mine, and I will repay.*" And we have sometimes viewed with astonishment the cup of trembling as it has passed round.

There is one circumstance connected with this station which should be mentioned, as it has a bearing on the Discipline. The Presbyterian Church in Putnam had generally a pious membership. They were closely allied to the Methodists by relationship and marriage connections. They had been in the habit, under all administrations, of communing with our people. For some time they had ceased to do so. Our people naturally inquired why they had discontinued communing. "Because," said they, "your elder has never given us the accustomed invitation." At our next quarterly conference some of our leading men introduced a resolution respectfully requesting the presiding elder to invite to our sacrament members of other Churches. The elder said he could not conscientiously do this, as the Discipline expressly showed that persons of other Churches could not be admitted without a token. I saw that a storm was gathering, and in order to allay it I rose and observed, "That as it regarded the token, I had never seen one in my life, and would be altogether at a loss to make one. We had been told that some Churches made them out of lead; but how, or with what tools, we knew not. Still, the presiding elder had the Discipline on his side, and it would be wrong to require him to go against his conscience; but if the Discipline was altered, conscience would be met. Now, the General Conference will meet in Pittsburg before our next quarterly conference, and I suggest that a committee be appointed to petition it on the subject." This idea gave another turn to the matter. They appointed a committee, and passed a resolution that the elder should lay the subject before all the quarterly conferences. I was chairman of the committee, and drew up a paper, with as much ginger in it as the solemnity of the occasion could bear. Presently we read, in the Pittsburg daily, that a petition was received from Putnam in regard to the sacrament of the Lord's Supper, and was referred to a committee. Presently we read that a petition, counter to the above, had been remitted by the presiding elder.

At last we read that the clause in the Discipline requiring a token, etc., had been struck out. At the next quarterly conference, on Saturday night, I reminded the elder that the "*token*" had been abolished, and our people would expect him to give an invitation to members of other Churches. He said he would not do it. After giving out several appointments, he said brother L. might give out his appointments. I invited all in good standing to meet us at the Lord's table on the Sabbath. They came, and we had a delightful communion. Now, if there is any credit due for flinging away that obsolete, or rather never-used "*token*," let the

33

Church of Putnam have her share. Did I say never used? I might add, used only by some of our Baptist brethren, when they flirt it in our face, as an evidence of our close communion. And this they have done often since the rule has been repealed. But we can say, "*Ou est le papier?*"

XXXI.

ASBURY CIRCUIT—HARMAR STATION.

1849. WE had been kindly stationed in Putnam in order to recover our health; and there was a fine prospect of restoration. But, at the next Conference, I was thrown on one of the most difficult circuits I ever rode, and my saddle disease returned in all its force. In riding up one hill and down another, my situation in the saddle became so painful that I often had to get down and walk. On one occasion I walked, and led my horse, seven miles through unbroken snow and mud; and, when I got home, felt as if I had taken my last promenade. But I made the best of it, and carried out a scheme which had been devised the previous year, and to all my other gettings I added the French language, so far as to find access to its literature. Perhaps, if I could have endured another year, I might have attacked the Hebrew, for my faculties were stretched out to their extreme tension by the things which I had suffered.

We had several revivals at different points, but had to loosen our grip of many of our spoils before the year was out. Indeed, in one place, we had to drop nearly all. The converts were of Baptist raising, and their relations appeared as if they would rather see them lost than to be united to the Methodists. They were most violent against them, and would say, "Wait till the 'Old Horn' comes." This was a nickname they had given to their preacher—intended as a compliment—who, they supposed, had all the treasures of wisdom. When Old Horn came, he decided that they had not begun to know any thing about true religion; they had only fallen into Methodist delusion. And, as he piqued himself on wit, he publicly caricatured Methodism, so as to place it before them in a ridiculous light. Through all this they could see his dishonesty, because he strongly urged them all to join his Church. Their high delusion would in a moment form an *experience* sufficient to introduce them into *his Church*. But they scorned his proposals, though they were driven back—some of them, we fear, to perdition. A number of them had given satisfactory evidence of a real conversion. And some held fast their confidence.

When the "Old Horn" had succeeded in scattering the Baptist children, he said, with great exultation, "I told you so; once in grace always in grace." I love good Baptists, whether preachers or members; and it has been my lot to know many such. But the preachers of that part of the country were dram-drinkers, and they were not ashamed of it. When they stopped at a house, the jug was immediately seen traveling to the grocery. One of the preachers was heard to say he did like to take a dram before preaching, because it took away the fear of man. This same man came out to the grove to hear Ebenezer Chase preach on temperance. He stretched himself along a log, and prepared to hear in such a way as might indicate his contempt of both the preacher and the cause. Chase had occasion to speak of ministers who were opposed to temperance, and, among other things, observed, "I have heard of a minister—not a hundred miles from here—who said he liked to take a dram before preaching, because it took away the fear of man, which is a snare." The gentleman sprang up into a decent position, and his face flushed a deeper red; and well it might, for the eyes of the whole congregation were fastened on him.

Ebenezer Chase was a Methodist preacher of the highest order. He was always successful; and lived in the affections of the people of his charge. And yet some of his distant friends hardly know that he has, years ago, reached the haven. We are almost tired of reading, for successive years, the eulogies of our classical brethren who have made good marks as they passed along, and are worthy of remembrance; but others, whose apostolic epistles are scattered over all the land, are laid by almost in silence. The reason is, those of blue ribbon and green spectacles can not—and ought not—forget their chums; and we of the saddle-bag class ought to do likewise—that is, when we get a chance. So,

Ebenezer, Ebenezer! "if departed spirits are permitted to review this world," look down complacently on one with whom thou hast taken sweet counsel in the days of thy pilgrimage, and accept this small record of thy worth. And let all who read say, amen.

My colleague on this circuit was Sanford Haines, a very promising young married man. He emigrated, next year, to Iowa, to enter on broad fields of future usefulness.

We took in many members; but, as a new circuit was made the year previous, we can not tell how many were taken from us, and consequently can not find what the increase was by the Minutes.

HARMAR STATION.

1851. This was a beautiful town at the junction of the Muskingum and Ohio Rivers. It was, for the time being, the residence of our presiding elder, who was once one of the brightest boys in our Xenia Sunday school—Uriah Heath. The town of Marietta was on the opposite bank. The towns were subject to partial overflows occasionally; but, through mercy, they were exempt during our sojourn. We had a pretty little meeting-house, but the ceiling was unusually low—only a few feet above the pulpit.

On a quarterly meeting occasion the house was closely crowded one night, and it was my lot to preach. The elder requested me to call up mourners before I was done. As I rose up in the vitiated atmosphere I felt very sensibly oppressed; I, however, finished my sermon, and was exhorting sinners, when all at once a singular unconsciousness—in regard to what I was saying—came over me. I suppose I talked ten minutes or a quarter of an hour, something that I could not comprehend then, and which I could not remember after. The thought struck me that I had been talking nonsense or something irrelevant to the occasion, and I sat down utterly dismayed. Mourners came up, and the elder carried on the meeting; but I got low in the pulpit, and felt greatly ashamed. When I got home I found that I could not remember the names of my near neighbors. When I learned from my elder that I had said nothing out of the way, and that he wondered that I staid in the pulpit, I felt greatly relieved in my mind. He stated that he had experienced the same thing occasionally. The doctor said it was prostration by too much labor and watching, and that I must rest. I was not able to continue the meeting, and as the elder was alone, and had to leave soon, the meeting was closed. A minister preached there one night, but just after he commenced he had to stop and order them to open all the windows. He believed his very life was in danger.

It was while here that I published my "Sea-Sermons." Brother J. F. Wright kindly undertook the supervision of the publication in Cincinnati.

When the manuscript was prepared and directed to its destination, I took it into an upper room, laid it in a chair, and kneeled down to spread it before the Lord with all my motives and purpose; but as I bowed down a powerful influence almost pressed me to the floor, and I felt that the work was approved. In my travels I had clear evidences of the efficacy of these sermons, *viva voce*, and since their publication I have received from distant parts, by correspondence, testimony of their utility. What may be in the future is unknown, but I believe, in presenting them before the Lord, I had a clear spiritual indication that they were accepted.

My motives as expressed to my fellow-men were these: There has been of late years a great reformation among seamen. Bethels have been established and chaplains have been appointed in many ports, both at home and abroad; and many cheering revivals have taken place. We believe that all this has been by the direction of a wise and holy God. When our Savior began to preach his everlasting Gospel, he chose his ministers principally from the sea. True, it was an inland sea—a lake; but still it was the sea of God's chosen nation. And in bringing in the latter-day glory, it should not be incredible that seamen should be called to bear an important part.

The author of this work spent the morning of his life on the sea, both before and abaft the mast. His heart and his affections still twine around his shipmates. The most lifelike dreams that come over him in the slumbers of the night are rigged in marine scenery. Then he is on board, either as a missionary or a sailor, but always under a sense of religious obligations. At such times the motions of the ship, the peculiar odor of the rigging, the saline savor of the Atlantic atmosphere, are all realized with vivid certainty; but he awakes, and finds himself securely moored by domestic associations in the far West. He reads of the sailors' happy meetings, of their bright conversions, and would love to mingle in their sincere and artless communion; but his lot forbids. While he rejoices in the abundant ministerial provision which is made for seamen while in port, he knows that their brief stay on land is a kind of parenthesis in their being— a time of extraordinary excitement—of meeting and greeting of friends and connections, if not a time of indulgences less innocent. Perhaps there is no time when the sailor is so accessible to the Gospel as when he is at home—on the mountain wave. Then he is removed from many powerful temptations, and the sober realities of life are upon him. Then he has opportunity, in his watches below, to read and meditate on religious truths. We can hardly look forward to any time when every vessel can be supplied with a living minister. These considerations have moved the author to put out this volume. It may serve as a pocket companion for the sailor. The author sends forth the book humbly imploring the God of the land and the sea to follow it with his blessing, and to make it useful to many,

> "When his poor, lisping, stammering tongue
> Lies silent in the grave."

Soon after we left Harmar many of the leading members of the Church were removed by death in the space of a few weeks.

XXXII.

FULTON STATION—GENERAL CONFER·
ENCE.

1852. At the time we labored here there was a very energetic Church. The members were well gifted in prayer and exhortation—male and female—and our large house was generally well filled. I attended always the weekly prayer meeting, and can not say we ever had a lifeless prayer meeting, even when the streets were almost impassable, and we were reduced to two or three. The occupation of the people—boat-building and kindred works—render the community movable and vacillating; and they sometimes experience sudden reverses in their income, but they are always generous according to their means. This is what God requires, and no more. The members were scattered about two miles along the river, and this made visiting very laborious. Still this was modified through the omnibuses that were constantly passing and repassing. It is moreover a place of alternate mud and dust in their extremes. For these reasons the preachers are not content to make it their abiding place, with the exception of brother Joseph Reeder, who is one of our comically good men, and who might, without irreverence, be called "the angel of the Church at Fulton;" and if the pattern should fall any way short, his pious and devoted wife will make it up.

This year I had to attend the General Conference. I confess candidly I had no ambition to gratify. Although I had been ambitious, and once grasped, under our political government, two offices at once, and panted after more, yet when I devoted myself to the itinerancy I renounced the spirit, and have ever since dodged all kinds of Church promotion. Some may think it did not require very hard dodging. It is my business to record my testimony, nevertheless. Still my heart was made glad by the election, because it was to me such a cheering demonstration of the affection of my fellow-laborers in the vineyard of the Lord. This was more than honor, or silver and gold. And then, about this time, I had a longing desire to revisit the sea-board, and especially Boston, because it was the only sea-port of consequence on our coast that I had not seen. The brethren of the Ohio Conference knew very well that I would not thunder in the North; and it was a pure expression of their esteem. Let it be understood that we do not find fault with those who desire distinguished places, because they think they can do more good; but we would warn them that the higher they climb up in the Methodist Episcopal Church the more thorns and briers they will pass through. I have never envied those who are in authority, for some must be. The love of God throws down all distinction; and he who is good is my brother, whether he wears the thorny miter of a Methodist bishopric, or roasts his venison by the wild fires of the trackless prairie.

On our way to the General Conference we left Cleveland about dusk, under a lowering atmosphere, with the lake sufficiently rough to induce seasickness in those who were not accustomed to voyaging. Late in the evening supper was set. As we had no idea how many hundred passengers were on board, at the signal given, we entered the dining-room, and saw a very long table crowded with eaters, and as many more, standing back on each side, awaiting their turn. Our happy forerunners ate as leisurely as if it had been a thanksgiving board. When they were shoveling it down I thought to myself it was a useless operation, especially as it regarded the ladies, some of whom appeared as if they had never seen good things before; for I believed they could not retain their delicious tenants — having been on deck taking a scientific view of the prognostications. When the dishes were changed, and the second signal given, I thought I would take a reef in my usual gentility; so made a dash, but it was not a dash in. There were so many there who had been rougher raised than myself. At the third course I succeeded in sitting down, with about two hundred of the cream of the gentility, as I thought.

After supper the gale freshened, and many were

seeking convenient stands about the gunwale where
they might slyly throw away their fifty cents' worth;
others were strolling about the cabin like buckeyed
cows. After a while gagging became so fashionable
that no one seemed to be ashamed—sovereign fashion! Some of our preachers made from three to
seven offerings to Neptune, if he deigns to range
through fresh-water seas. We did not, however,
charge them with idolatry, as their sacrifices were
unwilling. About midnight the chambermaids
made a great fuss running up and down the stairs
of the ladies' cabin. We asked one how matters
went on below. She said, "O, sir, I wish you could
see! they are scattered on the carpet, and in their
berths, and every-where; nothing but gagging, lam-
entation, and woe." But I had no craving desire
to behold the scene. I had a hungry time in wit-
nessing the ingress, and could dispense with beholding the outcome. At first I had some little apprehension of an attack, as it had been so many years
since I had followed the seas, and I thought there
would be a kind of disgrace in getting seasick on a
lake. But I had no nausea at all, and was good for
my breakfast. So I wandered about the decks, and
enjoyed the storm, which awakened so many remembrances in my mind that I could not sleep. As night
set in, something like the following conversation was
heard among the hands, on the between-decks:

"We may calculate on having a greasy time before morning."

"Why so?"

"Why, because I never in my life sailed with a white horse on board without smoking for it."

"You do n't say we have a white horse on this boat?"

"Yes, worse still, we have two as snow-white creters with us as you ever clapped your skylights on."

"You do n't say!"

"Well, I can give you a bit of comfort to splice on to that. We have about a dozen Methodist preachers above, if I rightly twig the cut of their jib, going to the Gineral Conference, as they call it."

"Goola! if I had known that, this child would not have put his foot on board, this trip. White horses, and Methodist preachers! Look out, boys, for a rip-sneezer!"

We could but meditate awhile on the exactness with which the traditions of superstition have been handed down from generation to generation. Sailors have been shy of ministerial passengers ever since Jonah was launched overboard. This superstition has been cherished more by the erroneous doctrine that the devil has peculiar privileges with the wind and the sea. This they take as granted, without any waste of rhetoric or logic; and as they know that preachers meddle a great deal with his matters, they conclude that Old Nick would not be so green as to let slip a fair opportunity of making them feel his wrath. If sailors would study the narrative of Jonah, in connection, they would see that the "Lord"—not Satan—"sent out a great wind into the sea." This is agreeable to the doctrine of the Bible: "It is He that commandeth the stormy wind, that lifteth up the waves thereof." Moreover, Jonah was following the counsel of the wicked one, in attempting to flee from his duty, and his God; and it would be more rational to suppose that his deceiver, if he had it in his power, would have afforded him every facility—a fair wind and smooth seas—in carrying out his flight, even beyond recovery. But, on the other hand, if it is the Lord who holds the helm of affairs on the land, and on the sea—blow high, or blow low—then it is highly unreasonable to suppose that, as a general thing, he will destroy his embassadors, whom he has so impressively sent to the perishing nations of the earth. Indeed, considering the multitude of ministers who are passing and repassing on the seas, instances of shipwreck are few and far between.

The case of the lamented Cookman stands out from the general rule of Providence in bold contradistinction. He and his shipmates sank down in one of the secret places of the Almighty; and the attendant circumstances have not yet reached the living. The sufferings of the crew and passengers, in the face of death and eternity, might have been sufficiently protracted to have admitted of serious consideration, deep contrition, and faith unfeigned;

and, under the administrations of such an able preacher, the most, if not all, of the sufferers might have found their homes in heaven. If this was so, who would not say that such a great salvation was worthy of the sacrifice of the most unblemished of our flock? Who would not say that God crowned his seraphic ministry with a most triumphant close? As the disjointed steamer makes her last plunge, methinks I see his released spirit bounding above the foaming surface of the stormy deep, and, in its homeward flight, carrying his last sheaves with him.

"Servant of God, well done!"

In the account of another steamship disaster, we are told that many of the passengers were preserved several days on the hurricane-deck. As the last flickerings of hope began to withdraw from their aching bosoms, it was asked, in all the agony of humbled nature, "Is there no Christian on board?" One who had carried himself throughout the passage with a meek and lowly bearing, but, nevertheless, had his life hid with Christ in God, felt, doubtless, something of that responsibility that our Savior entertained, when the high-priest said, "I adjure thee by the living God, tell us whether thou be the Christ?" And he slowly rose up, and said, "Friends, I am an unworthy servant of the Lord." Scarcely had the last word fallen from his lips, before he was surrounded by all the passengers, male and female, imploring him to pray for their wretched
34

souls. He fell on his knees, and the grace, the unction, the fire of God's love which had been pent up in his swelling bosom, like the flames of a laboring volcano, burst forth in mighty irruptions of confession, intercession, and praise. Mercy and light came down; confidence in the providence of God sprang up; a sweet serenity lighted up every countenance; holy purposes were formed, and the Lord, in answer to prayer, soon delivered them out of all their distress, and brought them to the desired haven. Thus does the Lord often afford to his ministers and people opportunities of working their passage, by the salvation of souls, without destroying their bodies.

At other times the Lord displays to his preachers his power and his glory, in forms in which they are no where seen but in a storm at sea, that their reverence may be deepened, their theology improved, their imagination corrected, their souls ballasted, and they better prepared to discourse of the attributes of the Almighty and his marvelous mercy to the children of men.

In the mean time, while we admit that the superstition of the sailors is fully as pious as the clairvoyance, prescience, and witchcraft pretendedly connected with animal magnetism and spiritual rappings, still the fog must be swept away. The "angels of the waters" are abroad and are at work. The holy Gospel, like the mystic albatross—feared by the wicked, revered by the good—is shedding its glorious light. And doubtless the time will come when sailors will fear carrying blacklegs more than carrying white horses—will fear packs of cards more than lots of Bibles—will fear bar-keepers and grog-bruisers more than Methodist preachers. Yea, in the storm and in the calm, in life and in death, they will know that all things shall work together for good to them who love the Lord; to them who are the called according to his purpose.

We pushed on toward Boston, expecting the city was looking hard for us, as they had never had a General Conference before; but when we put up at our tavern we found no one knew, either the tavern-keeper, lodgers, or attachés, where the Conference was to be held, or whether there was any such thing as a General Conference. We looked surprised at them, and they looked back, surprised at our surprise. The tavern lodged, but did not feed travelers. We got neat rooms, and were told that whenever we felt like eating, there was a separate establishment below, where we might be accommodated. This was found to be a great advantage. We were not obliged to pay for things we never ate. We might breakfast at any hour from sunrise to noon; and dine any hour from noon to night. If we had no appetite we might omit breakfast, or dinner, or supper, or all three. We might eat cheap things, or things costly, and we made up the opinion, if a man only has where to lay his head, he may live cheaper in Boston than he can any where else—in town or country; but he must pay as he goes—no chance to swindle a week's board. We, however, soon found our allotted homes. It was my good providence to be placed in a pious, intelligent, social family of the name of Chandler. It is astonishing to myself that, in the course of four or five weeks, I should have formed such a tender attachment to a family I had never seen before. But they have ever since had a place in the catalogue of my friends and relatives.

On my first Sabbath it was in my way to promenade the wharves. I can not express the tranquillity that pervaded my whole being, as I snuffed up the most pleasant of all earth's effluvium — the aroma of the shipping; and as I turned a corner where a large anchor—best bower—was planted in the earth, I slapped its flukes with my hand with so much affection and faith unfeigned, that it rasped my whole constitution, and almost made me dance Juba, as the negroes say; and tears of fond remembrance rolled down my cheeks. I preached in Boston and East Boston; but the happiest Sunday I had was at Scituate, a place principally peopled with sailors or those in connection with the sea. Here, standing on a gentle hill, the whole coast to my right could be seen almost to Cape Cod, while before me spread out the blue sea. Vessels, large and small, were coming in and going out, and scenes of by-gone days swept over my mind, and all the remembrances of youth beckoned me out;

but my anchor was cast in the West. How strange it is that the pleasurable excitements of the sea are engraved on our mind, while its disasters and toils have perished in the wake! This was also a day of unusual religious enjoyment with myself, and I believe with every body else.

The most exciting question of this General Conference was the pew question. Our readers all know the result. Whether it was in consequence of the unusually-long railroad ride, or sedentary work, or a return to our old delicious diet—oysters and fish—I know not, I was extremely sluggish, and, under commonplace debate, inclined to doze. One day the brethren were debating about a bishop for Africa. The great concern with them seemed to be the fatality of the climate and the danger a bishop would run in landing on the coast. We had to listen to, what seemed to me, exaggerated accounts of that horrid strip of earth, till I became somewhat torpid and overpowered with something which was part dreamy, part fanciful, and part a morbid invention of the mind; and methought I saw an American packet, backing and filling on the coast of Africa. Then I saw a native pirogue come out, and a letter sent on shore, announcing the arrival of a Methodist bishop. I looked and beheld a procession of colored brethren embark in a coaster, and making for the packet she laid her bowsprit on the tafferel of the ship. Then I saw the candidates shin out on the bowsprit, while the bishop touched their heads with the longest boat-hook on board, and said, "Take thou authority," etc. Then the captain cried out, "Fill away, boys! tail up for Boston, the land of immortality and life, where bishops never die!" I thought how many blasphemous sinners, for the mere sake of gain, had explored the sickly rivers and putrefying fens of Africa to steal or buy negroes, and had returned in safety; and yet how doubtful we were about trusting a bishop there for one week to do the work of God! I was roused by indignation, and felt like saying, if I could have slipped in a word, which I could not, "Mr. President, I do not desire the office of a bishop—if I did, it would be no sin, as it is a good work—but if it could be made consistent with our constitution to make me simply a nuncio for six months, I will go to Africa, sit one week in Conference, and ordain the preachers, and come back, or Mary Lorrain shall be left a widow on the banks of the *Belle Riviere.*"

The Conference being over we returned with astonishing rapidity. At Buffalo I took a carriage in the evening, in the midst of a thunder-storm, for the steamer. A gentleman and his wife were with me. I never heard a woman pray harder than she did for her husband to wait till the next day. She wept and declared that they were going as to the slaughter. I could not blame her in view of the ragged lightning and bursting thunder, that were playing over our heads; but he told her that she was asking what was impossible, his trunks and money were all on board. We got on board and put out on the dark lake, in the hight of the storm. After we had cleared the pier I went down in the cabin. A preacher put his head out of a berth, and said,

"O, here is brother Lorrain! I am so glad you are come! Now I feel safe!"

"Brother," said I, "look here, don't pin your faith on my sleeve. The Lord could drown me as easy as any one on board."

"Yes," said he, "but you know how to manage the thing."

I told him the boat was under the supervision of the captain, and if he chose to drive her to ruin, I would not rise in mutiny; but he need not be alarmed, all was well. We soon resumed the cars, and got to home—sweet home.

I found that, in my absence, the spirit-rappers had invaded my territory; but by the help of the Lord, we soon laid them as far as the Church was concerned. We had good times and large congregations the whole year. The Lord bless Fulton, and supply them with men of warm hearts and sound minds!

XXXIII.

BETHEL CAUSE.

1853–54. HAVING been solicited, for several years, to take an active part in the "Western Seamen's Friend Society," I at last consented. The principal work assigned me was to edit the "Western Pilot," a paper exclusively devoted to the Society. This work I attended to industriously for two years, attending to all the work—packing and directing to upward of two thousand subscribers. My Sabbath work was to assist the chaplain at the floating Bethel, and to travel, preach on the subject, make collections, and gather subscribers. I was first solicited by brother Thomas Cooper to engage in this work. He was a young minister of extraordinary promise.

There is an opinion which is entertained by some good members of the Church, which should be corrected. It is thought that the Bethel cause is a novelty—one of the eccentric experiments which the nineteenth century, fruitful in theories, has rolled up; and that its results are of doubtful disputation. This view is very erroneous. Our enterprise is coexistent with Christianity itself. The great High-Priest of our profession was, emphatically speaking, a Bethel minister. The ordinary arena of his labor was the sea-shore. He who reads the New Testament, keeping this assertion in sight, will be surprised in noticing how much of our Lord's ministry was about the lakes. Indeed, he admitted it himself, in that solemn warning that he gave to the towns and cities on their borders. He made occasional excursions to Jerusalem, and elsewhere; but we soon trace him back again to the waters; and it is said, *"And he began again to teach by the seaside."* He began *again*—that is, he returned to his accustomed field of labor.

Now, we contend that this course—singular as it was—was most reasonable; and that it is no new thing to preach on the sea-shore, or on the boats and wharves. In all ages, the seas and the water-courses have been in advance in wickedness, and usually tend to corrupt more deeply the land; therefore, there was both mercy and wisdom in our Savior's labors to save first those who were nearest to ruin. The prophet Esaias saw this beginning of the Gospel, where he said, "The land of Zebulon, and the land of Napthalim, by the way of the sea, beyond Jordan, Galilee of the Gentiles: the people that sat in darkness saw great light; and to those which sat in the region and shadow of death, light has sprung up." The waters still have a tendency to corrupt the world, and will have till their streams are purified by grace. When we send a missionary to heathen lands, he not only preaches the incomparable doctrines of the Gospel, but insists upon their purifying power. He shows that Christian faith works by love, and produces practical holiness in those who believe. But presently a ship comes into port bearing the flag of some Christian nation. The natives now expect to see a community of living saints. But when they see some of the crew staggering along the beach, under the influence of intoxicating drink; when they see others engaged in strife and bloody rows; when they see others invading their family peace, corrupting the youth, and spreading disgusting contagion through their community; and above all, when they hear the name of Christ, which the missionary has taught them to venerate, blasphemed by those whom they suppose to be his professed followers, their hopes sink within them, and they begin to conclude that, whatever may be the claims of the Gospel as a theory, it is worthless in its results—and they cling with renewed tenacity to their old and time-honored superstitions.

We once heard a converted Indian telling a large congregation of the dampening influence that the conduct of wicked white men had on him, even after he had admitted the truth of the Gospel, and was earnestly seeking its consolations. But he observed that in traveling through our settlements, he had become satisfied on that point. He met with a goodly number who practiced the virtues that his missionary had preached; and he found that among both the white folks and Indians, it was only those who *obeyed* the Gospel of Jesus Christ who felt its power. But if we confine our observations to our Western waters, who does not see their corrupting influence? Why is it that wickedness prevails so much more in our lake or river ports, than it does in our rural or inland villages? Why is it that in our great commercial cities the nearer you approach our water streets, or wharves, the deeper you descend among the haunts of sin? Here they have their grog-shops, their screens, their brothels, and unless the tide of iniquity, on the waters, is staid, it will grow with the growth, and strengthen with the strength of our ever-swelling population. Indeed, when we look at the great marts of Europe, such as London and Liverpool, we find whole streets and alleys abandoned by the reputable, and given up to dissipation, lasciviousness, and wantonness; and over these dreary wastes no Sabbath shines. Why should we wonder that Christ began, and continued during his mission, to preach on the sea-shore? Why should we call this a new enterprise?

As it regards the results, they can not be of doubtful cast; for our Savior was successful. The people heard him gladly. They followed him up and down, and around the coast, and frequently so pressed upon him, that he had to enter into vessels, in order to address the immense crowd that covered the landing. When he entered into a house, it was blockaded beyond ingress or egress. Many believed, and the Church of Christ was built up. He drew the principal part of his apostles from the sea. When the proud Pharisees said they were ignorant and unlearned men, they meant no more than that they were not scientific, or what we in our day would call classical men. They doubtless had some education, and were men of sound mind, good judgment, bland disposition, and well furnished with natural gifts, necessary to the ministry. They were the best men, all things considered, that could be selected out of the Christian Church at that time; and that Church was a Bethel. Our Lord did not mean to reflect on sanctified learning; for as soon as the Church could afford it, he added to them Saul of Tarsus, who helped them mightily. Our Lord began on the sea, and we have no doubt he will end there; for sailors are eminently calculated to carry the Gospel to the ends of the earth. We do not mean altogether as ministers proper. We know that well-educated ministers are necessary to head our missions; but God has reserved to himself great missionary power in the membership. An apostle says of them, "You are a chosen generation, a *royal priesthood!*" Saul did, unintentionally, great good while he was persecuting the saints; for then the brethren were scattered every-where—but as they went they *preached* Jesus and the resurrection. These were laymen; for we are told that the apostles stood their ground. God *sent* the membership—driving them before a gale of persecution.

So God will send converted sailors to be, under Christ, for salvation to the ends of the earth. He will send them by the force of circumstances, by love to their families, by a sense of the duty of providing for their own, by an undying attachment to their profession, on voyages the most distant and adventurous, and wherever they touch they will leave a savor of life unto life. A learned ministry will have the advantage in some respects — the sailor-laity in. others. Sailors are *physically* superior; they have passed through all kinds of calms and storms, sunshine and frost, and their constitutions have become acclimated to every latitude. They will not stand before the heathen with eyes almost destroyed by the midnight lamp, and each with a pair of green spectacles on his nose. They will not whisper with a voice rendered almost inaudible by pulmonary weakness; but standing on the uncovered deck, will lift up their voice like a trumpet, and show the people their transgression, and the idolatrous natives their sins. Again, sailors are superior in experience. The learned minister is needed, and so is the experienced layman. Those who are educated for the ministry go into the college about seventeen or eighteen years of age. They come out in ripened manhood. All this brightest part of their lives they have been excluded, in a measure, from the world; and what do they know of men, matters, and things? It is not so with the adventurous Christian sailor. He has been compelled to study human nature, in all its eccentric windings. He has marked it in its various working, in different positions, and under multiform circumstances; and he is able to pencil down the sinner's presumptuous cruise, with all its traverse sailing, backing and filling, and to rout him out of every hidden cove, and refuges of lies, till his sins become hateful, and he flies from himself to a sin-pardoning God.

But what do we mean by thus magnifying our work? Do we mean that the voice of the Lord is heard only on the waters, and that our brethren of the interior should forsake their comfortable tabernacles, and come down to pray with us on the sea-shore? No; but we do mean to battle the idea that our undertaking is a new thing. When some are solicited to lend a hand, they look wondrously wild, and say, "Why, brother, this is a new thing. We have never heard of it before; it has not been spread before our people before, and we must take time to consider." What! have we never heard of Christ preaching on the shores of Galilee; of his being pressed by the multitudes so as to be driven on board a ship, and being put to the necessity of shoving off from the shore and dropping anchor, lest the vessed should be swamped by the multitude crowding to hear the Word of Life? Have we never heard of his crossing and recrossing the lake, of the sailing, and rowing, and racing of vessels and boats to overtake him in his itinerant career?

Have we never heard of his excursion to the sea-
coast of Tyre and Sidon? Indeed, the greater part
of the Gospel scenery is laid about the sea and the
adjoining coasts. And we claim that the Bethel
work is not new, as far as its *essence* is concerned.
Then we claim that no cloud of *uncertainty* can rest
upon the result. Our Lord did not labor as one
beating the air—a great company believed. The
Bethel ministers do not now spend their strength
for naught. Where is the Church in Boston that is
accomplishing more than the mariners' Churches?
Where is the Church that is doing more permanent
good than the Norwegian Bethel and others in New
York? Here in the West much has been done on
the lakes, the rivers, the canals, and much more
will be done when the means of the Seamen Friend
society become more ample. But the crowning argument on this head—that which should sweep away
every vestige of mist from all minds—is the declara-
tion of the Bible.

"The abundance of the sea shall be converted
unto thee." Here that which is the duty of our
citizens is also their interest, and should, therefore,
be their delight—the regeneration of our waters is
the salvation of the land. The bread that is cast
upon them will be found after many days.

The character of the sailor is but partially understood by the bulk of mankind, especially that portion of it that dwells in the interior districts.
When the sailor comes rolling along through the

country, he is regarded as a rare curiosity. His
language, his gait, his habitudes are closely scanned;
and his manner of operating, although generally
founded on the true philosophy of things, and consequently strictly correct, is often a subject-matter
of ridicule. But Jack smiles at their botheration
in coiling against the sun, is diverted at their coming down their scuttles face foremost, instead of
bear-fashion, laughs heartily at their granny-knots,
and passes on in perfect good-humor. It is, moreover, thought by many that, 'bating the dangers
and occasional disasters to which seamen are exposed, their vocation is one of extraordinary pleasure and indolence. It is true that there are times
and seasons when the profession is pleasant and
even fascinating; but this state of things is liable
to sudden and grievous interruptions. The sailor
expects them, and his mind is at all times braced
sharp up for a sudden transition from a state of rest
and ease to labors the most arduous and sufferings
the most extreme. Indeed, there is something in
the unparalleled and terrific grandeur of the stripping gale, in connection with the pride of profession, that makes the sailor's heart swell with boundless ambition. And when the seas and skies appear
to be tumbled into lawless and sublime confusion,
he feels glad that he is there, and is proud to
consider himself a necessary item in the driving
tempest. Then it is that he is prepared for deeds
of mighty daring. We doubt, indeed, whether

there is any thing in all the pomp of war, the rattling of the martial drum, the clangor of the rousing trumpet, the roaring of cannon, the momentous vibrations of mighty empires poised in the scales of battle, which can rouse the ambition of mortal man, as the warring elements and rushing, white-crested billows rouse the ambition of the sailor.

> "With such mad seas the daring Gama fought
> For many a day, and many a dreadful night,
> Incessant, laboring round the stormy Cape."

There are often severe hardships endured in the ordinary merchant-service. We have been sometimes, for weeks off the coast of America, contending with driving gales, and adverse winds, accompanied with alternate showers of rain and snow; compelled to shift our clothes till not a dry garment could be found in the forecastle. In the mean time the wind would fall and rise continually, so as to keep the hands employed all the time in making and taking in sail. Often have we retired from the watch with our clothes soaking wet, tumbled, exhausted, into the berth, and under our friendly blankets, we have soon fallen into a delightful hydrological sweat; but still tormented with the idea that every moment we might hear the cry of "all hands ahoy!" while the indisputable certainty of having to bundle up at the expiration of four hours, diffused its bitterness through all our dreams. But what is all this in comparison with the suffer-

ings endured in other departments of sea service—
the exploring expeditions? True, these are few and
far between, and are sometimes of fatal termination;
their distress, perhaps, far exceeding the fancy of
a British poet, although that is sufficiently doleful:

"Miserable they! who, here entangled in the gathering ice,
Take their last look of the descending sun,
While, full of death, and fierce with tempest frost,
The long, long night, incumbent o'er their heads,
Falls horrible. Such was the Briton's fate,
As with first prow—what have not Britons dared?—
He for the passage sought, attempted since
So much in vain, and seeming to be shut
By jealous Nature with eternal bars,
In these fell regions—in Arzina caught,
And to the stormy deep his idle ship
Immediate sealed, he with his hapless crew,
Each full exerted at his several task,
Froze into statues; to the cordage glued
The sailor, and the pilot to the helm."

Multitudes engaged in the whale-fisheries pass
through labors more severe, sufferings as intense.
We have been speaking of the enterprise and pro-
verbial endurance of seamen in general, without
regard to national distinction. The Dutch, at an
early period, were preëminent in naval enterprise.
The English, at a later day, became famous. But
we must say it—and we likely would say it, if only
an emigrant of yesterday on these shores—that
American seamen, in this day, are rather in advance of all others in point of enterprise and marine
daring.

As early as the year 1775, the Americans had

more ships engaged in whaling than England, France, and Holland combined. Four thousand American sailors were then employed in this work. Mr. Burke, in speaking of the colonies in that day, holds this highly-complimentary language:

"Look at the manner in which the people of New England have of late carried on the whale-fishery. While we follow them among the trembling mountains of ice, and behold them penetrating into the deepest recesses of Hudson's Bay and Davis's Straits, while we are looking for them beneath the Arctic circle, we hear that they have pierced into the opposite region of polar cold—that they are at the antipodes, and engaged under the frozen Serpent of the South. Falkland Island, which seemed too remote and romantic an object for the grasp of national ambition, is but a stage and rest-ing-place in the progress of their victorious indus-try. Nor is the equatorial heat more discouraging to them than the accumulated Winter of both the poles. We know that, while some of them draw the line and strike the harpoon on the coast of Africa, others run the longitude, and pursue their gigantic game along the coast of Brazil. No ocean but what is vexed with their fisheries—no climate that is not witness to their toils. Neither the per-severance of Holland, nor the activity of France, nor the dexterous and firm sagacity of English en-terprise ever carried this perilous mode of hardy enterprise to the extent to which it has been pushed

by this recent people—a people who are still, as it
were, in the gristle, and not yet hardened into the
bone of manhood."

The American sailor is also superior in naval
warfare. We do not mean that he is hardier or
more fearless than the British tar. It is enough,
in these particulars, that the children be as their
fathers. But there are circumstances 'of national
usages and complexion that raise the American
above his fellows, as there are peculiarities that
damp the ardor of the English man-of-war's man.

First. The latter is generally in a forced service.
The merchantman sailor returns from the East or
West Indies with his well-earned shiners in his fob.
He hears that the press is hot, and, with all the
stealthy caution of a runaway slave, he attempts,
perhaps under cover of night, to reach his happy
home; but often, in sight of his own cottage lights,
he is seized by an unfeeling press-gang, and hurried
on board a tender. There are no family circumstances, however tender, that can move compassion
in the bosom of his captors. He is taken into service; and when the day of battle comes, his sailor
hardihood, the severity of the service, the force before, the force behind equalize what of fear may remain, and he faces the dreadful music, but feels but
little concern as it regards the victory or the defeat.

With the American sailor it is otherwise. His
may be called voluntary service. True, he may
have taken the bounty while "half-seas-over;" but

he lays the principal part of that indiscretion to himself, and soon makes up his mind to bear up for the two-year service. He goes on board with a full determination to sustain the honor of his flag; and in the day of trial he fights desperately.

Second. The English service is generally cruel and degrading, to a proverb. The frequent music of the lash brutalizes the unhappy sufferers till the dignity of manhood is all gone. Their pride of country is drained drop by drop, till their blood refuses to redden their brow at the sight of an approaching frigate. How can it be otherwise? Who can be proud of a country that delights to make the long furrows of slavery on his back? Indeed, they can not repress the idea that their worst enemies are those of their own ship. They stand, and go through all the evolutions of a battle, of course; but they care not how soon the cannons cease to roar, and they are permitted to enjoy the hospitalities of prisoners of war. There is less barbarity in our navy, and our men are not so deeply degraded. So far as we copy the example of England in this respect, it only works evil to our service.

The voluntary entrance of our seamen, the shortness of the service, the mildness of discipline, all conspire to buoy them up in their place; so that each man, in the tumult of battle, not only obeys the orders of his officers, but, so far as may be consistent with them, exercises his own personal knowledge and skill in dealing his blows on the enemy, so that he is soon dismantled, and compelled to strike. There is much in this. Officers might give orders for every thing to be done, which might lead to a favorable result; but, after all, the manner of doing them is more than half the battle. We know that the fear of disgrace, or the lash, might make things move like clock-work on board a frigate, but then the movement is *servile*, and not *intelligent*—an empty parade, destitute of that patriotism that swells the freeman's breast. It would be an easy matter for a slave, at the word of command, to point a cannon, and for another to apply the match; but American sailors, at the word of command, not only point the gun and apply the match, but they do all as experienced engineers who feel an interest in the result.

The Last War with England, although short, demonstrated the superior tact of our sailors in naval combat. Our Government, doubtless, glories in the fact. But would it not add additional luster to our stars, if it could be said that, while American* sailors excel in valor, in skill, in patriotism, they excel also in civility, in morality—yea, in pure and undefiled religion? Many in our merchant service have availed themselves of the watch below in improving their original stock of knowledge. Others, who were supremely ignorant, have learned to read. What might be done in our navy, by way of training our seamen in all that is great and glorious!

XXXIV.

COLLEGE AGENCY—MILFORD AND BA-
TAVIA CIRCUITS.

COLLEGE AGENCY.

1855. WE received an appointment as Agent for the Hillsboro Female College. As we were entering on this work some of the banks in Cincinnati broke, and many of the citizens of Highland county had deposited their money in them. This gave us a considerable backset. The first thing that struck me was, that the town people had not given the enterprise as generous a heading as they ought to have done. Of this the county complained, and we made known their complaints. At a subsequent meeting the citizens liberally enlarged their subscriptions, and we went forth with more boldness.

I felt a very deep interest in the institution, and thought that it would become the most famous of all our female schools. A preacher will say, " Yes, every brother thinks—for the time being—that his own appointment is the *great work;* and it is well that he can so think." We have, however, reasons above all this. The location is perhaps unparalleled in point of health. We still hope that the embarrassment of the institution will be, by some means, thrown off, and that it will rise up to the high destiny of which it is worthy. The subscription, when handed to me, amounted to about four thousand, six hundred dollars. That year, by enlargement of old subscriptions, and additional subscriptions, and shares sold, it was increased to about twelve thousand dollars. Although I helped at Conference to thank a brother for raising four hundred dollars for another school, by a rising vote, yet I was blessed—I expected nothing of this kind; and I got nothing. I never could understand why a Conference should thank an agent for doing the work assigned him, any more than they should thank a preacher for doing the work of a circuit. It is not in harmony with our theological hymnology—

"O that each in the day of his coming may say,
  I have fought my way through;
I have finished the *work* thou didst *give me* to do."

Indeed, it is hardly in keeping with our prosaic faith, if we hold to Wesley, who said, "Learning is good, but saving souls is better." Still the agent may do this. We attended several large meetings— one in particular, where we made a good haul for the College, and where, we humbly hoped, we helped to save souls. If we did, we trust the Lord has recorded it.

I pretty well explored the county, sold a number of shares, and got many promises for the future;

some of which I might have realized by continuing in that work, but my tenacious disorder forbade. So, in order to better my condition in regard to laborious riding, I—"jumped out of the frying-pan into the fire."

MILFORD CIRCUIT.

1856. We have a warm feeling for this circuit, because there are many of the members who have a just regard for temperance and all Christian graces. And those of them who have been unfortunately involved in the still-commerce, are in *other respects* good Methodists. They are warmly attached to our doctrines and usages, and firm defenders of our government, and in no instance have they risen in opposition to the Episcopacy.

They are strong against the frivolous fashions of the day, and seem as if they would die in defense of the customs of the fathers. Nevertheless, the chief labor of their lives has been in sustaining the distillery. And while they continue to do so, there is a part of the community who will never embark the welfare of their souls in the Methodist Church. We may have, from year to year, an ingathering of attachés of the distillery, or of Sunday school children, who have from infancy seen the dark column of smoke rolling over their heads, as regularly as the sun, and have never questioned its origin or end. And we are glad that such are accessible. But we will never assume that high position there

which the early organization of that society deserves, till the Church washes her hands of that
iniquity. It has ever been a rule in our ministry
to preach against the special sins of that division
of the work to which we have been appointed.
What would it avail to preach on the Blue Ridge
against a sin of some seaport—say smuggling—or
to preach in Vermont against the sin of raising
Indian corn for the distilleries? I can not conceive
of the feeling of the minister who can serve a
Church a whole year, and never touch on a besetting sin in that Church.

When I came to the circuit it was a serious question with me, "*What must I do?*" I saw clearly
that among a people who seemed, in many important
points, to love Methodism, I could shape my course
so as to be acceptable, if not popular. But could
I take this course and clear my skirts? I finally
concluded before the Lord to do my duty, if it
brought me on short allowance. Still I intended to
defer my battle till the people had got well acquainted with me; for I believed I had some good
points as well as they.

In the mean time Thanksgiving day was approaching, and a brother requested me to give notice that there would be preaching on that day. I
asked him who would preach. He said, "Never
mind; somebody will." So I gave it out, supposing
he was going to get some one from the city. When
the day arrived there were at first very few at the

meeting-house. I said, "Brother, you will have a small congregation to preach to."

"You must preach."

"I had rather not. You never told me that it was expected for me to preach; and, besides, the occasion, *thanksgiving*, might lead me to say something that might hurt the good feelings of some."

"O, never fear. We are a people who can not be hurt, if you preach the truth."

"God forbid we should preach any thing else!"

Presently we had a large congregation, and nearly all those of *the* traffic. They listened with the most profound attention, although I touched upon the sins of the nation, and especially drunkenness; for they love to see the drunkard, as a poor, singed goat, bear off the iniquity. But, toward the close, I called their attention to the *thanksgiving*. This was not the sermon; indeed, in many places, no sermon was preached. The thanksgiving is in the devotional exercises to follow. We must acknowledge the great mercies of God—bewail our misimprovement—promise for the future. I then observed that I was at a great loss about framing a prayer suitable to all present, for two classes are here; and, after a pause, said, I believe I will make two prayers. Then each member may make his choice, and carry it home. The first prayer might be something like this: "O Lord, we acknowledge our great obligations to thank thee for the mercies of the past year—a year of unusual plenty. Our pas-

tures are green and luxurious; our bottoms are •
bursting up with potatoes; plenty reigns around us.
We see it is our duty, after providing for our own
household, to be generous to the poor, to sustain the
missions, the Bible, Sunday school, and tract societies, and to do all the good we can with our abundant
means. Amen, and amen." The other might run
thus: "O Lord, it has been a year of uncommon
plenty. Our bottoms are crowded with corn, and
all the fruits of the earth are abundant. We feel
grateful, and mean to apply these blessings as we
have ever done. We will haul our wood to the
furnace, and our corn to the great crib, and help
to stir up the fires of the distillery; and we will
send down such a stream of blue-ruin as we have
never raised before. We know that, in so doing,
we will have a hard row to hoe; our own sons may
get to crooking their elbows too often. Then
friends, family, and fortune will all go; then will
come delirium tremens, insanity, death—and, last
of all, the drunkard's hell; but we will say, with
Hezekiah, 'truth and peace will be in our day.'
Nay-men, and nay-men."

About six months after, some said my last prayer
did not suit them. But I told them, whether it
suited them or not, they had fulfilled all that I had
promised the Lord for them. They had carried all
their corn and wood to the distillery, and, in so
doing, they had chosen that prayer. From that
time to the close of the year, I paid due attention

to the northern institution. Still, brother Fitch and myself took in about seventy-five new members on the circuit. We presented the following report on the subject of Temperance, at Conference:

Your Committee are compelled to admit, that, of late, there has been an increasing declension of the general temperance reformation. It is no uncommon thing now to see what has seldom been seen for the last twenty years—the sparkling and seducing decanter, unvailed, in our wedding and social parties, and ladies, yet in their teens, sipping, with shameless *sang froid*, what would craze a genuine teetotaler. In our national anniversaries and public banquets the old, barbarous custom of toasting ourselves sick, out of tender regard for the health of others, is greatly reviving; and the more scientifically liquors have been analyzed, and the more nakedly their ingredients have been turned up to the noonday sun, the more thirsty the intemperate seem for the ruinous draught. Our post-offices— the purity of which ought to be dear to every American citizen—are thrown too often into groggeries and dens of drunkenness, where females and children can not approach without being exposed to blasphemies and sickening exhibitions of human depravity. Our Church has always coöperated with every institution laboring to establish national and social Temperance in our land; but during the whole fight we have not neglected our own con-

cern—the lodge of Methodism—so that, notwithstanding the increase of our membership, we have
at this time less to do with intoxicating spirits
than we ever had.

With great delight we state that the cause of
Temperance in the Methodist Episcopal Church has
been continuous, onward, onward, from our organization.

"Bent on purpose grand and glorious,
Her banners move in course victorious."

The experience of many years has confirmed us
in the doctrine, that the religious reformation of
the drunkard is the most reliable—the most permanent. Lorenzo Dow used to say that there were
but two specifics in the case: one was to put an
eel in a quart of rum, and drink generously; the
other was the grace of God. We never had any
faith in his eel-bounce; but the grace of God we
can label, "Tried."

We know of only one medium now in connection
with the Church and still-house: "That corn!" O,
that corn! Some of our folks are still engaged in
that wicked and disreputable commerce. Our
brethren who may not have been thrown where
Satan's choice seats are may not be initiated into
the *modus operandi*. As soon as you approach
such a place, the black temple of Copper Nosey
looms up, like nothing else but the back door of
hell. As you advance you will encounter a toper
in almost every square, all in different stages of

progress. One is quite good-natured, and comfortably "how came ye so?" Another is raging and declaiming as if he were the Emperor of the Moon. A third is peaceably sleeping on the sidewalk, with his cheek slapped up against a curb-stone—

> "The flies creeping in, and the flies creeping out,
> And sporting his eyes and his nostrils about."

But here comes a team, superannuated and gaunt, and behind, mounted on a pyramid of corn, high and dignified, sits an exhorter, or, it may be, a local preacher. Our preacher dares not pass the last-mentioned case. He has a commission from the Church, and reins up, and, descending from his high estate, he roots the drunkard over with his muddy boot, and says, "Halloo, here! are you not ashamed to be lying here, dead drunk, in open daylight?"

The drunkard drawls out, "Ashamed enough! but you brought me to it!"

"How can you make that out?"

"Why, you carry your corn to the distillery; they make the sparkling whisky; I drink, and become fuddled; but you are 'the great first cause, least understood.'"

The drunkard rolls back on his curb pillow; the preacher drives on, lamenting the wickedness of these degenerate days, but scowls defiance at every Templar, Son, or Daughter he may meet.

The preacher in charge says, "I 'll have a big

meeting; that I will." "Do so," say the pious; for, as it was of old, so now there are some, even in Sardis, who have not defiled their garments. The meeting comes on; several are powerfully convicted; the big tears course down their cheeks; but still they come not. A friend says, "Try them another night; try them once more—only once more;" and so from week to week; but they come not. When you get their only reason why, it is, "We can not come and be surrounded, and talked to, and prayed with, by those who are living, as we believe, in mortal sin." The preacher sees that there is a class of people around which Methodism can never reach, till she washes her hands of this iniquity. He sees that he must battle the whole watch with the monster. Perhaps one may be ready to say, as Peter, "And what shall we have, therefore?" Truly, that is a question. Surely, you will have hard times, and may have to eat your own horse; but we hope that, in the spirit of martyrdom, you will say, "Let a hundred horses be devoured; but let the Church of God swing free."

"But," says another, "is there no one to whom we can look for help in this age of reformation?" You will have to gather instruction from behind the reformation. A pious Catholic woman was seen, weeping on the street. A passenger inquired what was the matter. "O, sir," said she, "I have lost my crucifix, and now I have nothing to pray to but *Jesus Christ!*" You must not lean on the outsiders,

though *temperate* they be. They will look complacently on, and be highly diverted, like the frontier
mother who stood in her cabin door and beheld,
with a smile, her husband engaged in mortal combat with a huge bear. When the hunter had gained
the victory, with the skin of his teeth, he upbraided
his wife for not coming down to his rescue, and
especially for smiling at the blood and sweat he had
shed. She coolly replied that she had never seen a
fight before in which she felt so little interest, as it
regarded who might whip. Funds they have, but
they must go for ice-cream, and oyster suppers, and
picnics, and costly music, so that the inebriates say
they have only changed the *complexion* of intemperance, and are like unto a man who boasts highly
of having quit tobacco chewing, but, nevertheless,
smokes like a locomotive.

Brethren, the minister of God has a work to do
in temperance that none other will or can do. His
temperance is not only a human virtue, but a
Christian grace; not only the temperance that
rejects manifest poison, but "temperance in all
things." He admires and indorses the temperance
that won Cyrus an empire; but he strikes for that
temperance at which God has priced the crown incorruptible. Our preachers, however, have much to
encourage them.

1. We know some who once traded with the
distillery who have abandoned it as a loathsome
thing, and we believe they would suffer martyr-

dom before they would be driven back to the practice.

2. Others are in a transit state. When we speak to them on the subject, they will smile and say, "Well, in truth, I do not like the business. I have thought some about quitting; but I can not see my way exactly clear just now, and for the present will have to do as I have done." We here bless God, and take courage. It requires only a little more effort to capsize a cake already half turned, and our late President Taylor said, in a similar case, "A little more grape, Captain Bragg!"

3. The best is, no Methodist believes in whisky-growing. Those who contend for the practice never advance one argument that half satisfies themselves. The discerning minister always discovers in them evident marks of painful conviction, and their whole demeanor but forcibly declares,

"We know the right, but still the wrong pursue."

"Then," it may be asked, "why do they do it?" We answer, There is a sin that underlies the whole transaction—a sin as fatal to the soul as drunkenness — *covetousness*. All Methodist farmers would prefer a clean trade, all things being equal; but the offer of two cents more on the bushel, or the paltry expense of toll, determines the will, and. drives the wagon to the still-house; and it is notorious that the most wealthy among them are penurious to a proverb. They stick to the poll-tax which the stewards adopt in their estimate; and they seem to think that it is the duty of the preacher—be he rich or be he poor—to bear one-half of the expenses of their wealthy circuits. If they can not come out of his pocket they must come out of his horse or his hide; for the doctrine is stereotyped on the *cerebrum* and *cerebellum*, "The leaner the hound the swifter the chase."

So we find, without elaborate search, that the idolatry of covetousness is the jackal of the still-house. When this calm and settled avarice is lashed into a tempest by the preaching of temperance, it becomes doubly distilled, and threats of starvation fall thick and heavy. True, they sometimes make a benevolent effort, when they go through the process of what is called, in those parts, "buying up the preacher"—a donation call. The preacher may be entirely ignorant of the design; but, whether he is or not, he will have the extreme mortification, when he comes to the footing of his quarterage, to find that he has been made to buy up himself, besides making presents to his own wife and children of some pretty toys, which smile in contrast with the furniture of the parsonage, but which will by no means make the pot boil.

What is the conclusion?

1. There is not a shadow of doubt resting on this body in regard to the man who stands day by day at his bar, dealing out poison and death to his neighbors' children, destroying the peace of families,

and inciting to desperate deeds, and ofttimes bloody murder. He is wicked—his act *immoral*.

2. Neither do you entertain a doubt concerning the merchant who supplies him, and is accessory; for if the first serves Baal a little, he serves him a great deal. He is not only a co-worker with that retailer, but with a hundred others, so that his guilt is out at compound interest. His standing partially behind the screen avails nothing. His bread and butter depend on the diligence with which his customers retail their drams. And in the same proportion he lays up gold and silver, he treasures up wrath against the day of wrath. His trade is *immoral*.

3. We need not say you have no doubts about the distiller. He has none about himself, and commonly he evinces no desire to rob any evangelical Church of livery to serve the devil in. His greatest claim on mercy is—he is no hypocrite. Nevertheless, he is *immoral*.

4. The whisky-growing farms are the only available arsenals of the vast army of intemperance, and the Methodist farmers who cultivate them, make it their business to roll the ammunition down to the nearest magazine of woe, and on the 23d or 25th of November offer thanksgiving to Almighty God for the *abundant harvest* of spiritual grape and canister. Now, neither the distiller nor the vender could carry on their work of desolation without the cultivator. So *he* has the unenviable distinction

of setting this vast machinery of insanity and death in motion. And if he who putteth the bottle to his neighbor's mouth is bending under the curse of the Almighty, what must we say of those mischievous commissaries who keep that bottle supplied with an inexhaustible stream of anguish and ruin? True, they plead their own cause; but who does not? But their two main points of defense are so weak that we can hardly attribute them to the instigation of the devil.

1. They say that whisky is made for medical purposes. But we answer that no conscientious and intelligent physician, in view of the late analysis of Ohio whisky, would prescribe it even for the bots. It is wicked to follow a business that does **more harm than good to our world.**

2. If every drop of it is made for medical purposes, still the world would breathe easier in the absence of a medicine which alternately saves *one* and kills a *thousand.*

3. Allowing all that is claimed, that the still is the sovereign specific, the fountain of health and immortality — the long-sought spring of Ponce de Leon — still this does not enter into the motives of our self-deceived brethren; because there is no medical benevolence in selling corn for forty cents per bushel to the distillery, while people in honest trade are giving only thirty-five. The same brethren clothe the naked every day when they rise, and feed the hungry every time they eat. They quote

often this passage: "Give strong drink to him who is ready to perish;" but neither will this meet their case. It is no benevolence in times of scarcity to give four gallons of whisky to him who is ready to perish with thirst, and by so doing take away a bushel of corn from him who is ready to perish with hunger. And, besides, they do not give at all, but sell at an advanced price. And this is their crying sin, that they sell corn to those who sell it in whisky, not only to the sober, but to those who are truly ready to perish — perhaps the finishing dose.

4. They are concerned about no other medicine. If whisky will not cure, the sick may go to—the grave. They do not grow rhubarb, poppies, nor even lobelia. The other main point is—*necessity*. What shall we do with "that corn?" "How shall we cultivate our land to profit?" We need not meet this defense before a body of men so well acquainted with our agricultural prosperity, the high price of provisions, and the countless mouths to be fed in this country.

Finally, we feel driven, logically and conscientiously, to present the following resolutions for the consideration of the Conference:

1. *Resolved*, That it is irreligious for our members to hold commerce with distilleries, saving such as distill *exclusively* for medical and mechanical purposes.

2. *Resolved*, As a ministerial body, in our place,

we do approve of our ministers preaching against the above evil—it is their *duty* to do so.

3. *Resolved,* We do most affectionately beseech the members of our Church not to engage in a speculation where the minute *good*, if any, is overpowered by such stupendous *evil*.

BATAVIA CIRCUIT.

1860–61. This was our last circuit. The first year I labored with brother James H. Herron, and two-thirds of the last year with brother Thomas Lee. At the close of the first year my health seemed to be getting better, and in all good faith I ventured on another appointment; but my complaint increased in violence, till I saw I would have to surrender. My external appearance was healthy, and I kept my suffering to myself, and forced myself through all kinds of weather and roads to my appointments, till the third quarterly meeting conference, when I made a statement of my peculiar affliction, and requested the presiding elder to grant me a dispensation. The brethren generally sympathized with me, and treated me in a Christian and genteel manner. I could say much good of this circuit, but find my work has been swelling beyond what I contemplated. At the Conference I asked for a superannuated relation, and my brethren granted it with all that affectionate and Christian spirit that has always distinguished them.

I saw that I could not continue and do my duty

without prematurely destroying myself; that there
were strong and healthy men anxious to enter the
field, and that it was altogether right that I should
superannuate. And seeing it was my duty, what else
remained to me but to march? And may the Lord
so prepare my soul by grace and judgment that
when I see my pathway clear, to march, even when
it must be to the air of Roslin Castle!

XXXV.

MISCELLANEOUS WORK.

As we have been in the habit of corresponding with public papers and periodicals, it may be expected that we will say something on this subject. We commenced very early in life. 'Bating our first attempts, known only to ourself—highly approved to-day and utterly condemned to-morrow—our first adventure, of course in poetry, was an answer to my oldest sister's address to the Petersburg volunteers before their departure. We can not remember one line of that heroic effort, and we would not attempt to rouse it up from its sweet and long oblivion.

After moving to New Orleans I assisted my brother some in a lively, and, among the American population, a popular paper. After entering the traveling connection, I wrote occasionally for the Advocate. When the Ladies' Repository was started, it seems that our great men did not give it that help which might have been expected from them. Bishop Hamline had a hard work on hand, but he was sufficient. At no subsequent period has that periodical been more in accordance with the taste of our membership, although some of the most accomplished of our ministry have directed it. We continued our help, such as it was, under succeeding editors, till their correspondence has swelled beyond their disposal. We have written also for papers of a political cast; and the most part of the Western Pilot is original—professedly or not. We might fill a large volume with these occasional productions, but this would be foreign to our work; and being closely allied to the passing events of the time, their chief interest would now find no place. We will, however, close with a sample of this part of our labor.

THERE IS SURELY BUT ONE STEP BETWEEN EARTH AND HEAVEN.

While seated in my study, my mind adverted to Mrs. Sarah Edwards, the accomplished consort of President Jonathan Edwards, and the daughter of James Pierpont, an eminent and useful minister of New Haven. It is said, she was a young lady of uncommon beauty—a beauty which was rendered unrivaled by that rare loveliness of expression which is the result of a combination of intelligence, cheerfulness, and benevolence. She possessed an unusual share of natural talent, highly improved by a liberal and polished education. She was gentle and polite, and all her conduct and conversation were under the government of Christian charity. She was one of those distinguished flowers which, consecrated to God in the bud, prove no vain sacrifice. It is said she in a remarkable manner exhibited the life and power of religion when only five years of age. This early piety grew with her growth, and strengthened with her strength. Her uncommon devotion to God arrested the attention of Mr. Edwards several years before their union, and he recorded the following testimony of her worth: "They say there is a young lady in New Haven, who is beloved of the great Being who made and governs the world; and that there are certain seasons in which this great Being, in some way or other, comes invisibly to her, and fills her mind with exceeding sweet delight, and that she hardly cares for any thing except to meditate on him; that she expects after a little while to be caught up to heaven, being assured that he loves her too well to let her remain at a distance from him always. There she is to dwell with him, and to be ravished with his love and delight forever. Therefore, if you present all the world before her, with the richest of its treasures, she disregards it, and is unmindful of any pain or affliction. She has a strange sweetness in her mind, and singular purity in her affections; is most just and conscientious in all her conduct, and you could not persuade her to any thing wrong or sinful if you would give her all the world, lest she should offend this great Being. She is of a wonderful sweetness, calmness, and universal benevolence of mind, especially after this great God has manifested himself to her mind. She will sometimes go about from place to place, singing sweetly, and seems to be always full of joy and pleasure, and no one knows for what. She loves to be alone, walking in the fields and groves, and seems to have some invisible being conversing with her." Perhaps there never was a more congenial couple than Edwards and his guileless partner— such a duplicate as Thomson would have called a "*matchless* pair," the only shadow of difference this—

"Hers the mild luster of the blooming morn,
And his the radiance of the rising day."

Mrs. Edwards was a judicious and faithful mistress of a family. She was not only alive to the domestic duties that naturally fall into the province of the female, but, as her husband was sometimes pressed beyond measure in his ministerial work, she relieved him much of those perplexing and outdoor concerns which commonly belong to paternal supervision. This shows the superiority of her mind, for she was not drilled to it by Eastern usages. She also saw that, in the multitudinous business of her husband, he might have to lament in the end, "I have kept the vineyard of others, but my own vineyard I have not kept;" so she took, in a great measure, the religious education of the children on herself. She did not, like some mothers, wait till her children should get more sense before she would attend to their best interest. She was like that ma-

tron saint who, when she awakened her children in
the morning, implored God that they might, in early
life, "awake to righteousness, and sin not;" when
she washed their bodies, she prayed that God might
wash their souls in the laver of regeneration; when
she dressed them, she prayed that they might be
found in the wedding garment at the coming of the
Lord; and when she gave them the breast, she
called on God, with strong cries and tears, that she
might not nourish and raise a child for the devil.
But Mrs. Edwards did not stop here. She helped
much her husband in his ministerial work. She
was eminently qualified to do this. Her conversation was in heaven. It was not conversation about
religion, about its doctrines, its truths, its duties—
her conversation was *religion itself*, the very heaven
of love. She encouraged and promoted female meetings, and was prompt to take up her cross at every
call. There was no gloom in her theology. Her
religion was the religion of joy in the Holy Ghost.
It is perfectly overwhelming to read some of her
spiritual enjoyments left on record. On one occasion she writes: "At the same time my heart and
soul all flowed out in love to Christ, so that there
seemed to be a constant flowing and reflowing of
heavenly love from Christ's heart to mine, and I
appeared to myself to float and swim in those bright,
sweet beams of the love of Christ, like the motes
swimming in the beams of the sun, or streams of
light which came in at the windows. My soul re-

mained in a kind of heavenly elysium. So far as I am capable of making a comparison, I think that what I felt each minute, during the continuance of the whole time, was worth more than all the outward joy and comfort which I had experienced in my whole life put together." At another time, she writes: "So intense were my feelings, when speaking of these things, that I could not forbear rising up, and leaping with joy and exultation. I felt, at the same time, an exceeding strong and tender affection for the children of God, and realized, in a manner exceedingly sweet and ravishing, the meaning of Christ's prayer, 'That they all may be one, as thou, Father, art in me, and I in thee, that they also may be one in us.' This union seemed to me an inconceivable, excellent, and sweet oneness; and, at the same time, I felt that oneness in my soul with the children of God. A hymn was sung, but when these words were read,

'My sighs at length are turned to songs,
The Comforter is come,'

so conscious was I of the joyful presence of the Holy Spirit, I could scarcely refrain from leaping with transports of joy."

Here my mind wandered from this pattern-mistress of a parsonage to the sisters Fletcher and Rogers, and a number of holy women on this side of the sea, embraced in my own memory; and all these were singularly fond of the communion of saints—an interchange of religious views and experience. Then it struck me, may not an exercise, so dear to the saints in all ages on earth, even enter into the inexplicable promise, "*the joys of thy Lord?*" Then I exclaimed, "Surely, there is but one step between earth and heaven!"

Then one of those reveries which sometimes take possession of my mind came over me, and methought my soul soared aloft beyond the bounds of time and sense—yea, was permitted to behold in the unfading groves of paradise the blood-washed throng. As the last lovely melody of celestial music died away on the air, a spirit of unearthly beauty arose, and in a voice far beyond the stretch of mortal tune, addressed the mute and listening multitudes.

NATHANAEL.—"Brethren beloved, I stand before this congregated election, as a peculiar case of happy and facile transfer from the economy of Mount Zion, into all the blessings of the new and everlasting covenant. Born and raised an Israelite, I was zealous of the law, the sacrifices, and the traditions of the fathers. They were weighty and imposing, and even in the deadness of the letter were transcendently superior to the vain and empty shows, and indecent and lascivious sacrifices and offerings of the idolatrous Gentiles. Moreover, I discovered, from time to time, that beyond the outward exhibition of our mysteries and rights, there was a deeply-hidden spirituality that I could but partially apprehend. This drew my soul out in frequent and fervent prayer and meditation, especially as in that day it was thought that the time of the promise drew nigh. Sometimes I experienced what I believed to be signal manifestations of Divine power. On a certain occasion, while deeply engaged under a tree, I was suddenly overwhelmed by an unearthly influence. It seemed as if celestial spirits were hovering all around me, and as if the Divine arms were underneath and round about me, and something seemed to whisper, 'Hold up thy head, thy redemption draweth nigh.' Soon after this I met with Philip of Bethsaida, and he said unto me, 'We have found him of whom Moses in the law, and the prophets, did write.' A bare allusion to our much-loved and long looked-for Messiah, struck a cord which vibrated through soul and body; but when he added, 'Jesus of Nazareth,' my spirit sunk within me, and I said rather petulantly, 'Can any good thing come out of Nazareth?' His answer, though short, was indicative of strong confidence, 'Come and see.' It, moreover, struck with force a principle established within me; one that was afterward so often insisted on by our beloved brother Paul— 'Prove all things and hold fast to that which is good.' How forcible are right words! And when I saw the Savior, his exterior mien and Godlike carriage struck me with solemn but delightful awe. His first salutation was, 'Behold an Israelite, indeed, in whom there is no guile!' Here I felt thrown into a very delicate difficulty. I might

have used a little voluntary humility, in denying
the allegation; but I could not do so without denying and departing from my true character; for,
through the mercy of the God of Abraham, and a
conflict of faith and prayer, I had gotten the victory over all guile and hypocrisy, and had often
sung with growing delight, 'Blessed is the man to
whom the Lord imputeth not iniquity; and in whose
spirit there is no guile.' So I stood up in my integrity, like Job, and answered, 'How knoweth thou
me?' But when he said, 'Before Philip called thee,
when thou wast under the fig-tree, I saw thee,' my
very soul appeared to melt down into wonder, love,
and praise. For I knew that no mortal eye had
witnessed what had there transpired between God
and my poor soul under that shade—the blessed
fig-tree; and I immediately exclaimed, 'Rabbi,
Rabbi! thou art the Son of God; thou art the
King of Israel!' In that hour I began to comprehend the mystery, hid from the foundation of the
world. All my prejudices, and views, and sentiments which were not of God's right-hand planting
began to wither and die, and I sweetly and gradually entered into the new and heavenly Jerusalem.
What was commenced, through the faith in a coming
Messiah, was consummated in the powerful out-
pouring of the day of Pentecost—a day to be held
in remembrance through the countless cycles of an
endless immortality. Brethren, I have had my
warfare, and my afflictions, which were common to

the Church of the First-Born; and, O, my last bitter conflict! But they are all left on the other
side of the river. They are as though they had
not been—while my soul swims in a sea of glory,
with God eternally shut in. Halleluiah to God, for
this heaven of love—this continuity of bliss!"

Here, as this Christian patriarch ceased, a glow
of holy sympathy lighted up the innumerable host,
and the orchestra of heaven struck a peal for which
the laws of mortal interlocution have made no provision. Then one, who appeared to be as great a
favorite in heaven as he had been among the saints
on earth, rose to address the happy assemblage.

SIMON PETER.—"Holy and beloved, the salutation of our Lord to Nathanael was the highest encomium ever conferred on man in his mortal state.
As it regards myself, in my unregenerated state,
ambition was my shrine. I gloried in being a son
of Abraham, and was zealous of the law. There
was nothing, however chivalrous or grand, that
was predicted of the coming Messiah as a mighty
conqueror and martial leader, which was too glowing
for my ambitious spirit. Believing in Jesus of Nazareth, I at first attached myself to his interests, in the
full conviction that it was he who would restore the
kingdom to Israel. Strange it was, that this conviction should abide after I had well marked his
humility of spirit, his benevolent bearing, and his
extreme deadness to the honors of the world and
the pride of life! I honestly aspired after power

and distinction under his administration. However, above all these selfish breathings of my soul, there arose an undying attachment to the Savior. I counted not my life dear in the defense of his person and his claims. And on that awful night, when he predicted that he would be forsaken of all before the morning-light, I thought this could not, and should not be; and you remember with what vehemence I exclaimed, 'Though all men forsake you, yet will not I.' This I believed, because I knew that I had animal courage enough to carry it out, even unto death. And I was right glad when he inquired if we had swords. From the purpose of dying for him that night, if necessary, I did not waver for a moment—no, not even when the mob approached, for then I drew my sword and made my charge. But when I saw the immaculate Jesus calmly extend his arm of power and close the wound my blade had made; when he said, 'Put up thy sword; for he who takes the sword shall perish by the sword;' when I saw that his kingdom was to be established in righteousness, and not with the shout of the warrior and garments stained with blood; when I saw that it was moral power and suffering by which he was to conquer, my heart seemed to die within me—and I shamefully fled. Still I could not give him up; all my interest appeared to center in the mysterious sufferer. I turned, and followed at a distance, and at last entered into the judgment-hall. But O, what unnat-

ural tremors coursed along my nerves! and when I
was challenged as a follower of Christ—challenged,
brethren, by a maid-servant—I denied my best, my
greatest friend. And when they seemed resolved to
fasten the charge upon me, and I found that the
mild language that Jesus had taught me was likely
to betray me—O, shame on my guilty cowardice!—
I cursed and swore most infamously. Just then the
cock's shrill clarion pierced through my soul. I
looked toward the bar at the silent Lamb, and his
eyes of reproof, swimming in tears of compassion,
rested on me; and well might it be said I went out
and wept *bitterly*. O, the days of indescribable anguish—almost of despair—that I suffered till the
morning of the resurrection! Still I loved the
Lord, and I could not abandon the assembly of his
saints. Strange, that they bore with the backslider! I was permitted to mingle my tears with
his sorrowing disciples. The spirit had almost failed
before the God that made it, when, on the glorious
morning of the third day, certain sisters broke in upon
our conference, exclaiming, with unbridled joy, 'The
Lord has risen from the dead! We have seen, we
have heard him—he has spoken to us; and we have
a message from the Lord to you, O brethren! He
sent us to say to Peter and the brethren, "Behold!
I go before you into Galilee."' 'O, not to me!
Did he say Peter?' 'Yes, Simon; he not only
mentioned *thee*, but mentioned thee *first:* "Go and
tell *Peter* and the brethren," were the words of our

risen Jesus.' O, what unspeakable joy sprung up in my soul! And I said in my heart, 'Blessed be the God and Father of our Lord Jesus Christ, who has begotten us again unto a lively hope to an inheritance which is incorruptible, undefiled, and that fadeth not away.' But my joy and peace were increased in our interview on the sea-shore, where he renewed my commission as often as I had denied him on that horrible night. 'Feed my sheep.' On the day of Pentecost a full consecration was sealed on my soul; and, feeling that I was under greater obligation to speak well of the Lord than others, because in me much had been forgiven, I sprang to my feet. O, what light then shone on my soul! The plan of salvation stood before me in all its unfolded splendor. I saw that the Gospel was not intended merely to free us from the Roman yoke; but I saw — yea, felt — that it delivered us out of the hands of all our enemies, that we might walk before God in righteousness and in holiness all the days of our lives.

"Through many trials and much tribulation I have reached the bright goal. And now let my pretended successors below boast about Rome and the patrimony of St. Peter! What was my patrimony on earth but a broken net, and a shattered bark, and a daily death? Here is the patrimony that fadeth not away; and the idea that it is not for me only, but for all the blood-washed saints, enhances its worth and highly sharpens my relish. Yes, it fadeth not away! The roses of heaven will blush a deeper red; the lilies will shed a more dazzling white, while eternal ages are onward rolling—'it fadeth not away!' Alleluiah!"

SAUL OF TARSUS.—"I once said I was the chief of sinners. Some of our more modern friends on earth have since gone to extensive pains to soften or whitewash that sentence. They have said that Paul felt as all young converts feel, who knowing the sore of their own hearts, and being ignorant of the secret convictions of others, are disposed to write hard things against themselves. Little do they know of the divine impulse under which we wrote and spoke. The storms of life all over and heaven gained, I am not disposed to retract a single word. Sin draws the shades of its complexion from the circumstances attending its commission. There might have been those in my day, who might have been guilty of sins which Saul of Tarsus even would have shuddered at; but they had not Saul's culture, Saul's education, Saul's opportunities. I was well-read in the sacred writings and the commentaries of the most approved Rabbis; but I carried with me all the time the most unmistakable mark of the beast of hell—*the spirit of persecution.* Bigotry congealed all the kindly streams of human nature. I pursued even tender females in my wrath, and I persecuted the Church of God beyond measure. It is well for me that remorse can not enter heaven; that tears can not stain the golden streets of the New Jerusalem. Some men's sins go before them to judgment; the sins of some follow after. The day of retribution came. At the gates of Lystra the cup of trembling was pressed to my lips. I drank the bitterness of Stephen's martyrdom, with the heavy interest of the anguish of *resuscitation*, which Stephen never felt. I, too, was persecuted, buffeted, whipped, imprisoned, and shipwrecked; but I gloried in my afflictions, because I saw the retributive justice of God, and because I knew that they would work out for me a far more exceeding and eternal weight of glory. Well do I remember the throes of the new birth through which I passed on my way to Damascus. While breathing out threatening and slaughter against the disciples of the Lord, the power of God arrested me. 'Saul, Saul, why persecutest thou me?' And I said, 'Who art thou, Lord?' I knew that I had persecuted much and rather indiscriminately, and began to suspect that in the heat of my zeal I had torn up some wheat with the tares; and my inquiry was, in what *instance*, in *whose case* I had offended the Lord. But, O! how was my whole soul dismayed when I heard that hated name—'Jesus' of Nazareth! I saw my whole work condemned, and myself involved in black despair. For three days I ate no pleasant bread and drank no reviving cordial. All was midnight darkness. Then I bethought me of the means of grace, and kneeled before the Lord. Hope sprang into my soul, and I began to look for deliverance. While sitting in darkness and in the shadow of death, the door was opened; Ananias, one of the persecuted, stood before me. He might have said, 'O, thou proud and haughty persecutor of my brethren and sisters in the kingdom and patience of Jesus Christ, has my God humbled thee at last?' But no; he gently approached, laid his hand upon my head and said, 'Saul—*brother* Saul, the Lord—even Jesus who appeared unto thee in the way—hath sent me that thou mightest receive thy sight, and be filled with the Holy Ghost.' The scales fell from my eyes, and blindness from my mind, I saw light in God's light, and praised him from a feeling sense of his pardoning love. And having obtained help of God, I persevered in the way—enduring the cross, despising the shame, and am now exalted to the kingdom on high. And now the greatest boast I make in heaven's courts is this—'*a sinner saved by grace!*'"

Here, again, I exclaimed, "Surely, there is but one step between earth and heaven!" But a voice within said, "Yes; but in that step what trials 'in number, measure, weight,' may come! In that mysterious tread, temptations, sorrows, bereavements, sometimes shake the elect to his solid foundation."

THE END.